BREAKING AND HOLDING

ADVANCE READER COPY

This is an uncorrected proof.
The price and publication date
are subject to change.

ISBN-13: 9781503936713
ISBN-10: 1503936716
358 pages - $14.95
Release Date: August 2, 2016

BREAKING AND HOLDING

A NOVEL

JUDY FOGARTY

This is a work of fiction. Names, characters, organizations, places, events, and incidents are either products of the author's imagination or are used fictitiously.

Published by Lake Union Publishing, Seattle www.apub.com

ISBN-13: 9781503936713
ISBN-10: 1503936716

Cover design by Danielle Fiorella

Printed in the United States of America

For Mike

CHAPTER 1

This isn't my story. It's Patricia and Terry's. But in the summer of 1978, their lives were wound around mine like strands of twine around a spool. Twine. Rope. Barbed wire by August.

I still have the notes I took out of habit that summer, not knowing what else to do. I have Patricia's journal too, which was left at the beach house on Kiawah Island in the aftermath. Even now, five years later, I find it too painful to read.

I have the moist heat of the Carolina coast, even here in New York. I see the rivers and smell the salt marsh, sweet with life and bitingly sour. I hear the perpetual respiration of the ocean, rolling us toward what I called date certain—September 1, 1978, the beginning of the Labor Day weekend.

I have me, interloper turned housemate. A his-and-hers confidante, counselor, friend. Speaking truth to love. Lying to power. A fascinated witness, in the middle of it all, the place I hate most to be.

On the first of June, I took in everything at once and made sense of nothing. Patricia was sitting on the side of the bed. The sheets had been stripped and lay on the floor beside a haphazard pile of her husband's suits. The arms and legs of coats and trousers were at odd angles, as if limbs inside were broken or dislocated. Dress shirts were in another pile. Pockets monogrammed *JC*. She hadn't answered the door, hadn't responded when I stepped inside and called her name. She'd ignored the click of my heels on the heart pine floor.

"Dear God," I said, "what's wrong?"

Her eyes were downcast, her shoulders round. "Where is my husband, Lynn?" she said, without looking up.

"He's finalizing the presentation. He's changed the ad campaign so many times, the art director may walk." Silence. "He said you were upset when you called. He asked me to come."

He'd asked me, his personal assistant, to assist his wife. He asked often when short on patience or time. Or when baffled, like today. When he couldn't intuit the problem. When, unarmed with strategy and tactics, he was afraid his temper would flare.

I sat down beside her, and she looked at me at last, blue eyes brimming, tears threatening a mudslide from her lashes. "I want to leave Jack," she said. "I want you to help me."

I looked away. The golf wear I'd purchased for her was in a box on her dresser. I'd purchased lessons for her too, at Jack's direction. A shopping bag of books sat at her feet. On the bedside table were more books, a pink compact of birth control pills, and her contact lens case.

"I want to show you something," she said. "Something you may know about." She picked up her contact case. "And I don't mean my lens. I'm *sure* you know about that."

I wasn't supposed to. No one was, but in The Curren Company everyone did. Custom tinted, the lens was Jack's solution to the problem of her mismatched eyes, for making the gray of her left match the cornflower blue of her right. He had no solution for their mismatched ages—her twenty-six years, his forty-nine. None for their mismatched lives.

She twisted the *R* cap open. In the white well, a black pearl button was another eye. Omniscient, unsympathetic, unblinking.

"It isn't mine, Lynn. I found it." She patted the mattress. "Here."

I took in a choppy breath, whitecaps of air. "You can't

possibly think Jack would do that."

"Be unfaithful? Or be unfaithful in our bed?" She laid the button in her palm, made a fist, and passed her other hand over it. She uncurled her fingers, and like a failed magician, stared at what now looked like the head of a nail hammered into her palm. "Do you know who, Lynn? A client? Someone at the office?"

"That's a question for Jack," I said.

"I've wondered *who* all week." Tears rimming, clinging. "And I've wondered about this button. Was it on a skirt? A dress? A blouse? What color? Black on black? White, pink, yellow? Was it alone on a sleeve or in a long row of buttons? Front or back? V-neckline or mandarin?" She dropped the button back in the case. "How did this button come to be lost? Was it loose? Were they hurrying? Afraid I'd come home? Was she resisting? Was he rough?" Now the mudslide. "I look at this button and see my husband's hands."

She returned the case to the table and said, "I found something else." She took a black pinstripe coat from the floor, slid her hand into a pocket. "I don't know what I was looking for. A note. A phone number."

She removed a one-inch square package, which I imagined felt cold to her touch. I sighed, knowing too much about their marriage, knowing she'd never touched a condom before. She removed the wrapper. She pulled the condom over her finger.

"A covering," she said, "like my lens." She turned to me. "He wants to take care of me. And he does. But by controlling me." She dropped the condom in her lap. "He is standing in the way of everything I want in my life."

In one swift motion, she removed the contact lens I had never seen her without. The difference in color was so dramatic that the gray eye appeared much larger than the blue, and almost off-center. I managed not to shudder, but I stared. It was chilling. It was also telling. Two people inside her stared back at me. One docile, one determined. My helpless friend, my boss's new foe.

She laid her head on my shoulder. "I could find the strength to leave him if I were like you, Lynn. But I'm not. And I'm not sure I can."

She went into the bathroom, dropped the condom in the trash, and stared at the mirror. I wanted to go to her but knew if I hugged her she'd sob. I scanned the room until my eyes met Raggedy Ann's.

The goddamn doll, Jack called her. A gift for Patricia's third birthday, handmade by her mother, Raggedy Ann wore the traditional white apron over her dress, but the yarn stitched luxuriantly into her head was yellow instead of red, and her big button eyes were mismatched. Over the years her painted smile had faded, but those eyes shone as if new.

"I disobeyed him this morning," Patricia said, stepping back into the bedroom. She straightened the doll's apron and went on in a sunny half whisper. "I went to Harlem, to the public library, which he told me not to do. I volunteered for a program called Read and Reach for the Stars. I sat on the floor and read to children for hours. I can't remember the last time I was that happy."

"You're exaggerating. Every time you open a novel you're happy, or go to a reading or a concert or a play."

"Don't tell Jack," she said. "About Harlem. Or the button. Especially the button."

I stood to go. "I have to get back. He needs me. He wants the Kiawah account badly."

"Wait, Lynn. I went to the Book Mart today. The Gotham." She dug through the shopping bag of books, found the one she wanted to show me.

My eyebrows arched at the title. I'd bought the book the day it was published, read it in one rainy Saturday sitting. "This is 1978, Patricia. You're five years late."

"No, three. Three years married and three years late in doing something other than what my husband tells me to." She returned the book to the bag. "Do you think I'll like it?"

I hesitated. "Yes."

At The Curren Company, the clucking of typewriters had ceased. The workday had stolen the crisp starch of morning. Jack had rolled his shirtsleeves and loosened his tie.

"She's fine," I said, and he nodded, a thank-you in his eyes. "Or she's better at least."

I switched off the overhead projector, sure he'd rehearsed the presentation in my absence. I turned off the fluorescents, hoping the soft light of the tall brass lamps on his credenza would persuade him to wrap things up and go home. Instead, he asked about the executives, twelve hours and a handshake away.

"What should I know about them professionally, Lynn?"

I handed him my report on the management team. "The CEO thinks an oceanfront golf resort in South Carolina doesn't need an advertising agency in New York."

He looked at me over his reading glasses. The challenge in his eyes was as bright as the lights of the city, framed by the floor-to-ceiling windows of his corner office, thirty-fourth floor. The squeaking of his leather chair as he rocked and skimmed my work became the only sound in the room.

He leaned forward, forearms on his desk. "What should I know about them personally?"

"Golf. The director of sales is a member of Pine Valley. The CEO, of Augusta."

"That's good," he said, "though I haven't played golf in a year."

"The director of marketing and his wife play tennis," I said.

"Tennis."

"Careful, Jack. Your scorn is showing."

"I don't know one damn thing—"

"The current rivalry is Connors-Borg—the American bad boy versus the stoic European. The 'Ice Borg' or 'Ice Man,' whose mere presence on court causes women to 'Borgasm.'"

He laughed for the first time all day. "*All* women? You?"

I went on. "The new wunderkind is John McEnroe. He's nineteen, just turned pro. Wimbledon begins on the twenty-sixth. You might suggest Mr. and Mrs. Director of Marketing fly up for the U.S. Open in August. You might offer them The Curren Company box."

"Since when does my company have a box?"

"I have one reserved," I said, and he smiled. "I need to let them know. Do you want—"

"Go with it. And thank you, Lynn. I hope my sincerity is showing."

With his chair tilted back to the maximum angle, he took a moment to relax. When he rocked forward again, he lit a cigarette and studied me. "What is it?"

Smoke curled between us. "Patricia."

"You said she was fine."

I tried to decide whether husband or wife deserved my loyalty. "Jack."

He clamped the Viceroy between his lips and began scribbling tactics on a yellow legal pad, leaving me to wonder if he'd heard and ignored me or tuned me—and Patricia—out completely. On this night, at least, I chose Patricia. I told him only, "She bought *Fear of Flying.*" I had to say it twice before his eyes met mine.

"Patricia has never been afraid to fly," he said.

"It's a novel, Jack. It's a feminist novel. I wouldn't call it militant feminism—"

"Is there another brand?"

His smile was a familiar invitation to banter, but I was tired.

I stayed on task. “It’s not self- help. It’s fiction, but not what she usually reads. I think she’s trying—” I braked as he raised his hand.

“You can’t fix my wife, Lynn. Please.” He let out a smoky sigh. “I can’t get her beyond when I was seven. She can’t finish the sentence even for me. If I can’t help her—” He crushed out the thought with the cigarette. “Children are orphaned,” he said. “Children are broken and they recover. For whatever reason, Patricia did not.”

He swiveled his chair, and we looked at her photograph together. I saw an inmate in a sterling frame.

He cleared his throat. “Mail the May P&Ls when you get them. To Kiawah. To the beach house.”

He gave me a meeting-is-over nod. He picked up a portfolio with one hand and his briefcase with the other. Scuffed with twenty-two years of accomplishment, leather cracking around the handles, it was the only thing he was sentimental about. Patricia had given him a new one for Christmas. He’d had me return it the following day.

We crossed the room and paused ceremoniously at the large framed collection of ads on the wall beside the door—newspaper and magazine ads, some color, some black and white. They comprised the award-winning print campaign that had taken an Iowa dairy farm, its failing product, and The Curren Company from regional obscurity to national renown—a print campaign built around seven-year-old Patricia. Her hysteria at the initial photo shoot was the only reason Jack had impulsively changed the shot, headline, and strategy. Without knowing it, he had also changed his life.

He set his briefcase on the floor and I watched the ritual. He touched the frame as he did at the beginning and end of each day, as if dipping his fingers into a font of holy success or brushing them against a corporate mezuzah.

He said for the first time, “Thank God she was broken.”

In the elevator, I thought of the rules I'd learned from coworkers on my first day at the office.

Never say, the agency wouldn't be where it is today without that campaign.

Or, the little girl made the man, made him a success.

Never in any context say, trophy wife.

Never say, Jack is superstitious.

Or, he married Patricia sixteen years after the ad campaign, when he needed another bit of luck.

As for the last one, I knew better. Beautiful, virginal, helpless, she was an intriguing challenge he couldn't resist. I tried again. "About Patricia."

"You're my assistant. She's my dependent, and I don't mean on a tax return."

"You say that like you're proud."

"Don't analyze. Just assist." He gave me the disarming smile he used with tough clients.

"That doesn't work with me," I said, and when he chuckled, I persisted. "It's not only the novel. It's something I can't quite grasp, but it's there. Something is stirring. It's atypical."

"Is it problematic?"

I met his gaze head-on. "I don't know, Jack. I really don't."

"Noted," he said. But it wasn't. I could tell.

Often that summer I wondered if I should have given him a stronger warning that night. I might have, if I'd known what Patricia would do. I imagined her taking a job, a trip, too many sleeping pills, even divorcing him. I imagined many things. I knew only one: if the self-worth she sought led her to the fault line of infidelity, if it fractured inescapably or she chose to cross it, I would not tell her husband. I owed her that much.

The black pearl button was mine.

CHAPTER 2

Day 7. Kiawah Island. Pen in hand, Patricia looked at the ocean, as overwhelming to her as the journal before her, its empty pages waiting to be filled.

Vacation. Off course. Jack is working at the Kiawah sales office, giving his new client the time he'd promised me. He apologizes but leaves the beach house at eight and doesn't come back until six.

She hadn't missed him really. She'd missed Lynn instead. She would have spent her time differently if Lynn had been there. As it was, she hadn't left the house. Not to work, not to play. Only occasionally to walk the beach.

She'd hoped to read there rather than inside. But the dunes had grown taller daily in her mind, and the sea oats had issued warnings, not welcomes. They didn't nod. They swayed left to right, shaking their heads in a breezy, continuous *no.* Midweek a seagull had flown into the sliding glass door and fallen to the deck. Not stunned. Dead. She'd asked Jack to get rid of it, but he'd only kicked it to the sand below.

"For the time being," he'd said.

But he'd meant for the rest of their time there, and she didn't want to walk past it or even see it again. He'd no more pleased her with that response than by having an employee drive the car down from New York, and then offering to drive the rental car and let her drive the Porsche, as if she loved it like he did.

She hadn't told him that she'd asked Lynn to pack three boxes of her books from home and send them along. *Not in Lynn's job description,* Jack would have said or, *that's ridiculous.* But Lynn understood what he couldn't: that Patricia needed books on shelves to feel at home, as others needed photos or art on walls. A day later, when Jack had tried to lift them out of the Porsche's hatchback luggage area, he'd pulled a muscle in his back, cursed furiously, and refused to bring them inside all week.

"You can read in New York," he'd said. "I want you to *do* something here. Anything you want besides read. Please."

He'd suggested she take a day trip to Charleston, but she hadn't. She hadn't gone to the Kiawah Island Club either. She'd moved no closer to a golf tee than Joan Didion's *Play It as It Lays.* She hadn't confronted Jack either. She might as well have swallowed the button and the memory of it, or left both in the trash with the condom.

Last day, she thought. *Last chance. Get out of the house. Move. Do. Act.*

She changed into a swimsuit, added a towel to her bag, dropped her rings in a dresser drawer, and reached for the Sea & Ski. Ten minutes later she was climbing the steps to the club's pool, with its bird's-eye view of the beach on one side and the tennis courts on the other. *Her objective,* Jack would say, *was to strike up a conversation, make friends.* But it was hot and the pool was deserted. On the courts only one match was in play. She chose a chair facing the ocean and took *Ward No. 6 and Other Stories* from her bag. She studied Anton Chekhov's photo on the cover—goatee, flat cap, double-breasted greatcoat, intelligence in his handsome face, genius in his eyes. She opened the anthology reverently, only to have communion interrupted by the arrival of three women.

"Hi," she forced herself to say. "I'm Patricia Curren."

Ann, Becky, and Candace responded in kind.

Midforties, she decided. *Cookie-cutter women. A, B, and C from the same alphabet.* They settled on the other side of the pool.

Was it her? The angle of the sun? A breeze off the ocean she was missing? Was it Chekhov and the yellow highlighter in her hand? She dropped both in her bag, watched the waves for a moment, lay back, and eavesdropped.

"Which player?"

"The one in ready-position perfection. The one with the very fine ass."

"If his shorts were shorter or tighter he couldn't get them on."

"Or off."

"He must have a tailor. Those shorts must be custom-made."

She turned her attention to the on-court whops and thwacks, trying to discern the sounds of success and failure. She adjusted her chair and rolled over to tan her back, resting her chin on her hands. The player turned toward the pool and pulled off his shirt. He used it to wipe sweat from his face and arms, then tossed it to a corner of the court.

"Michelangelo's *David*," sighed A, B, or C. Patricia had forgotten who was who.

She sighed too, but at the cliché. *He wasn't David.* He had the thighs and calves of Bourdelle's *Hercules* and broader shoulders than *David*, though the abdomen was right. Maybe that was it—a haughtiness she unintentionally conveyed.

"He has legs like that dancer Barry-something," said A, B, or C.

Baryshnikov, she wanted to say. *Mikhail.*

"Legs like Vilas."

"Vilas?" she murmured. *Who is Vilas? See, Patricia? You don't know everything.*

She went to the outdoor café for an iced tea—sweet tea, this was South Carolina—then back to her chair. She tried *Fear of Flying* and couldn't help her studious self. She took out the highlighter.

Five chapters later, long after the women had left, she ventured into the pool, clutching the railing, sliding her feet over the steps, then moving cautiously forward until the aqua water rippled below her breasts. The sun, straight up and searing her skin, advised her to put on her cover-up and go home. She took heed. Back on the deck, she picked up her beach bag, or book bag, and winced as its straps bit her shoulder. She started for the parking lot.

She didn't stop at the tennis pro shop. Something stopped *her*, or so she told herself as she stepped inside. It was small, unmanned, and jam-packed with merchandise. She considered the apparel and equipment—dresses, socks, shoes, rackets displayed on the wall. She walked across the shop and onto the rear veranda.

David was on the far side of the court directly before her, shirtless still, alone, working on his serve—tossing, coiling, releasing, leaping, connecting. It was balletic. Unnoticed, she watched until he'd served the last of the yellow balls from a wire basket. He was starting toward the near side of the court to collect them when he saw her. He stopped, pulled on his shirt, and approached. She turned to go. Or meant to.

He looked up at her from the base of the steps. "Hi."

"Hi. I was just . . . I'm just—"

"It's Thursday. We close at twelve on Thursdays."

"I'm sorry. The door was open."

"I guess I forgot to lock it." He smiled and shrugged. "So I guess we're not closed."

They stepped into the shop together, and she drew a breath infused with sunbaked skin and sweat, indistinguishable as his or hers. The hint of chlorine was definitely hers. Her suit was still wet, her cover-up damp.

"You must have spent the morning at the pool."

"Yes."

"Really hot today, huh?"

"Yes."

"So what do you need?"

"Lessons."

"Do you play?"

"No, I've never played." *I've never played anything,* she thought.

"There's a beginners' clinic on Tuesdays. I can sign you up."

"No, I . . . I'm leaving tomorrow. I wanted a lesson later today. Just one."

"One?" He raised his eyebrows. "It takes more than onc. And we're closed."

"I was supposed to take golf lessons but didn't want—" She stopped because he'd stopped listening. He was staring out the window at Jack's ridiculous car.

"Is that your Porsche?"

"Yes."

He whistled softly. "A 928?"

She had no idea. "Yes." *He loves cars,* she thought. *Like Jack.*

But unlike Jack, he had no gray in his curly honey-colored hair. His sideburns were longer and wider than Jack's, but not as well filled in. His eyes were hazel, not dark.

He glanced at her ring-less left hand and at the car again. "I'm not supposed to teach adults. Me and Baze—he's my doubles partner—we're just here for the summer to help run the kids' tennis camp. Pretty cool gig. We fill in at the shop, so the pro and assistant pro can take vacation time, but we only teach kids. And we're closed. I'm off. I'm going to the beach."

"That's fine then."

"But if you really want that lesson—that one and only lesson." He grinned. "I'll do it." When she didn't respond, he said, "Today. Like, now."

She glanced at the rack of short white tennis dresses. "I don't have—"

"Pick something out. Take your time. I'll work on my serve

a little more and come back and help you with a racket."

She needed to go back to the beach house, take a bath, and pack. She and Jack were going to dinner at six and home in the morning on an early flight.

He folded his arms. He unfolded them and scratched his earlobe. "So, the lesson," he said. "Yes or no?"

The ladies' locker room was an igloo—large white rectangular tiles, a hidden thermostat set too low. She took a quick shower to wash away the chlorine and slipped into a pair of frilly pink tennis panties. She pulled out the ball pockets on both sides and tucked them in again. She had no bra but didn't need one: Every dress she tried on bound her breasts. Even the best fitting, a Chris Evert design, felt like a corset.

In soft new tennis shoes, she padded to the window of the pro shop, where she watched *David* serve ball after ball. She removed an advance copy of the June issue of *Panache* from her bag and took the only seat in the shop, the tall revolving stool behind the cashier's counter. The publication, a local *People* of sorts, was new and floundering. In a flutter of pages she found the article about the advertising mogul whose success knew no end, whose company was gobbling up smaller agencies and even modeling agencies, who was surrounded in the lead photo by a dozen models. She studied them, wondering if her husband had betrayed her with one of the twelve. All were looking at him in the same moonstruck way. But Jack, smiling and looking straight ahead, gave no clue.

The article was a puff piece, practically an advertorial. The more she read, the more certain she became that he'd approved every word of the piece. She stopped at the penultimate paragraph, where she was described in words so worn they confirmed the involvement of TCC's public relations arm, of the vice president who maintained and polished the company's brand. Jack's brand.

Princess Grace pretty. As blonde and classically beautiful as her husband is dark and handsome. Enigmatic and refreshingly shy, unlike countless women seen on his arm in recent years when he was a mainstay on most-eligible-bachelors lists. The enviable shape of a model, but lacking the tiny, enchanting flaw that today allows a career to take flight. Perfect features instead, starting with her eyes, a captivating blue.

Emphatically she closed the magazine just as David-Hercules-Baryshnikov, or whoever he was, opened the door.

Say something, she told herself, *anything.* Why was it such a challenge? She nodded at the price tags and cash she'd laid on the counter. They exchanged places, his body brushing against hers. She returned the magazine to her bag as he laid his racket on the counter. He opened the register and counted change into her hand.

"That's too much," she said, giving him ten dollars back and wondering what caused him to blush—his mistake or his gaze, as stuck in her cleavage as a cab in Manhattan traffic. "I'm not athletic. You can probably tell."

He lifted his eyes. "How could I tell?"

"I'm . . . I don't know . . . an imposter in this dress."

"So, want to forget the lesson and go to the beach with me?"

As he smiled, she had a bizarre image of her finger tracing his lips and dancing across his teeth. A slight center overlap suggested he'd been a borderline candidate for braces but hadn't worn them. He'd been left instead with a tiny, enchanting flaw.

"No. I only want the lesson." Apprehension was tying the laces of the corset now. "I have to be home by four. I have dinner plans."

He left the register, brought them face-to-face. "I'll get you back in time." He waited but she didn't respond. He started to slip his hands into his pockets but stopped. He removed a tennis ball and stared at it as if he'd forgotten it was there. He bounced it a few times, returned it to his pocket. He tucked his racket under his arm, as if it were a shield he might need. He looked at her again with a flash of self-doubt. "I'll get you back."

"All right," she heard herself say. "Cool. Let's get the hell out of here."

"But the dress." She fingered the hem.

"You're keeping it, right? For that one and only lesson you'll take someday?" He locked the back door. "We can change at my place. And we'll need your car, okay? 'Cause I don't even have a car, except for a piece-of-crap Valiant me and Baze share." At the front door, he turned out the light. "Ready?"

She couldn't see herself wriggling back into her still-damp swimsuit in the home of a man she'd just met, but she drove to a group of villas, as directed, and stopped at number twenty-three. She followed him inside and into the stench of locker rooms and gritty men and boys.

"I'll change first and then pack the car," he said, starting down the hall. "And don't use this bathroom." He paused to pull a door closed. "We gotta call a plumber."

When he'd disappeared into his bedroom, she pushed her sunglasses to the top of her head. Over the kitchen's half wall, she saw a cupcake, with tall swirls of chocolate icing, on the table. With a couple of steps, she saw bowls in the sink, cereal fossils in the bowls.

In the living room, her eyes skipped over takeout boxes and beer cans to the bookcases. Bare. She'd have nothing to talk about. Newspapers on the floor were open to sports sections.

On one side of the fireplace, Cheryl Tiegs, in a pink bikini, was posted to the wall. Farrah Fawcett was posted to the other side, her smile wide, her frosted hair flowing, her nipples erect in her red one-piece swimsuit. On both posters, someone had drawn cartoon speech bubbles with black marker.

Happy birthday, Terry. Can I blow your candle? said Farrah.

Key party? Three party? said Cheryl. *You, me, and Baze?*

"Room's all yours," he said, returning.

In his bedroom, she picked up a large packet on his dresser and read the return address: University of Texas Tennis. *Jesus God*, she thought, *he could be eighteen.* She went into his bathroom to change and back into the bedroom, away from a ring in the toilet, curly hair on the vanity, a dripping faucet, and a sink littered with the morning's shave.

"I am not attracted to this man," she said, pushing the bedroom door closed, her fingers grazing the jockstrap hanging on the doorknob.

This is wrong, she thought. She undressed.

A mistake. She put on her black maillot and cover-up.

There will be consequences. She opened the door.

He was standing there, blocking her exit, his knuckles poised to knock. "Ready?"

She listened to water plopping in the sink until the air-conditioning kicked on with a roar. She shivered from a swoosh of air from the vent overhead. She nodded at the burnt-orange logo on his T-shirt. "Do you go there?"

He held up his hand, grasping his middle and ring fingers with his thumb and extending his index and little fingers. "Hook 'em Horns." He picked up her bag. "I wanted California really bad. UCLA mostly or Southern Cal. But Texas was the only Division One school that wanted me—enough to offer a full scholarship anyways. Well, University of Florida did. But I live in Orlando and wanted to get as far away from home as I could. Austin's been great."

"What position do you play?" *Are there positions?* she wondered.

"Number three. Singles and doubles. But there's a tournament here starting Monday. The Challenger Series, which is new. If I can beat my friend Freddie, who plays number one for us, Coach might move me up to two. Freddie's coming in town to play, and I'm hoping he's in my half of the draw. Or what would be great is that he's in the other half and I play him in the final. But Freddie's tough. And only a sophomore."

"You're a senior?" She hoped to God.

"Yeah. But Freddie's better than me. On clay, for sure. Not hard court."

"Have you played on grass?"

"A lot." He laughed. "Want to smoke a J?"

"No."

"Do you ever? Ever get bent?"

"No." She wasn't sure what he meant but was sure that she didn't. Ever. "If you're a senior, you're what—twenty-one?"

"Twenty-three. As of yesterday." He seemed to hear questions she wasn't asking and to answer in defensive fragments. "I got held back. When I was a kid. I was sick. A lot." Defense became offense. "That's a weird question. How old are *you*?"

"Twenty-six."

"For real? You act older."

She followed him to the door of the villa but stayed inside. She rubbed her left thumb against her naked ring finger. *How old?* she wondered. *Midthirties, like Lynn? Dearest Lynn, coppery and green-eyed. Confidence in her step, an energetic bounce in her short auburn hair. Determined, assertive, driven like Jack.*

"Are you coming?" David-Hercules-Baryshnikov called, but his voice was distant. The nearer voice, in her head, was her husband's.

"She's good with clients," Jack said once of his assistant. "Great conversationalist. Perceptive. Reassuring. She senses things, like a psychic. And competitive? She can hold her own. But don't tell her," he said. "I like her as she is—confident. I don't want her cocky."

Patricia told Lynn immediately, knowing how much his praise meant to her and how often he withheld it. "It's a gift," Patricia said. "Holding your own. Jack's got it. You've got it."

"I had four brothers." Lynn laughed. "Two older. Two younger. I learned to hold my own."

"Better than where I was," Patricia said. "No siblings, no parents after seven."

"Be proud," Lynn said. "You've held your own too."

But she hadn't. She'd barely held on. Then, now. Always?

Back in bright sunlight, she squinted at a cooler, a Frisbee, two beach chairs, and David-Hercules-Baryshnikov wearing sunglasses, a T-shirt, flip-flops, and cutoff jeans—tight, short, frayed, vertical split in the right front leg, a sliver of white upper thigh.

"So," he said.

"So?"

"Can I have your keys?"

"Just one key." She handed it over.

"And I'm driving, right? Since I know where we're going."

He didn't wait for an answer. He opened the hatchback, slid the boxes toward the front seats, and began packing, like she should have been packing for home. As he leaned into the car to add her bag and adjust the beach chairs a final time, her eyes fell upon a quarter-sized circle of white cheek. She looked away when he turned but not quickly enough. He slid his hands into his back pockets.

"Sorry," he said. "Is that going to bother you? It's laundry day. All my other shorts need washing."

"Excuse me?"

He pulled her sunglasses from the top of her head to the bridge of her nose. "You're excused." In the car, he seemed ready to swoon as he looked over the dashboard and turned the key. "Got any tapes?" he said, and when she shook her head, he turned on the radio. Static. “Is that what you listen to?” He began punching buttons.

Someone suggested that she “Prove It All Night.”

“Good?” he said, but he seemed to sense her dismay. He punched again and waited for a reaction. “Waylon and Willie? No? What do you like? Sex Pistols or something?”

“No . . . I . . . What’s your name?”

“Terry. Terry Sloan,” he said. “Yours?”

“I’m Patricia,” she said. “Curren.”

She said no more—nothing while he drove through familiar parts of the community. Nothing miles later when he took a left, into a future neighborhood where only two homes were under construction. Nothing when he turned right, into an area where the only sign of development was an unpaved road. With no end in sight, it paralleled the beach, which was visible through oaks, palmetto trees, and underbrush.

“Would you mind if I drive kinda fast now?” She looked at the massive oaks lining the road.

“If you don’t want me to, just say so.” He waited. “But I’d sure love to.”

“All right. But be careful.”

She tried to remember what Jack had said about the car’s maximum speed as Terry turned road into runway. She imagined the car’s wheels leaving the ground, folding into the chassis.

“Too fast?” the pilot shouted above the engine’s roar.

She tried to take off her sunglasses to see the speedometer more clearly, and she accidentally knocked them to the floorboard. She read ninety before the wind, rushing through the windows, began whipping her hair into her face, flogging her eyes.

“Stop,” she shouted as he took a sharp curve.

And it happened. He lost control. For a few seconds the Porsche careened up an embankment, hurling sand and debris into the car and into her eyes. Her eyelids came down like window shades yanked far past the point of retraction. As he completed the curve, she was thrown against the door so hard that she might as well have been thrown from the car. She felt a hatchet in her brain, claws in her eyes, and at last, a whiplashing stop.

Behind eyelids unable to roll back up, black gave way to the cold bright white of confusion, of clenched teeth, of snow, of the breast of a gull, dead on the beach. Dead near the deck. Three days dead now. Unmoved. Unmoving.

"Shit. I'm sorry," he said. "I overdid it."

Arms pressed hard against her ribs, she folded forward, face toward her knees. Nothing could cool the pain in her head, but a fierce waterfall splashed out of her eyes. She rubbed them and when she opened them, the digging and scratching had stopped. She reached for her sunglasses on the floor and without looking at him put them on. She listened to waves slap the beach.

"Are you okay?" he asked. "I didn't mean to go that fast. It just got away from me."

He sounded like a six-year-old boy who really was sorry—but because he'd been bad? Or because he'd been caught? "Get out."

"What?"

"Get out of my car. I'm leaving."

"Why? Aren't we going to the beach? This is the beach I want to go—"

"I don't like the way you drove my car and—"

"I was only going eighty-five."

"Liar. Get out." She turned her head.

"Are you gonna leave me here? Fifteen miles from fucking nowhere? Will you look at me? Will you please fucking look at me for a minute?"

"Will you stop saying that word? It's offensive to me. Everything about you offends me."

"Fine. I'll get my stuff out of the back and you can go. Or do you want to keep my cooler and leave me in the heat with nothing to drink?" He muttered something as he yanked the key from the ignition. While he unloaded, she lifted her body over the gearshift and into the driver's seat. She adjusted it as he slammed the hatchback closed. She needed to calm down, needed to get back to the beach house and put on her rings. With her head pounding, she clutched the steering wheel tightly, and still her hands trembled. She stared at them, then at the ignition. She raised her eyes and looked for Terry Sloan, but the man, the mistake she'd made, had disappeared into the short stretch of woods between the road and the beach. She forced herself out of the car and around to the back.

Damnit. He had done it on purpose. She was certain of that. Damnit. Damnit. He had taken her key.

She made a hot, shaky trek toward the sound of the ocean and paused at the edge of a shining expanse of sand. The beach was untarnished by walkers, runners, and sunbathers; undisturbed by shell collectors and readers; invaded and solely occupied by a man in a chair facing the ocean. She stopped at the empty chair beside him, wondering how he could think she would stay.

"I screwed up," he said, without looking at her. "I'm really sorry."

His hair was wet. Saltwater beads clung to his body. She noticed her bag for the first time. He'd taken that too.

"Sorry about the car, but mostly about the key. I put it in my pocket by mistake and went swimming. My back pocket. With the hole."

"God." Her knees gave way. She sank to the sand.

"You've got a spare, right?"

"In New York."

"Oh."

She sat back on her heels. "Jesus God."

"A dealer can make a new one for you. I'll pay."

He offered his hand to help her back up, but she pushed it away, managed to stand on her own, and walk toward the ocean. Weaving slightly, as if she'd had too much to drink, she pressed her hand against her forehead. The situation and the futility of trying to explain it to Jack aggravated the pain.

"If you want me to," he called, "I'll walk back and get the Valiant."

She folded her arms and looked down, watching again and again as the ocean, flat and frothy, slid in to greet her and withdrew hurriedly, as if its waves, like Terry, didn't know what to do, how to soothe her. She felt rather than heard him approaching, his bare feet stealthy upon the sand. When he reached her, she turned her back and looked down the desolate beach.

"It's only six miles or so," he said. "A 10k. I can walk it easy. I run, see? Did a half marathon in February."

"Then *run.* Don't walk."

"I will, if you want. But what I think we should do is hang out for a while. We can catch a ride back. Somebody will come along."

She faced him. "It looks like a popular spot." Her voice was weak, but her tone as sarcastic as she'd intended it to be. "I'm sure we'll be overrun any minute."

"That's what I like about this beach," he said. "Not too many people know it's here. If you've got to be stuck somewhere, this is a pretty nice place." He waited through a breezy silence. "I don't know what happened. Hell, nothing falls out of my pockets because my shorts are so tight. I've got a thirty-two-inch waist, so I gotta buy shorts to fit my waist, which makes them fit the rest of me so tight that girls are always staring and—well, not all girls, but some."

"Narcissus."

"I don't know what that means." The wind hummed, then whistled. "It's bad?"

"I deserve an apology."

"I'm sorry. I swear." He went on, his sunglasses preventing her from measuring his sincerity. "I admit I wanted to drive fast, and once I got going, I couldn't help it."

"If it feels good, do it?"

"Sometimes I'm selfish. I admit that too, okay? Sometimes I'm a—"

"Bastard?" It felt good to say it. She should have said it to Jack a thousand times but hadn't even once. "Do you know what *bastard* means?"

"Yeah, and I'm a bastard. And I'm so fucked up you don't want anything to do with me."

"Tell me something I don't know."

"I'm trying to apologize. Again. I'm fucking trying—"

"I want an apology without your favorite word."

"Tricia, I—"

"*Pa*tricia."

"*Pa*tricia. But I want to call you Tricia. 'Cause if I call you Patricia, then you'll call me Terrence, and I hate that. So, all I can say—" He hesitated. "Tricia," he said. "I wish I hadn't done it. And if I can make it up to you, I will."

"Just get me home and away from you. I have to be home by four. Four." She started back to the chairs and her bag, desperate for a minute alone.

"Hey, Baze is coming out here in a while. So can we just hang out till then? Enjoy the beach together?"

She spun toward him, intending to shout no. But as he walked toward her, the clouds above the horizon began to spin like cotton candy around a twirling cone. The world went sugary, sticky white, and she grabbed his shoulder for support.

"I'm going to pass out."

"Holy shit." He helped her to the empty chair.

She was weak and sweating, but the spinning stopped and the world was full of color again. "Thanks."

He sat down beside her and pointed to the right side of his forehead. "You've got a bad bump."

She touched the same spot on hers. "God. It's a baseball." She adjusted the slope of the back of her chair from ninety to forty-five degrees and closed her eyes. "That's the second time I almost blacked out. Or whitened out. I must have a concussion."

"Take off your shades."

"Why?"

"If I can see your eyes, I can tell. If your pupils are dilated—" He leaned toward her, carefully removed her sunglasses, and frowned.

"What is it?" she said. He looked shocked and concerned. "Am I concussed?"

"No, I—you're fine. I just hadn't noticed that before . . . that your eyes are different."

"Jesus God." She turned away, her lens lost in the turbulence, her key in the ocean.

"What? I shouldn't have said that? Did I say the wrong thing?"

"Yes."

"Why? I think it's kinda cool."

"It's abnormal," she said, thankful for spares at the beach house. No spare key, but a lifetime of lenses. "I'm abnormal. And my head is hurting."

"It's not a concussion, though. Your eyes look fine. If you had a concussion you'd be mixed up. Like you wouldn't know where you are or why you're here."

"I don't know why I'm here."

"With me, you mean."

"Yes."

He gave a one-shouldered shrug. "Anyways, if you had a

concussion you'd be talking crazy, making no sense."

"I need something to drink."

"Michelob or Bud?"

"No water? Or soft drinks?"

"Sorry." He took a Styrofoam cup from the top of the cooler, scooped it full of ice, and offered it to her.

"I want something to *drink*," she said.

"It's gonna melt, you know."

"Really?" she snapped.

He set the cup on the sand and turned his chair toward hers. She faced the ocean; he faced the dunes. He wrapped three of the ice cubes in a corner of a towel and gingerly pressed the compress against her forehead.

"Jesus God."

"Why do you keep saying that?"

"I am pleading to be delivered from this beach and from you." *Jesus God,* she prayed silently, *tell me what to do. I am here, I know, for betraying my husband in heart and mind. And even though he has betrayed me, You have imprisoned me on this empty beach, with a concussion and a boy who has the body of* David *and* Hercules *and the heart of Iago. Please tell me if I should push his hand from my head or leave it there because I have head trauma and might need him.*

"Tricia, if—"

"*Pa*tricia."

"*Pa*tricia. I'll do anything you want."

She tried to relax, let her body go limp, let her head rest on the back of the uncomfortable chair. "The dead bird," she whispered, confused.

"Maybe you do have a concussion."

"I have to be home," she managed.

"By four. I know. That's the third time you've told me."

A tear pooled under the rim of her sunglasses. Hidden, she hoped, but she felt its slow slide. He took the compress away and laid the tip of his finger upon the tear. She squeezed her eyes shut to dam a stream. Uselessly shut. He laid his palm against her face.

"Sorry," he said. "It's my fault."

"Yes," she returned, "and no." She leaned to the right, letting the weight of her head rest in his hand. "I'm so . . . so—"

"Fucked up?"

"Yes. So badly that you don't want anything to do with me." Wind. And waves.

"Can I help?"

"Keep your hand there."

He lowered his elbow slowly onto the arm of his chair for support. "Okay, but why don't you try to sleep? I'll put your chair all the way back, and I'll stay right here. I won't leave you."

"How could you? You lost my key."

She was blessed with an hour-long nap but cursed with a nightmare: Jack walking the beach, in a coat and tie, searching for her, shouting her name. When she woke, Terry helped her sit up. He gave her the cup—water now—and she drank thirstily.

"Want something to eat?" He offered Peanut M&M's. "No thanks."

"They've been in the cooler. They're cold. They're good that way."

"I don't want them." She wiped sweat from her forehead. "God, it's so hot."

"Do you want to take off that cover dress and go swimming with me? Cool off?"

"I would rather dive into a book. Will you hand me my bag?"

"So, do you live in New York?"

"Yes." She opened *Ward No. 6.*

"You like it there?"

"Very much." She felt locked up in *Ward No. 6.*

His pleasantries continued: Did she like the island? Was she here for the summer? Was she renting? So she owned a place?

"Yes."

"What are you reading?"

"I'm not reading anything because you keep interrupting me."

"No, seriously, what are you reading?"

She showed him the cover and he nodded appreciatively. "Cheekhov."

"Chekhov."

Silence, then: "I was kidding. I know how to say it. I've read a lot of books by him."

"He didn't write books. Only stories and plays."

"That's a book in your hands, isn't it?"

"An anthology of stories."

"Stories, then. I read a lot."

"I've got other books in my bag, if you want something."

He explored. "Always read five books at a time?"

"No, but I always keep several with me, especially on the beach or a plane, to be sure I have something for every mood and situation."

He stopped browsing and looked at her. "When you're locked out of your car and stuck with an a-hole, is Cheekhov—"

"Chekhov."

He looked embarrassed. "That's what I meant," he said. He picked up *Fear of Flying.*

"Not that one," she cried. He dropped it as if he'd been burned. It hit the beach, not the bag.

"Sorry," he said. He brushed away the sand and exchanged it for *To the Lighthouse.* While his finger slid left to right on the page, his lips shaped every word. He looked up. "The second sentence in this book is twelve lines long."

"Are you afraid of Virginia Woolf?"

"That's a movie, right?"

"A play first. Edward Albee."

"*Who's Afraid of Virginia's Wolf?*"

"Oh my God."

"What?"

"You are unbelievable."

"For fuck's sake. I was kidding." He closed the book and stole a glance at the cover. "You think I don't know who Virginia Woolf is? All I said was this book has long sentences."

"Afraid of long sentences?"

He tossed the novel into her bag. "I'm severely dyslexic." Wind. Waves. "That's why I got held back. Twice," he added. Then he said, "I'm kidding."

"You're not dyslexic?"

"Not if you're gonna look at me like I'm stupid. And I'm not reading anymore. The waves look great. I'm going swimming." He took resolute steps toward the ocean, stopped, and turned to her. "Will you come in with me?" She shook her head. "Okay, don't." More steps and a spin. "Why won't you come in?"

She couldn't decide if the question had the ring of a tantrum or a plea. Tennis brat? Boy? Or a species more rare—the insecure, vulnerable male? How had Narcissus become Achilles? And how had she so easily found his heel? At the edge of the ocean he gestured to her as waves built, crested, and smashed. She shook her head.

He couldn't read, and she couldn't play tennis or swim. She was as landlocked—physically and emotionally—on this island as she was in the city with Jack, as she'd been on a dairy farm in Iowa. Just as orphaned and afraid. Excepting Lynn, her family and friends were from fiction. She was afraid of the water, afraid to speak or act, afraid of everything really. Her only spine was that of the book in her hand.

She watched him venture deeper, floating over mild-mannered waves, diving through tall ones that threatened to swallow him. He waited patiently and made a choice. He timed it, raced the curve of frothy white water with a strong freestyle, and bodysurfed into water so shallow she thought he would scrape his face on the sand. He turned and headed back for more.

Prowess, strength, rhythm—they were there in the water as they had been on court.

David-Hercules-Baryshnikov. Vigorous, sculpted, tall.

Narcissus-Iago-Achilles. Self-centered, evil, weak.

Terry Sloan. Holding ice in a towel on her forehead, touching a tear on her cheek.

"You should have come in," he said.

She had just shed her cover-up, unable to bear the heat any longer. He put his sunglasses on, and she couldn't see in their reflective lenses if and how he was looking at her body.

"I liked watching," she said. "You caught waves at exactly the right moment."

He seemed pleased with himself and with her for noticing. He sat down beside her and together they watched the V-formation flight of a flock of pelicans. He pointed to the ocean.

"See the dolphins. Straight ahead." Two surfaced, disappeared, and surfaced as they made their way through the water. "So, Tricia."

She thought he sounded unsure of himself. When she turned, he looked unsure too. "That tournament starts Monday. Want to come? See me play?"

"No."

He shrugged. "Do you want to take a walk?"

"No."

"Want a beer?"

"No."

"Throw the Frisbee?"

"No."

"You hate me, don't you? Because of the car. Which isn't

exactly fair, because I did ask if I could drive fast, and you didn't say no."

"I'm not good at saying no. I've never been able to."

"You just said no to me four times in a row, so you must be getting better. I can get you to say yes to me right now, though, to anything I ask for."

"Why would I say yes to you?"

He took time in answering. "Because I have your key."

"You found it in the ocean? That's incredible."

"Yeah, I—" He paused. "Don't get mad, okay? The truth is, I've had it the whole time. But I wanted you to know I was really sorry, and the only way to keep you with me long enough to apologize was to keep the key."

"And keep me here for hours."

"I'll give it back. All you have to do is say yes to one thing."

"Oh please. I was starting to like you."

"I want you to say my name. Because you haven't said it all day, and that's bugging the shit out of me."

"Terry," she said slowly, "give me my key."

"Tricia, I will." Standing, he struggled to work his hand into his pocket. "If I can get it."

"Just kidding?"

"No." He tried to stifle a grin. "There's some pretty funny things I could say. Like, your hands are smaller, so maybe you should try. If I was really an asshole, I'd say shit like that."

"You just did."

He laughed. "You're kinda fun when you're kidding."

"I wasn't kidding," she said, trying to remember if anyone had ever called her fun. He placed the key in her hand. "Thank you, Terry. Let's go." She put on her cover-up. He slipped her bag over his shoulder, picked up the chairs and cooler, and they started back to her car.

"Want me to drive?"

"No."

"Your head is hurting. I think I should. I'll go slow."

"It's a no."

"I must be really good for you, because you're saying no all the time now."

"Nothing about you is good for me, Terry."

He looked at his feet as she started the car. He looked out the window as they rode to his villa.

He said nothing until she pulled into the driveway. "What about the dead bird?"

She listened to the engine. "The seagull. It was dead on the deck first. I swept it off, but it's beside the steps now, decaying, and smelling worse than your villa. I don't know why, but I haven't been able to get near it, even to get rid of it. But I'm sure I can do it now. Saying no so many times made me stronger."

"I'm a pretty good dead bird handler if you—"

"No. But thanks."

"So, Tricia, can I kiss you?"

"Have you lost your mind? No."

"Kiss you good-bye? Just on the cheek? Where that first tear was?" He was smiling.

And kidding? "How fast were you driving my car?"

"Maybe a hundred." He touched her cheek. "Just right there?"

"No, Terry, you can't kiss me good-bye."

"See how I'm helping you? You said no three more times. I'm counting."

"Don't kiss me good-bye. Tell me good-bye, Terry. Because that's what this is: good-bye."

Dressed and ready for dinner, with time to spare, she went to the suitcase she'd ignored all week and took out a gray metal box of five-by-seven index cards, untouched for three years, abandoned for Jack, who asked for all of her attention in exchange for a pittance of his. In the living room, on the sofa, she cradled the box in her arms before setting it on the coffee table. What else could she cradle? He wouldn't give her a child. She'd asked so often that he'd said not to ask again, that he wouldn't talk about a family until he was ready.

Taking out the first card, she began to transfuse her aborted PhD dissertation. Her notes for "Anton Chekhov: The Genre Paradox in the Major Plays" stole an untracked hour, and Jack came in so suddenly that she couldn't pack the cards away. But that was a good thing. He'd notice the metal box, ask about it, and she'd broach the subject—NYU, completing her degree.

They're not mutually exclusive, she would say, *our marriage and my PhD.* She rose slowly as he walked toward her.

"You look beautiful, princess," he said.

"It's the dress. Lynn chose it."

He smiled, as unaware of the box as of the clump of makeup hiding the bump on her forehead, covering her guilt and anxiety. He moved to the bar and took a pack of cigarettes from the carton there. "I need to check in with Lynn," he said, picking up the phone. "Ten minutes. Then we'll go."

She packed the cards back into the box and the box back into the suitcase. On impulse, she took the magazine from her bag and laid it on the coffee table.

As they drove toward the clubhouse, he went over the names of their guests for dinner: the Kiawah executives and their wives. "I'm sorry it's not just the two of us, but this is necessary. They're clients." Gently he added, "And you're my wife. Please help me entertain. Please don't sit at dinner and say nothing, like a mouse in a corner."

"I'll try," she said, "but it's always hard to break in. You talk business nonstop with clients. Their wives talk hair, weight, shoes, shopping, and golf. They're older. They're different." They colored the gray in their hair for their husbands, not the gray of an eye.

"Talk about anything. You're intelligent, informed. Talk about what you're reading."

"You don't care what I'm reading. Why would they?" She shifted in her seat, rubbed her wedding ring like a magic lamp, wishing for charm and verve. They said nothing more until he'd handed the keys to the valet.

"Please try," he said, drawing her close. "For me."

She did well with the introductions but fell silent.

Drinks, soup, salad. Hair, weight, golf.

She turned to the other conversation at the table.

"The objective is creating urgency," Kiawah's director of marketing was saying. The CEO and director of sales concurred. They wanted to make their mark on the TCC ad campaign that would be revised in accordance with Jack's strategic goals. She marveled at her husband, listening as if they were the experts. She thought of Lynn's fight for a place at his boardroom table and her own meager fight for a useful place at dinner.

"Fear of loss. A reason to buy now." This was the director of sales.

"So the ad photo," said the CEO, "should be the signature hole, Jack. Number six."

Jack laughed good-naturedly. "Which I triple-bogeyed twice this week."

"The signature hole," the director of marketing continued, "with a husband and wife walking off the green, arm in arm, living the good life. With a headline like: 'Dream Tomorrow, Live Today,' then some dots, the photo, more dots—what do you call that? The dots—"

"An ellipsis," she said. Clients, babbling wives, Jack—all turned to her as if they'd forgotten she was there. The silence wasn't dead, but alive and brutal. "Though correctly, it's used for an omission or—"

"It's a headline, princess," Jack said. "Not an essay." He fired a quick burst of laughter. Then everyone laughed and she tried to laugh too.

"So," the director of sales resumed. "More dots and then 'on Kiawah Island.'"

"Nice," Jack said, but she knew he didn't mean it. As he charmed them, she sipped her coffee, thinking of the dots in her life she longed to connect to dreams.

"Jack," she said as they reentered the beach house. With a hand on his arm, she stopped him in the foyer. "I want to go back to school, to NYU, for my doctorate in comparative lit." She saw that she'd caught him off guard, but he recovered and kissed her.

His words, like the kiss, were fatherly. "I don't think we can manage that."

"We? Or *me?*" she said quietly. "I can't manage it?"

He took a note from his pocket. "Let's talk about this tomorrow. On the plane." He picked up the phone in the kitchen. "I have a call to return."

"And I have nothing. NYU is the answer."

He stopped dialing. "What is the question, Patricia?" He hung up the receiver and gave her his full attention. "Tell me, because I don't understand. What is the goddamn question?"

"You don't love me, Jack. You love an idea of me."

"One more time, Patricia: You were a concept in 1960, not '75. I never turned you—excuse me, my concept of you—over to PR." He took off his coat, hung it over a chair.

"I'm not what you thought. I'm not what you want. I feel like an item on your task list." She noted the deep breath he drew, signaling a tactical shift.

"You're my A-1," he said. "The A-1 of my life."

"But you never start with me. You never even end with me.

You delegate me. To Lynn." He tensed and dialed again, even as she continued. "I love Lynn, but as Lynn, not your proxy. I don't want Lynn as my date for plays and concerts because you'd rather work. I don't want her shopping for me and dressing me to please you."

"Tom," he said. He listened and paced. "No. The creative is not uninspired. I saw the boards. It's the best work we've done for them." His voice rose. "The account exec is uninspired. That's you, Tom."

A pattern took shape, one she knew and hated. He would lose his temper in a string of *goddamnits* and, without warning, twist 180 degrees to sympathetic calm. *How can I help?* he would say. Then he'd take charge. He'd take care of Tom or whomever, whatever. He'd take over and find a solution to the problem, then bask in his prowess with an almost sexual satisfaction. But tonight the *goddamnits* were louder than usual, the string of them longer. She'd taught herself to turn his tirades into white noise, but this one was blood red. She closed her eyes, opened them to the mantel where a clock marked the time and the tide: eight fifteen and almost dead low. She was dead low already. Princess Grace pretty. Emily Dickinson lonely.

"How can I help?" Jack asked Tom, his voice calm now, but his shoulders still heaving.

She opened the heavy sliding glass door, stepped out on the deck, and thought of the bird. "Don't look down," she murmured. "Look straight ahead." Shielding the left side of her face with her hand, she hurried across the deck and down the steps. She made the climb up the dunes and scampered down. She strode across the sand, stopped near the water's edge.

With the sun setting behind her, she watched three suntanned, towheaded children build a sand castle. Only after they'd packed up their buckets and shovels and gone home with their parents did she wade into the ocean up to her knees. She felt sand eroding beneath her feet as the undertow swirled at her ankles.

She went back to the house, and as she stepped inside, Jack swirled the Scotch in his glass. "Why did you go out?" he asked, with a lingering trace of a scowl.

Thinking he'd only twisted ninety degrees this time, she pulled her hair over her shoulder and began to braid nervously. "Fresh air," she said. "The beach. Sunset."

He glanced at the magazine, asked how she liked the article.

"Fine." She unbraided and braided again. "Except for the photo of you and a dozen women."

"The photo wasn't my idea. If it displeases you, I'm sorry." He tapped his finger against the glass in his hand. "What's wrong, Patricia?" He looked genuinely concerned. "Help me understand how I'm failing you."

"I want something for *me*. I want to work too. When I hear you talk about the agency—"

"You don't hear me. You drift off. You daydream."

"Please listen. When you talk about work, I hear a hum. It's the same with Lynn."

"I didn't marry Lynn."

"But you admire her. You've said so. And I do too. When either one of you says *market share* or *focus group* or *double truck* or *demographics*, there's a buzz. I feel it. I want it too. I'm not a watch to be worn on your arm. I'm not a pet to be groomed, a model to be dressed—"

"Lose the metaphors, Patricia. Tell me what you want or need that I haven't given you. Just one thing. One specific thing. Besides a degree."

"What I've always wanted: A child. One specific child."

"You've got a doll. Isn't that enough?"

He walked to the sliding glass door. He looked at the ocean, though there was nothing of the day left to see. Just darkness. A void.

"Please don't tell me again that it's not in the five-year plan,

Jack."

"I shouldn't have to. I've told you a hundred times."

"You'll be fifty-four in five years."

"It's not in the five-year plan."

"Is our marriage a business plan?" She wanted to be indignant not hurt, to demand instead of beg. But when he faced her, she felt tears welling. "If it is, I want a—"

"You don't know *what* you want."

He'd broken in loudly, as if he'd known what was coming and wouldn't let her say it.

"A degree and a child are two different things, Patricia."

And a divorce, she thought, i*s a drastically different third.* But he was right. She didn't know what she wanted other than to fill the hollow inside her.

"There's your child," Jack said tightly. "She's seven."

He pointed so deliberately at something behind her that she turned, but she didn't see a child in the mirror above the mantel. She saw a woman in a carnival fun house, stretched by her husband in painful ways, compressed in others, pulled apart, and doubled into someone she wasn't and didn't want to be. She closed her eyes and when she opened them again, the thick, dry dust of the nothingness inside her seemed to have settled over the glass. She wanted to imprint her palm there or take a finger to it and write her name, but as she raised her hand, Jack sailed his highball glass across the room into her reflection. She cried out as if he'd struck her, cringed as the mirror shattered. It hung on the wall for an impossible moment before crashing to the floor.

"Patricia," he said calmly and she faced him. "Why don't we talk about how you've failed *me?* Just once, let's talk about that." He waited. "Can't think of anything to say?" She shook her head. "Sometimes, Patricia, you are so beautiful to me that you still take my breath away. But you are so colorless sometimes I can hardly see you. And so hopelessly introverted I can hardly stand you." He started down the hall. "Come to bed."

No, she thought. But with Jack, she couldn't even murmur that tiny critical word.

She took her journal and a pen from a drawer in the kitchen, and leaning back against the refrigerator, she tried to recount the good things he'd brought to her life.

Protection. Security. Care. No, control.

Six weeks of romance in the city in the spring, of having him all to herself. *The agency be damned,* he'd said when he'd begun that vacation.

He'd given her two glorious weeks in Lake Como, and brought her home to New York and a surprise gift he'd had readied while they were away: the conversion of the third bedroom of the town house into a library and two treasures from Bauman Rare Books that he'd called a sound investment.

"North of twenty-five grand," he'd said of the 1926 first edition, first printing of *The Sun Also Rises,* signed by Hemingway, and an 1884 edition of Whitman's *Leaves of Grass.*

She'd taken them into her hands and looked at one hundred new hardbacks, each tied with a bow. "I will love you, Jack," she'd said, "for the rest of my life."

The next day, he'd gone back to work. Three months later, Lynn had appeared at her side for the theater, the ballet, the 92nd Street Y—for every event Jack didn't want to attend. Now, three years later, he referred to her library as her $450,000 mouse hole, and six days of vacation were too many to ask of him.

At the table, she recorded in a surprisingly steady hand the description of her husband she'd crafted, without the help of a PR team.

Jack. I-me-mine power. Control. Caretaking. A proclivity to intimidate. Conceit masquerading as confidence. Duplicity. Extreme volatility. Machine-gun laughter. Fast, cold, humiliating. Lovemaking, the same.

She waited until the bedroom was dark and she was sure he had fallen asleep. But when she slipped into bed, he turned on the light.

"You should slit my throat, princess, with a piece of that mirror. I damn well deserve it."

Extraordinary good looks, she added in her mind as he pulled her toward him and forced himself into sex that was raw and dry.

He was always so handsome in her eyes, even through tears when they were done. She had taught herself to cry without making a sound but couldn't deceive him. She could roll away. She could squeeze her eyes shut and rest her cheek on the mat of dark hair on his chest. She could press her lips together, as she did then, and try to wait for darkness.

"I understood the first time, princess. Your first time. I don't understand this time, and every time between then and now."

"I'm sorry. It's a reflex."

"A reflex. I come and you cry."

She looked at the ceiling fan. The spinning of its blades seemed too fast, its whirring too loud. She turned out the light. "I don't want to go home," she said softly. The fan whirred on. He asked her why. "I want to spend the summer here."

"I don't understand."

He needs Lynn, she thought, *to explain me.*

"Stay alone? Why? You don't like the beach or the club. You've shown no interest in Charleston. You've done nothing but read here."

"Please let me stay."

"What is this? Women's lib? Self-gratification? Is this Lynn?"

Above the fan, she heard a clicking—her vertebrae, one at a time, locking into place. "I'm going to stay, Jack. All summer."

He sighed deeply. "All right. I'll come back for Labor Day weekend. We'll spend it here and then go home." He slipped his arm around her. "Stay, Patricia, if that's what you want. But my guess is you won't last a week."

Patricia was on a park bench in White Point Garden. Jack was on a plane.

Along the Battery of Charleston Harbor, a pair of runners were pounding the riverfront promenade as the city shook off the night. The sun picked up a corner of a dewy gray curtain and began unrolling the morning, one blade of grass at a time. Within hours, the park would be sullied by heat and haze. But for the moment the air was clear, the temperature was pleasant, and the Ashley and Cooper Rivers, converging in the harbor, were a double-dosed tranquilizer.

She waited in the stony silence of monuments honoring three hundred years of history. She waited until there was movement in the High Battery's antebellum homes, until a couple brought coffee and a newspaper to their porch. Until city residents were heading for the office and tourists overran the park. Until children were climbing upon Civil War cannons and a saxophonist headed to the bandstand to play for change. Until vacationers climbed into horse-drawn carriages to see the city from its narrow cobblestone streets.

"Make the most of your time here," Jack had said at the airport. "It won't come again."

Had he meant that time was fleeting? Or that he was her timekeeper and would allot her only this single season on her own? She glanced at her watch and moved on.

In the Charleston County Library, Patricia drew in the smell of books—of pages, shelves, stacks, and years. It was the same in Harlem as in the rest of Manhattan or Iowa City. The same at Sarah Lawrence College, for a child and her parents.

Her index cards were in the tote bag on her shoulder, but on her way to Reference, she paused in the Children's Department. A program called Story Time Friday had only one child waiting and no adult volunteers. So she settled on the floor with *Madeline* and five-year-old Melanie, whose skin was as smooth and dark as coffee beans.

She read with her father's pauses and her mother's lyricism, drawing other children in. Aboard *The Little Engine That Could* she took them to *The House at Pooh Corner* and spent an hour there. Upon Melanie's request, she reread *Madeline,* and when Miss Clavel turned out the light a final time, there were twelve little children not in two straight lines but in a circle at her feet. Mothers stood listening against the wall. One sat in a child-sized chair. When Patricia rose to leave, the librarian came in and led all of the listeners in a chorus of *please come back next week.*

Walking down Calhoun Street, Patricia made commitments: Friday mornings for Story Time and afternoons for research—on a dissertation yet to be approved, by a committee yet formed, at a university yet to accept her.

She stepped into a clothing boutique, where Jack couldn't approve clothes Lynn chose for her.

When she started home, it was late afternoon.

She turned into the circular driveway of the beach house and parked the Porsche directly in front of the porch. A half hour later, energized by a shower, a new white tube top, and a new paisley wrap skirt, she went back to the car and made a futile attempt to lift the smallest box of books. She groaned. Lynn should have packed twice as many boxes at half the weight. She stood upright, pulled her still-damp hair over her shoulder, and absentmindedly began to braid, thinking she would have to carry the books inside a few at a time. She leaned into the car, tugged at the box again. As she gave up, Terry rode up on a bicycle.

"Dead bird patrol." He dismounted. "We've had a report."

"What in Jesus God's name are you doing here?"

"What are *you* doing here? You told me you were leaving today."

"Change of plans."

He put his hands in his pockets, jingled change. "I saw you drive by the courts a while ago. Saw the car." His eyes telegraphed nervousness in a code of shifts and blinks. "I was worried about you." He gestured toward her forehead.

"How did you find my house?"

"Detectives." He tried a grin. "I hired a couple of the older kids from camp, told them I'd pay five bucks if they could find a house with a white Porsche. They took off on their bikes and were back in no time."

"They were lucky. The car is usually in the garage." She wished it were right now. "Will you leave, or must I take out a restraining order?"

He folded his arms. He scratched his earlobe. "I'm not here to bug you. I'm a good Catholic boy trying to repent for yesterday. I was thinking I could move the bird for you as my penance. I'll even move the boxes."

"I can get them."

"Yeah, well, I saw you trying to get them when I rode up." He waited but she gave him nothing. "You want a confession? I was an a-hole. I'm trying to apologize, okay?"

"I accept."

"Good." He brushed past her and lifted the smallest box. "What's in here?"

"Books. Part of my library from home." She led him inside. "There. Put them by the fireplace." He handled the second box with less ease than the first, and she thought he approached the third with apprehension. "Don't hurt your back. Lift with your legs." *With your Herculean quadriceps,* she thought.

"I can pick up a box." But he grimaced. "Son of a bitch." He hurried up the steps and to the fireplace, let the box hit the floor with a thud. He ambled to the sliding glass door. "Decent. Nice view."

When he turned toward her again, her first impulse was to run to the bedroom for a bra and a shirtwaist dress. Her second was to enjoy the reversal of yesterday's roles.

"Is this top going to bother you? It's laundry day. All my other tops need washing." She almost laughed at his discomfort.

"Well, you're dressed kinda—" He paused. "Summery."

"You don't have the eyes of a good Catholic boy."

"Then give me a penance. The bird, okay? Out there?"

She had forgotten how large it was, how plump its chest, the sharp angle at which its neck was twisted, the blood that had dried beneath its eyes and caked like a pillow beneath its head. She had forgotten the odor and the ants. They burrowed into feathers. Flies buzzed, landed, and rubbed their front legs together, preparing to feast.

"Flew into the glass," he said. "Couldn't see it coming. Got a shovel?"

"No."

"A rake? Or a bucket?"

"No and no."

"Am I playing Twenty Questions?"

"Yes. I—no. It's a summer home. It's my first time here."

"How about garbage bags?"

She went to the pantry and returned with two. She followed him to the door but stayed inside, saying she didn't want to watch. When the task was done, she thanked him. *Too gratefully,* she decided as he started across the room. "You're leaving?" *Too disappointedly.*

"Nope. I'm washing my hands before I unpack your books." At the kitchen sink he looked out the window. "You've got a visitor," he said, stepping to the front door.

"Wait," she cried on a desperate breath.

She saw the pink roses first, then the deliverer behind them. Short, pudgy, his khaki uniform dark with sweat, he struggled with the weight of the arrangement until Terry took it off his hands and carried it to the coffee table. She tried a quick count—three dozen. She plucked the small envelope from its plastic holder and read the card: *Miss you already—Jack.*

"From your boyfriend?" Terry said.

"No, my . . . my cousin. I've been helping her out of a very bad marriage. It's been a struggle, but she's filed for divorce."

"That's too bad."

"The divorce? No, it's good."

"It's a sin, is what it is. Maybe not at first, but when they start screwing other people it is. It makes those other people sinners too."

"You don't really believe that, do you?"

"I told you. I'm a good Catholic boy. Parochial school. Nuns. All that stuff sticks."

"And the last time you went to confession?"

"A little while ago," he said with a laugh.

"I'm not your priest. And I don't agree. They're mismatched. They're wrong for each other."

"So why did she marry him?"

She stared at the roses. "Patterns."

"Patterns?"

"They first met when she was seven. He owned—still owns—an advertising agency. Her grandparents entered her photo in a contest, and she was chosen as a model for an ad campaign. She didn't want to be a model." She paused. "She was traumatized."

"By having her picture made?"

"Yes. They liked her in the contest photo." It had been black and white. "But not when they saw her." In color. "They were talking fast, using terms that frightened her."

Color-correct. Can't we color-correct her eye?

"They kept changing locations, moving her about."

The photographer wants a tree in the shot. Pick a tree, Jack. Any tree.

"She was hysterical until he stepped in and took charge. He had her sit on his knee."

Can you wink, honey? Can you wink at me?

"He charmed her. He promised to take care of her and he did. For a year of commercials, photo shoots, and events, he was there. He smiled, told her what to do, and she did it."

"That's how they met, not why she married him. She didn't marry him when she was seven, did she?"

She sighed. "For the product's fifteenth anniversary—"

"What was the product?"

"That's irrelevant."

"Would I know it?"

"Yes."

"Would I use it?"

"Is this Twenty Questions?"

He chuckled. "Finish the story."

"Years later, he thought about using her for the product's fifteenth anniversary campaign. He found her, brought her to New York, and started a personal campaign instead. He took her to dinner, took her to bed. The patterns were reestablished. Six weeks later she married him."

"Because he told her to?"

"He's a persuasive, powerful man. She is, or was, needy and weak."

"Pretty weak reason for getting married."

"She thought she loved him. Maybe she did, but with a child's love. Both had an image of the other and how things would be. Both got it wrong."

"Well, anyways, your cousin must love you a lot, 'cause

that's a shitload of flowers."

"They need water."

Filling a pitcher in the kitchen, which was open to the living room, she watched as he sat down on the hearth and began unpacking her books. He read opening lines—lips moving, index finger tracking—then looked up and answered the question she was about to ask.

"I'm trying to figure you out," he said. "There might be clues in here."

"I wanted to do that at the villa, but you didn't have any books."

"Because I'm a dumb-ass?"

"No. I didn't mean it like that. That's in your heel. Head, rather. Your head, not mine."

"There are dumb jocks and there are dyslexic jocks, Tricia. I'm dyslexic."

Beside him again, she poured water into the vase, watching carefully so she'd know when to stop. For the same reason, she ventured with the same kind of care: "You're self-conscious, aren't you? About your reading?"

"My not reading? I do read. Just not good."

"*Well.* You mean *well. Good* is an adjective."

"Are we playing school?"

She put the half-empty pitcher on the table. "You needed the adverb *well.*"

"Well, I'm not going to reading class. Unless you've got *Alice and Jerry* somewhere."

She thought for a moment. "I have the perfect book for you." With eager hands, she dug through the open box, then directed him to open another.

"You really love this stuff, don't you?" He took the book she'd chosen into his hands. "*Peter Pan*? You want me to read *Peter Pan*?"

"Yes. It's ostensibly a children's book, but it has a

wonderfully humorous adult connotation. The social allegories—" She tried to rein in her enthusiasm. "I wouldn't have had it shipped from home if I didn't love it. I wasn't insulting you." Stop? "I understand dyslexia."

"Fuck."

She drew back. "I didn't mean—"

"No, it's not that." He laid the book on the table. "I forgot to call somebody, and it's important. Can I use the phone?"

"In the kitchen," she said.

He said "Nona" into the receiver before dropping his voice too low for her to hear. As he talked, he picked up a pen and a paper napkin. He copied Patricia's number from the phone and stashed the napkin in the pocket of his shirt. He rode a wave of silence back into the room.

Who is Nona? she wanted to ask. Instead, she looked at the inner hearth of the fireplace. She wished for a spark, flames, and a popping and crackling of wood. For sound of any kind.

"So," he said. "Want to unpack your books?"

He looked at her breasts again. She thought of his cutoffs from the day before. It was getting dark outside and dangerous inside.

"You should go," she said. "I was in Charleston all day and I'm tired." She put her hands on his arms and turned him toward the door, but she picked up *Peter Pan* and followed him onto the porch. He smiled as she gave him the book.

"What did you do in Charleston?"

"I went to the library. I read to children."

"What are you gonna do now?"

"Crawl into bed and read to myself until I fall asleep."

"Why don't I crawl in too? You can read to me."

"Not funny," she said, but she smiled. "What would I read? Cheekhov? Virginia's Wolf?"

"Not funny." But they laughed to a new level of ease with each other before falling silent yet again.

"That's all you've got, isn't it?" he said. "Your books."

"No. I—" She looked away.

He said quietly, "Did that hurt?"

"Yes, actually."

He shrugged. "All I've got is tennis. You've got lines on a page. I've got lines on a court." She heard truth, with a whisper of sadness. She noticed the last two digits of her phone number, peeping from his pocket. "It's two five at the end," she said, "not five two."

He winced. "Twos and fives, *b's* and *d's*. Big problems." They listened to crickets and cicadas.

He said slowly, "I play at two on Monday, if you want to come."

"I'd like to. I will."

"That's great. Thanks." He kept his eyes on hers, as if he might find something there that would tell him what to do next. Gently he touched her cheek. "That's where that tear was. Where I wanted to kiss you yesterday, but you said no. So, this is what I'm gonna do when I want to kiss you." Another touch. "So you'll know."

She looked up at him. He was taller than Jack. She put her hands on his shoulders, broader than Jack's. On tiptoe, she brushed her lips against his. He took a slow step forward, and she, a slow step back, wondering whether the warmth was coming from his body, hers, or something between them.

"So you'll be there?" he said. "I have to ask again, 'cause you're looking shifty eyed, by which I mean blue-eyed—which isn't really you."

"I've worn the lens a long time."

"I bet you can see my match better without it."

"It's cosmetic. It doesn't affect how I see."

"Sure? 'Cause you'll want to see every shot I hit that clips a line, where the other guy can't quite get it." He paused. "Promise me one thing. Promise me you won't ever tell me you'll be there and not show up. 'Cause that's happened before. A lot. And it hurt."

"If I tell you I'll be there, Terry, I will. Promise."

CHAPTER 3

Jack had been back in the office for only two days when the IRS auditors told him they wouldn't wrap up as scheduled. He met with them early in the morning and spent the rest of the day alone, door closed to everyone, even me. At five, he asked me to come in and offered me a cigarette as I sat down. I shook my head.

He lit up and exhaled, smoke streaming from his mouth and nose. "Bill Kiernan was in here yesterday, raising hell about corporate giving and a $50,000 commitment I made to sponsor a ballet."

"I know. I overheard."

"'The company can't afford it,' he tells me. 'My company,' I had to say to my CFO." He frowned with furrows in his brow so deep that I wondered what problems had plowed them. He laughed sharply. "I had no choice about the ballet. The broad who pitched it was so goddamn good I wanted to hire her. Wynona Warren," he said. "That was her stage name, and she still uses it when she's fund-raising for the ballet. She's sharp. Persuasive."

"Whoever she is, and however sharp she is, she's not the reason you've been in here alone all day."

"No." He closed his eyes and turned his head slowly to the right, grimacing as if he'd slept wrong. "Tom Padgett didn't get the Polaroid account. He lost Blue Nun wine. That's the fourth account in two months."

"Four hundred thousand in billings."

"Four twenty and change."

"That justifies Kiernan's concern," I said.

Glowering at me, he ground out his cigarette. "Fair point."

I'd never been afraid to tell Jack what I thought, but something told me to tread carefully this time. I put my elbows on the table and laced my fingers for a chin rest. I tried to hear him think in the uncanny way I'd always been able to when I sat beside him in meetings. I had an exclusive ticket to the train of his thought, but this time there were multiple trains at a junction, in a pileup, jumbled and engineless.

"What else?" I asked. I thought he'd add Patricia or his family.

He financially supported his brother, who had arrived at Khe Sanh in time for the Tet Offensive and come home a quadriplegic. He'd put three nephews through college, but the third had recently been expelled from Penn State for possession of cocaine. He'd refused the nursing home option for his ailing mother, paying instead for round-the-clock care at home. He owed her that and more, he said once, for the years she'd worked not only a day job but weekend shifts as a Waffle House waitress too. That was after his father, a longshoreman, was sentenced to a maximum-security correctional facility in Philadelphia for beating a supervisor into a permanently disabled heap on the docks. He'd told only me—not even Patricia—about the charge and conviction: aggravated assault with extreme indifference to human life.

I said, "What else, Jack?"

"The auditors. The young guy."

"Wollensky?"

"Wollensky. The corporate hole. He says they'll need another week, but he was vague. He wouldn't say why. Tomorrow, I want you to pull the last three—no, five—years of financials. I want to go through them line by line."

"Why don't you have Kiernan—"

He shook his head, then tapped his fingertips together. "Because I don't think Wollensky has found a mistake. I think he's found something purposefully irregular. If I'm right,

Kiernan is behind it. And I have no idea what it is."

"We'll find it," I said, but he didn't nod or smile. "Where there's a problem, there's a solution," I reminded him. He cited that cliché so often to employees and clients that it seemed like a company tagline. He responded to me with another, his mantra.

"Whatever it takes," he said.

For the rest of the week his door remained closed, but I was an insider now. We worked together at times, independently at others, poring over ledgers and spreadsheets. He was in a meeting when I stumbled into a web of discrepancies, spun so thin as to have gone unnoticed until then. It stuck messily to my fingers as they trembled over columns and rows. Kiernan's accounting had been far too creative.

My heart banged around in my chest as, standing with Jack at the conference table in his office, I showed him a general ledger for a TCC subsidiary that didn't exist. He studied the numbers before him, his five-o'clock shadow seeming to darken as his face paled. I would have felt better if he'd shouted, but he stood stock-still. I put my hand over his. He nodded in gratitude but didn't seem comforted. He moved to the chair behind his desk and sat quietly. Didn't rock, didn't even smoke.

"Kiernan," he said, eyes focused across the room.

"Do you want me to call him?"

"No. You'd better keep the son of a bitch away from me."

I tried to change direction. "At least we know. We have a trail to follow."

"We have *lines* to follow," he said. "*Lines* Bill Kiernan crossed. We have his failures—of ethics, of regulation."

And loyalty. I read that thought so clearly that Jack might as well have said it. Knowing how deeply that failure hurt him, I marveled at whatever double standard allowed him—allowed *us*— to cheat on his wife.

"But you're right, Lynn. We know. We have direction." He stood and looked at me. "I'm relieved. And I'm grateful."

"Personal Assistant is a misnomer," I reminded him. "I do much more for you. I—"

"Have an MBA. I know. I know."

"An MBA from your alma mater. One of only twelve women, class of '73."

"My alma mater is Harvard. Not Harvard-Radcliffe. There's a difference."

I let it go. No sparring tonight.

He knew why I'd accepted the entry-level job: for the future he'd promised me and the chance to work with and learn from him during his meteoric rise. He knew he used me like an MBA and paid me like a secretary—$14,000 a year.

For the umpteenth time, he said a promotion was long overdue.

For the first time I saw myself as Patricia, knowing I should leave him but unable to.

He insisted that the audit, Kiernan, and the company were off-limits during dinner at La Grenouille. "We'll have nothing to talk about," I said, but I knew where we were headed.

"I haven't had a conversation with my wife since I've been back in the city." He scratched his temple. "You were right. Something's up. I've called seven times, left seven messages. She's ignoring the phone. Or ignoring me."

"She's made it a week," I said.

"But I know Patricia. She's reading twenty-four hours a day. She'll come home a recluse if I'm not careful. She'll slip away from me, from the whole damn world."

He coughed. Nervously, I thought.

"Would you call her, Lynn?"

"She asked me not to for a while. She wants to be totally on her own. Besides, if she's not answering the phone, she's not answering the phone."

"But if *you* leave a message, she'll call back. She'll open up to you."

I looked at his wedding band. "I'd rather not."

He swallowed hard, cleared his throat. "Then help me understand this island sojourn. I don't know if she's trying to break out of her shell or slipping further into it."

"The former, Jack."

He tugged at the knot in his tie. "She can't manage."

"Not as long as you're micromanaging her."

"She can't function on her own."

"She wants to try for three months. Without you. Without me. Let her try."

"Goddamnit, Lynn." He slammed his hand against the table. I flinched. He did it twice more in quick succession. Heads turned in time for the fourth, most emphatic, slam. Our waiter scurried toward us, but Jack waved him away. I'd seen that sequence a hundred times. I knew the number of slams and number of seconds between them. I'd seen them directed at many a coworker but not at me. Never at me.

"I am letting her try," he said. "I love my wife, and I'm letting her do this ridiculous thing that makes me so mad I could knock her head off."

"Don't say—"

"I could knock her goddamn gorgeous head off."

"Damnit. Calm down."

He stared at his hand as if it weren't his, his fingers surely stinging. He took a swig of his drink.

"You sounded like you meant that," I said.

He looked pained. "I am not my father. You know that. And you know me, Lynn. I don't want anything I touch, professionally or personally, to fail. That includes my marriage."

"Jack." My shoulders tightened. "I care about you both, but I've been in the middle too long. Let me out."

"Call her."

We locked eyes, and as always I blinked first. I didn't commit but said, "I'll try."

He raised his glass in a half salute, as if only now his workday had ended. "At least her messages amuse me. Day before yesterday, she asked me to ship her the goddamn doll."

I shrugged. "Bring her in. I'll—"

He waved his hand, telling me not to bother.

"In today's message, she said she's taken up tennis. I find that bizarre, don't you?"

"You wanted her to take up golf. Why not tennis?"

"Patricia bashing balls at someone across the net? Competing?"

As suddenly as he'd slammed the table, he began to laugh what Patricia called his machine-gun laugh. Round upon cruel, ugly round.

When his ammunition ran out, I said, "I'm leaving. I'll take a cab."

His smile vanished. "It's been a helluva week. Stay with me, Lynn."

His eyes zipped me open like a suitcase. He offered me a cigarette and I said, "I'm trying to quit."

"This isn't the time. We have the audit. Too much to do. Too many hours ahead." He put a Viceroy to his lips and opened his lighter. It hissed and flashed. I watched the flame until he extinguished it with a snap. He tapped the bottom of the package on the table. Again he offered me one.

Again I refused, my words slow and hanging in the air between us, as though I'd written each one in bold black letters and added an exclamation point. "I am trying to quit."

"Smoking?"

"And the other."

His eyes burned into mine, but this time he blinked first. "I'm asking, Lynn. Will you stay with me tonight?" He laid a cigarette on the table between us.

"Bastard," I said. "You're relentless."

"I need you right now."

"You've needed me for years. Admit it."

"I need you," he said and smiled. "But you don't need me. That's how you're different and what I love about you. I don't have to take care of you like everyone else in my life—my other employees, my family, my wife."

"But you thrive on caretaking and solving problems. Taking care of everyone builds you up, especially Patricia."

"You're so unlike her," he said. "Independent. Strong. You have no needs, Lynn."

"I'm not an automaton," I protested.

Plates and flatware clattered as a busboy cleared a table nearby. I wished those sounds were loud enough to overpower my thoughts. I'd trained like a weight lifter, not with barbells, but with an advanced degree, with on-the-job hours that grew longer as assignments grew harder, with seminars, professional organizations, and with Jack Curren, who smiled at me now, seeing only strength, even as I struggled to be strong.

"A drink," he said. "Just one. At the town house." When I didn't answer, the indomitable Jack Curren bowed his head. "Lynn," he said, looking up again, "please."

In the cab, as Jack gave the driver his address, Patricia might as well have been sitting between us. I remembered the sparks of anger I'd felt three years ago, when he'd added assisting his new wife to my job description.

I'd expected her to be my grunt work, the dues I had to pay, so I consoled myself with the idea of having a curious peek into their marriage and a priority ticket to cultural events in the city. But in concert halls and art galleries, at her beloved 92nd Street Y and Lincoln Center, I found I had an interpreter who understood the arts so intuitively that I might as well have been sitting beside the author, poet, choreographer, or composer. She was as right-brained as Jack and I were left, and while she and I easily found common center ground, he tried for six months and gave up. That was after she'd put him through *Equus* and Mahler's *Fifth* in one weekend and he'd fallen asleep during both.

"I learn so much from you," I said over coffee, after we'd heard Grace Paley read at the Y. "Sometimes I think I'm learning more from you than from Jack."

She shrugged and smiled. "Maybe. But you can't make a career out of what I teach."

"I can't," I said. "But you could."

"I'm learning from you too, Lynn," she said. I looked at her dubiously and she went on. "Purpose, goals, commitment, going after what you want." Her eyes glimmered for a moment. "I'm learning to stand up to him. Or I'm trying."

We stood to go. "They're very different things," I said. "Earning a living and literature."

"And one is inarguably more important than the other."

"We do have to eat," I said, "and a roof overhead never hurts."

"Lynn," she said, her eyes dancing. "I meant literature."

I slipped my arm through hers as we left P.J. Clarke's, both of us happy and laughing.

Two blocks from the town house, I told the driver we'd changed our plans and gave him my address. I turned to Jack. Light and shadow danced over his face.

"I'm closing the file," I said. "Not just for tonight."

His silence seemed interminable. Finally, he said, "Noted."

I waited for him to say accepted but he didn't. "I wish I could archive it," I said. "I hate myself for what we did."

His transformation from my lover to solely my mentor again was visible and easy, almost slick. "Guilt is a useless emotion, Lynn."

"I wish it hadn't happened," I said. And after a moment—damn him—he gave me an avuncular smile.

"Regret," he said, "is as useless as guilt."

I went inside alone. Getting ready for bed, I thought of the career goals I'd shared with him early on, the corporate ladder I planned to climb: rung one, his personal assistant; rung two, assistant account executive; three, junior account exec; four, account exec; five, director of strategic planning or group account director. He'd smiled so wryly that I'd stopped at four. His idea for my advancement, he'd countered, was a move up to copywriting, where I could provide the right perspective for the women's products TCC represented. I'd asked if he taunted me sometimes for amusement, just to see how far I'd bend.

I threw away the pack of Virginia Slims I'd stashed in a drawer in case of an emergency. "Resist," I said. "Whatever it takes."

I curled up in bed like a child. Hugging my spare pillow in one arm, I pulled the covers tight. I told myself it was the company I loved, not Jack. In spite of my lowly title and meager salary, I'd played a significant role in the company's success and would continue to. I'd give him an ultimatum and surely he'd give me the promotion. And I'd be validated and happy Monday through Friday, walking into his office, seeing him at his desk, working with him in a higher capacity. I would be tireless, creative, innovative, strategic—all of the things we valued in each other. I would understand him in a way that Patricia would never be able to, and try to help him understand her, but only if he treated us both as he should.

I lay awake for hours that night, keeping company with my useless emotions and imperceptible needs.

CHAPTER 4

Patricia fell in love with tennis. Or watching tennis. Or Terry playing tennis. Or Terry.

She loved watching him without her lens.

The way he bounced the ball six times—always six—before serving. The way he wiped sweat from his brow with his forearm or the tail of his shirt. His grunts. The squeak of his shoes on the court. The way he talked to himself—encouraging, scorning. The occasional fuck he mouthed after unforced errors, the spontaneous fist pump after exceptional winners.

The power in his groundstrokes, the touch in his volley. Crosscourt backhands. Forehands up the line. Crashing overheads, sweet aces, sweeter drop shots. The things his doubles partner, Baze, admired aloud when they watched Terry together—things she still didn't understand, like kick serve or inside-out forehand.

She loved it all, and all of Terry. Head, shoulders, knees, toes. Thighs, calves, and ass in tailor-made shorts.

She loved how he looked up at her in the bleachers after a match ended and he'd shaken hands with a defeated opponent at the net. The way he touched his cheek from the court and smiled when she touched hers. The way his smile grew as he climbed the steps of the temporary stadium constructed for the tournament and sat down with her. She loved the sweat on his forehead, seeping from his sideburns, shimmering on his arms and legs. The smell of his pure perspiration. His victorious, imperfect, enchanting grin.

"Björn beat Guillermo," he said, after his first-round match. "At 1, 1, and 3."

"Oh. I didn't see that match." He looked confused.

"I didn't see any others. I just came for yours."

His lips twitched as he tried not to laugh. "The French Open, Tricia. Borg beat Vilas at Roland Garros. In Paris."

"Oops." She blushed, and though embarrassed, felt at ease. At least she'd learned who Vilas was.

"I'm kinda hungry," he said. "Want to make me some dinner? *Us*, I mean. Make *us* some dinner? Or *us* make us some dinner? At your place. Or I'll make you some dinner."

She drove him to the villa to shower and then to the beach house for the omelets and toast he suggested. They walked on the beach and watched television until he fell asleep on her couch, and she woke him and drove him home. The sequence became as routine as the solid wins he chalked up in the tournament's early rounds. Yet he remained dismissive of his success.

"Why do you insist that the other guy is no good or playing badly?" she asked after his quarterfinal. She, Terry, and Baze were sitting together in the grass, watching a doubles match on one of the field courts. "Why don't you think you're good and playing well?"

"I'm playing okay."

"Get real," Baze chided. "You've worked your ass off for a year, and you're playing great. You massacred Keith Yarbrough this morning."

"Yarbrough was nothing."

"He whipped my ass yesterday."

"I guess that makes you nothing too." He laughed as Baze threw a mock punch, but grew serious again. "I've got Richard Ferris or Larry Wyrick next. They're playing now. Know anything about Ferris?"

"You'll have Wyrick. I saw his match yesterday. Wicked serve. He brings a lot of heat, but mixes it up some too. Every serve is off the same frigging toss. Hard to get a bead on it."

"But he's weak off the backhand wing? So I should—"

"Terry, you haven't dropped a set in three matches, and you want me to tell you what to do? You sure as hell don't want me to when we're playing doubles."

They had lost their match an hour before, but neither seemed bothered by the defeat. Unlike the team they'd played, their strategizing had sometimes seemed like bickering.

"It's like I'm married and playing with my wife," Baze said. "I'd divorce you if I didn't love you so." He wrapped Terry in a headlock and tried to kiss his cheek. They wrestled, laughing, until Terry pushed him away. "You can have him, Tricia," Baze said. "I'm leaving."

"Divorce is a sin," Terry called after him. He lay back in the grass, hands behind his head, feet crossed at his ankles, eyes closed. "I'm thinking I should call my mom. She wanted to come, but I don't usually play too good when she's watching, and this one's important to me." He yawned. "So I called her yesterday and told her I got beat."

"You lied to your mother?" She'd sounded judgmental, though she hadn't meant to.

Terry sat up. "She's lied to me my whole life, Tricia. Her name is Helen. I spell it with two Ls. Hell-en." He picked a few blades of grass, studied them, discarded them, and looked at her. "There's this kid at camp. Carson Dressler. His mom is my mom all over again. He's eight, see? And she's getting him ready for a Wimbledon final. She hasn't missed one minute of camp—not a drill, not a match. There are plenty of moms there some of the time, but Mrs. Dressler is there all of the time, and most days when we're done, she asks me questions forever, while Carson stands there wanting to go to the pool like the other kids." He picked twenty-two blades, with Tricia counting silently. "The kid's a natural, and she's gonna destroy him. Give him a couple of years and he'll be nervous as hell when he plays. Like me."

"You don't seem nervous."

"That's why we've been eating omelets all week—because anything else would have me throwing up. I'm always nervous, and I hate that. And I'm dyslexic. And I'm always telling you stuff I don't tell anybody else. I don't know why." He took off his socks and shoes and curled his toes in the grass. "I'm telling you this too: Nona."

"Nona?"

"I've gotta get to the final because of Nona McClelland, this lady who might sponsor me when I turn pro. She's great, Tricia. So damn nice to me. I met her at the NCAAs in May, and she was, like, 'Show me what you can do this summer, and we'll talk about a sponsorship.' So I've gotta have this final and I've gotta have this championship, 'cause I've gotta have Nona, no matter what. I don't have the money to go on the tour without her." He began picking grass again. "She's got connections. She can get me a wild card in the qualifying rounds of the Open. Pull some strings, which I don't feel exactly right about, but I can't quite make it on my own. My ranking is three slots too low. Just three."

"The U.S. Open?" she said. "I do know about that."

He laughed. "I thought you might, since it's been in New York for a while. Like about fifty years." He grew obviously wistful. "I want that too, Tricia. The Open." He traded his shoes and socks for the flip-flops in his bag. "If I get to the final, I'll play Freddie. He got a walkover in the semis, so he's already in. I've never beaten Freddie, not even in practice at school."

"But you're playing so well."

"I'm playing the best I've ever played, but a lot of it's luck. You know how some people have blind luck?" He ran his hand through her hair. "I've got blonde luck."

"It's you, Terry. Not luck. Not me."

"Just the same, don't miss that final, okay? Or my semi tomorrow at nine."

"I'll be there, but not as your good-luck charm. I'll be there because I want to be."

She was not only there; she was early. She waited eagerly through the warm-up and then watched in dismay as he double-faulted twice on important points and netted easy shots. He lost the first set, but improved in the second. They played to 6–all and a tiebreaker, which made Tricia so nervous that she closed her eyes for most of the fourteen points, including the eight Terry won to take the breaker and set. When Wyrick tired late in the third, his big serve failed him, and Terry won the set and the match, 2–6, 7–6, 7–5.

"You didn't need to be nervous today," she told him as they got into her car. "I was nervous enough for both of us."

He nodded grimly as she turned the key in the ignition, but when she put her hand on the gearshift, he placed his over hers. He started to speak but seemed unable. Tried again, shrugged, and said, "Let's go."

Since he'd played the early match that day, she offered omelets for lunch instead of dinner. He ate a banana instead, said his stomach wasn't right, and stretched out on his back on the sofa. He bent his knees, making room for her to join him.

She touched his right forearm. "This one is larger. Tennis?" He nodded and she said, "I like that. And—" They had not touched each other, other than holding hands, other than the kiss on the porch before the tournament began. Feeling warm now, as she had then, she walked her fingers slowly along his shin. "This tennis tan. You look like you're wearing white socks, even when you aren't."

"You're kidding me, right? 'Cause I hate that." A short laugh. "What else? My ugly, blistered feet? My cold feet? They got cold in the car today, when I tried to tell you—wait, they're getting cold again." He slid them under her rear. "That's better. Warmer. Anyways, what I wanted to tell you was, I want to thimble you."

"What?"

"I want to give you a thimble." Obvious amazement filled his eyes. "You don't get it?"

"I've cooked omelets all week. Do I have to sew too?"

"It's not that kind of thimble."

"Tell me then, and don't look so gleeful. I'm stymied. I admit it. Now tell."

"Think about it, Tricia. It'll come to you, and you're gonna feel stupid when it does."

His glee subsided as she drove him home. By the time she pulled up at the villa, he was fidgeting anxiously with the tape she'd helped him place over a blistered finger.

"Are you okay, Terry?"

"I don't know. One minute I'm psyched, the next I'm freaked out." He gnawed on a callus in his palm. "You won't see me again, Tricia, till you're in the stands," he said, "'cause Nona's coming in and taking me to dinner. And I don't know why the fuck I did it, but I called my mom. She's flying in. I've gotta pick her up at ten, drop her at a hotel, and get back to the island and get some sleep. In the morning, I'll have to be focused. Totally. Which is why I've gotta give you something now." He took a three-by-five envelope from his tennis bag and slid it behind the sun visor, passenger side. "For you, but don't open it till after the final."

"Then why leave it in my car to tempt me?"

"'Cause I've got Nona, my mom, and the final on my mind, and if I don't put it here, I'll probably lose it. So just hang on to this envelope—"

"Until you've won," she broke in.

"One more thing," he said. He got getting out of the car. He closed the door, leaned in through the window, and grinned. "Thimble."

"Thimble," she whispered, laying her head on her pillow

that night. At the sound of the alarm in the morning, she thought: *thimble.* Then: *Terry. Sunday. Final. Smoke.*

She moved down the hall to the kitchen. Smoke in the air. Faint and stale. Coffee. Brewed. A full carafe.

She went to the living room. Ashtray. Viceroys. Briefcase. Shoes on the deck. She looked at the beach. Husband on the dunes. Barefoot. Trouser cuffs rolled.

She felt her lungs lock as Jack approached the deck. He brushed off his feet, slipped on his shoes, and reached for the door.

The glass slid open, and the color of the past few days slid too. Slid away. The world went back to black and white and hot, glaring contrast. She stared at Jack's open shirt—black moss on skin blanched white. She thought about Terry—skin polished bronze by the sun, not a hair above his navel. She stared at the shadow on Jack's face, long past five o'clock, and thought of the spotty stubble along Terry's jaw.

"I didn't want to wake you," Jack said.

"Why are you here?"

"You'd know if you'd answer your phone for a change. Or check your messages. Or call me back."

She looked across the room at the answering machine and the red blinking light she'd ignored. "What are you doing here, Jack? Why were you walking on the beach?"

Beneath his raven-black eyes, half moons were so dark and puffy she thought she should prick them with a needle, relieve the pressure. She gave him his cigarettes. He sank into a chair.

"I was walking," he said. "I was trying to think."

"About what? What's happened?"

"It's the company, Patricia. It's TCC."

She forced herself forward and sat down at his feet.

"Tell me." She tried to concentrate as he talked about the audit.

She heard *phantom subsidiaries.* And remembered what a

thimble was.

She heard *duplicate sets of P&Ls and balance sheets*. And remembered Wendy offering to give Peter a kiss; Peter not knowing what a kiss was, holding out his hand; Wendy not wanting to embarrass him, giving him a thimble instead.

"I don't understand," she said.

"You don't understand? Or it doesn't matter?" He went to the bar and took a bottle of Macallan from the cabinet below.

"Jack, don't." Alarm in her voice. "It's not even nine."

A glug of Scotch. A splash of water. The ice was in his accusation: "The agency has never mattered to you, Patricia."

"Of course it has. But you'll have to explain these terms. I'm not Lynn."

He took a step toward her. "Can you understand fictitious transactions? You, with your inordinate love of fiction?"

"I can't possibly understand if you're going to condescend."

"I am personally and corporately leveraged to the max, Patricia. TCC has a balloon note due in October on the loan for the acquisition of the other agencies—five hundred K. The agency, I learned yesterday, owes 4.2 million in taxes. Back taxes. Four goddamn years' worth."

"How is that possible?"

He raised his voice. "Have you heard anything I've said? Bill Kiernan understated revenues. Purposely. By design."

A vein throbbed at his temple so fiercely she thought it might burst.

"But if Bill—"

"It's accounting fraud. A crime. It's my company." He slammed his hand, palm open, against the wall. "And I want you with me. I want my wife at home. Now."

The phone rang, jarring Patricia. *Jesus God,* she prayed, *don't let it be Terry.*

The same ring steadied Jack. "That's Lynn," he said, heading for the phone. "She's in Kiernan's office, going through every scrap of paper she can find. Our flight is at two, Patricia. Pack. We're going home."

"No," she said impulsively. And courageously, "No."

He clutched the receiver but did not lift it. "No?"

The answering machine picked up, and they listened together. "There are five not three subsidiaries that exist on paper only, Jack. For God's sake, call me."

He stared at the wall. "No, Mrs. Curren? Why not?" He did not face her. "Do you want to lie on the beach and read while I fight for everything it's taken me twenty-two years to build?"

"If you need me, I'll come. But tomorrow night, Jack. Not today." She watched his shoulders rising and falling, his back expanding and contracting. As he composed himself with measured breathing, a timpanist played a slow ostinato in her head. His inhalations boomed at one pitch, his exhalations at another. "I can't come today." She grasped for a reason to stay on the island, other than a tennis match. "I have a job. At the library. I have to work tomorrow." He faced her, and her heart pounded like a snare drum in double time. "I have a job."

She held her breath as Jack threw back his head and laughed. His well-stocked armory sustained him until he was back at the bar.

"It's true, Jack." Words tumbled out of her. "There's a children's program at the library, but it isn't well publicized or well attended. I've been thinking the agency could design a poster." He was suddenly so still she thought she had slain him.

"I'm losing the agency, and you're asking me for posters?"

"Yes . . . I . . . No . . . I shouldn't have. I know you're upset. I'll do what you want. But what I want—" She put her hands to her forehead and closed her eyes. She pushed back her hair, stretched her spine. "I'm staying here tonight. I have responsibilities. In the fall I want to go back to school." She pointed to the card box on the coffee table. "Those are notes from three years ago, from grad school, from Iowa. I want those notes to become a dissertation. I want my PhD."

"Do you?" He refilled his glass with Macallan—his oasis, she knew, in the desert of their marriage. He walked slowly toward her, drink in one hand, bottle in the other. He stopped at the coffee table and stared at the box. "Do you?"

"Yes."

"Noted. Accepted."

"I don't think you mean it," she said. "You've had too much Scotch."

"You're right." He looked at his glass. "I have. I don't need this." He looked at the bottle of Macallan, and then looking at her, turned it over and drowned her dissertation.

When she could move, she rushed to the metal box and fell to her knees as Jack went back to the phone.

"Lynn," he said as she picked up the box. She tried to dump its contents on the floor, but the cards were packed so tightly that she emptied only whiskey.

"Oh, dear God."

"Which accounts, Lynn?"

Jack continued to speak, but to Patricia his words were the buzz of an appliance, the growling of a blender. She raced upstairs, and kneeling on the catwalk, pulled the cards out in sections. She fanned them out like a dealer in a card game and tossed hand after losing hand to the floor.

But it wasn't poker. Or even Crazy Eights. Or crazy husband.

It was crazy wife. Crazy to have married him, crazier to have stayed, craziest to stay on.

She examined the cards one at a time. Those that were wet, she blotted on the ivory carpet, not caring about ink stains or the barroom smell. She laid them out in long rows to dry, crawling backward on her knees along the catwalk and into one of the upstairs bedrooms. If she'd checked the messages, if she'd known he was coming, she might not be fashioning a mosaic of hundreds of handwritten notes—some unscathed, some decipherable, some eradicated.

She reached the last of the cards, the red, blue, and black bibliography. The color-coded references were running and smearing. She sat back on her heels. She closed her eyes, and when she opened them again, saw battalions of fuzzy black spiders. They crawled toward her on angular spindly legs, crossing the red-and-blue network of arteries and veins on the floor.

TCC was Jack's lifeblood. The dissertation was hers.

Pulse. Pulse. "Goddamnit. Goddamnit," he shouted. "How the hell did he do it, Lynn?"

She floated numbly down the stairs and past the kitchen, where Jack was slamming the receiver against the wall again and again. She expected the plaster to crack but didn't care. She took a shower she could not feel, slipped on a tube top and pair of shorts. She took four boxes of contacts and her case from a drawer. Four boxes, six blue lenses in each.

She went back to the kitchen, cemetery-silent now.

Sitting at the table, with his eyes glued to spreadsheets, Jack said, "I'm sorry, princess. I lost all sense of what I was doing. You'll have to forgive me." He took a sip of black coffee, gave in to a hacking cough, and slowly drained his cup.

She went to the sink, where the gaping drain transfixed her. She turned the water on full blast and watched its stream. She turned on the garbage disposal, which gulped and clattered.

Jack glanced at her and went on with his work. Patricia proceeded with hers. Twenty-four lenses. One at a time. Gulp. Chop. Grind. Dispose.

She marveled at his concentration, broken neither by noise nor the abrupt stark silence that followed the completion of her task. She marveled even more at the steadiness of her hand as she picked up the carafe of coffee and walked to the table. She stood beside Jack, wondering whether she should smash the glass carafe or simply pour. She decided to pour, to drench his spreadsheets. But when he lifted his eyes, she refilled his cup.

"You've forgotten your lens." He looked at her summery clothes. "I would prefer my wife not be dressed for a beach party when we arrive in the city. The flight is at two."

"I'm not going, Jack. If you'd like reasons, besides my job and what you've done to my dissertation, here's another." She laid her contact case in the center of his spreadsheets. "Open it," she said. "Not the left side. That's my lens." The only lens she had left. "Open the right side."

Slowly, he said, "I am working." He went on, sledgehammering every word. "I do not have time for games."

"Open the case," she said. "See what I found in our bed."

He laid his pencil on the spreadsheet, just under the title as precisely as if he were underlining it. "Get dressed."

"Found in our bed," she said again. He didn't respond. "It's a black button, a pearl, from another woman's dress. Or blouse or skirt. Which one, Jack? You know. I don't."

He did not move, other than clenching his jaw. She listened to a clock in her mind, a foreboding ticking. Without warning, Jack knocked the case from the table with the back of his hand, with a swipe so violent that its follow-through struck her forearm and propelled him to his feet. She dropped the carafe, and its crash upon the floor coincided with the thud of her back as he shoved her against the wall. He clamped her shoulders, dug in his fingers.

"I don't have time for this," he shouted, his face close to hers. "Do you understand?" She tried to turn away but his hands flew from her shoulders to her head. Holding fistfuls of her hair, he forced her to look at him.

"Let go," she whispered. "You're scaring me. Please."

He dropped his voice. "Do you understand me?"

"Yes," she whispered.

"Yes?" He pulled her head up and down, again and again, in a torturous nod.

"Yes," she cried.

He dropped his hands. He looked at the glass around them, then spun and kicked a large jagged chunk across the floor. He followed it to the opposite wall and faced her.

"I'm sorry." He held out his hands, palms up. He took a step toward her.

"Stop."

"What do you expect me to do?" Fists to his hips. "You're my wife. You cry in our bed. You *cry.*"

"You're not the victim here."

"You are lifeless," he said.

"Who is she, Jack?"

He shouted, "I deserved her." He began to pace. He rubbed the back of his neck. Regaining control, he measured his words, doled them out slowly. "I'm sorry. Jesus. It was nothing, Patricia. And it is over. I can't talk about it right now."

"Do you think you can table it? Move it to next week's agenda?"

"Today my agenda is TCC. It is potential indictment. Can you understand that? How about bankruptcy?"

"It's our marriage that is bankrupt."

"Then make a goddamn deposit," he said flatly. "For once in your life, don't withdraw." He looked at the spreadsheets, and with businesslike calm began packing his briefcase as meticulously as he always did. He closed it, buckled it, and pocketed his readers. He laid her plane ticket on the table. "Pack."

"No." She straightened her shoulders, adjusted her stance, prepared for another attack. But if he struck her, wouldn't a rigid stance hurt rather than help? She tried to relax but drew only one deep breath before realizing she didn't need to.

Jack's eyes were blank. Clearly flummoxed, he reached for his briefcase as needily as she sometimes reached for Raggedy Ann. He picked up his suitcase on his way to the door. He paused there to say, "Call me when you're ready to come home. Not before. I have nothing else to say to you, Patricia." And he was gone.

She looked at her feet and shins, at the tingling pink splotches left by hot coffee.

She looked at the clock. Already eleven. But if the first set had been close and hard-fought, she could make it in time for the start of the second.

She waited with other latecomers at the stadium gate until play paused for the changeover. As Terry and Freddie changed sides of the court, she raced up the steps. She took the only seat she could find—a half seat really, on the end of a row. Two players she recognized from earlier in the week slid left to give her more room.

"What's happening?" she asked no one in particular.

A man below her proclaimed, "It's a drubbing."

"The first set was a twenty-minute breadstick," said the player beside her, "and the best serve-and-volley tennis I've ever seen Freddie Tyler play. Now he's up a set and a break."

Behind her, two teenaged girls commiserated. They wanted the cute guy with curly hair to win.

From below. "Ready to go? This isn't worth watching."

From her left, "Freddie's in his head." And, "Like always."

The third game began with Terry serving. Poorly. But he fought his way back from love–40 and held for only the second time in the match. Freddie opened the fourth game with a rare double fault, caught an unlucky net cord on the second point, and with an unforced error on the third, gave Terry his first break point of the match—a triple break opportunity.

"Terry breaks him here or it's over," said the player beside her.

"He will," she said, and Terry did, with a topspin lob that Freddie scrambled to and reached, but dumped into the net. "He'll come back," she said. "Don't you think he will?"

"Maybe." The player introduced himself as Jeff Penrose and his friend as Sam Holt.

"I'm . . ." She paused. "Tricia. Tricia Curren." *Blue-and-gray-eyed Tricia,* she thought.

The hard-fought set continued on serve to 6–all and a seemingly endless, heart-stopping tiebreaker. Twenty-four points later, Terry won it, 13–11.

"He's not going away now," Jeff said. "Not after clawing his way back." But Sam said, "He'll cave. Like always."

"He won't," Tricia said.

Jeff said, "Are you doing anything tonight?"

"Yes." She would be celebrating. With Terry.

The final set began, with Freddie trying to serve and volley and to chip and charge, while Terry slugged returns and bludgeoned passing shots crosscourt and down the line. The lob continued to work for him, offensively and defensively. Each time Freddie retreated to the baseline, Terry pinned him there in long steady rallies, pushed him back farther, and waited for a short ball to clobber or an unforced error from Freddie.

"Where did this come from?" Jeff asked.

"He's like a battering ram," Sam answered.

Like the teens behind Tricia, the entire crowd was now cheering for the player who had battled back from a set down. Heart booming, hands quaking, she hoped he could withstand the pressure, and if necessary, the loss, after fighting so hard and coming so close.

Freddie stepped up to serve at 5–all. He won the first point, and when he served the second, Terry took the ball early and nailed the return.

"Circus shot," Sam said, applauding with the crowd.

It was 15–all.

"Circus shot," Jeff echoed on the following point.

Now 15–30.

Serve. Return.

Crisp volley from Freddie. Aggressive topspin lob from Terry, over Freddie's head and out of reach.

Now 15–40. Double break point.

Fault, and a weak second serve from Freddie. A scorching return from Terry, unanswered. Game, Terry. Freddie, broken.

With the championship on his racket, Terry fidgeted through the changeover. He stepped up to serve, took three quick points, and stared trancelike at his teammate across the net. Championship point. He double-faulted for 40–15, netted an easy forehand for 40–30, and fell into a long rally on the following point before hitting an inside-out forehand that Freddie couldn't handle.

Game, set, match, championship.

The crowd reacted with a resounding ovation, which after a few boisterous whoops faded to steady applause. Tricia jumped to her feet as everyone rose. She expected Terry to jump too, but he gave only a fist pump that seemed more thankful than boastful and headed to the net to shake hands.

He began scanning the bleachers, but he didn't find her until she waved. He looked stunned, quizzical, and then so happy that she expected him to take the celebratory leap then. He touched his cheek, and before she could respond, began making his way to the side of the court, through tournament organizers and volunteers who offered congratulations, through the group of excited campers Baze was trying to hold back.

He is coming to me, she thought, but he wasn't. He was heading toward two women waiting courtside, neither acknowledging the other's presence. Not knowing her place in the hierarchy, Tricia held back at the bottom of the steps.

Both women were attractive. Jack's age, she assumed.

The first looked like Lynn had dressed her in country-club casual—sleeveless polo, golf skort, a gold cuff bracelet on one wrist, stacked bangle bracelets on the other. She looked like a client wife. His mother, Tricia decided, as the woman hugged him. He stood rigid, hands at his sides, before melting into a reciprocal embrace. He clung to her but then broke away, looking flustered. His mother was frowning and speaking rapidly. She didn't stop until the second woman slipped gracefully between them.

"Nona," Tricia said to herself, intrigued.

Terry's potential sponsor was tall and slender, with her dark hair pulled straight back and the end of her French braid pinned under. Her short cotton dress was made almost too short by long shapely legs. No jewelry. Large round sunglasses. She hugged him, and when she drew back, her pale green dress was splotched with sweat. Terry looked embarrassed and apologetic. But Nona laughed and he laughed too until a tournament official led him back to center court.

The ceremony was brief, and when it concluded, Terry said something to Baze, who started toward Tricia. With the trophy wrapped in one arm, Terry let Nona lock her arm through his other. She swept him toward the pro shop, his visibly disgruntled mother trailing behind.

"Tricia," Baze said, "Terry said to tell you he'll call you."

In the stranglehold of disappointment, she took a breath, but it swirled like a hostage in her throat while her lungs scraped up a ransom. "Couldn't he tell me himself?"

"He has to go to lunch with Nona and Two-Ls Hellen, which looks like a catfight waiting to happen. Then he's going to Hilton Head with Nona. To her house. To spend the night."

"Why?"

"Hmmm." Baze turned his baseball cap around, brim in the back. He took on an exaggerated frown and stroked his chin.

"She wants to get laid?"

Tricia choked out a laugh. "Do you ever stop joking?"

"Sometimes, but that was too good to resist. Seriously, though, Nona wants to work up an agreement. Finalize the gigolo-ship. I mean, sponsorship."

"You're not funny."

"But he'll call you. As soon as he can."

She went home to the beach house. She went through the index cards for a second time and cried a little—for her lost dissertation and the phone call that didn't come. She slept so fitfully that she gave up in the early morning. She went to the kitchen and walked directly to the phone. Jack's tantrum hadn't cracked it or the plaster around it. But maybe the line was dead.

She lifted the receiver. The healthy line purred. Terry hadn't been trying to call for hours, as she'd hoped.

Only Anton Chekhov was calling now. She would spend today, tomorrow, and every day in the library. She would begin again. But first.

First, she went into the garage, bare feet on concrete. She got into her car on the passenger side and pulled the sun visor down.

CHAPTER 5

It was early morning. Quiet. Except for birdsong. Looking at the view from the patio, Terry understood why Nona McClelland, who also owned homes on Long Island and in Atlanta, had chosen the river instead of the beach on Hilton Head Island. He loved the beach, but at that moment, the absence of the audible comings and goings of the ocean seemed like a blessing, as did Nona.

He looked at the pool. He looked to his left at Nona's tennis court, then to his right at the boardwalk, which led to her floating dock and the river. He looked at the phone and thought about Tricia, who had missed the coin toss, the warm-up, the start; who had missed the first set; who hadn't been there when he looked for her after the first game of the second. Or after the third game, when he'd looked up and given up. He had no idea when she'd come in, no idea what he'd say when he called, no idea how bad he'd feel if he got her machine.

"Hello, this is Patricia. If you'll leave a message, I'll call you back soon."

You broke your fucking promise, he wanted to say, had every right to say. But at the tone, he said simply, "Tricia, it's me. I'm at Nona's, which I wasn't planning on, but I had to, 'cause she wants to get to know me better. I think she's gonna sponsor me but she hasn't said for sure. After lunch yesterday, she dragged me all over Charleston while she met up with friends. I was gonna call you once we got here, but I was so damn tired I crashed after dinner. Anyways, I hope you opened your present—the tickets—and that you're going with me Wednesday. 'Cause that play, *The Seagull,* is by Cheekhov, which you probably know. So call me, okay? Nona won't mind— 843-752-4994."

Shit, he thought, as he hung up. *Five two or two five? What had he said?* He tried to think of a reason other than dyslexia to call her back but had no chance. He heard, "Good morning," and said, "Nona, hi."

She had a smile that happened slowly. It tantalized him as he waited for its full expanse and the shifting of a tiny birthmark just above her upper lip. It was so black, flat, and perfectly round that it looked like a dot she'd drawn with the tip of a permanent marker. With her dark hair swept up and her eyes as black as slick, shiny crude oil, she looked like an actress he'd seen in a movie. An older actress, whose name he didn't know.

She was a marathoner, he'd learned the night before, which was why she was so damn skinny. Ropy calves. Zero body fat. She was dressed for running, and looked tit-less in her jog bra, except that her nipples were hard.

He answered questions over breakfast—yes, he'd slept well, he'd had everything he needed, the eggs were fine, not too runny. She was from Atlanta, dropped her r's—said othuh instead of other—and never quit talking.

"I'd love for you to run with me, angel, but you've earned the right to rest today. What a battle yesterday! What a warrior you were!" She babbled on until the phone rang. As she said hello, she gave another slow smile, as if the caller could see as well as hear her. She handed him the phone and he smiled too.

"Tricia," he said.

Nona raised an eyebrow. It looked like the top of an unhappy question mark.

From the other end of the line: "Who is Tricia?"

"Mom." He ground the receiver against his ear.

"Who is Tricia?" she snapped.

"She's nobody. A friend. I'll call you back, Mom. Me and Nona are having breakfast."

Helen Sloan dropped her voice to an angry whisper. "Listen

to me, Terry. You do not need that woman Nona McClelland. I have the money now, and I want you away from her."

He glanced at Nona, wondered what she could hear. He couldn't help asking, "Where did you get it, Mom?"

"Come home. I'll explain."

"Where, Mom? From who?"

Nona picked up the newspaper, rattled it open.

His mother said, "From your father."

"Unh-unh." His vocal cords were taut as racket strings. "Dream on."

"Terry, I have important things to tell you."

"Thanks for calling, Mom, and saying again how good I played. Catch you later." He hung up and started to stand, but Nona's housekeeper, snow-haired, black-skinned, and uniformed—gray dress, white apron—was creaking to the table, age and arthritis in every step. Ola Mae poured more coffee for Nona, who added cream and with her spoon began making such leisurely figure eights in her cup that he knew he wasn't excused. "Sorry, Nona. I don't know how she got your number."

"It's a public listing, angel. I don't mind. She must have been very proud yesterday."

"Yeah, she was."

But Nona was looking at him as if she'd overheard what his mother had said after the match and wanted to comfort him. She laid her hand over his, already sweating in the warm, greasy sun.

"Terry, angel, I was more impressed by your comeback than I would have been if you'd beaten Freddie in straight sets at love. And I know how talented Freddie is, how machinelike."

He withdrew his unworthy hand. "I didn't even know where I was in the first set."

"I can't tell you, angel, because I've completely forgotten it due to the second and third. She sipped her coffee. "Did you know that I danced, angel? With NYCB."

He knew he was supposed to get it but didn't.

"New York City Ballet. When I was your age, there were six months in which I accomplished more with one teacher than in all the years I danced. He was revered, the most highly sought teacher in the city. But I argued with him once, and I'll never forget it. I complained that he wasn't pushing me hard enough, wasn't picking me apart, finding every weakness. He listened patiently, indulging me, I suppose, which infuriated me. I ended by shouting, 'You see only the best in me.' And he said quietly, 'That is where we begin, Nona. That is the only way to do it.'"

He tried hard to swallow a feeling he couldn't name. "My friend kinda says that too."

Nona put her napkin on the table. "I'll run now before it gets hotter. Then I'd like a tennis lesson." She stood up. "What are you reading, angel?"

"Oh, this? It's—I'm not really reading it." He'd turned the book facedown on the table, but Nona read the title on the spine.

"I saw Mary Martin in *Peter Pan.* Broadway, opening night, 1955. She was splendid."

"My friend gave this to me. She reads all the time." And she's calling me now, he hoped as the phone rang again. Nona answered, gave him the receiver again. "Hello."

"Listen to me, Terry."

He looked at Nona, thought about saying: *The reason for* Peter Pan*, Nona, is that I can't even fucking read, because my mother put a racket in my hand when I was five and got me a tennis coach instead of a tutor.* Instead: "Aren't you going running?"

"What?" his mother said loudly.

Nona sat down. "Another cup of coffee, angel."

"Come home, Terry."

"I can't."

His mother, shrieking: “Then you’d better ask her to start supporting you *now.*”

Nona smiled. “I’ll be glad to, angel.”

“If you don’t come home, you won’t get a cent from me for the rest of the summer or for the fall. Do you know how many unforced errors you had in the first set?”

He felt his face reddening.

“There’s an extension in your room,” Nona offered.

“Hold on, Mom.” He hurried upstairs, picked up the phone. “Mom?”

“Fifteen unforced.”

He wasn’t sure Nona had clicked out of the conversation, but Two Ls wasn’t waiting. “You panicked.”

“Why are you calling me here?”

“Because you’re making a mistake.” The serrated edge in her voice wasn’t that of a paring knife but of a rusty old saw in a shed. “You need a coach, not a sponsor. You won’t keep a sponsor, even her, if you play like you did yesterday. You didn’t start well. You didn’t adjust.”

“Are you drinking, Mom?” he shot back. “Why don’t you have a drink? It’s not too early. Not for you. I like you better drunk. And best of all, passed out.” He slammed the receiver into its cradle and sat down on the bed, then took the phone into his lap. He called her back, knowing she wouldn’t answer. She would take out her skill saw instead. She would abandon him, turn her back, disappear. He had to record his apology. “I didn’t mean it, Mom. ’Cause you’ve been sober for two years. You’ve done awesome. I’ll come home as soon as I leave here. Baze can cover for me. And I know I sucked in the first set. I’m working on the mental thing, like you want. I’m getting better. I won, didn’t I?”

He lay down on the bed and was six years old again.

He wore pale blue pajamas with tennis balls and pairs of rackets crossed at their throats, patterned like the bedspread and the wallpaper border. Rod Laver looked down from posters on the wall. His mother looked down at him too.

"Don't cry. Did something happen at practice? At school? Did you have to read aloud?"

"Everybody reads better than me. And the girls laugh. Sometimes Matt makes fun of me. And even Joey laughs."

"But it doesn't matter, does it? Because everybody is different, right?"

"Yes."

"And everybody is special?"

"Yes."

"And you can do something better than anyone else. Hmm?"

"Yes."

"What can you do, Terry?"

"Play tennis."

She kissed his forehead. "Yes, my little ace. You're right."

"Mommy." Afraid. "I want to skip practice tomorrow."

She tweaked his chin, played with his curls. Her fingernails were orange. They were long and pointed. Her bracelet sounded like bells, her voice like a song.

"Not if you love me, little ace. If you love me, you'll go."

He rolled toward the wall, ten again, and grounded.

She said it was because he'd made two Fs and a D, but he knew it was because he'd been losing.

He rolled onto his belly, fourteen again, in the car with her, stopped for a red light.

She turned to him and slapped his head with both hands as if she would never stop. She said it was because he'd back-talked her, but it was because he'd double-faulted three times in a row. And because she was drunk.

He rolled to his back and was sixteen.

He didn't have his house key and she didn't have hers. The spare was in the shed. The padlock wasn't fastened. He threw the door open and flipped the switch, but the bulb had burned out. He felt his way forward in the windowless shed, got the key from the hook on the back wall, turned, and stopped. The bright afternoon had turned his mother into a black silhouette, unmoving, waiting in the doorway.

He sat up on the bed like a jack-in-the-box, dialed, and sighed as the recording began. "Tricia," he said at the tone. He halted in the swift cool breath of the door swinging into the room.

"I've decided to go shopping instead of running," Nona said pleasantly. "There's a mall in Savannah. I'd like you to come with me."

He hung up. "Sure. That will be great." *Great,* he thought, *shopping not negotiating, not one damn word about the sponsorship.* He gave her the reliable smile he'd given so many teachers, his please-give-me-a-D-not-an-F smile. "After that, can we start on the agreement?"

"Not while you're distracted."

"Distracted?" He thought she looked annoyed. "No, I'm—all I'm thinking about is tennis and the sponsorship." He paused, then played on. "And you, Nona."

"No distractions," she said, fastening her eyes on his. "No Tricia. No girls."

She wanted to shop for him first, Nona said, in case they went out to dinner.

She made selections. He tried them on, losing count of the times he went in and out of the dressing room and followed marching orders to the three-way mirror. He looked at himself in three-piece suits, with coat lapels so wide they looked like wings. She dressed him in flared, high- waisted polyester pants so tight that the seam crawled like a snake in the crack of his ass. He buttoned satin shirts all the way up. She unbuttoned them halfway down.

When she went to the lingerie department to shop for herself, he felt so awkward that he asked for a furlough. She gave him an hour, which he spent playing Space Invaders in an arcade before meeting her back at her car. She had four bags of clothes for him, and the only thing he liked was a green-and-gold plaid cotton shirt he'd picked out and she'd said he looked irresistible wearing. She handed him a book, *I'm Ok – You're Ok,* and started the car.

"I bought this for you, angel. You'll love it. It explains how the things we hear repeatedly in childhood, especially negative things, become tapes that play in our heads even as adults. It will teach you how to turn them off. You'll find it more interesting than *Peter Pan.*"

"Thanks," he said, knowing he wouldn't read it.

After lunch, he gave her the tennis lesson she wanted and played a match with her, using a handicap scoring system she'd devised.

"My rules," she said, before straight-setting him.

By afternoon they were in her boat with a picnic supper. They crossed Calibogue Sound and anchored in the May River, where they stayed so long and with a cooler so full of beer that he was one-too-many drunk when they started home. Or two- or three-too-many.

He was loving the colors of the sunset and thunderheads, loving the smell of the salt marsh. It had been offensive to him years ago—sour, like towels left twisted in the washer for days or a dead bird decaying on the beach. But in time, on Kiawah, the marsh had become the smell of the summer to him, of the coastal South, of something natural and alive. Like a girl, wanting and waiting. Like sex about to be. Sex over and done. Two people satisfied, complete.

Like he and Tricia would be, he was thinking, as he turned on the shower, stripped, and waited for the water to warm. If

Tricia were with him, her skin would be like his, pink with too much sun, crusty with the salt of the river. She would taste salty when he lifted her hair and kissed her shoulder before they stepped into the shower, before she turned to him. He had held her hand, run his fingers through her hair, kissed her once, and touched her cheek. Now he wanted to touch her everywhere, wanted to so bad he could hardly stand it.

He showered and went to bed, to silk sheets, cold and slippery. He closed his eyes. Beer sloshed in his belly while anxiety burrowed like worms in his brain. He worried that Tricia's reason for not calling back was the same reason she'd been late for the match: she didn't give a shit.

That she would go to *The Seagull* alone or give his ticket to somebody else. Somebody smart like her, who would understand the damn play.

That he wasn't focusing on the important ticket—the one Nona held, to clay, grass, and hard courts all over the world, to a coach and success as a pro. The ticket away from Two Ls.

That Two-Ns Nona had changed her mind and there wasn't going to be an agreement. That he shouldn't have gotten so drunk in the boat.

That he drank too much way too often and might end up like his mother. That he'd made a dumb-ass mistake by asking Tricia to call him at Nona's. That Tricia was a mistake and could cost him a sponsorship.

He made another call, and at the annoying beep, left her a final message: "Don't call me, okay?

No matter what." He hung up the phone and passed out.

Minus the phone calls and shopping, Monday and Tuesday were reruns of Sunday—tennis lessons, matches, the river, and no agreement. To angel, the place no longer felt like heaven but hell. Like a "Hotel California" he could never leave.

But Wednesday was different. He ran six miles with Nona, and afterward they sat together on the side of her pool, bare feet dangling in the water.

"I suppose it's time to get you back to Kiawah," she said. "I can't keep you here forever, can I?"

"I wish you could, Nona. 'Cause it's relaxing, and being with you is nice. But camp's my job and I need to get back."

"I'll give you up today, angel, but you'll come back soon. That's part of our agreement."

He thought he'd melted and slid right into the pool. "You're gonna do it?"

"Of course. Did you think I wouldn't? Dollars don't matter to me, angel. You do. And I'll give you everything you need. You don't have to sign anything." She laced her fingers through his. "Call it a handshake agreement." With her free hand she turned his face toward hers. "All I require for now is that you focus on tennis with no distractions and spend time with me whenever you can. That's not too much, is it?"

"That's nothing." But it felt like a lot.

"Don't worry about our agreement, or me, or anything, angel."

But Nona had put worry worms in his head. He didn't like her calling him angel, or planting her hand on his thigh on the drive back to Kiawah. He wished he were back in Austin playing number two. Or one. He was tired of Nona and his mom and glad to be done with Tricia. He was sick of the summer and camp.

Nah, he decided. Not camp. Not really.

The Wednesday-afternoon group was his favorite, and those seven- and eight-year-olds were glad to have him back. At five thirty, when their session ended each day, he chose one kid as champ and awarded him or her a pack of Peanut M&M's—

always a different kid, not the one who had hit the best shot, showed the most improvement, or even tried the hardest, but the one who guessed the random number he was thinking of.

“Terry.”

“Mrs. Dressler, hi.” He gave her son a high five. “Good job today.”

“I want to talk about Carson’s backhand. Have you got a minute?”

“Surc.” Thc problcm was that one of Mrs. Dressler’s minutes was equal to ten of anyone else’s. Luckily Baze intervened to tell him someone had called the pro shop and was waiting for him at the villa. He apologized to Mrs. Dressler and got into the Valiant with Baze.

“Who called?” Terry asked. “Who’s waiting? Tricia?”

“Yep. What’s wrong? You look sick.”

He massaged his forearm. “You want to go to a fucking play tonight?”

“You say you’re going to fuck her tonight?”

“No, asshole. I said, do you want to go instead of me?”

“Sure, I’d like to fuck her.” Baze started the car.

“Asshole. Drive slow. I gotta think, ’cause Nona said no girls.”

“So what does that mean? Just boys? Or just Nona?”

“Just no girls. No Tricia.”

The Porsche, engine idling, windows up and air-conditioning on, was parked in the street in front of the villa. Baze pulled into their driveway. Terry stared at the villa door.

“Tricia’s a distraction,” he said.

“No shit.”

“I can’t go.”

“Fine with me. But the distraction is getting out of her car, I’m getting out of this one, and you need to get out too.” Baze opened the car door and said, “Terry, one question: How would Nona know?”

Terry looked over his shoulder at Tricia, standing by the Porsche. Her pink dress was heart-shaped across her breasts and clinging so tightly all the way to her slender waist that all he could think of was a valentine. Thin straps were tied around her neck.

She turned her palms out, obviously asking what was wrong, but he couldn't move to answer her. He sat there until her smile faded. She turned and opened her car door. He looked at her bare shoulders and upper back, the crisscrossing of straps, like shoelaces, down to her waist. He wondered how in the hell he would get her out of that dress. She faced him again, holding the tickets over the heart of her dress. He hurried easily toward her, stopped a foot away, folded his arms, tugged his earlobe nervously, and smiled.

"I wasn't sure I should come," she said, "after you told me not to call."

"At Nona's. That's all I meant. I couldn't talk there."

"I thought I'd at least get a thimble."

"I can't. I'm scared you're not real. Scared if I touch you, you'll disappear." She laughed the happiest laugh he'd ever heard from her. "You look so perfect, I'm afraid I'd mess you up, 'cause I'd thimble you so hard I'd give you a concussion and make you cry."

"You'll only make me cry if we're late for the play. Get your shower."

The villa seemed darker and dirtier than ever to him, but before he could apologize, she asked him to hurry. Baze, heating canned ravioli in the open kitchen, said, "Take your time, man. I'll entertain."

Terry took a step toward the hall but turned back again. "I wish I had a coat and tie."

"You can wear your tailor-made shorts for all I care."

He grinned. "You just want to see Cheekhov."

"I just want to be with you. And Terry, I— The play is long.

We might be too tired to drive back."

He frowned in confusion. "Thirty miles is all."

"There's an inn."

She looked anxious, and in the silence Terry looked at Baze, hovering at the stove. He began dragging a spoon around the pot with more care and patience than Chef Boyardee required.

"Just simmering," he said pleasantly. "Ignore him," Terry told Tricia.

She dropped her voice. "There's an inn I love in the French Quarter."

He waited a moment to make sure she wasn't kidding. The stirring, which had stopped, began again. They both turned to Baze.

"Sizzling now," he said. "Anybody want some?"

Terry took her hand and led her away from the kitchen. "So this inn," he said.

"I made a reservation."

She sounded breathless. He tried to sound calm. "I'll have to get back early for camp in the morning." She nodded and he chuckled. "Tricia, every square inch of your skin I can see is as pink as your dress." He kissed her cheek. "Don't go anywhere."

He had dressed, packed his razor and toothbrush in his bag, and was staring at his—or somebody's—reflection in the mirror when Baze opened the bedroom door.

"John," Baze said, extending his hand. "John Travolta, how are you?"

"I look like a dork, right?" He didn't wait for an answer. He peeled off the polyester and reached for his khakis. While he changed, Baze positioned himself at the door.

"Nice shirt," Baze said. "Nice plaid."

"Thanks." Three steps later, bag in hand, Terry said, "Move." Baze didn't. "What is this?"

"A warning. Don't go. She's worse than a distraction. She's

bad news."

Terry waited for a punch line but there was none. "Why?"

"She doesn't talk. I couldn't get her to say anything. It's like she's up to something. Something no good. She's yanking your chain. I don't know how I know, but I do."

Terry said, "Out of my way." Baze stepped aside. "And stay put, right there. Till Tricia and me are out of here."

"Yes sir."

Tricia moved to the villa's front door, as if she couldn't wait to get to Charleston. Terry walked to her, dropped his bag, and stepped in close. He knew she thought he was going to kiss her. Instead, he ran his index finger slowly along the top of her valentine dress. Then he hooked his finger slightly over the edge, and began again—from one side, slowly following the curve to the dip in the center, to the other side and back again. She turned her head and closed her eyes.

"Tricia," he said.

When she looked at him, blue and gray, he uncurled his finger, slid it down across her dress, over her nipple, and around, tracing. He cupped her breast and kissed her.

"Wait," she managed, but he kissed her as he'd imagined kissing her—long and deep, not wanting to stop, her hand on his face, then their arms around each other. He changed to quick kisses, letting her punctuate them. "Terry . . . the play . . . I don't want to miss—" He let her step back. "When I saw the tickets—" A sigh. "I don't know what I can say or how I can thank you. Do you want to drive?" She handed him the key.

"Is that my thank-you?"

"For now. Fifty-five, though. No faster."

"What I was thinking," he said as the Porsche hummed toward Charleston, "when I started all that back at the door, was that if we made love before the play, then we could make love afterward too. We could even go back to the car and do it during intermission." He glanced at her. "You like that. You're smiling."

"Terry, there are four acts." She laughed. "Four acts, three intermissions. That would be five times, counting before and after."

"Good thing I'm an athlete," he said. "And the longer I play, Tricia, the better I get."

On Queen Street in Charleston, Tricia set a brisk pace, in spite of stiletto heels. She lectured like a professor of history as they walked hand in hand: Charleston's great fire of 1740, the Civil War, historic building preservation, and the Dock Street Theatre.

"It's the country's first building designed just for theatrical performance."

"How the hell do you know so much?" Terry asked. She started to answer but held back. "Because you read, right? You can say it. What else?"

"DuBose Heyward was a resident writer here."

He was supposed to know who that was but didn't.

"*Porgy and Bess*—Heyward and his wife wrote the play, which became the Gershwin opera. And Martha Graham danced here."

He didn't know who that was either but thought he could impress Nona with the name.

As they turned onto Church Street, he felt out of place. It was the theater's three stories and stout brownstone columns, or the idea of four acts by a man whose name he couldn't get right. But Tricia took his hand, dragged him into the lobby and up the curved staircase, making him feel great again and proud. Every man in the theater was watching her. Women were watching her too, or watching their men watch her.

"You even chose wonderful seats," she said as they were ushered to the center box.

"Yeah, they're great, huh?" The chairs were straight backed and wooden. At least he wouldn't fall asleep. "I'm gonna try to like this because I like you, as much as you like—" He lowered his voice. "Is it Chekhov or Cheekhov?"

"Chekhov. But Cheekhov is fine. I like it." She touched his cheek as the house lights dimmed. Staying focused was easier than he expected. The characters weren't speaking everyday language but seemed real enough. He was getting it, and yet, he wasn't. The program said *The Seagull — A Comedy*, and while the audience gave out a collective chuckle now and then, nothing seemed funny to him. Occasionally his gaze wandered, but only as far as Tricia, barely visible in the darkness, her face full of thought and involvement.

They spent the first intermission in the theater's courtyard, where he was glad to see a bar. Beer and white wine. Many smiles. Few words.

"You seem to be enjoying it," she said when they were back in their seats. She looked worried when he didn't answer. "Are you?"

"Yeah," he said, "but is this next act where the laughs are? It has a good ending, right?"

"It's Chekhov. It's tragicomedy. It's—"

"Almost over?" He laughed. "Nah, just kidding."

The lights went down, the curtain went up, the conversational hum of the audience faded, and *The Seagull* flew on. Hours later, after applause and standing ovations, Terry and Tricia stepped back into the night.

"A Chekhov moon?" Terry repeated, looking at the sky and referencing the conversation she'd had with another playgoer as they left the theater. She slipped her arm through his and they started toward the inn.

"Mood. Chekhovian mood."

"I don't know what that means."

"No matter. Tell me what you thought of the play. Twenty-five words or less."

"This isn't a test, is it, professor? 'Cause if it is, I'm going to flunk. I tried but I didn't get it. I thought—you want to know honestly what I thought?" She nodded. "I thought the whole thing was screwed up, because everybody loved somebody who loved some-other-damn-body-else. And everybody was unhappy and wanted something, but not enough to go after it. I hated his mother because she treated him so bad. I didn't like it that the good guy didn't get the girl, and I sure don't know why it's called a comedy. But mostly? I wish Konstantin hadn't blown his brains out at the end. I know I didn't get it—"

"Yes, you did." She stopped on the sidewalk, put her hands on his arms. "It's a story of hopelessly misplaced love. That's life, isn't it? And you're right: almost everyone wanted to change and talked of change, but never acted upon what they wanted, and life slipped away. That's life, too, isn't it? And that's Chekhov."

Here at last was the comedy—Tricia, happy and unaware, talking energetically on the sidewalk, the nightlife crowd parting and walking around them, her giddiness floating up and away like bubbles blown from a ring.

"Tricia," he finally said, "calm down."

She winced, and giggling, dropped her forehead to his chest. "I'm sorry. I'm impassioned and silly." She looked up. "I'm practically reciting research. I have notes—"

He felt something vanish in a soundless pop. "Notes for what?"

"Had. I had notes for a PhD dissertation," she said. "I had to give it up. But I hope to go back to it soon."

Those words were bubbles too, but clustered and weighty, hanging in the muggy night. He tried to dispel the new mood—Chekhovian or otherwise—that had come over her. "I heard the bell ring, professor. That class is over. I'm teaching the next one. You're taking it, right?"

"I want to, but first we have to talk. I have to tell you why I was late for the final."

He led her out of the mainstream and onto a quiet side street. "Tricia." He placed his hands on her waist and thought he'd captured a hummingbird. He sensed tiny wings flitting, a heart pattering. "You were late. You had a reason or you would have been there on time. I guess it's gonna hurt me, 'cause it looks like it's hurting you."

"Yes."

He pressed his lips together, struggled, and told her the truth. "I've just had the best week of my life. I played my best tennis. I beat Freddie. I won a tournament. I got a sponsor. But most of all, there was you. And I'm pretty sure I'm about to have the best night of my life. So can you wait and tell me tomorrow? 'Cause right now all I want is to make love with you."

Bad serve, he thought, *a fault.* She wasn't responding. No way he'd risk a double. But she didn't call it out. Instead, she slipped her hand behind his neck and brought his lips to hers in a light invitation to rally.

Welcome to the landmark Vendue Inn, built as early as 1783 in the legendary French Quarter and recognized by the Preservation Society of Charleston for sensitive rehabilitation. Around every corner, you'll discover antiques, heirlooms, original art, and heritage quilts. You'll enjoy our elegant sitting rooms, the Music Room, and the Reading Room.

Terry returned the brochure to the chest where he'd found it and, from a wing chair in the corner of the lobby, tried to ignore the awkwardness he felt.

Tricia checking in, handing over her credit card.

A couple giving him the hairy eyeball while waiting for the elevator.

A short, shiny-faced man sauntering into the inn, stopping, and looking directly at him. Staring, really. Causing Terry to shift in his chair and wonder how he could feel so uneasy under the gaze of a worm of a guy. His black hair was slicked back by a glob, not a dab, of something. And if that weren't enough to make him a certifiable putz, he was wearing a pair of red-and-yellow plaid pants. Lemon-peel yellow and fire-engine red.

The guy looked Tricia up and down, and with another glance at Terry took his place in line behind her to wait his turn to check in. He took two steps toward the crisscrossed laces. The dipshit was close. Way too close.

Terry stood and winced as he knocked an ashtray to the wood floor. It clattered but did not break. He carefully placed it back on the chest with the brochure as Tricia came back to him.

"There's a reading room," he said.

"I know." She smiled. "And a rooftop bar, if you want a drink."

He shook his head, and only when they were alone in the elevator did he relax. "Do I look like a gigolo?" he asked.

She broke off a piece of a chocolate chip cookie she'd picked up at the desk and fed it to him. "Do I look like I need to pay someone to have sex with me?"

"I guess not," he said.

"Room four."

She smiled. She gave him the key. He unlocked the door and together they stepped inside. He scanned the room.

"This looks like—" *You,* he wanted to say but didn't. Too cheesy?

"Fill-in-the-blank, teacher? How about *romantic*?"

She crossed the room to admire a rosebud in a crystal vase on the mantel, and his eyes took in the exposed brick walls, fireplace, and high four-poster bed. He looked at her, knowing what he wanted but unable to move ten yards across the floor. He longed for voices in the hall, the bell of the elevator, a door opening and closing—anything to break the silence. He'd staked the role of teacher for himself but needed his student to lead, to come to him and unbutton the shirt he was supposed to look irresistible wearing.

She unbuckled the ankle straps of her shoes and slipped them off. She walked to him and freed him. She put her arms around his neck. And so it began. Holding Tricia. Kissing Tricia. On and on.

Finally she stopped him. She did unbutton his shirt, but before she could slip it off him, he was untying the straps around her neck, thinking about the crisscrossed laces in back, watching the valentine rising and falling with the rush of her breathing, heavy like his. He kissed her again, his hands on her rib cage, her breasts. He fumbled blindly with the bow on the back of her dress at her waist while she unbuckled his belt.

The bow was stubborn. His fingers were clumsy; his hands, unsteady. He stopped kissing her, and with his hands on her shoulders, turned her away from him. As if he had planned it, they faced themselves in a cheval mirror. Their eyes met in the large oval glass, but hers began darting from ceiling to floor, as if she were frightened and trying to be brave.

He stepped back to examine the bow, defeated it easily, slipped his fingers inside the laces to feel her skin, slid the sides of the dress apart. Up over her head or down over her hips? Again their eyes met in the mirror, and at the timid, unspoken direction of hers, he sent the pink cotton rustling to the floor. Still behind her, watching in the mirror, he wrapped his arms around her waist, just below her bare breasts, and kissed her neck. She turned her head shyly, as if she couldn't watch, couldn't look at herself wearing only barely there lace panties. He kissed her cheek, then the corner of her mouth, and as his hands began to move, he lost her.

"I can't," she said.

He managed a husky, "What?"

"I can't."

He choked on, "Why?"

She stiffened and pushed his hands away, turning the mirror into a storefront window where a mannequin needed to be dressed—where a life-size fiberglass doll couldn't move, flinch, or blink her lifeless eyes. "Tricia, look at me."

His hands on her shoulders begged her to face him, but she refused.

Damn, he thought, watching her face in the mirror. *Damn. She's going to cry.*

"Tricia, it's me, just me. And whatever it is, it's okay." He massaged her shoulders until she wriggled free. She faced him, not speaking, but not crying either. "Tricia, help me out," he said. "I'll do whatever you want, but I don't know what that is." Nothing. "Want to go back?"

She shook her head. "It's late."

"It's twelve thirty. I'm not gonna fall asleep at the wheel."

"Can't we stay here?"

He expelled a long, slow stream of air. He gestured to his right. "I can sleep in that chair."

"That's silly."

"You're gonna sleep in the chair?" She shook her head. "Tricia, tell me what you want, okay? 'Cause I'm stupid and—"

"Terry, you're not. You understood the play perfectly."

"Okay, I'm a genius, but you're way too complicated for me." She bit her lower lip, tears pooled, and he backpedaled. "I didn't mean that in a bad way. I—okay, we'll stay. That's a big bed, you can sleep all the way over on one side and I'll sleep on the other." He waited. She nodded but didn't move. He decided to lighten things up. Or try to. "So, you're on the right and I'm on the left, and if you change your mind, you can meet me in the middle." He tossed her overnight bag to the bed. "So, do you want to get dressed?"

"I didn't bring anything to sleep in. I didn't think I needed to."

He pursed his lips and exchanged her bag for his. "You want one of my T-shirts?"

"No, I'll be okay."

"Unh-unh." He looked straight at her breasts. "You can't walk around dressed like that. Or undressed or half undressed like that. Please don't ask me to sleep in the bed with you half undressed. 'Cause I'm having a hard enough time as it is."

"I can see that."

"Yeah, well." He walked toward her, T-shirt in hand. "Come on. This will look good on you. And you know what? It's good we didn't do it, 'cause I've imagined it for so long and it was always so perfect that the real thing was gonna be a letdown."

"That hurts my feelings."

He tried to decide whether that was a complaint or a subtle invitation. "It might have been great, but not perfect. Nothing's perfect, right? That's just life. Just Cheekhov. Here, put this on." She shook her head. "I'm the teacher, and there's a dress code in my class." He gathered the sides of the shirt in his hands as if preparing to dress a child. She pushed her lips into a pout that was sexy, not childlike. He stepped in, raised the shirt, pulled it over her head and down to her waist, and suddenly she was kissing him again. Like before. And his hands were underneath the soft white cotton, touching and caressing her breasts like he'd not had the chance to before. Then the T-shirt was off, and they were standing a foot apart, looking at each other as if they weren't sure whether to be amused or aroused. Aroused won out, but she still looked uncertain.

"Do you want me to take these off?" she asked, slipping her thumbs inside her panties and rolling the top of them slightly over and down.

"I want you to do whatever you want, Tricia."

"I'm used to someone telling me what to do."

"Tricia," he said slowly, "if that's true, if everybody you've ever been with treated you like that, then . . ." He'd seen that look once before—when she admitted having only lines on a page in her life. "Then you've always been with the wrong son of a bitch."

"I know."

"Now you're not."

She ran her hands over his chest and belly, followed the line of soft hair from his navel to his belt. She pushed his shirt off his shoulders. It fell to the floor on top of her dress. She undressed him. His belt, pants, and boxers fell on top of his shirt. She added her panties to the pile.

She looked at him freely now and boldly. Then, hands moving, mouths reconnecting, bodies pressing one against the other, they made their way across the room.

"Which side of the bed do you want?" he asked, lying down beside her, his fingers on her thighs, then between them. "Left side or right side?"

"Terry."

He thought she said no again but wasn't sure. He felt rather than heard soft sounds on his ear. He couldn't interpret them as consent or refusal or fear. His mouth left hers, moved to her throat and her breasts.

"Left side or right side?" He would do what she wanted.

"Inside, Terry. Inside of me. Please."

"Shhh." Done, spent, lying on his back, still holding her, Terry placed his index finger over her lips. He smiled, and with a dare in his eyes, slowly removed it.

"Terry—"

"Shhh." He whispered an answer to the silent why on her lips: "Don't talk. Don't wake me up. I'm dreaming I made love with this perfect girl, and even though nothing's perfect, it was fucking perfect. Or perfect fucking. If I keep dreaming, I'll get to do it again."

"You're not dreaming. Pinch yourself to make sure you're awake."

"Pinch?"

She nodded, and when he pinched her nipple, she cried with mock indignation, "Ow."

"Shhh," he hissed.

Okay, she mouthed, pinching him back. She went into the bathroom. He went to the champagne bucket, popped the cork, and she laughed. "That surely woke you. Now can I talk?"

He watched her get back in bed, arrange the pillows against the headboard, lean back against them. No dream, he told himself. She's real. Everything's real. He pulled the ice bucket stand to the side of the bed and spilled a little champagne as he poured two glasses. He handed one to her and raised the other.

"To Tricia." He got in bed beside her. "To Tinker Bell, Wendy, the girl of my dreams." He clinked his glass against hers, put it to his lips, felt his nose tingle. "Your turn."

"To Terry. To Pete. To Chekhov and Cheekhov, who made this possible." Another clink. She ran her fingers around the rim of her glass, listened to its hum. She drank a sip and placed her glass on the bedside table.

"Don't you like it?" he said. "Don't you want to sleep?"

"Tricia, if the only son of a bitches you've made love with—"

"Sons of bitches," she said lightly.

"Sons, then," he said. "But all that matters is this: if the only thing Tom, Dick, or Harry ever did was roll over and go to sleep afterward, then you made rotten choices. No way I'm sleeping. I'm teaching. I'm assigning you to pull an all-nighter with me."

He tried to measure her smile. Genuine, he decided. As much as he hated reading, he didn't mind reading her, or trying. It was becoming easier, but there were pages and chapters he hadn't even skimmed yet, and some of the pages he'd already turned were still as blank and white as the sheets on the bed. She lifted his arm and nestled under it, a cozy protective wing.

"Pete from Neverland." She ran a finger across his lips, his teeth. "That was never-before-land for me. No-one-else-land. No one has made that happen before."

He'd feel like a dumb-ass if he'd misunderstood, but he risked the low percentage shot to make sure. "So, like, are you saying, like, you've never, like—"

"There were three *likes* in that sentence. But, like, yes." She smiled, covered her eyes with her hands, then spread her fingers for a peek. "I've read The *Joy of Sex* but I've never known it. I'm twenty-six years old. It was a first. My first. And I'm embarrassed."

He took her hands from her face. "Why? Don't be."

"There's another first—something I've never told anyone but want to tell you. Every time I've had sex in my life, I've cried afterward. Except this time."

She sat up straight and raised her eyebrows to ask what he thought, but he couldn't even manage *you're kidding me, right?*

"Give me a half hour," he finally said, "and I'll prove it wasn't a fluke. And you're lucky, 'cause even though you were perfect the first time, I'm giving you a quiz for extra credit. Twenty Questions." As he poured more champagne for both of them, she looked uneasy and expanded the space between them. "We're gonna play. 'Cause even though you just told me a lot, you still know more about me than I know about you. You know dyslexia, bad nerves, some about my mom." He paused. "But I don't know hardly anything about you."

"I don't want to play."

"Try. It'll be fun. Here we go: Did you like the play?"

"Yes."

"Were those tickets the coolest present anybody ever gave you?"

"Yes."

"Did you think you'd ever be lucky enough to fuck me?"

She laughed. "No. Yes. Yes and no. I don't know."

"What do you do?" No answer. "For a living."

"That's not yes or no. Retract it. Rephrase it."

"In New York, are you a teacher? Like at a college? English and books?"

"No, but I would like to be."

"You'd be a great teacher." He kissed her as she slipped under his wing again. "You'd be lecturing every day just like you were talking to me on the street tonight. Nobody would daydream in class 'cause you'd be talking excited and happy and making things interesting. Every guy with a pulse would take your class, and guys would line up at your door during office hours. But"—he held up a finger to make a point—"you'd give killer exams, and assign lots of papers, and mark everything up so bad that the school wouldn't be able to keep you in red pens."

She gave up a happy laugh, and to him the sound was champagne glasses clinking and ringing.

"I would want my students to learn," she said. "And I've always wanted to teach. My parents both taught literature at Sarah Lawrence College, in Bronxville, thirty minutes from New York City by train. I was always with them—in their offices, in the library, in their classes. I'd sit in the back and listen to lectures, even though I couldn't understand."

"I bet you came close."

She shook her head. "They were brilliant. I was only a child. But a very happy child. I wrote a poem about the campus when I was six:

Summers wear green.
Winters wear snow.
Buildings wear ivy
Wherever I go."

She laid her head on his shoulder, and with her eyes closed, relaxed into a slow neck roll, a turnstile to a happy past. He wanted to follow but had no token. Slapped back by cold metal arms, he waited for her return to the present and was glad when she picked up her champagne.

"I loved my eyes then. Blue from my father, gray from my mother. Special eyes, they said, for a very special girl." She sighed, still smiling. She sipped champagne and snuggled close to him again. "They read to me constantly. There are children's books I still know by heart. I wanted so much to be like them that I learned to read when I was very young."

"Cheekhov at three?"

"No, but I was always reading something, and they were too. That's the sound of my childhood—pages turning."

She fell silent, and he knew she was listening to those pages. He tried to listen with her, but he'd never been read to, and emptiness throbbed like an earache. "Are you and your parents still close?"

"Here," she said, handing him her champagne, her voice changing in one clipped word.

Puzzled, he put her glass on the nightstand and his beside it. She lay on her side, propped up on her elbow.

"My parents are dead. They died together."

He winced. "I'm sorry."

"It was my birthday."

"Jesus."

"I was seven."

Leaning in, he kissed her lightly. She responded as if she wanted to make love again but drew back as a storm built in her eyes and gave way to a blue-gray flash flood.

"When I was seven," she said again. *Seven* went under with a sob. He kissed her forehead while moving his hand into the valley between her hip and ribs, then into the small of her back. He pulled her closer.

"I want to tell, Terry."

"Tell how they died?"

"And why. My fault. I've never told. I need to."

"Then tell me," he said. "I'll be first again."

She lay down on her back as if too weak to do more. "When I was—" She raised her hands, showed him five fingers of one, two of the other. Terry covered them with his hand, pulled them to his lips, and kissed them. "Seven," she said, her eyes dry now and vacant. "When I was seven," she said, and went on.

"My parents died in a head-on collision. On impact. They were speeding."

So began the exclusive he sensed she'd been privately writing for years and chosen him to receive. She was mechanical, her voice tinny. He was overwhelmed with responsibility.

"I saw police photos a child should never have seen. The car—" Her voice changed as if she'd stepped onto a tightrope. "The car was crumpled from end to end. My mother was trapped inside." She rolled onto her side, away from him, though not far. "My father was thrown from the car. His head was crushed. His neck was broken. It was twisted. The way it was twisted—" She stopped and started: "That's why—" And stopped again.

"The seagull," he said, "by the deck." He rubbed her arm, shoulder to wrist.

"Terry, you can't imagine how much I needed you to move that godforsaken bird."

He moved closer, comforting, spooning. "You almost didn't let me in that day."

"Please don't move."

She said it so urgently that it startled him, as if she saw something he couldn't see—a bug on the wall, a monster in the closet. She grew so still he thought she'd fallen asleep, but then she faced him.

He said instinctively, "It wasn't your fault."

"It was." She looked certain and solemn. "I took the life of my father and my mother. Of Marcus and—" She shaped her lips into an m and shook her head. "I think of myself as Daddy's girl, but it's my mother's name I can't even say." She tried again.

"Mary?" he said. She signaled with her hands that there was more. "Mary Jane?" he guessed, and she shook her head. "Mary Beth? Mary Ann?"

"Uh," she managed. "Marianna?"

"Marianna," she said, and in a grateful whisper, "thank you. That's the first time in nineteen years I've said—" She had to whisper but said again, "Marianna."

"Pretty name." He waited. "More?"

"My parents were going away for a weeklong conference at Princeton. They had never left me before and I didn't want them to. They left me with our next-door neighbors, who had teenaged children. Two girls. And a—" She stopped and nodded at him to fill in the blank.

"Boy," he said.

"Daryl."

"How old?" He felt his chest tighten.

"Fourteen. But it's not what you think."

"Good," he said, relieved.

But she added, "Not exactly."

He braced for a tidal wave of truth.

"Things were fine until the third day, my birthday. The kids were babysitting me that night, and when Daryl went out, he made me go too. To a carnival, he said, to have fun with his friends. We went through dark streets. We took shortcuts through woods. And when we got there, they took me to freak shows—dwarves, dead Siamese twin babies in a jar, the legless lady. They left me in the hall of mirrors. They forced me onto the Tilt-A-Whirl alone and laughed at me while I spun and screamed. When it was over, I was so dizzy and frightened I couldn't stand up. The man who took tickets—he was like a freak too. He smelled. He was dirty. His teeth were crooked and brown. He grabbed my braids. I—" She shook her head. "I can't do it."

"Get outside of it, Tricia. Watch it like a movie." That was what he tried to do with the shed. "It's not happening to you. It's somebody in a book. Just read me the story."

"The carnie pulled—"

She shut her eyes and opened them again. He hoped the glaze in them would protect her. "The carnie pulled Patricia's hair and said, 'What do you got there, girlie? What's those eyes?' She looked at the gate, hoping to run away, but the boys were waiting. One called out, 'They don't match. They're devil's eyes.' The carnie, still holding Patricia's braids, said, 'No, this girlie's got witch's eyes. You better light a fire, boys. Burn her up.' Daryl shouted, 'At the stake.' The man laughed and pushed her toward them. He said, 'Burn little witchy at the stake.' Two boys grabbed Patricia, but she clawed like a cat. She got away from them somehow and ran to the woods. But they chased her and caught her."

Tricia struggled for air in quick little sniffs that gave way to panicked gasps. Memory wrinkled her face into a rubbery mask.

"Tricia," he said gently, "turn the page. Can you turn it?"

Tears raced down her cheeks like runners toward a finish line. "The boys took off the helpless child's clothes. They touched her. All of them. Touched everywhere. She was crying when she should have been screaming for help. 'Pick a tree,' Daryl ordered. 'Pick a tree for a stake.' They took off their belts. They rolled their shirts and used them to tie her to a tree. A skinny little tree. A sapling. Young and fragile like she was. They held cigarette lighters in front of her face, flicked them on.

'I'll burn her pigtails first,' Daryl said, laughing. 'They'll burn fast.' But when he grabbed a braid, she screamed for the first time. And screamed until they ran."

Tricia bit her lip and began to sob. He held her in his arms. "It's okay," he said. "I'm here. I've got you." He kissed the top of her head, and as she regained control, he kissed her lips, nose, cheeks, chin. He kissed her until she rolled onto her back and looked at the ceiling as if for constellations.

"Someone found me," she told him. "A couple. A man and his wife. They took me to the hospital and called the police. It took hours to locate my parents, but at last my mother was on the phone, telling me they would be there soon, promising they would drive fast. I kept saying, 'Fast, Mommy, fast, fast.'" She pulled the white down comforter to her chin, let soundless tears drip into puffy folds. "But they drove too fast, Terry. They never came. The hospital chaplain came. My parents' friends, faculty friends I knew well. Someone with a psychologist. They all came to tell me my parents were dead."

Calmly she unspooled the rest of the story: a different life on a farm in Iowa; her well-intentioned grandparents, loving her, proudly displaying her like an object, but always lamenting her eyes; the story of the carnival spreading like wildfire through the small Midwestern town; children at school, ridiculing, ostracizing, even fearing the witch.

"I withdrew," she concluded. "All I wanted to do was read, and that's what I've done. You were right. Just lines on a page."

"Till now," he heard himself say, not knowing what he meant. "Because you've told it," he explained—to himself? To her? "So things are different now. You're free."

She began moving her hands along his face as if she were blind and trying to discover who he was and what he looked like. She kissed him and whispered, "Thank you for the firsts."

Looking at her in the long silence that followed, he wondered why first felt empty, what else he wanted and why.

"Twenty Questions," she said, her voice light and rippling. "Number one: Will you turn out the light? It's nearly three, I'm exhausted, and you've got camp tomorrow."

He crossed the room to turn off the chandelier, glanced over his shoulder, caught her staring. He flipped the switch and walked to the lamp glowing beside the bed. He reached for the chain and held it, letting her watch him grow hard.

"Question two," she said. "Meet me in the middle?" He pulled them into darkness.

She touched him, and he postponed his own question: What was it she'd wanted to tell him after the play?

She kissed him, and he decided to hold the question forever, because forever was a summer and nothing more. He'd go back to Austin; she'd go back to New York.

He entered her and wondered if there was someone else in her life. He told himself it didn't matter. But when they came, together, he knew that it did and why.

Only. He wanted *first and only.* He lay still, waiting for the emotional response to recede with the physical one, knowing even then that it wouldn't.

Her nudge was gentle but woke him. In the morning light, he rolled over and tried to say hi, but she stopped him, her finger on his lips.

"Shhh. I'm having this incredible dream."

"No you're not. Neither one of us is dreaming. It's real."

He smiled at her—smiled in the bed, in the shower, at breakfast, and in the car as he drove them all the way back to Kiawah.

"Hey," he said, "that other thing you wanted to tell me? About why you were late for my match?"

"We checked in at the Vendue after midnight," she said. "So we didn't make love for the first time last night; we made love for the first time this morning, which makes today the best day of my life. Can I tell you tomorrow?"

"If you want. But if it's going to fuck things up with us, don't ever tell me."

"I have to, Terry. And you're speeding."

He tried but couldn't slow the car or his thoughts: There is somebody else, who sends roses but doesn't treat her right, who can't make her come, who rolls over and goes to sleep. A Tom, Dick, or Harry. But Terry knew he could beat him, on court, in bed, in every way.

The campers were already warming up when he pulled into the parking lot, but he took time to take a T-shirt from his bag. "I'm leaving this in the car," he said. "It will be my reason for having to come to your house this afternoon. I'll have to get it."

"You don't need a reason. You have a standing invitation."

"And you're real, right?" He waited for her nod and touched her cheek. "I'm just checking."

She smiled and touched his. "I'm just making sure."

CHAPTER 6

Jack met with the auditors for over four hours in the conference room, then with his attorney, Aaron Silver, whom I found arrogant and had never trusted. I sat at my desk, wondering why he didn't want me beside him as usual, taking notes, recording minutiae that might prove important later. But without warning, I'd been shut out again, along with everyone else.

Our senior account execs were in and out of my office, asking what was going on. So was Bill Kiernan, pale and fidgety. *Not feeling well,* he said at midmorning, and *not expecting to be back*, as he left for lunch. Barbara Fox, our administrative assistant, ordered lunch in for Jack and Aaron. Over the course of the afternoon, five men arrived, their dress and bearing as professional as their faces were unfamiliar. I listened for their names as they checked in with Barbara, whose desk was in the center of the suite comprised of Jack's office, my office, and the conference room. I flipped through my Rolodex, a duplicate of Jack's, and finding none of them, assumed Aaron had brought them in. I checked the phone book and learned that they were accountants, corporate tax specialists, and a corporate criminal defense attorney.

In the late afternoon, when Jack buzzed Barbara for "more goddamn coffee," I volunteered to take in a fresh pot. My opening of the conference room door guillotined conversation. I stepped into a smoky conspiracy. There were ash heaps in ashtrays. Around the table, cigarette flames glowed like tranquilized fireflies.

The newly assembled team scrutinized me as I carried a carafe to the hot plate. I stalled. I straightened mugs, checked sugar and cream. I looked at Jack, who offered an apologetic smile, telling me he knew I felt spurned and hated serving coffee. I filled one mug and walked to the head of the eighteen-foot mahogany table, polished so luxuriously that I thought I might see my reflection and Jack's. I gave him his coffee. I reached for an ashtray to empty it.

"Not necessary," Jack said. "Thank you, Lynn."

On the stretch of hardwood between the antique Oriental rug and the door of their sanctum, the clicking of my pumps resounded with discriminatory and personal rejection.

The meeting broke at seven. Aaron and Jack moved back to his office. When Aaron left and I went in, Jack was standing at the window, looking out.

"What's going on?" I joined him at the glass.

"I have no choice."

"About what?"

"Saving the company."

"What did they recommend?"

He went back to his desk, started to pack his briefcase.

"Tell me, Jack. Let me help you. Whatever it takes."

He shook his head, not in refusal, but as he often did when I'd missed a point he was trying to make. "It's important to me that you don't know what I'm going to do." He gave up a cough that sounded more like bronchitis than nervousness. "You above everyone else mustn't know. Do you understand, Lynn?"

I closed my eyes but still saw the fall of the man I so admired. He might as well have jumped from the thirty-fourth floor. "You're trying to protect me."

"Yes."

He snapped his briefcase closed and walked away. For the first time, he forgot the ritual. He didn't touch the picture frame at the door.

I relapsed. I began not only smoking again, but chain-smoking, inhaling as hungrily as Jack did, exhaling as violently. Over the next two weeks he gave me long, complicated assignments, none of them related to the audit. I ran meetings for him, made decisions with newly granted authority. When he woke me at home with a phone call just past midnight, I didn't know what to expect.

"The media plan for Kiawah is done." He was hoarse. With exhaustion, I assumed. "The presentation is Friday. I'd like you to make it."

He waited for me to react, but I couldn't, even when I heard the impatient drumming of his fingers. He went on. "Stunned, Lynn? Why? You've earned your chance. The plan is solid. I've okayed it. You only have to present and get their approval."

"Tom Padgett?"

"I let him go. I need another account exec. I'd like to have a woman, to have you."

Maintain, I told myself. Don't gush, don't be giddy. Act as he would. "You'll walk me through the plan in the morning?"

"Now."

I didn't feel sharp, but I grabbed a pen and tablet. My impulse was to jot down the emotions he'd stirred and served me—excitement, gratitude, pride. Instead, standing at the rickety card table that served as my desk at home, I consumed objectives, strategies, and tactics like a glutton.

"You're going to Kiawah in the morning, Lynn. That will give you a day to settle in and prepare. It's a 6:00 a.m. flight. It's all Barbara could get this late."

Doubt crackled. "So this is a snap decision?"

"Yes and no. You've been asking. I've been considering." He said nothing for a moment, then went on. "I want you to work on-site, get to know the team, get the feel of the place. I want you on the island until we launch the rebrand."

"That will be months." I lit a cigarette to kill a bitter aftertaste.

"You can stay with Patricia."

I, the glutton, had been feasting on pap. "Salary, Jack?"

"Twenty-five."

I did the math in my head. "I won't work for fifty-seven cents on the dollar of what the other execs—the males—are paid." I paced as I waited for his answer, loving and despising him, one more than the other, though I didn't know which.

"All right, thirty," he said. "Merit increase in a year."

"Accepted." I swallowed my surprise and switched subjects before he could change his mind. "Patricia knows I'm coming?"

"We're not speaking, remember? Not since I flew down to get her and she refused to come home. Not even through messages, except for one. She said she's been getting prank phone calls and had the number changed. The new one—take this down—is 843-227-1318. For an emergency, she said. That's the only reason I should call."

"Call her in the morning, while I'm on the plane."

"You're not an emergency, Lynn."

I stared at the receiver's cord—black, coiled, twisted. "What am I, Jack?" He said without hesitation, "You are exactly what you want to be."

I walked as far across the room as I could, straightening the cord that tethered me to him, pulling it as tight as I dared.

"You're a necessity," he said.

"A necessity," I said. "Nice, Jack."

"That's a compliment."

"That's cold and clinical. It's also unclear. I'm necessary for the agency? For Patricia?" I took a long pull on my cigarette. "For you?" I heard his lighter, heard him smoking.

"For the agency, you're as necessary as I am, Lynn, and an account exec now."

"Yes." And a personal assistant still. "Call your wife," I said.

"Why? She won't answer. Surprise her, Lynn. She'll like

that."

I knocked and smiled from the beach house porch. "Say hello to the first female account exec at TCC."

Patricia stared at me blankly. "Congratulations."

"Jack has given me the Kiawah Island account," I said. She stood motionless in the doorway, unsmiling. "I'm to stay with you." She was speechless. "My luggage didn't make the connection. They'll deliver it." I slit the quiet morning open by forcing a laugh. "Can I come in?"

I looked beyond her as a man ambled into the room. Barefoot, gym shorts, no shirt. She stepped aside, and feeling wooden and unable to move, I somehow forced my way across the threshold into a new triangle. She introduced me as her best friend, and I sounded wooden too, as I said hello. I tried to light a cigarette and she snapped, "Don't smoke in here."

"Why?" If ever I'd needed a cigarette, it was then.

"Terry's an athlete."

"It won't bother me," he said. He looked from Patricia to me to Patricia and said, "Well, it might." Then: "I've gotta get to camp." He started toward the bedroom but turned back to her.

"In the dryer," she said.

He smiled, apparently not noticing that she was trembling, and with a casual *thanks*, he headed to the laundry room for a shirt, then back to the bedroom to dress. Patricia leaned against the wall, closed her eyes.

"Don't tell Jack," she said.

I looked at beer cans on the coffee table. I saw an empty bottle of Boone's Farm wine in the kitchen, tried to envision Patricia drinking Strawberry Hill. I looked around the living room, stared at a crystal jar full of Peanut M&M's. I saw shoes at the door and shook my head—not at his Nikes but at her Candie's, molded plastic heels, leather strap across the toe.

Outside and poolside, his-and-hers clothes were entwined and sleeping in the sun.

Like the snap of a hypnotist's fingers, the sound of a bedroom room door closing brought Patricia out of her trance and into a rigid posture; she stood as if facing a firing squad. The man looked younger step-by-step as he passed through the room again and kissed her good-bye. I clenched my jaw and glared at her. Uselessly. She looked at the floor. I heard the garage door growl open and the Porsche crank, and held my indignation as he backed into the street.

"Patricia. That man is driving Jack's car." I looked into eerie eyes I'd seen only once before, expecting them to fill, but their gaze was steely. The gray one seemed to swell like a balloon. "Did he sleep here? Are you sleeping with him?"

"You can't tell Jack," she said. "Let's go to the beach and talk. Give me a chance, Lynn. Please."

"I don't have my clothes."

"I'll dress you for once."

Her bathing suits wouldn't have fit me, so she gave me shorts and a T-shirt—the Rolling Stones, Some Girls tour, Myrtle Beach, SC, 6/22/78. "Did you go to that concert?" I tried to sound casual instead of appalled.

"No. Terry did. He brought it back for me. He loves to give me presents."

"So does your husband."

"No," she said sharply.

It wasn't the roar of a lion, but neither was it the squeak of a mouse.

"Jack gives me extravagant gifts. Jack can afford to. And most of the time, you choose them. Terry makes six dollars an hour and chooses them himself. It's different."

"All right. I understand."

She smiled for the first time. "It's different, and it's endearing."

"Are you smitten?" I cried. She shrugged and I fumed. I jerked the clothes from her hands. "Where do you want me?" I asked. "Besides back in New York."

"Upstairs, the beachside room. So you'll have a phone."

"I'll change there."

"Close the bedroom door when you start back down, okay?" She said it again when I reached the midpoint landing. "Lynn, close the door when—"

"I heard you the first timc."

I continued my stomp up the stairs, walked to the window, and looked down. The pool, the dunes, the beach, the ocean—everything shimmered in the sun. Even the air shimmered, beckoning me to play with possibilities: Who he was, how they met, what they had in common, who seduced whom. I wondered about their first time making love and thought about mine and Jack's.

Six months ago, after landing an important account in Charleston, he and I had taken a day off to celebrate at the beach house. We'd had a glass of champagne on the deck before he led me upstairs to show me the second-floor view.

In the sunlit bedroom, desire danced on my skin, my breasts, my lips. Danced frantically on my tongue, daring me to taste the mix of cigarettes and champagne in his mouth. Fear, just as lively and quick, danced too. Jack would break me, prove me no different from any other woman in his workaday world. He would use me to sate the hunger he'd told me Patricia couldn't, drink me like luxurious Drambuie enriching his after-dinner Scotch.

His mouth, on mine, was crushing, as I'd known it would be. He surprised me only by stopping to ask, "Are you sure?"

"No," I said, or *fear* said, though I was aching inside.

He stepped back. "Why? It's no more intimate than your living with me ten hours a day, calming me down when no one else can. Reeling me in, reading my thoughts, finishing my sentences." He paused. "You inhabit my mind. You're inside my head."

I did. I was. And he was sincere.

"It's not a power play, Lynn. It's a longtime want."

Having shed only our suit jackets before champagne, we unbuttoned each other's shirts, mine solid blue, his pinstriped pink. No boy and girl fumbling. We were man and woman, sure-handed, welcoming sights imagined but unseen until now.

He wanted me too, always had. I'd mind-read it. Now he'd admitted it.

I ran my fingers through the hair on his chest, as thick and dark as his five-o'clock shadow had suggested. He kissed my neck, my shoulders and chest—smattered with pale freckles as he must have guessed from the same smattering on my arms. He pulled me into him, pressed us together, and we fell from grace to the floor.

I forced myself away from the window, the ocean, and that slice of a memory. I fixed my eyes on the phone.

I inhaled, imagining my fingers punching in Jack's number.

I exhaled, felt his fingers inside me again.

Inhaled and heard myself saying, "Jack, Patricia has a lover."

Exhaled and heard, "Patricia, the black pearl button was mine."

Inhaled the courage to tell her the truth.

Exhaled all hope of forgiveness.

My betrayal would cut her more deeply than Jack's had. The bleeding might never stop. My six-month offense was unpardonable. And if I counted thinking about it, I'd slept with him for years.

I left the room, so lost in thought that I forgot to close the door. Downstairs again, I followed her to the beach.

"I'm going to try to leave Jack," she said once we were settled. "I think I'm strong enough. But I may need your help."

I wanted to smoke but couldn't light my cigarette until she cupped her hands to block the breeze. I noted the progression from New York's *I want to leave* to Kiawah's *I'm going to try to leave*, from *I want you to help me* to *I may need your help.*

"I've never even had a job, paid bills, filed a tax return. I've never lived alone. Even in college I lived with my grandparents." She patiently tucked her hair under a hat with a Texas Longhorns logo on the brim. "I dread those things. And I want them."

I smoked my cigarette and buried the filter in the sand. "I can't help you, Patricia. I can't lie to Jack. And I can't let this go on with you and your lover."

"Jack has a lover too. Remember? I still have her button."

I listened to the beating of waves on the sand. I longed for the honking of yellow taxicabs and for the city's summer heat, trapped between skyscrapers, nowhere to go, like me. I would gladly have traded the rejuvenating salt of the air and sweetness of Sea & Ski for the staleness of garbage yet to be cleared, and homelessness; the smell of pretzel and hot dog stands on the street; a whiff of crisp dry-cleaned suits in crowds, heads down and pushing en masse to the office; the tang of sweaty tourists, heads up and gawking in Times Square.

I felt the circular, caring movement of my friend's fingers as she rubbed lotion on my face, pale with life in the office, my life with her husband.

"I think she's a model," Patricia said.

"Whoever she is—was—doesn't matter. It's over. He's so wrapped up in the audit he doesn't have time for anything else. It meant nothing to him. He loves you."

"No. Jack loves Jack. And TCC," she said. "He doesn't even know me."

I thought of the many times in his office, in the early days of their marriage, that I'd related something new I'd learned about her. "Really?" he'd say in surprise, and if I went on at any length, his eyes would glaze over and he'd break in with something like, "Did you see the six plus six forecast?"

Still I persisted. "He loves you, Patricia. He will never let you go. You'd better understand that." She rubbed her temple with her bare left hand as if I were making her goddamn gorgeous head ache. "And you love Jack. It's just that the two of you are so diametrically opposed—"

"Lynn," she said, "Terry is so dyslexic he can hardly read, and until a few weeks ago he'd never heard of Virginia Woolf."

"Oh stop. Don't say you're in love with him. Tell me it's recreational sex or your way of settling the score."

"It isn't. And I don't like the way you called Terry my lover."

The beach became a tundra in spite of ninety-degree heat. We went up to the house for lunch, then back to the sand for more cold, silent sweltering. Only when Terry arrived and went into the ocean did Patricia and I begin to talk again.

She told me about reading to children in Charleston, needing a family one day, wanting to go back to school, the Scotch in her index cards. She rehashed things I'd heard many times before and described him with a well-rehearsed litany, from *I-me-mine power* to *extreme volatility.*

"The volatility is getting worse," she said.

"It's the audit," I insisted. "The problem he can't solve in a way he finds acceptable. It's killing him." We watched Terry walk out of the ocean in a slow reveal—shoulders, chest, tight belly. "And what you're doing, Patricia? This would really kill him."

"It's turnabout, Lynn. It's fair."

"But it isn't play?"

She didn't answer. Terry was walking toward us and smiling. He gave her a quick kiss and insisted on fixing dinner.

He touched her cheek and she touched his. Then he did it again, left-handed. She did the same, and the legs of this new triangle turned spindly and unstable. I felt the sand turning to mush and my chair sinking in the messiest bog of a middle I'd ever known. Before leaving us, Terry kissed her again, so intensely that I had to look away.

When he was out of earshot, I turned to her. "Does he know you're married?"

She got up, walked to the water's edge. I went after her and we stood together, letting the ocean cool our feet.

"Does he know you're married?"

"I've tried to tell him, but he resists. He doesn't want to know, I swear. And I'm afraid to tell him. I'm afraid he'll leave, and I'm the happiest I've ever been right now."

"You're lying to both of them."

She looked at the horizon. "Yes."

I glanced at my watch and left her there. I trudged back up the beach. I folded my chair, stepped into the flip-flops she'd loaned me. "Patricia." I had to shout to be heard and to accommodate my anger. "I'm not lying to anyone. I'm going inside. I'm going to call Jack."

I didn't have to call Jack. It was five, the hour we'd agreed upon for a daily check-in. Jack was calling me. Terry reached for the phone in the kitchen, responding to a scarcely audible ring. Patricia, who had chased me, spewing *waits* and *pleases*, was finally catching up.

Terry said, "Hello," and looked baffled as the ringing continued upstairs.

"It's for me," I said, climbing.

Patricia said, "I had a second line installed, Lynn. Just for you."

Not for me, I wanted to protest, *for your lover, to prevent Terry's answering a call from Jack or overhearing a message.* Prank phone calls, she'd told her husband. I slammed the bedroom door.

"Hi, Jack."

He rushed through pleasantries and on to tomorrow's presentation. As I listened, Patricia opened the door but stayed halfway in and halfway out of the room, halfway in and out of her parallel lives.

"The CEO will scoff at two hundred grand for print," Jack was saying.

"I'm prepared for that."

"Then you're ready," he said. "Put Patricia on the phone." I said nothing and he said it again. Loudly.

Patricia shook her head. "He told me he had nothing to say to me until I'm ready to come home. I'm not."

"She's about to shower, Jack. We just came in from the beach."

"Put her on the phone."

Patricia came to me, gave my hand a squeeze, as desperate as the plea in her eyes.

"I can't, Jack."

He snorted. "Tell her to call me."

As he hung up, she and I sat down on the bed. Her hand quaked in mine like a nine on the Richter scale but slowed as she told me about the night of firsts, sex that fired nerve endings she didn't know she had, and about making it past when I was seven. "Terry is the only one who will ever know, so don't ask, Lynn. Just help me, please."

"Patricia," I said, my own hand quivering. "What would have happened if Jack had come to Kiawah to pitch the media plan? If Jack had come to the door instead of me? What will happen if he shows up next week to check on the account?"

I tried to answer the question myself, but as well as I knew him, I had no idea. I came up with the best possible scenario: he would be stunned into inaction, so totally perplexed by both of us that he would resort to a legal pad and make a strategic plan.

It was unlikely but not impossible, and—God—so much better than any loss of temper or crime of passion that might have played out in my mind. I tried like a medium at a séance to channel him but couldn't. It was a terrifying failure.

"I want to leave him," she told me. "I'm surer every day. And I'm stronger every day. But there's a piece inside me that is scared to death. I need this summer to be sure."

I owed her. But I owed Jack too.

"I need this island," she said.

I needed absolution.

"He mentors you, but you mentor me, Lynn. All I'm asking for is time."

In my head, my sigh sounded like a storm wind. "One month, Patricia." It was the sixth of July.

On my second day on the island, we began to establish a routine. Patricia, after writing in her journal, went to the Charleston library. Terry went to kids' camp. I went to the Kiawah office.

I welcomed my first solo presentation, relieved to be absorbed in a professional challenge instead of a moral dilemma. I called Jack at five to tell him how well things had gone—that apart from an increase in Golf Digest ads, the Kiawah team had accepted the plan intact. I basked in my mentor's praises as long as I dared and ended the call before he could ask for his wife.

"Help me with this picnic," she said as I joined her in the kitchen. "Terry will be home soon and we'll go to the beach. His best friend is coming too."

"Not for me, I hope."

"No, of course not."

I was taken aback, but before I could ask exactly what she meant, the front door opened and someone called, "Foxes, here are your wild and crazy guys!"

The impersonation rang so true that I expected Dan Aykroyd or Steve Martin to shimmy-strut into the kitchen in plaid pants, a floral shirt, and a flat cap.

"This is Baze," Terry said. "Don't believe anything he says."

"Chris Bazemore," said his friend. "Baze." Tall and beanpole thin, he tilted his chin upward to toss his shaggy dark bangs out of his eyes. "And believe everything."

I sought clarification. "Patricia?"

"You've gotta quit calling her that," Terry said with a laugh. "Every time you say Patricia, I start looking around, like some other girl must be here She's Tricia."

Tricia/Patricia abandoned the grapes, shrimp salad, and me. She rinsed her hands and reached for a towel, but Terry was kissing her before she could dry them. He whispered something, and she smiled and led him down the hall.

"Did he say tennis lesson?" I asked Baze. "Aren't we going out on the beach?"

"Code," he said. "*Lesson* is code. *I want to give you a lesson* is code for *I want to get laid.* Or *rally.* That's a good one. *Terry, let's rally.*" He began packing a cooler. "Are you a beer drinker, Lynn? It's Lynn, right?"

"Yes. And yes on the beer."

"Here for the summer?"

"Indefinitely."

"Let me give you the skinny." He raised an index finger. "Always knock before you come in the house. You never know where and how you'll find them—whose hand up whose shirt or down whose shorts." He poured a bag of ice over the beer and picked up the cooler. "Let's go."

"Shouldn't we wait?"

"I'm not that patient. She likes his forehand. A lot of forehand."

"Code again?"

"You bet."

I looked at the kitchen counter and a cookbook she'd purchased. I read a note she'd left that morning: *Baby, grocery store today.* To her list of staples, he'd added *Bud, twelve-pack.*

"They're playing house," Baze said, watching me wad up the note. I trashed it, and picked up the beach bag full of towels. "Of course, if I wanted to play house," he said, "I'd pick a beach house too. And then there's the Porsche."

I felt protective. "Is that the attraction?"

"Nope. And it's not that they're fucking each other's brains out. Or that she reads to him, like Wendy to Peter, she says. Poetry and classical lit. *Mrs. Dalloway* put him to sleep so she switched to *The Great Gatsby.*"

"Her favorite novel," I said.

"Not mine. Bad ending."

He studied me as I imagined bad endings of my own. He seemed to be trying to decide if he could trust me.

"I should tell you, Lynn. Terry's got problems. He's my best friend, but—" He tapped his temple.

"Psychological problems?" I made a silent list of disorders that started with manic depression and ended with sociopathy.

"Psycho and physio. Both kinds of logical." He looked at the floor and back at me. "Terry's sick."

He offered nothing more, and I resisted the urge to ask but only until we reached the beach.

The tide was retreating. My restraint went out with a wave. "Sick?"

"Both kinds of sick. Lovesick and sex sick. They're both sick." He opened our chairs, planted them in the sand. He took off his sunglasses. "I think it's contagious. We'd better quarantine them. Or," he said with a grin, "we could vaccinate each other."

I laughed. "In your dreams."

He pulled off his T-shirt, pulled a tab on a Budweiser, and gave it to me. “You play tennis, Lynn? Know anything about it?”

“I know that Billie Jean King beat Bobby Riggs in the Battle of the Sexes.”

“That’s what I thought you’d say. It doesn’t matter that he was fifty-five years old, right? And she was ranked two in the world.”

“What was the score?” I said lightly as he opened a beer for himself.

He raised his Budweiser. “Touché.”

I didn’t have to work on the weekend but wanted to get out of the house. I spent Saturday getting to know Charleston, which Jack wanted to position as an amenity of the island. On Sunday morning, I rode the resort’s Gary Player course in a golf cart with the head pro and toured the Kiawah Inn with the general manager. Under an overcast, darkening sky, I looked at real estate with the two top salesmen—at homes blending into the subtle grays and greens of the landscape, at live oaks preserved instead of cleared. The target market, according to the salesmen, was retirees from the Northeast and Midwest, most of whom were still choosing Florida.

Sales*men*. No women on staff.

When a bolt of lightning slashed through the sky and it began to rain, I went back to the house and a Wimbledon bacchanalia. There were empty champagne bottles on the bar. Baze was in the kitchen making Pimm’s Cups. Terry was on the sofa in the living room, and Patricia—no, Tricia was in his lap, feeding him strawberries and cream while he played with the ruffles of her peasant blouse. She wore a choker of plastic flowers, and her hair was pulled back by two tortoiseshell combs.

“We’re wasted,” Baze announced. “We’re done. So is

Connors. Borg is up two sets and a break."

"Tricia is wasted?"

At the sound of my voice, she turned toward me and gave me a dazed smile. She tried to stand but teetered and fell back into Terry's lap, her tiered skirt almost up to her panties.

She waved to me. "Come watch Wimby with us."

"Pimm's, Lynn?" Baze said.

"No, thanks."

Tricia made her way to me. She gave me the warmest of hugs and told me she loved me. When she pulled back, I touched the choker, a cheap curiosity.

"From Terry," she said.

"I have work to do." I started upstairs.

"Don't work, Lynn," she said. "Play."

From the landing I turned to her, but my eyes flew over her shoulder to the couch, where Baze had joined Terry. Baze was cutting lines of cocaine on the glass-topped coffee table.

"No," I said. The razor blade clicked on. "No," I said loudly over the sound of thunder. "Stop." Terry and Baze looked up at me simultaneously, like one man—or boy—with two heads. They turned to each other with the same precision, then back to me. "Not in this house," I said. "Not while I'm here."

Tricia cocked her head and looked at me. *Which of her bleary eyes,* I wondered, *is the dominant one? And which of her personalities?* I started on a march to the coffee table.

"You're not the mother," she said, but I faced her, and she cowered as if I were Jack. "Or if you are, you weren't here," she said. "You were out."

"Patricia," I said, "do you even know what they're doing?"

"Who?" she said.

"Thing One and Thing Two," Baze quipped.

I seethed. Tricia swayed. She locked her knees, and with her body stiff and straight, made a clockwise loop—right, back, left, and forward. I grabbed her arms before she toppled.

"Look at me, Tricia. I'm your friend," I said, and she nodded. I dropped my voice. "Jack is your husband."

"He has my doll," she whispered, eyes wide. "I want her back. When you talk to him, tell him I want—" Again she swayed.

"I've got her," Terry said, approaching us. He looked high but concerned as he slipped one arm below her buckling knees, the other around her shoulders.

"Forget the threshold, buddy," said Baze. "Get her to the bathroom."

He was right. She was going to be sick. Terry carried her down the hall, leaving me alone with Baze.

"No more coke here," I said.

"Got it, Mother."

"I'm no one's mother," I said.

"Anybody's babe?"

"No. But we do seem to need an adult here."

Baze picked up the bowl of strawberries and the bowl of whipped cream, and paused beside me on his way to the kitchen. "Hungry?"

The strawberries were perfectly formed, fragrant, and that just-ripe shade of red. I wanted to resist but hadn't had lunch and was famished.

"Pick a good one," Baze said.

And I did. It was tart at first, like his sense of humor, but an overpowering sweetness stayed with me.

He tossed his bangs out of his eyes and smiled. "Pimm's, Lynn?"

"No," I said. "I'm the grown-up. I'm going upstairs." I felt him watching me all the way up to the catwalk.

"Lynn," he said.

"Hmm?" I stopped and looked down.

"I'm your ally."

"I doubt it." I didn't get a clever retort as expected. "What is our unlikely alliance for?"

"Not for. Against."

"Against what?" I said.

Without smiling, he said, "Bad endings."

Discomfort shivered down my spine. "I don't need an ally."

"Everybody needs one sometime," he said. "And when you do, you've got me. And I've got you." At last he grinned. "Babe."

Weird, I wrote. I didn't have a journal, like Patricia, but a lined yellow tablet. *Everything is weird here. It's a muddle. A mess. And I'm in the goddamn middle.* I tore the page up and wrote again. *Summer 1978—Notes for JC.*

I started a bullet point list of all that had happened since I'd arrived, beginning with events in the beach house. By the time I got to a list for the Kiawah office, I put down the pen and phoned him. I got no answer at the office so I tried him at home.

He slurred his hello so badly that I asked what was wrong. He said he hadn't slept well all week or at all last night. He had to catch up, sleep today—had to—if he was going to function tomorrow and accomplish all he needed to before Monday morning.

"So you were napping?" I said.

"Trying. I thought a Macallan would help."

"A drink or a bottle? You sound like you're working on a bottle."

"Let me talk to Patricia," he said. "Get her. Now."

"Hold on." That would be a great conversation—both of them drunk. Everyone was drunk, except me. I opened the door, waited several moments as if I'd gone to find her, and closed it again. "She won't talk," I said.

"She will," he shouted. I opened my arm, held the phone as far away from me as I could. "If I have to come get her, I will. She has to talk to me."

"If you're going to yell—" I yelled too. "I'm going to hang up." He said something calmly and I returned the receiver to my ear.

"What should I do?" he said.

"God, Jack. I don't know. Mail her the doll."

"The goddamn security-blanket doll." His voice grew huskier with every word. "If she needs security, tell her to suck her thumb, since she won't suck anything else."

I didn't have to consciously disconnect us. My hand moved of its own accord. I pressed and held the button, not releasing it even when he called back. Four strident rings screamed for me to pick up, but I made him record a message instead.

"I shouldn't have said that. I'm sorry. I lost—I keep losing control." He paused before adding, "And I won't send the doll back."

He hung up with a dull, flat click, but I knew there was more to come. The message seemed as open-ended as the summer. I carried the lined yellow tablet with my notes to the bed, forced it under the mattress where Tricia would never find it. I turned back to the phone as it rang again. I waited through three rings, then picked up.

"I can't send the doll," he said.

"Why?" When he didn't answer, I changed my question. "What? What did you do?"

"I tore off her eyes."

I sighed a long whoosh of frustration. "Jesus, Jack. I'm starting to think you need help." I was surprised that he didn't disagree. "Get Barbara to buy new buttons and sew them on. Fix the doll and send her here."

"I can't, Lynn. I tore her apart."

"Why do they do it?" I complained to Baze weeks later. "There's a bedroom fifty feet away. Are they taunting me? For amusement?"

"Taunting us?" he said. "I'm a secondary witness, sunshine."

I didn't tell him that intermittent problems with the air-conditioning upstairs often forced me to move to the downstairs guest room to sleep. I didn't confess that I left my door open as they always did, and lay awake listening to their lovemaking across the hall.

Instead, when we were sitting by the pool, watching Terry try to teach Tricia to swim, I told Baze about watching *Coming Home* on HBO with them. When it began, they were lying on the floor on a couple of pillows, space between them. An hour later, I heard her roll toward him. After that, there was no movement or sound until tandem breathing increased in volume and pace, and in a slow simultaneous swish of euphoric exhalation, returned to normal.

"I don't even know what happened," I said.

"No?"

"They never even moved. Is that possible?"

"I don't know. We could test it ourselves."

"No. And wipe that grin off your face. We're friends, remember? And I'm twelve years older." I was never sure how to take Baze but loved having him around. I appreciated him most of all when we came in from the beach in the middle of a Sunday and did catch them in the act. Naked and standing, they froze when I opened the sliding glass door. And I froze. Tricia was backed up against the column between the living room and kitchen, her body shielded by Terry's. She looked at me over his shoulder with eyes that said *oops*. Terry turned his head to see who was at the door. He looked embarrassed and alarmed, but my eyes left his face and free-fell to his golden-brown shoulders and back, across private tan lines, along his magnificent legs, across tennis tan lines, and to his feet. I couldn't look away. My eyes climbed up again.

If Baze froze, he thawed in a second. "Terry, Tricia, how are you?" He sauntered past them on his way to the refrigerator to restock our cooler as planned. "Good to see you." He called to me from the kitchen. "Michelob?"

I smothered a laugh. "That's fine."

The beer took care of our thirst but did nothing for the heat on the beach.

"Has she always been oversexed?" Baze said as we walked to the ocean to cool off.

"No. She's always hated sex." I didn't tell him her husband had told me so.

As the undertow tugged us out, I tried to tug him in. I was lonely in the middle, frightened sometimes. "Baze." I touched his arm. "I need to talk."

"Fine, but don't tell me anything I can't tell Terry." He dove into a wave, which knocked me back, and came out on the other side. "She's bad news, right? Bad ending waiting to happen?"

"I'm trying to rewrite it. I need your help."

"We're allies, Lynn. Not liars. At least I'm not, where my friend is concerned. Whatever it is—you tell me, I tell Terry. Or maybe you should tell him."

He dove again into a cresting wave. I tried to follow but, a second too late, I slammed into a flat wet wall. Blinking salt water out of my eyes, pushing my hair off my forehead and behind my ears, I started back to our chairs. Waves punished me all the way in, and Baze joined me a moment later.

"It's not my place to tell Terry," I said.

Baze sighed and conceded. "I know. And it wouldn't matter if you did. He's so damn happy he can't hear a thing."

"Want to walk?" I said, standing.

He put on his Longhorns hat, tugged the brim down low over his forehead. He handed me the suntan lotion. "Slather my back," he said, "and I'll slather your front."

I laughed. The Sea & Ski laughed too in a series of burps and squirts. Seagulls shrieked and circled overhead. As we set out, his mood darkened.

"Lynn, would somebody be having Tricia watched?"

"Watched?" *No* and *why* were trapped in my throat, small brittle bones I couldn't get down or cough up.

"Shadowed, followed, tailed." In a flutter of wings the seagulls abandoned us for a child throwing crackers on the beach. "There's a guy hanging around the courts, but only when Tricia's watching Terry practice. He came into the shop once, after she'd picked Terry up. I was in the back, stringing a racket, but I heard him ask the assistant pro about the chick with the Porsche. That's not much to go on, I know, but—bad vibes. Totally." We walked on, pausing for sandpipers scurrying across our path. "Every time I see him, I feel like something isn't right."

"It's your imagination," I said. I'd needed only a moment to dislodge the splinter of possibility: Jack had no reason to have her watched; Jack had *me.*

"It's my gut."

"Maybe someone's having *Terry* watched."

"Like who?" He angled us to the ocean's edge and dipped his hat into the remnants of a wave, bathing our feet. "The only person who would have someone watching Terry is his mom." He swept his hair from his forehead and to the right, wrung the excess water from his hat, and returned it to his head, brim in back. "His mom," he said. "Or his sponsor. Something's definitely not right about her." We resumed our walk.

"You're paranoid."

He turned his face to mine. "Say what you want. Say I don't know jack shit or—"

I stumbled and stopped so abruptly that he halted midsentence. I looked down, wondering if I'd been tripped by Jack or something else. I saw only sand.

"Ghost crab," Baze said, pointing a few feet ahead.

So perfect was the camouflage that I could barely see that ghost, but as we watched it scuttle away, I knew it had scuttled over my toes. "Let's go back," I said. "It's getting late."

But Baze didn't move. "I may not know much, Lynn, but I know this about my friend: he's got an ego the size of an English pea."

I watched a pelican dive-bomb and snag a fish.

"Seriously. Terry's made of glass."

"Come on," I said, but he didn't budge.

"You missed the reading last night. Chapter four. You'd gone to bed."

"I've read *Gatsby*," I said. "I don't need to hear it."

"It was the part about Jordan Baker, the other girl. The one who left somebody's car out in the rain and lied about it. The golf champion who cheated."

"I remember," I said. I took his hand and pulled him along. We walked close to the ocean, which ran in and out, playing tag with our feet.

"I didn't tell Terry about that guy. He'd think I was making it up. He thinks I don't like Tricia, but I do. I just don't trust her."

With the lightness of the ghost crab, a memory slipped through my mind. I looked back through the day's rearview mirror at the morning, at a car crawling slowly past the beach house, trapping me in the driveway for a few extra seconds when I was already late for a meeting.

"The man at the pro shop," I said, "what did he look like?"

"The tail? He looked like a prick who doesn't belong on the island, like a weasel who thinks he can put on a pair of golf pants and look like a club member with a four handicap." Baze relaxed enough to laugh. "Trouble is, he picked the tackiest pair of madras pants I've ever seen and wears them all the damn time. Ugly frigging pants. Red-and-yellow plaid."

CHAPTER 7

The ocean was glassy, as if the undertow, so fierce all week, had worn itself out. Miniature waves fizzled at the edge of an endless pool, glimmering in the morning sun. There was no brcczc, thc tidc was going out, and at lcast for now, Terry and Tricia had the beach to themselves. He paid attention to the sounds of their feet together: their cheeping and squeaking in thick sugary sand; their rhythmic padding on sand that was dry and compact; their quiet thumping on sand that was damp and ridged, striated like his belly, Tricia had said; their happy splashing in the shallow slough left over from last night's high tide; their crunching on the carpet of tiny shells that stretched into the ocean.

He was asleep in his chair when Tricia tapped his shoulder and said, "Watch this."

Young parents were walking their toddling daughter to the slough. She wore a swimsuit with pink-and-yellow flowers, a pink hat, and pink sunglasses with heart-shaped frames. Her cheeks were pink too, and full and round. Her smile was wide.

"Is that you when you were little?" he asked.

"I was a library baby, not a beach baby. But I think she's precious."

In the slough, the child stepped onto a Styrofoam surfboard, pink too, three feet long by two feet wide, and trapped in the soft wet sand. Pleased, she looked up at her parents. Then she looked left at Tricia and Terry, as if for applause. She stepped off the board and on again, resumed her stance, and smiled. On, stand, smile, off. On, stand, smile, off.

"If you'd been a beach baby, you would have been her," he said, lying down again. He wasn't sure how much time passed before Tricia tapped his shoulder again.

The little girl was alone in the slough now, her parents watching from their chairs nearby, and a boy, her size, halted the beach walk his mother was taking by scrambling out of her arms. Wearing baggy blue shorts and a red baseball cap, he walked with a waddle like the girl's. Face-to-face, they sized each other up. Too young to talk, Terry decided, or too shy.

The boy's mother stayed a step away, exchanging smiles with the girl's parents as they watched their children. The girl stepped off her surfboard, inviting the boy to step up. For at least five minutes, they took turns. On, stand, smile, off.

"If that was me, I would have kissed her by now," Terry said, "or knocked her off her board and given her a concussion."

"Very funny."

"Worked with you."

The children began chasing each other. They plopped down in the slough with splash landings and laughed. They shared buckets and shovels, dug and built together. When at last they tired, the girl ran to her parents to be cuddled. The boy's mother swung him to her hip, readjusted his cap, kissed him, and continued up the beach.

Tricia went back to her book.

Terry lay back down on his belly, head turned toward her, eyes closed. "When I was little," he said, words slow and tentative. "Bigger than that, but not much, I used to hang on to my mom— her leg, her arm, her hand. All the time. I wouldn't let go. When I got older, I hung on with tennis." He opened his eyes and found Tricia watching him and listening, caring more for his story than the one she was reading. "It was the only way I could. But if I won 6–3, 6–4, it should have been 6–1, 6–2. It was always, *You'll do better next time,* and then it got to be *Do better.* And Tricia, I was doing the best I could." He dug in the sand with his fingers, adjusted his chair, and sat up. "She hated the parents whose kids were better than me. Hell, she even hated other kids." He watched the family in the ocean, the father tossing his child in the air and catching her. As the threesome started in toward the beach, they stopped in shallow water and faced the horizon. The mother took one tiny hand, the father the other, and as each foot-high wave rolled in and broke, they cried "jump" and lifted their daughter up and over.

"I never had that," Terry said.

"I only had it for a while."

Tricia, it seemed, could watch them for hours, but he'd had enough. He went to the slough and picked up the girl's yellow plastic shovel. He started a castle and was dripping it with soft, wet sand when Tricia joined him.

"You finish this," he said. "I'll dig the moat."

As the family headed back to their spot, the girl darted into the slough only to stop and frown at Terry. She rolled her lower lip into a pout.

"You've got her shovel," Tricia said. He laughed, and handing it over, earned a smile before she raced back to her parents.

"Tricia," Terry said, "quit staring. You look so happy, you look goofy." He smashed the castle into a pillow for his head and lay down on his back in the shallow slough.

She began running her fingers along the edge of his cutoffs. "You know what I once called your thighs? Early on. When I thought about them."

"You thought about my thighs?"

"Yes. I called them your Herculean thighs. But your calves are Herculean too."

He closed his eyes, wishing the family would leave. He raised his head and shoulders, and she ran her hand over the six-pack of his belly. Resting on his elbows, he watched her hand.

"Terry." She sighed. "I love children."

He dropped back down, lost his hard-on. "Why are you telling me that?"

A shrug in her answer. “I’ve told you everything else.”

“Well, I’m twenty-three and I don’t think about shit like that. Ever. The last thing in the world I want is a kid. I’d be an a-hole dad. I’d be terrible.”

“What makes you say that?” She took her hand away and waited. “Your father? You’ve never mentioned your father.”

He sat up and stared at the dunes. The sea oats were still.

“Tell me about your father.”

The sea oats were pale, the color of straw.

“Which one, Tricia? ’Cause I’ve got two.” He let her absorb what he’d said. “The day I found out about the second one, I lost a tennis match, and my mom beat the shit out of me, or tried to. She was so drunk she couldn’t, so she locked me in a shed. And left me there.” He felt tight in his throat and tight in his chest. “I’m going up now, okay? I gotta be by myself.”

At the courts, late on the following afternoon, she read on the pro shop’s veranda while he practiced his serve—effortlessly, accurately, muscle memory at work. He wasn’t thinking of the ball or his racket, only of Tricia—how she’d told him she was sorry for probing and let the whole thing die, buried it in the sand, no questions asked. He served, ball after ball. She read, page after page.

“Hey, you,” she called from a rocking chair on the veranda. “Hey, shirtless. I love you without a shirt.”

“Hey, you.” He sliced one out wide. “Want a lesson?”

She waited patiently as he walked the court, collecting balls with a pickup basket. He guzzled water from a jug and took a seat in the rocker beside hers. He leaned forward, feet on the ground, elbows on his knees. With his left hand, he rubbed the calluses on his right that never went away. He explored a new blister on the tip of his middle finger and looked at her.

“About the shed.” He wondered if her nod meant *go on* or *I know* or just *whatever it is, it's okay.* He listened to the dialogue of a doubles match two courts away and the trilling of birds nearby. He gnawed a callus.

She eased his palm from his mouth. "Baby, don't."

"I lost that match on purpose," he said. She said nothing. "You gonna ask why?"

"You'll tell me when you're ready."

He was ready hours later, at moonrise, after they'd walked miles on the beach and come to rest on the wooden swing in front of the dunes. Its chain creaked and groaned. So did his memory.

"It was the regional high school championships. A big deal. My team was good. No way we could lose. So, we're warming up, right? And my mom comes in with this man. It was really crowded, so I guess she thought no one would notice. How stupid was that? I guess she was drunk." He paused. "'Cause she's an alcoholic, Tricia." He clenched his fists. "And I hate her for that." He watched her uncurl his fingers one at a time. "Anyways, I can't help but notice. My teammates notice." He was reliving it as he told it. "They were my friends and had been to my house a lot. They knew my dad. Barely knew him. 'Cause my whole life he's never wanted anything to do with me, never even seen me play." Silence. "My friends were joking, 'cause the way she's looking at this man is, like, obvious. I'm sixteen, see? I'm embarrassed, and first I'm thinking she's whoring around with this asshole. Second, I'm thinking she always has been, and third—" He had to stop. Breathing hurt. Thinking hurt too. Telling, he knew, would hurt most of all. "Third, I'm thinking he's my father."

She placed his hand between her hands. "Why would you think that?"

"Everybody thought that. He looked just like me. Or I

looked like him, whichever is right. There's my mother letting me and the whole world know she's cheated on my dad for sixteen years, 'cause she was fucking this guy before I was born and still fucking him. So I threw the match to piss her off." He waited for Tricia to make it okay, but clouds ate the moon and he could hardly see her.

"Maybe your mother loved him, Terry. Maybe her marriage was a mistake."

"You're gonna defend her?" His voice was thick with disappointment, as thick as the sludge churning in his stomach. "It was black in that shed. No windows. I went in to get the spare key and when I handed it to her, she dropped it on the ground, and the next thing, she started slapping me. Mostly I stood there, taking it, like a couple of other times she hit me. But that just seemed to make her madder. Finally I tried to grab her hands and she pushed me. Hard. I fell backward over something. She started picking things up and throwing them at me. I don't even know what. I was crouching on the floor, trying to protect myself, arms over my head. Next thing, I heard the door slam and the padlock click. And she left. It was May. Florida. Steaming hot." He steeled himself to say it again. "And she left me."

Tricia slid her arm around his shoulder, and gave him a comforting squeeze. "How long?"

"Four hours. Maybe five. It was way after dark when she let me out. And she didn't say a word. Wouldn't even look at me. So I walked off. Walked around the neighborhood for a while. A teammate lived close, but I couldn't go to his house, because—" He listened to the ocean, calling him to swim in darkness. "After I threw my match, my teammate sprained an ankle and had to retire. And we lost the championship because of what I'd done."

"It's okay, Terry. You were young. You were hurt. Look at me, Terry."

But he couldn't. "All I could do was walk, and when I got tired of that, I went back home and got back in the fucking shed. I sat there all night. Things had never been good with me and her and never were going to be after that. But it wouldn't have happened—none of it would have happened—if there hadn't been him."

Tricia kissed his cheek and said gently, "So this isn't about only your mother. It's about your father too."

He leapt up. The heavy wooden swing bounced back so hard and flew backward so fast that Tricia would have fallen out if he hadn't grabbed the chain. She put her feet on the sand.

"It's *her.* Not him. It's her and the shed. You're not getting it, Tricia. No more talk. Come on."

He walked too fast up and over the dunes, holding her wrist so tightly that she tried to break away. He wouldn't let her. Even when she stumbled, he kept going at his own rough, selfish pace. He planned to make love to her that way too but couldn't. They were generous and slow, like always, tantalizing each other almost to torment, aching with a shared promise of release, keeping that promise.

Afterward, lying in bed, in the dark, he picked up his story. "I started seeing him around more after that. She never sat with him again, but he was there. I think now he'd always been there. After matches, she'd usually be gone a couple of hours. I had my own car by then, so I followed her once to make sure they were together. I found out that he'd been the tennis pro at a club in Miami, that he'd played on the tour and been ranked in the top twenty." He took a break. Tricia's fingers were combing his hair, her kisses draining the last of his strength, drawing his pain into her mouth to blend it with hers and swallow it away. "He's why I'm playing tennis, why my dad—my dad at home—hates me. My real dad is why she wanted me to win so bad, and why I felt so bad when I lost. I always had this feeling when I lost. This one thing. I don't know what to call it."

He got up and turned the lamp on, needing acceptance in her eyes, but he couldn't face her. Sitting on the side of the bed, he stared at his feet. He felt her move to him, studied her feet beside his. She even had beautiful feet. Toenails painted pink. Like the valentine dress.

She whispered, "Shame."

How had he not known it? "I felt ashamed."

In silence they sat side by side like children, but not happy ones like the two on the beach. They sat naked—shoulders rounded, heads hanging, weighted with the past. "I still feel it sometimes," he said.

"But not now?" She rubbed his back.

"No, not with you, never with you. But I feel so—I don't know."

"Naked?"

He chuckled. "I know I'm naked, Tricia."

"Your body is naked, but your soul is too now, Terry. You're body-and-soul naked, like I was at the Vendue. Sharing-healing-saving naked."

"Hey," he said, his finger under her chin, lifting her face to his. "That's enough for one night. No more soul baring and sharing. I'm wiped out. This is Vendue Two. My Vendue. All we need is champagne." *And each other,* he wanted to add. *Nah, too cheesy.*

"And each other," she said.

Match point. Mini-tournament over. Camp over. Ten days until the next session began in August. He wanted to scamper with the kids, not to their mothers but to Tricia, who was getting out of her car in the parking lot. Wearing her beach cover-up, she hurried toward the pro shop, as if she couldn't wait to take him from work to play. She would have everything ready—cooler, picnic basket, beach bag—so once they were on the beach they could party hardy all night long.

The porch was congested as he started up the steps—moms, kids, women from Kiawah's league team. He was looking beyond them at Tricia, who was coming toward him. He didn't see Mrs. Dressler until they were face-to-face on the porch.

"Terry."

"Mrs. Dressler, hi." *Hi and bye,* he said silently, determined not to let her keep him there. "Carson played great. I'd never thought we'd see an eight-year-old make it to the final. Jeffrey, who won—"

"Jeffrey, who won," she repeated. "Jeffrey won. Do you know why?"

"Well, Jeffrey's eleven, for starters." He tried to smile. "He's a really big kid besides."

"Carson has played Jeffrey four times in local tournaments and never lost to him. Not once. Not until you switched him to a two-handed backhand."

He tried to keep things quiet. "When I suggested it, you thought it was a good idea."

"Twelve backhand errors."

He pressed his lips together, planted his feet firmly on the concrete to keep from turning to the crowd she had drawn and saying, *Can you believe this shit? She was counting.*

"Jean." Someone reached for Mrs. Dressler's arm. The gathering circle of mothers and campers began to buzz and close in. Baze was at its edge. So was Tricia. "It's been a great week. Don't spoil it."

Someone else added: "Terry's been great. The kids—"

"You took his game apart on court and left it there," Mrs. Dressler said. "You picked him apart, day by day. It will take him six months to get over losing today."

You, Terry wanted to say. *It will take you six months, you mean.* He was shaking. His hands, even his legs were shaking. His lips too, as he tried to explain. "Mrs. Dressler, we made a change. It's like two steps forward . . ." Was that it? Was that right? He couldn't think. "No wait. It's one step forward, two steps—"

"That's exactly what it is," she said, her voice so shrill that a hush fell over the audience. "Exactly what you've done. You've pushed him backward."

"Wait. I said it wrong. What I mean is, he's gotta go one step back and then he'll go forward real far—"

"Oh shut up. You're as stupid as I heard you were, Terry Sloan. You've undone every bit of decent coaching I've paid for in the past two years. You've destroyed his confidence, his motivation—"

"Mom." Carson tugged at her arm.

"You know nothing about teaching or coaching or children. You know nothing about winning. And I know everything about you. I've checked rankings and scores. I've asked around on the circuit. You can't close out a match. You choke. You lose."

"Mommy, don't." Tears came to Carson's eyes.

"For God's sake, Jean," someone said.

Terry's chin dropped to his chest, his head as heavy as a bowling ball. A ball in a gutter. Where it belonged. He sensed Baze starting to step forward, the head pro holding him back.

"I warned everyone from the club general manager on down that you were a mistake—for the club and most of all for the children. You will be gone by morning. I'll have you fired. And every member of this tennis club and every club in the area will know why. I'll make sure of that. You won't work again in a private club, tearing kids down. That's the only way you can build yourself up, isn't it, Terry Sloan?"

"I'm sorry," he said. He listened to Carson crying, and another child too, in the face of rage they couldn't understand. Mrs. Dressler grabbed Terry's wrist and ground in her nails. *Deeper,* he wanted to say. He wanted to nod and bleed and say he was sorry for every fault and unforced error, every game, set, and match he'd lost in his life.

"Terry," Tricia said softly, close by, to his right.

And Baze. "Let's go, man."

It was Mrs. Dressler who left instead, and women and children who filed out after her as silent as a congregation on Holy Thursday.

"Let's go home," Tricia whispered.

He looked up without seeing. "You and Baze go. I'm gonna walk."

"I'll walk with you."

"No."

"Do you need to talk?"

"No." But he was thinking *yes*.

"Do you want to be alone?"

"Yes." *God, no.*

"Shall I leave?"

He didn't want her ever to leave. "You and Baze and Lynn go ahead to the beach. I'll catch up."

His plan was to haul ass home and hide, but he could only plod. He felt like crawling. He hoped he didn't throw up on the sidewalk, with Mrs. Dressler or Mrs. Anybody and her kids riding by.

When he made it to the empty beach house, he ran to the bedroom, then the bathroom, slamming doors behind him. He leaned over the toilet and waited, but nothing happened. He took his bathing suit from the shower rod, where he'd hung it to dry, and put it on.

He grabbed the doorknob but couldn't turn it.

He couldn't get out. He had to get out.

He tightened his grip, turned the knob but couldn't pull the door open. The room was stuffy and hot. The room.

The shed.

He bolted back to the toilet and fell to his knees. He threw up everything in his stomach, would have thrown up his guts if he'd had any.

He let go of the cold, glossy porcelain rim. He sat back on his heels, waited for the weakness to pass. He brushed his teeth. He walked down the hall and straight to the sliding glass door. He stopped, wishing Tricia were there.

"Terry."

He turned and found her sitting cross-legged on the floor, in the corner, at the bookshelf. He'd walked right by her as he rushed through the house and again as he'd started out.

"I decided to wait. You don't mind, do you?"

He whispered, "No."

"What do you need from me, Terry?"

"I need to—" To cry like a two-year-old, he wanted to confess. "Pepto-Bismol."

"Because of what happened?"

"Yeah. And 'cause I thought you'd left, which is stupid, I know, since I told you to go. But I wanted you to be here."

"I am. The only place I'm going is to get your Pepto."

He shook his head. "Nah, don't. I don't need it." He went to the sofa, stretched out on his back, and made room for her to sit too. "Tricia," he said, "I'm so fucked up." As she had the day he won the semifinal, she ran her fingers up and down his shins, over his knees and thighs. "You know what I want?" he said.

"Uh-oh." She smiled. "Did I start something?"

"No. I—I want you to read to me. Anything. Whatever you want. Just read to me, Tricia, like I'm a kid."

"All children, except one, grow up. They soon know that they will grow up, and the way Wendy knew was this. One day when she was two years old she was playing in a garden, and she plucked another flower and ran with it to her mother. I suppose she must have looked rather delightful, for Mrs. Darling put her hand to her heart and cried, 'Oh, why can't you remain like this for ever!' This was all that passed between them on the subject, but henceforth Wendy knew that she must

grow up. You always know after you are two. Two is the beginning of the end."

"Why did you stop?"

A sigh. "That sentence bothers me. For a long time I thought it was clever and funny. But now I find it sad."

"I can't believe you picked up that book."

"Why not? The last time we were sitting like this, you said you wanted to give me a thimble."

He took *Peter Pan* from her hands and slid his feet under her rear. He skimmed the next paragraph. "Tricia, that kiss in the corner—in the corner of her mother's mouth that Wendy can't ever get." She nodded and he went on. "You've got one too, that thing I wouldn't let you tell me that night at the Vendue Inn, and you didn't want to tell me that next morning. I know I said I didn't want it if it would fuck things up between us." His mouth felt stale and dry. "But now I think I'd better get it, no matter what it is."

She looked down at him and shook her head. "Not today, not after Mrs. Dressler."

"I gotta have it." He touched the corner of her mouth. "I'm gonna keep trying to get it." She nodded. Her eyes were sad. "I won't quit. I'll play five sets, if I have to. Count 'em—one, two, three, four, five." *But two,* he imagined her saying. *Two is the beginning of the end.* "I'm in love with you, Tricia. You know that, don't you? I love you." He lost his breath saying it for the first time, and his heart stopped—or he wished it would—when she didn't say anything back. A minute ticked by. Or two or ten, each one without her saying she loved him too. At least he knew now, and knew he loved her anyway. He drew a deep breath and exhaled heavily. "I can't say it ever again. It nearly killed me." He touched her cheek. "So that's what this means now."

"Terry." She touched his cheek and said, "Too."

§

"Don't lift your head so high out of the water, Tricia," he said in the pool a few days later. "Take a stroke, turn your head, and breathe low, under your armpit. Try again."

She gave up, grabbed a float and hung on. "Terry."

He thought she looked worried. "Yeah?"

"You need to call your mother. Baze is right. He shouldn't have to make excuses for your not being at the villa, especially if she's calling every day, like he says."

"I worry about you drowning every day. This is a lesson. I want you to swim."

"I want you to call her. Or tell me why you won't."

"Because all she'll want to talk about is tennis." He let himself sink to the bottom of the pool, stayed underwater as long as he could. When he came back up, he tugged the float away from her, but she lunged and locked her arms around his neck.

"Can we skip psychiatrist tonight?" he said. "Let's play the other kind of doctor. Like, you show me yours and I'll show you mine."

She didn't laugh. "I lost my mother; I loved her; I still love her; I want her. You have your mother and don't want her at all."

He carried her to the shallow end and planted her feet on the bottom, harder than he'd meant to. "You swim one length, shallow to deep, and I'll call her."

She looked skeptical. "Promise?"

"Promise."

She looked at the opposite end of the pool. She closed her eyes, puffed her cheeks out with air, and pushed off. Stunned, he watched her perfect body swim thirty imperfect yards in the strangest dog paddle he'd even seen. He slashed through the water and was at her side by the time she grabbed the wall. She blinked chlorinated drops from her eyes.

"Tricia, that was unbelievable." He laughed, watching her

pant. "That was great."

"Inside," she ordered. "Call your mother."

He talked her into taking a shower with him first, only to find afterward that the towel around her wet body was a cocoon. He couldn't get the butterfly back, he knew, until he'd made the call. At the dresser, combing her hair, Tricia watched him in the mirror as he picked up the phone. He sat down on the bed, thought for a minute, and dialed Nona. She had also called that morning, according to Baze.

"Hi, it's Terry," he said, pressing the receiver tightly against his ear, trapping Nona's voice there. To his surprise, there was nothing to hear. "Sorry I haven't called you back till now. I've been busy with camp and—"

"You're on break."

He wondered how she knew. He licked his lips. They were chapped. Too much sun. "Yeah, I've been practicing a lot and running and all."

"I'm interested in *and all*."

He cradled the phone with his chin. "So, how are you?"

"Lonely."

He couldn't tell if she was teasing, flirting, or telling the truth. His mouth felt worse than his lips. Even his tongue felt chapped.

"We're taking a trip, Terry. We're leaving Saturday afternoon."

He wondered why he wasn't her angel tonight.

"There's a WCT tournament in Atlanta," she said. "You're playing."

"I can't get in. I tried back in June. I was too late for the qualies."

"I know the tournament director and the president of the Atlanta Athletic Club. You're in. The qualies start Sunday. Play well, and you'll have a wild card slot in the U.S. Open qualies. I've called in a favor."

He was silent. Then, "Is that, like, legal?"

"Not exactly. And you'll have to make it to the quarters in Atlanta."

He glanced at Tricia, who mouthed, *Legal?* What's wrong? He turned away.

"You'll spend Friday with me. Be here by 9:00 in the morning and spend the night."

He hesitated. "I'd do better staying here where I've got somebody to hit with. Get in a last good day of practice. You want me ready, right? And focused?"

"Solely on tennis. We agreed. And you agreed to spend time with me."

He frowned and Tricia frowned too. "I've got plans for Friday."

"Bring your plans."

"Ma'am?"

"You have plans with friends? Bring your friends. If they're so important to you, I need to meet them. Bring your doubles partner to hit with you."

"Bring Baze?"

"And anyone else you'd like to bring. We'll make it a party."

"Okay." He scrambled, parched lips twitching. Muscles were twitching too, deep inside of him, close to the bone. "But I'll just bring Baze. 'Cause that's really all there is."

"Terry," Nona said flatly. "Bring the blonde."

His heart skipped toward his throat, his brain toward his belly. He felt and heard their bloody collision. "Bring what?"

"Bring the blonde."

Nona hung up. He did too, slowly, forcing his eyes to Tricia's. "I've gotta go to Nona's."

"That was your mother. You promised to call your mother." Sparks flashed in her eyes. "It wasn't your mother?"

"It was Nona. And I've gotta go there Friday."

Tricia dropped the towel. She stepped into panties and pulled on a T-shirt. She was going to sleep in clothes for the first time all summer, if she slept with him at all. A pang of fear suggested to him that July, not two, was the beginning of the end.

"Don't be mad, okay?" he said. "Please. You can go too." Nothing. "Will you go to Nona's with me?"

"No. Why should I?"

"She wants to meet you. And you'll love her. She's a dancer. Like, ballet and stuff. Or she used to be. And she loves plays, like you. All that." He watched the blonde turn out the light. In darkness, in bed, in clothes, she was at least in his arms. "I need you to go. It's important." He touched her cheek. She touched his and whispered a begrudging *too.* "Will you go, Tricia?"

"Absolutely not."

CHAPTER 8

As August began, I saw the sparkle in the sand disappear. The line of the horizon vanished in the thickness of the air. The ocean, reflecting the hazy gray sky, was a tub of lukewarm bathwater, sure to leave a scummy ring if drained. Storm clouds teased with afternoon rumbles but gave no rain, no relief.

Jellyfish invaded. A solitary herald washed up on the beach, and from that point on, they rode in and out on the tide. They had no appetite for Tricia's perfect skin, but Terry, Baze, and I were mildly stung several times.

The four of us suffered random bouts of crossness and passed them virally to one another. On the sixth, when Pope Paul VI died, we fell into an argument that began with the validity of the one, holy, catholic, and apostolic church as the only true church. It moved through birth control and test-tube babies—the first had been born in July—to adultery and divorce, which pitted an emotional Tricia against a staunch Terry. He left us sitting at the kitchen table to go to Mass.

"That's hypocritical," Tricia said, starting after him. "You never go to Mass. You haven't gone all summer." He handed her the keys to the Porsche and drove the Valiant.

On another day, even Terry and Baze wrangled over which movie to see. "*Jaws 2* is still playing," said Baze, and Terry shook his head. "Why not?"

"I've spent the summer getting Tricia unafraid of the ocean. No *Jaws 2*."

"Okay. *Animal House*."

"Nah. Too crass."

"*Crass?* Whose word is that, Terry?"

"Mine."

"Horseshit. That's Tricia talking."

"It isn't."

"You're so pussy whipped, it's not even funny anymore."

In July that exchange would have ended there with a laugh. But in August, it went on.

"Fuck you, Baze."

"No, fuck her. Fuck Tricia."

I heard this secondhand from Baze hours later. We were sitting on the deck; Tricia and Terry had gone to see *Grease* for a second time.

"I don't know why I said it. It's just August. It's hot as hell. Summer's about to go belly-up, and Austin's about to come crashing down."

"I've never heard you complain about Austin."

"It's senior year," he said, "and it ought to be good, but I've got personal stuff to deal with when I get back."

He looked so troubled that I didn't ask, *Like what?*

"Real-world stuff," he said, and he opened a beer. "Like what happens after graduation."

"Tennis? Will you—"

"Hell no. I'm not good enough." He looked at me hard.

"And neither is Terry?"

"I don't know," he said. "But I've got better sense than to try." He took a beer from the cooler. "Last one," he said. "We can share." After a long sip, he passed it to me.

The can was ice-cold. I'd worked outdoors all day, with a photographer. I was sure he'd gotten what I wanted for a new brochure, and I was ready to relax. I took a sip and handed it back. "So what will you do, Baze?"

He smiled. "Whatever you tell me to, Obi-Lynn Kenobi. I've got a job if I want it. Assistant controller. It's a nice offer. The money's good."

"The company? "

"Solid."

"Where?"

"Chicago, which is good."

"Cold but good," I said. "I'm from there."

"Me too," he said.

I laughed in surprise. "That's crazy. We've spent the summer here together and that never came up."

"Lynn," he said, turning somber. "There's a lot of shit that never came up."

I saw no point in tap-dancing again around bad news, plaid pants, and the other jack shit we were never going to talk about. "So the job," I said. "What's the problem?"

"Family business. Not my family. But this family I know is handing me the job on a platter. I feel like they'll own me. I'd rather find my own damn job."

"That's noble but if that's your only hesitation—"

"It's a complicated family. Wealthy. The president is divorced and has five children. I'd say it's Ewing Oil, but it's not sons; it's daughters. And they're spoiled. Every damn one of them."

"Do they work there?"

"No. But they're—involved. They're everywhere and they're into everything. There's the ex-wife and the wicked stepmother. Too damn much estrogen."

"Excuse me?" I took the beer from his hand.

"Sorry," he said. "Give that back. I'm thirsty."

"I'm finishing it," I said. "For spite."

He laughed but grew thoughtful again. "Would you take it? If you were me?"

"On the basis of what you've told me—" I stopped as he grimaced. He was surely holding something back. "Baze," I said. "You've got time. Why don't you ask if you can spend a week at the company over Christmas and shadow the current assistant controller."

"There isn't one," he said, seemingly embarrassed.

"They're making the job just for me."

"Then shadow the controller. Get a feel for the corporate culture and the people you'll work with. Hang out nine to five for a week. Trust your instincts. You'll know."

He rose. "That's good, Lynn. August just got better."

"Maybe," I said. I looked at the sand dunes. But August was sure to get worse. In less than a month, Jack would come to the island to spend Labor Day weekend with his wife and take her home to New York. The summer had burned like a low-grade fever but was going to spike. I couldn't stop it.

"Thanks, Lynn," he said.

"Sure." When he kissed my cheek, I turned to him, my lips parting in surprise, or in an invitation he looked ready to accept. "I'm your ally," I said.

He stepped back, and we shared a wistful smile.

"Everybody needs one, Lynn."

I gazed at the dunes again.

I dreamed I was at an unfamiliar airport, trapped in the middle of a baggage claim carousel. Terry, Tricia, and Jack were on the outside, watching in confusion as their belongings went round. They wanted me to identify their baggage, tell them what to take and what to leave behind. Then the three of them were lying on their backs on the carousel, circling before me one at a time, talking to me earnestly like patients on the proverbial couch. When the carousel screeched to a stop and they all rushed toward me, I woke and went downstairs.

I was making coffee in the kitchen when the white roses were delivered. Tricia was still asleep, so Terry answered the door. He brought them to the breakfast table, nodded at the envelope that held the card.

"Opening that would be really shitty of me, right?" I grabbed the envelope so he had no chance.

"That's why I like having you around, Lynn," he said, "because if you weren't here, I might have opened it. Of course, if you weren't here, looking like you just saw a fucking ghost, I wouldn't have even thought about opening it." He took the vase back into his hands. "I'm getting rid of these in the dunes down the beach. You get rid of the card, so I'm not tempted."

Princess, I read, *I wish you were here. All my love—Jack.*

A half hour later, Terry was at the door of my bedroom/office. The only thing I saw when I turned to him was Tricia's journal in his hands.

"What about this?" he said.

"What about it?" My question boomed through anxiety's megaphone. I stared at the book of pliable brown leather, knowing one tiny yank of the leather cord, tied in a bow to hold the book closed, could spill conflict and indecision, pros and cons, thoughts of lover and husband.

"She left it on the table on the deck," he said. "I'm thinking I should read it."

"No," I said, like parent to child, teacher to student. "You know better. Give it to me." He handed it over—*gladly,* I thought. He sat down on the bed, folded his arms.

"Help me, Obi-Lynn Kenobi." His tone was desperate. "Tell me what to do, 'cause she's getting complicated."

Complicated, I thought, *and melancholy and petulant in equal measure, with Terry bearing the brunt of it all.* She'd been snapping at him and correcting him ruthlessly. But she always begged his forgiveness with her body, and he repeatedly granted it with his.

She'd stopped reading *Gatsby* to him at chapter seven. She'd switched to W. S. Merwin.

"I don't get poems," he said. "Not those anyways. I want *Gatsby.* I want the end."

"You won't like it," she said. "It's like *The Seagull.* The bad guy ends up with the girl." She'd given the novel to me for safekeeping. I'd finished it alone, hating Fitzgerald's three-dead climax.

"Tell me what to do," Terry said again. "You're her friend. You're a girl."

"I'm a woman." *A grown-up,* I thought. The only one around.

"Tell me what to do," he said, "before she fucks us up."

"I don't want to be in the middle of you and Princess Leia."

He lay back on the bed, fingers laced behind his head. "Give me a minute. I'm getting my courage." He sat up again. "Somebody else, right?"

I straightened files on my desk and met his gaze. "Talk to Tricia, not me."

"He's out of the picture?"

"No comment."

"But he loves her."

"Yes."

"Does she love him too?"

He looked so forlorn I couldn't even speak.

So he did: "Help me, Obi-Lynn Kenobi. You're my only hope."

Jack continued to call daily. He never mentioned the audit, and conversations about the Kiawah account grew shorter and shorter. "Put her on the phone," he said.

"I can't make her talk to you. I've tried." I watched Tricia and Terry from my second-floor window. He chased her to the ocean, seized her, and hoisted her over his shoulder. She mock-pounded his back and mock-kicked her legs until they were deep in the water. As she slid down his chest into his arms, I wondered how Jack believed in himself so much that the possibility of another man hadn't occurred to him.

"I don't understand her," Jack said, "but I love her."

I believed him. Tricia never did. His love for her might have been indefinitely second to his love and lust for TCC: at forty-nine, he was still too young to slow down and far too shy of his goals. His love for her might have sprung from ownership instead of communion, from his ego instead of his heart. But whatever its source, his love was unwavering.

A furious hacking disrupted my thoughts and left Jack hoarse and breathing hard. "Bronchitis," he said. "Scofus called in an antibiotic."

"Good," I said, but my heart skipped a beat. I'd never met Adam Scofus, but I'd talked to him by phone often when Jack wasn't available at the office. I knew Adam as his roommate from Harvard, his closest friend, and the man he'd fished with since the sixties—twice a year, all over the world. I also knew him as a renowned pulmonologist and radiation oncologist at MD Anderson in Houston.

Tricia's stream-of-consciousness journaling was yet to inspire a decision. "I don't know what to do." She was sitting on the same sunflower of the duvet cover where Terry had sat the day before, looking at me with the same despair. She massaged her ring finger, where not even a tan line was left of her marriage. "I've been afraid since I was seven. I'm afraid now."

I nodded, thinking she meant afraid of change and uncertainty. Apart from his temper there was not much of either with Jack. He was reliably absorbed in his work. He handled everything for her, made wise decisions, and provided for her. He had been unfaithful, but she had too now. He was committed to her—or his concept of her. He believed in his concept of their marriage.

"This event is date-certain," I said. "Jack will come to the island." I took her hand. I wanted to address her by name but had no idea who she was at that moment. "Who do you want?" I asked and wagered, “Patricia.” She jerked her hand away, looking hurt by my failure to perceive.

“Terry,” she whispered. “I want Terry.”

“Then tell Terry the truth. Don’t you think he suspects there’s someone else?”

“What he doesn’t suspect is that I’m married. He despises infidelity, Lynn. You know that.” She drew a deep breath. “I’m afraid he’ll despise me, afraid he’ll leave. I want to hang on until Labor Day. Selfish, I know, and wrong. But I want to have Terry as long as I can.”

“And Jack?”

She took a long time to answer. “A part of me loves Jack, or did. But never *to the depth and breadth and height—*”

“This isn’t a poem,” I said.

“I loved him with *my childhood’s faith.*”

“Don’t,” I said. I knew every line of the timeworn sonnet. Jack had chosen it and forced me to read it at their wedding, along with her obscure Sara Teasdale choice. I’d practiced both obsessively, and at the ceremony I’d willed myself through them. “This is your life. And Terry’s. And Jack’s.”

“I need to leave him.”

“You’ve gone from thinking, to wanting, to needing to leave him. If you’re going to do it, then do it.”

“I’m afraid,” she said, solemn and still now. “Jack must never find out about Terry. Even after I divorce him, he must never know. He would come after me with a chain saw.”

“You mean he’d come after Terry.”

“No, me. If I know anything about Jack, I know this: Jack would come after me.”

In spite of her gorgeous head and a doll ripped apart, I didn’t think she was right. I wondered which of us knew him better, hoped I’d never have to find out.

“Oh Lynn,” Tricia said, hiding her face in her hands. “Lynn, how did I get here?”

CHAPTER 9

Lying on a blanket on the beach in midafternoon, Tricia ran her fingers slowly over Terry's face, neck, breastbone, belly. He responded in kind. Touch, smile, her turn, his. Touch, smile, his turn, hers. Hands intimate and bold. She moved closer, burrowing her face in his neck.

"Do you know what I love?" she said. "The smell of you. Or smells of you. This one, salty and sweaty on the beach. The running smell, which is sweat alone. And the tennis one, with a hint of leather, when your hand smells like the grip of your racket."

"You got a favorite?"

She smiled. "Tennis."

"Then after September, when you go back to New York and I go back to school, I'll put some socks and wristbands in a box and mail them to you." Those words startled her more than the incoming ocean as it grazed her feet. Terry removed her sunglasses. "Good," he said. "That's the first time I'm glad to see tears in your eyes, 'cause they're telling me you'll be coming to Austin sometimes. Right?" When she didn't respond, he put his thumb beneath her chin and gently manipulated a nod. "I gotta be back on the second for practice. Classes start on the fifteenth."

More water washed over their feet. She started to get up and pull the blanket higher on the beach, but he draped his arm and leg over her to hold her there.

"We've got time yet," he said, but a larger wave broke on their ankles and water raced to their hips. "Or maybe we don't."

What broke next for Tricia wasn't a wave but a revelation. As they slid their blanket to dry sand, she adopted Jack's left-brained methodology: the objective, at its simplest, was leaving her husband for the man she loved; the strategy was building the strength to do it; but the tactics— what were the tactics? In a burst of energy she said, “I’m going to the house.”

“I’ll go too.”

“No, stay.” She stepped into her flip-flops and looked at Terry, his quizzical frown. “Don’t worry, baby. I need some time. I have things to do before Friday.” She kissed him and smiled. “Before we go to Nona’s.”

“You’re gonna go?”

“Yes. For you.”

“Fifty thousand two hundred dollars,” she repeated. Not in a certificate of deposit. No restrictions, taxes, penalties. Available for immediate withdrawal. A trust fund from her parents. All she had. “Thank you.” She pressed and released the button to end the call and start another.

“Directory assistance. City and state, please.”

“I need graduate admissions at two universities. The University of Iowa. That’s Iowa City. And NYU in New York.” She wrote down the numbers.

“May I assist you with anything else?”

She looked at the tablet before her, doodled, tried to think pros and cons—Terry was twenty- three, a college senior. They had never talked long-term. Theirs was an insular world, without other women, competition, or interference. So many cons. Still she said, “The University of Texas.”

“Arlington, Austin, Brownsville, Dallas—”

“Austin.”

The five-o’clock shadow of a storm was grim. The tide was racing in. The light was dimming. She held Terry’s hand as they walked to the water's edge; then she said, "Stop. I'm going in alone."

He folded his arms, and she tugged his earlobe before he had a chance to. "Why?"

"It's a tactic."

He stared at her blankly. "You going to war or something?"

"War with my past, my helplessness, things I fear. This is one of them, and if I can do this, I can do other things too. Things I need to do."

"Yeah, okay. But not now. It's rough. How about tomorrow?"

"I won't go so deep that I can't touch bottom. If things go wrong, you'll dash in and save me, won't you?"

"If you go under, I'll have a heart attack before I can dash in. If anything happens to you, I'll drop dead on the sand. Try it tomorrow, Tricia, at low tide."

"I've had a wonderful swim instructor. I'll be fine, and then I'll be stronger. It's a tactic. It's important to me." She kissed him and started into the surf.

"Hey," he called. She turned back and listened. "If you get caught in the undertow, don't fight it. Swim parallel to the beach until you come out of it."

She nodded and went on. A wave splashed her knees. A wave struck her thighs. A wave whipped her chest. The undertow swirled, but she didn't turn back. If she could make it beyond the line where the waves were peaking and exploding, the ocean would be calmer. So would she. A wave lifted her off the sandy floor. She turned her back to the next one and jumped, as Terry always did. They were coming faster now, higher and harder. She squeezed her eyes shut, dove through a fierce one, and crossed the line she'd sought. She lay back and floated, rising and falling on swells. Waves continued to break, but between her and the beach.

She'd made it. She could go back to Terry.

She tried to stand and did not panic when she realized she'd inadvertently broken her promise: she couldn't touch bottom. She dog-paddled until she could place both feet on the sand again and started back to the beach. The waves helped her along, sometimes with force that caught her by surprise; but sometimes, together with the undertow, they undid bits of her forward progress. She was waist deep, then shoulder deep again, but she persevered. Terry, who had inched his way toward her, was grinning. She gave a fist pump and stopped.

She tried to discern what was floating toward her from the left—a silvery blanket, large enough for a king-size bed. She glanced at Terry, who returned the fist pump. She looked back to the blanket, not understanding but realizing she could not escape it by running—not in, back out, or to the right. Without warning a wave behind her threw her underwater and into the bedding.

"Jesus God," she cried as she surfaced in Terry's arms. She coughed out the salt water she'd taken in and struggled to breathe through the pain. Pain from her breast to her knee, like jagged glass scraping her flesh and digging through to her muscles. Terry's eyes told her something was badly wrong. Hers poured tears.

"You're okay," he kept saying. But then he asked, "Are you okay?" When she nodded, he stood her on the sand, looked at her, and said, "Jesus God," instead of *holy shit.*

"What is it?" she cried but he didn't answer. He picked her up again and ran. "Stop, Terry. I'm going to pass out."

"You've been stung. Bad, but you're okay." He was panting. "Jesus Christ."

There was pain, only pain. But gradually she became aware of the couch beneath her, of Baze, Lynn, and Terry around her, of frantic discussion about what to do. Lynn lobbied for the emergency room. Baze and Terry argued ice versus water versus alcohol versus meat tenderizer.

"Vinegar," Baze was saying.

"Baking soda," Terry said. "A paste with warm water."

She heard Lynn in the kitchen, then saw a silver flash of tweezers as Terry knelt beside her. "This might hurt," he said.

"It already hurts," she tried to say.

"There's some tentacles."

"Pull them out fast," Baze said. "Not slow. Here, let me do it. You're shaking, man."

"No."

"Let me," said Lynn.

And Terry shouted, "No."

Baze took the tweezers out of his hand and worked on her leg while Lynn, with a second pair, worked on her breast. Tears flowed.

"Almost done," Baze said, but she no longer cared. She turned her head toward Terry, who was leaning against the wall as if too weak to stand. When he saw her looking at him, he returned to the sofa and forced a half smile, which failed to reassure her.

She closed her eyes and opened them again when Lynn said, "Take these."

With his arm behind her head, Terry helped her sit up. He held a glass of water to her lips and she swallowed Tylenol and Benadryl. "That will help the pain and the swelling. And I've got this baking soda, which is gonna help too."

Lying down again, she welcomed the warm paste and his touch, first on her breast.

"Man-of-war," Baze said.

"Hot jellies," Terry argued. "A brood."

"A blanket," she said. She realized how softly she had spoken as Terry leaned toward her, turning his ear toward her lips. "Blanket."

"Like a blanket," he said to Baze. He continued with the paste. Along her ribs. The left side of her belly. Her leg.

"You're getting sleepy, huh? That's the Benadryl, but it will take the welts down. You want to go to the bedroom? I can carry you."

"Later." She hoped he could read her lips because she heard nothing as she spoke. "Tell me when. I'm right here."

Baze turned on the television, kept the volume low. She listened to the faraway drone of a baseball game, heard Baze say the Yankees were coming back, that they'd be playing in the Series again. She sensed Terry settling onto the floor beside her, his back against the sofa. She opened her eyes and watched as he stretched his legs out. He crossed, uncrossed, and crossed his feet at his ankles. He folded and unfolded his hands. She closed her eyes again and heard his soft call: "Obi-Lynn." She felt the sofa cushion shift as Lynn sat down near her feet.

"I shouldn't have let her go in," Terry said. "It was rough. I knew better."

"She needed to do it."

"But if I—"

"Jellyfish stung her," Lynn said. "But *you'd* have stung her if you'd tried to stop or control her. It would have been worse, hurt her much more."

Yes, she wanted to say, *true.* But she left it to Lynn to convince him.

Baze said, "Terry, she's okay."

Lynn said, "She's going to be fine."

Tricia smiled inwardly. What did Lynn know about jellyfish? They weren't exactly floating around on Fifth Avenue.

"If she has a scar for the rest of her life, every time I touch her I'll feel like I should—"

The rest of my life. She sighed contentedly, though fighting sleep and pain.

"If she has a scar for the rest of her life," Lynn told him, "she'll have earned it. She'll be proud, and she'll thank you for it."

"Obi-Lynn," Terry said, his voice warm and full of relief. "Don't tell Tricia, but I love you too."

"Back off, bud," said Baze. "Lynn's mine."

"I'm everybody's," Lynn said with a quiet laugh, which to Tricia didn't ring true. As Terry lifted her and carried her toward the bedroom, she struggled to hear Lynn and Baze.

"Why the melancholy smile, Lynn?"

"I'm everybody's and nobody's," she said.

"By choice," Baze pointed out.

"Of course. Career choice."

"Let me know when that changes," Baze said, "and I'll make my move."

"Angel, oh angel," Nona said, and the dance began. She opened her arms, and with a measured turning of her wrists made a hug a requirement and her driveway a stage. Terry responded and when Nona pulled back slowly, she said, "I'm so glad you're here."

As she turned to Tricia with a smile, her white jersey wrap skirt flared and floated. In a Danskin leotard, Nona was in fashion, but she seemed in costume to Tricia. Before Terry could introduce them, she said, "And Patricia. What a pleasure, doll, to have you here with angel." She took Tricia's hand and half curtsied. She air-kissed her cheeks. "I'm ecstatic, doll. Thrilled." She clucked and cooed until Baze and Lynn arrived. She went to the Valiant and greeted them, though with less affectation.

Lynn looked uncomfortable; Baze looked amused. They saw through this woman, just like Tricia did. But Terry was beaming.

"She loves you, Tricia." He chuckled and added, "Doll."

"She's not going to call me that all weekend, is she?"

"Did you see how she smiled as soon as she saw you? One split second and something clicked. She fell in love with you. I knew she would. That's important, Tricia, 'cause I gotta keep her happy. I gotta make her love me, which means she's gotta love you."

"Is that why you wanted me to wear the lens?" she said edgily.

Terry stopped smiling, put his hands on hips. "That was your idea. You said you'd feel self-conscious with somebody new. All I said was okay."

He was right. She'd had him stop roadside so she could insert it with less risk of dropping it and losing it in the car. "I thought you'd dissuade me. I wanted you to try, but you didn't."

His eyes bounced from Tricia to Nona like a tennis ball. The rally ended with Tricia. "Don't get complicated," he said, his eyes as fearful as if he were facing triple break point. "Not here. Please, Tricia. Things are going great. Can't you see?"

Tricia, however, sensed something awry.

It was the arch of Nona's eyebrow, the obsequious welcome.

It was Ola Mae, when Terry put Tricia's bag in his room. "No Sirree," the housekeeper said, her tone as stout as she was. "No unmarrieds in the bed. Not in Miz Nona's house. Ladies go here." She pointed to the room with twin beds across the hall.

It was Terry, leaving immediately to go running with Nona.

It was the scene Tricia watched from the window of the ladies' bedroom an hour later: the return of the glistening runners. Terry said something to make Nona laugh before taking off his shoes and socks and jumping in the pool. Feet together, arms at his sides, a no-splash knifelike entry. He surfaced in time to watch Nona, in black shorts and white jog bra, follow him in. He gave her the float that was already in the pool and climbed out to get another. His pale gray shorts, drenched, thin, and clinging, were more provocative than the threadbare cutoffs he'd worn on their first day on the beach together.

The scene was so colorfully propped and styled that Jack could have been directing a photo shoot: the chartreuse floats, the aqua water of the pool, the deep kelly-green of the manicured lawn, the yellow-and-coral floral accents, the wispy clouds in a periwinkle sky. But the models were mismatched. Where was casting? Running clothes instead of swimwear. Where was wardrobe? And who was advertising what?

They talked as they floated side by side. Nona drizzled water over his back and shoulders, then spread it like sunscreen.

Intimacy. They were selling intimacy.

As the day rolled through morning and early afternoon, Terry and Nona continued to nettle her. When the five of them were in the boat, Captain Nona suggested water-skiing, and Terry announced, as Jack might have, "Tricia can't ski. She can barely swim." While everyone else skied—even Nona with Terry at the wheel—Tricia stayed silent and dry beneath her cover-up.

Lunch was enjoyable for Tricia, but Nona's tennis lesson was not. While she, Lynn, and Baze watched from the pool deck, the coquette on court inspired gigolo quips from Baze.

"You're not funny," Tricia finally said. "I want you to stop."

Baze took a long swig of beer. "Let me explain this, sweetheart. It's not just tennis. Terry's playing great but there are a lot of players who are better than he is and need sponsors."

Lynn looked up from the magazine she was reading as Nona gave her instructor a playful push at the net. "She's just flirting, Tricia."

"She's just horny, Tricia." This from Baze. "Horny and rich. She needs Terry. Terry needs her. Believe me, he'll play her to the max."

Tricia stared at the river until Terry rejoined them, without

Nona at his side for the first time that day. He and Baze were going out in the boat again, he said, and Nona was going to spend time with Tricia and Lynn. "Isn't she great?"

Tricia said, "I'm going to take a nap."

She lay in bed for hours, knowing what was wrong. Patricia was back. Patricia had been on the boat and been afraid—of the water, skiing, falling, failing. It was Patricia who had refused to take off her cover-up because of the jellyfish sting. Patricia who could not change her life any more than she could change the course of the river, who was flailing in currents of helplessness.

But it was Tricia who swam and broke free. She looked at a welt on her knee—the tip of a magenta funnel that darkened as it ran up her inner thigh to an ugly clash with the orange of her high-necked maillot. Beneath her suit, the welts were crimson, short around her hip, longer around her waist, and fat and mean across her breast. She'd earned them. She'd swum in the ocean alone.

Start over, she told herself, *for Terry's sake.*

With Terry and Baze still on the river, Tricia joined Lynn and Nona on the pool deck for sweet tea, tangy with lemon, fragrant with mint. At the table, in the shade of its umbrella, Nona's arched eyebrow no longer seemed wicked but suggested I'm listening carefully so that I understand you, because you're important to me. Her dark eyes worked hard to make sure she was understood in return, and sometimes she opened them unnaturally wide, as if she were still a ballerina engaging her audience in the upper balcony.

"Terry says you were a dancer," Tricia said.

"Oh yes." Happily Nona recounted her life in ballet slippers and pointe shoes—her first recital at three, Clara in *The Nutcracker* at eight with the Atlanta Ballet, summer intensives in New York as a teen, Juilliard as a freshman, a City Ballet audition at nineteen. The story rolled on and on, and Tricia glanced at Lynn, expecting her to roll her eyes in boredom. But she seemed captivated by the pool, as if something important was slowly sinking to the bottom and she might be called upon to dive in for retrieval or rescue.

"I had seven fabulous years with the company," Nona was saying, "and Balanchine. I danced Swanhilde in *Coppélia* at twenty-four, Aurora in *Sleeping Beauty* at twenty-five." A regretful pause. "That was it. I had to stop."

"Why?" Patricia said, but only silence followed. Feeling awkward, she glanced at Lynn for guidance, but Lynn looked—what? Bewildered? Alarmed? Patricia turned back to Nona and said hurriedly, "I'm sorry. I didn't mean to pry."

"It was 1955," Nona said, "so there were four possibilities: failure, injury, a man, or a pregnancy." She hesitated. "I never failed. I was never injured. But I was two for four."

Tricia chased what she assumed was a happy ending and a change of subject. "You had a baby." But she'd brought on another silence, graver than the one before.

"My baby was stillborn."

No one moved. The pool rippled without a sound. Finally Tricia managed, "I'm so sorry."

Nona pressed her fingertips against her temples, tucked loose strands of dark hair behind her ears. "I carried him to term," she said, as if that absolved her of failure. "Robert and I had been married for six months when our boy was born." She took her sunglasses from the table and put them on. "A precaution. I never know when I'll break."

"I'm sorry," Tricia murmured again.

Nona held up a hand. "There's nothing you can say or do; nor was there much I could do at the time. Valium was medicine's answer for everything in the fifties, including postpartum depression. I wanted Valium. I thought I needed it. But it destroyed my comeback and almost destroyed my life. If anyone knows the power of addiction, I do." She rose, called by pink geraniums nearby. She deadheaded them patiently, as if Lynn and Tricia were no longer there. She plucked yellow leaves from a large white hibiscus and returned to the table. "Valium didn't save me," she said. With a grateful smile, she added, "My husband did." For a half hour she spun highlights of their fourteen-year marriage, then willed her way through the crash of his company plane to the details of her second major depressive episode.

"I fought my way out of that one by running. Only one year later I ran the New York Marathon and was suddenly alive again and ready for something new. I began fund-raising for NYCB and for nonprofits involving children and dance."

"What about tennis?" Lynn asked.

"I took it up when I took up running, began to love to play and watch it played. I attended all four majors for several years. In May, when I went to the NCAA Championships for the first time, I decided to launch my own nonprofit—to help a young player, as my mother had always helped me. I would never have made it as a dancer without my mother. I would have crumbled under the pressure and competition without her belief in me." She glanced at her watch. "It's six, ladies. Teatime—sweet teatime—is over."

Ola Mae brought drinks on a tray. "Wine for Miz Patricia and vodka tonic for Miz Lynn. I asked Mr. Terry early this morning." She seemed pleased with herself. "And for you, Miz Nona." She placed a cigarette, lighter, and ashtray beside a glass of iced coffee.

"It's incongruous," Nona said. "A runner, smoking. But I'm a dancer first and foremost, and dancers have always smoked to stay thin." She lit her cigarette. "Anyone else?"

"I'd like one," Lynn said. Generous Ola Mae gave her two.

A hum grew louder as a boat skipped over the river and began to slow. With Nona and Lynn, Tricia watched through the trees as Terry brought it home.

"My son would have been twenty-three this year," Nona said, her words clouds of smoke. "He and Terry have the same birthday."

"That's why you chose him?" Tricia said. For a son, she thought, not a gigolo.

"June 5th, 1955. His birthday is the reason I chose him, but remarkably, he has everything I'd wanted—natural talent, crushing insecurities, the quintessential sports mother who has broken him down." She turned toward Tricia. "He's like a child—so needy that I want to hold him and protect him. And he plays such a beautiful game. Agree, Patricia?" Nona waited. "A beautiful player, child, son, man."

Tricia said only, "A beautiful player."

"Yes." Nona took off her sunglasses. "But enough about Terry and enough about me. Let's talk about you, Patricia."

"My life story pales beside yours, Nona."

"I don't think so." Nona looked at her cigarette, ground it out in the ashtray mercilessly. She looked up again with her wide stage eyes. She smiled at Tricia but spoke as if she had no pulse. "I know your husband," she said. "I know Jack."

The puttering of the boat's motor stopped, as if Terry had heard Jack's name too.

Tricia couldn't speak, so Lynn did. "You're Wynona Warren."

"That's my maiden name and stage name. I am Mrs. Wynona—Nona—McClelland, by marriage." She stared curiously at Lynn. "Have we met?"

"No, but I work with Jack. He mentioned you once." Lynn turned to Tricia. "TCC sponsored a ballet."

"Silver Level last year," said Nona, "for a night of the Ravel Festival. The ballet was Chaconne. That's where I met you,

Patricia."

"I don't recall."

"I was unmemorable, doll? Nondescript? I certainly remember you. You wore white. A short, backless A-line. You looked beautiful. Your photograph in Jack's office is also beautiful. I was there a few months ago on behalf of this year's festival. He renewed at the Gold Level. Fifty thousand."

Lynn picked up her cigarette and borrowed Nona's lighter. Her hand seemed steady but she had to flip the starter wheel three times before managing a flame. Nona smiled the smile that Terry had called mysterious and Tricia now found torturous.

"Your husband is a generous man, Patricia, and the agency, a good corporate citizen. It is Patricia, correct? Not Tricia. Jack introduced you as Patricia, his wife."

"Terry and I are friends." Her words were mousy squeaks, Nona's laugh a playful yip.

"Friends who live together and are indiscreet on the deck, in the dunes, in the ocean. Sometimes the beach only appears deserted, doll."

"It's a meaningless relationship," Lynn said. She took a deep pull on her cigarette.

"Meaningless?" Nona's eyebrow arched. "In whose opinion? Jack's? Of course not. Jack doesn't know about Terry, does he? Does Terry know about Jack? I think not."

In the boat, Terry and Baze positioned fenders and knotted lines around cleats on the dock. They began reorganizing the gear for the next day's outing.

Nona began a round of fouetté turns. Had she been dancing, she would have brought an audience to its feet, but she was speaking, and at the umbrella table, every word was an effortless extension of her leg and a kick to Tricia's throat, every spin a breath-stealing threat.

"But my relationship with Terry isn't meaningless either.

Yet here he is risking my sponsorship and the U.S. Open, all for you, doll. My sponsorship, which he wants and needs. He is breaking the no-girls clause of our agreement. He is lying to me. I have a legal right to break our contract now, to upend his career on the tour before it's begun." She nodded at the extra cigarette. "I'll take that," she said to Lynn. "I'm upset. Frankly, I'm hurt." She began to smoke in thoughtful silence, which gnawed at Tricia's attempted calm. "Terry is an investment for me, and you're a distraction for Terry. The game you're playing is hurting his game."

"That's not true."

"Please don't argue, Patricia. I'm not trying to hurt you, but I have Terry's best interest at heart." She paused. "And my own interest. He's not a financial investment for me. He's an emotional investment, from which I expect deep dividends. Distractions decrease returns."

Terry and Baze started up the boardwalk. Tricia tried to pretend it was a treadmill, that they would walk but never arrive.

"I can't bear him lying to me, doll, as a result of your lying to him about your marriage."

"Please," Tricia said. She turned to Lynn, and seeing only blank eyes, pinned a whimper to the back of her throat. "Please don't tell Terry."

"That's not my intention. And you won't tell him either." Nona leveled her gaze. "You won't hurt my son."

Tricia sat back in the wrought iron chair, hoping to support her spine, to stop its disintegration into chalky dust.

Nona pulled up like a ballerina, her slender chest high and triumphant. She looked toward the river. "And I won't tell poor, unsuspecting Jack. I won't have to."

Again Tricia looked to Lynn, who looked as upset as Tricia had ever seen her.

"I'm sorry, doll," Nona said, words like syrup. "So sorry

you're leaving us in the middle of the night. Unexpectedly. From your twin bed, not Terry's king. Leaving while angel sleeps."

"That would hurt him."

"I'll help him understand. Someone is ill. You had to go. Your mother? Your father?"

Tricia said only, "He'll be hurt and suspicious. He'll expect me to call."

"Yes, that's right." Nona nodded, and as if she and Tricia were coconspirators, gave up a pensive, "Hmmm." She snapped her fingers in an aha that looked more like a command for a pet than a solution. "But you didn't want to wake him, not in the middle of the night. You were so considerate, doll. I was still awake, and when I saw you to the door, you asked me to tell him you'd call in a week or so." Her broad smile seemed ready to pull her face apart. "But you won't call, Patricia. Do you understand me? And if he calls you, you'll hang up. He and I will go to Atlanta as planned, and by week's end, he'll have played so well and be so excited about the Open, he'll have forgotten your name. With my help," Nona added, syrup thinning to venom. "You will never call Terry because if you do—" She delivered the bite: "I'll call Jack."

Terry and Baze were approaching, were a hundred yards away.

"You'll leave my home tonight, Kiawah tomorrow morning, and Terry forever."

Fifty yards.

"You'll go back to New York or I'll phone New York: 212-780-5000."

Twenty yards.

"That's the office, correct?"

Ten.

Tricia said, "Yes."

Five, four, three, two, one.

§

Terry and Baze stepped into the thick fog of crisis. Lynn turned her eyes downward. Baze trained his on Lynn. Nona's were full of anticipation. Terry's were happy and blind.

"I'd like to sit on the dock," Tricia said to him.

"Why?" Nona's words danced. They were playful and ballerina-light. "We're all together again. Dinner's almost ready. Please don't go, doll."

"Come with me, Terry."

But Terry took up Nona's cause. "Why?"

The question landed on Tricia's ear with a thud. "Please," she said. When he shook his head, she committed an act of desperation she thought he'd understand. She turned away from Nona, made a C with her left thumb and index finger, pulled her eye open, and removed the lens.

Terry looked confused. "Jesus, Tricia." Then worried, then afraid—the way he'd looked on court against Freddie when facing triple break point. "What are you doing?"

Nona stretched her neck left and right, a periscope searching for its target. She hissed to Lynn, "Does she have a glass eye?"

Tricia started across the pool deck, expecting the sound of Terry's footsteps behind her. She heard the solitary slapping of her flip-flops and Nona instead: "Stay, Terry. Goodness, we've been apart all afternoon."

On the dock, Tricia—Patricia?—struggled and worked the dry lens back into her eye. In a fetal sit, she wrapped her arms around her shins. She'd called the bank, requested applications, swum in the ocean. She'd grown stronger but not strong enough. She'd survived hot jellies, but now there was Nona. She squeezed her calves, and with her head on her knees, longed to go back to summer's beginning, to an honest summer with Terry.

She heard her mother reading *Alice's Adventures in Wonderland*:

And once she remembered trying to box her own ears for having cheated herself in a game of croquet she was playing against herself, for this curious child was very fond of pretending to be two people. "But it's no use now," thought poor Alice, "to pretend to be two people! Why, there's hardly enough of me left to make one respectable person!

"He'll come," she told the river, but she sat alone until dusk, then went to the house.

"Are you all right, doll? We've been waiting, and the boys are ravenous." Nona led Tricia to the dining room. "Come as you are."

"No, Nona." Everyone looked refreshed. She wanted the shine and fragrance of shampooed hair, the sheen of lotion on smooth, clean skin, a summery sundress, energy renewed. Nona noted that Ola Mae was ready to serve, clean up, and go home. "Please start without me," Tricia said. She went upstairs to the assigned ladies' bedroom. She called her husband, and when he picked up, gave him no chance to say hello. "Jack."

"Patricia." He sounded astonished.

"I'm ready to come home."

"Patricia."

Yes. Patricia. Patricia. Patricia was crying. "Tomorrow. I'm coming home."

Jack was silent. Then, "I'll be out of town for several days. I have a meeting. An appointment I can't change."

"Where, Jack? I'll come there." She tried not to sniffle. She heard him light a cigarette, heard him say, "Houston."

By the time she sat down to dinner, she was an intruder, an outsider to new inside jokes and the animated chatter at the table. She drank two glasses of wine and started on a third to catch up with the caravan ahead of her. She pulled even with Terry, Lynn, and Baze as Ola Mae served homemade peach ice cream and gingersnaps. Terry and Baze ate like greedy boys but Patricia and Lynn stayed with wine. She saw Terry freshen Nona's drink and realized that their hostess, while encouraging their overindulgence, was drinking club soda with a twist of lime.

Patricia's eyes, cloudy with chardonnay, were a problem. Or Nona's were, she decided. They moved from guest to guest as she babbled gaily, the coquette from the court holding court at the table. Occasionally, though, Nona fell silent, and with her head, mouth, and eyebrows deathly still, her eyes moved around the table.

It was reptilian. No. It was wine. And panic.

It was Jack, somehow present. No. It was Nona.

Of course Nona knew Jack. She *was* Jack—shrewd, controlling, charming. Intimidating Patricia. Beguiling Terry, taking his hand as she rose, dragging him along. She might as well have collared him, Patricia was thinking as she, Lynn, and Baze followed them into what was not the expected pool house but a studio with a wooden floor, mirrored walls, and a ballet barre.

"You're gonna dance, Nona?" Terry asked.

"Yes, angel. I always dance when I have a partner. Give me a minute."

Nona released Terry's hand. She slipped behind a decorative three-panel screen, giving Patricia the chance she wanted. "Terry—" The anger in his eyes made her gasp.

"What's wrong with you, Tricia? You've been weird all day—leaving us all, taking naps, going to the dock, being late for dinner. Are you trying to fuck this up for me?"

The ballerina emerged in pink ballet slippers, pink tights, and a black camisole leotard with a square neckline and a high-cut leg line. "Not one word," she said sharply, intending the order for Patricia, but everyone obeyed. All watched as she stretched, first on the floor, then at the barre. The scooped back of the leotard couldn't have been lower. She moved to the stereo, spinning in piqué turns.

For Patricia, everything was spinning.

Lynn pulled her gently aside. "You look pale."

"Why didn't you tell me?"

"I didn't know at first. By the time I realized who she was, I had no chance."

"I've had too much to drink," she said weakly, feeling wine burning in her throat. Then, loudly, to everyone: "Excuse me. I'm dizzy. I need some fresh air."

The line she walked toward the house was not straight like the line the ballerina had spun. She felt exhausted but she pushed on.

"What are you doing?" Lynn asked, catching up with her.

"I'm leaving. I have to."

"You don't. I'll call Barbara Fox and tell her not to put Nona through to Jack. Not to give him any messages from her."

She forced her shoulders back. "I'm going to Jack. Either I'll stay with him like a sweet little wife from the 1950s, or I'll find the strength to tell him I'm leaving him. If he doesn't take out the chain saw, I'll come back. I'll tell Terry I'm married and hope he still wants me." Her legs felt collapsible. She almost went down.

"You can't possibly drive back to Kiawah tonight. You'll have an accident." The idea seemed lovely. Like her parents. Dead on impact.

"I'll go with you," Lynn said.

"No. I won't let you. I don't want anyone taking care of me anymore. I'm going alone. I'll go inside and sleep for an hour or two. Then I'll disappear."

"Lynn," Baze called, coming out of the studio. "I'm going to the river for a swim. Come with me."

"Go, Lynn," Patricia said. "Leave me on my own."

"I'll get my suit," Lynn called to Baze, but with worry for Patricia in her voice.

"Skinny dipping." Baze laughed.

"I think I'll just watch."

Lynn moved toward Baze and, through the open window of the studio, Patricia heard Terry: "I'll be your doubles partner, Nona, but not this."

"I'll do the work," Nona said. "You'll only lift and hold me."

Watching from the pool deck, Patricia became the audience for their brightly lit *pas de deux*. "Down on one knee, angel, and when I come to you, put your hands on my waist and look slowly up at me."

In the strong hands of her partner, Nona executed a perfect *arabesque penchée*—extending one leg straight and high, pointing her toes, bending at the waist, leaning toward Terry while sliding her hands beside his face and beyond in long graceful lines, bending deeper, leg higher, lips almost brushing his as together they raised their faces and stopped, chin to chin. Nona stood straight again, as did Terry.

"Now, a fish, angel. I'll count, and on four, catch me with your right hand here, just under my arm. Your left here. Not my knee. Higher. Yes."

If Terry was her son, this was incest, or child abuse. Inside the house, Tricia managed the stairs and a reservation on a Delta flight: departure from Charleston at nine in the morning, a long layover in Atlanta, Houston at five. A one-way reservation.

She set her alarm, and at its 3:00 a.m. cry, turned on the bedside lamp. Lynn had come in and was sleeping soundly, snoring. She imagined Terry sleeping soundly too, his would-be mother and lover standing guard at his door.

She found the hall empty. She opened the door to Terry's room, moved quietly in the dark to the bed, sat down on the near side, the right side, Terry's side. He always slept on the right. She reached for him but her palm sank to the mattress. She turned on the lamp. The bed was undisturbed. A look out the window showed her inky darkness. It seeped into her slowly, through what felt like a pinprick in her throat.

The house was quiet. A single light downstairs showed her all she needed to see: no one asleep on a couch or in the sunroom, Nona's closed bedroom door.

She turned on only the parking lights as she backed the Porsche out of the driveway. She turned on the brights at the end of the street. "*Stop,*" the sign read, and she imagined reading more. *Stop your island foolishness. Go back to your husband, Patricia. Go home.*

CHAPTER 10

A helluva way to wake up, Terry thought. Falling off a float at dawn into water chilled by the night. Like a wet dog, he shook water from his hair but not the sludge from his head. Still half drunk, he got back on the float. He turned his face toward the river, hoping for a sobering breath of fresh salt air. He drew in chlorine instead, which stung the inside of his nose. He watched the scarlet globe in the sky, its slow-motion rising. He closed his eyes. He felt a gradual warming, inside and outside his body. His naked body. He always slept naked. With Tricia.

"Holy shit." He rolled off the float, and standing in the pool, remembered.

He was alone in the studio with Nona, turning, lifting and lowering her, having a nightcap at the pool, doing whatever she said. He looked wearily at Baze and Lynn as they came in from the river and said good night.

"I gotta go to sleep, Nona," he'd said. "'Cause I'm about to pass out. I could go to sleep right here in this chair. Or on that float there, which is looking pretty good right now."

"Go ahead, angel," she'd said, rising. "Sleep there. I want you to." She gave his hand a squeeze. "Sweet dreams. Good night."

She'd left and he'd pulled off his clothes in the dark. Because he always slept naked. Because Nona had told him to sleep on the float. Because climbing the stairs seemed like a chore. Because Tricia had been a bitch all day.

Late-night memories out. Hangover in. "Shit," he said, head pounding.

He turned toward the house and Nona, walking toward him with the colors of the sunrise in her satin robe and a rolled pink towel in her hands.

"Good morning." She stopped at the edge of the pool.

"Hi." He nodded at the table. "Would you put that towel there with my clothes?"

She didn't. She held it. "Breakfast?"

"I'll wait for Tricia."

Nona looked dismayed. "She's gone, angel. She's no longer here."

"She's what?"

"She left in the middle of the night. I saw her out."

Hammers to his head.

"She phoned home to check her messages and learned that her mother is critically ill."

A bludgeon to his skull. "Her mother?"

"Yes, her father had left her an urgent message."

He stared at his sponsor. His stomach cramped. "I don't think so, Nona." It was easier than accusing her of lying.

"Her father said she should come right away."

"I've got to go too." The water resisted as he moved toward the steps. He remembered his nakedness and stopped. Nona repositioned the towel in her arms, held it like a baby.

"You mustn't go, angel."

"I have to. She'll need me."

"I need you too. We have Atlanta."

"I'll try to get back, but I've gotta go to Tricia. Put that towel there."

She wrapped it tightly in her arms, pressed it to her breasts. "No, angel. If you want my sponsorship, you will not go."

"Nona, I—" He looked down through the water at his brown legs and white feet, thought about Tricia's fingers on his shins.

I love this. This tennis tan.

He looked through water that was perfectly clear and decisions that weren't. His eyes climbed the pool steps one by one, skipped over the gleeful colors of Nona's robe, past her forced smiled, up to the dare in her eyes. "You're kidding me, right? It's you or her?"

"You want to play tennis, Terry. I can help you. Patricia cannot. Don't you want me?"

He heard a whistle, absurd and familiar, starting high and sliding low. He looked up at a boulder falling from a cliff. He was Wile E. Coyote, flat on his back, arms and legs splayed. It was all coming down.

He walked out of the pool, asked for the towel with an open hand. She tightened her hold on the terry-cloth roll. He tried to read the messages in her eyes: she was hurt, she was furious; she loved him, she hated him; she was turned off, she was turned on. He felt her eyes drilling into his back as he went to the table. He pulled his boxers and shorts up his wet legs.

He turned back to Nona, who'd hung the towel over a chair. She examined her fingernails. She retied the sash of her bathrobe, fingered the fringe at its edge. She brushed something—an eyelash? a tear?—from her cheek and looked up. "If you don't care about me, don't you at least care about my money?"

He was thinking how stupid he would be to give up a sponsorship for an uncertainty, to give up hard cash in hand for a summer of a girl. A complicated, no-promises girl, with a kiss in the corner of her mouth.

"I'm forty-five years old, angel," Nona said. "I'm alone. I'm lonely."

"I can't fix that, Nona." He folded his arms, stuffed his fists in his armpits. "Is that what you want me for? 'Cause I thought it was my tennis." Silence. "It's not my tennis?"

"No distractions, Terry. No Patricia. Make a choice."

"Tricia," he said. "I choose Tricia."

§

In the beach house driveway, the Valiant shuddered like a racehorse pushed too hard, lathered, and ready to be put out of its misery. On the porch he reached for the doorknob as Tricia opened the door. She dropped her eyes.

"What's going on?" he said. "What's wrong?"

"Where are Lynn and Baze?"

"I left them. I couldn't wake Baze. He kept saying 'later,' and I didn't want to wait." Still looking down, she said, "How will they get back?"

He ignored her question. He moved into the foyer, stopped at the luggage beside the wall. A lot of luggage. Clothes for weeks.

He faced her. She was wearing a dress he'd never seen. Her hair looked like Farrah Fawcett's. There was color on her cheeks and lips, even her eyelids. Both eyes were blue. Blue ice picks. Chipping their way through his breastbone. "Where are you going?" Nothing. "Are you leaving? For good? Are you leaving . . . me?"

"I'm going to Houston."

"Houston? Why?"

A cab pulled into the driveway with a long mournful call. "I have to go, Terry. I can't miss my flight."

His eyes took their own flight around the room, looking for the place where the walls were going to start crumbling and caving in on him.

"Terry, I have something to tell you."

He imagined asking: Is there someone else? Imagined her saying yes. *Let me make love to you,* he would say, *before you go to him, so I'll have a chance.* But like a wimp, he just said, "Unh-unh. Don't tell me now and walk out the door. You've waited this long. Wait till you get back." The summer was crumbling, not the walls. "Are you coming back?"

She took a step toward her bags and Terry brushed past her. From the porch, he shouted to the cabbie that she wasn't ready.

He closed the door. His upper lip quivered.

"I want to make love to you, Tricia." He eased the tote bag of books from her hand. She moved her fingers over the stubble on his chin, as if it were one more thing to remember him by, the feel of it, the sandpaper sound. She would remember it along with the smell of him. "I want to make love to you. The cab can wait. I'll pay."

"We can't make love. I'm dressed. I've got my period. The cab is here."

"Not one of those things is a reason not to."

"I could miss my flight."

"That's a reason to do it. For me anyways. I don't want you to go. That's one reason to do it, and another reason is that—" He stopped abruptly. He touched her cheek.

"Too," she said, touching his.

"Don't cry, Tricia, okay? You'll fuck up all that makeup you never wear when you're with me, 'cause you don't have to." He slid his hand into her hair, which was hard and sticky. He wanted to say, *You're going to meet somebody, aren't you? The somebody who sends you roses.* But instead he asked, "Are you coming back?"

"I don't know. I know where I'm going now, but not where I'll go after that."

It wasn't much, but it was the best thing he'd heard. With his hands on her arms and both lips quivering now, he kissed her and fought on. "Come to Atlanta."

"No," she said, eyes brimming. "You'll be with Nona."

"Nona fired me. Or I fired her."

Tricia was fighting too, a battle with tears. "Did you sleep with her?"

Her jealous whine was the second-best thing he'd heard. "Holy shit, Tricia. Is that what you think? No, I didn't sleep with her. I would never sleep with her."

"Promise?"

"I swear. She's as old as my mother. She acts like my mother. That would be worse—" He shook his head. "Tricia, I would never do that. I swear on my life."

"But you weren't in your bed." She began to cry.

"I was in the pool. Passed out on a float. I'm done with Nona. She said you or her. I picked you." He watched her eyes shift from jealousy to terror he didn't understand.

"Oh God, was she angry?"

"Probably but—"

"She'll do something to hurt you. To hurt us."

"It's okay, Tricia. I swear." He moved his hands to her waist and up and down her rib cage. "I'll find another sponsor. Maybe in Atlanta. I'm entered in the tournament and I'm gonna play. I might have to stay in a Motel 6, but I'm going and I'm gonna play. Play good." His determination put a light in her eyes so bright that he thought she'd changed her mind, that she would open the door and dismiss the cab with a wave. Instead, she took a check from her checkbook, signed it, and gave it to him, along with most of the cash in her wallet. He tried to protest.

"Take it, Terry, please. If you love me, you'll take it."

He folded the bills and check and put them in his pocket. "I'll have to qualify. But I will. I'll make the main draw, which starts Wednesday. I'm just in it till I lose, which could be the first round. It's a thirty-two draw, and some pretty good pros use the tournament as a warm-up for the Open."

"You won't lose."

"I'm gonna lose sometime, Tricia. But maybe I can handle it now. Better than before anyways. Before you." He wanted to trap her smile, but it was nimble and fled. "Do one last thing for me, Tricia. Come to Atlanta. Promise me you'll come see me play. One last time."

"I can't promise that, Terry."

He looked down, thinking how happy she'd made him all

summer, fearing she'd make him equally sad. He raised his eyes, and his gaze followed hers to the cab. "Tricia, listen to me. I've got a big idea. Really big. For you and me. I've been working on it. Come see me play and I'll tell you the big idea." He forced a leaden shrug. "Either you'll like it or you won't."

She put her hand behind his head and drew him to her. He wanted to keep the kiss going until the cabbie grew impatient and left, but she broke away and picked up her tote bag.

"Tricia," he said, "come to Atlanta. To the Atlanta Athletic Club. If you do, I'll trade you the big idea for that other kiss." He touched the corner of her lips where it resided. "For whatever the hell we've tap-danced around all summer." She nodded and closed her eyes. He said, "We'll fix it. We'll know what to do."

He carried her bags to the cab, kissed her once more, and helped her inside. He stepped back and studied her through the window. She touched her cheek. He touched his and said, "Too."

What the hell? he wondered. *What's different?* It wasn't the eyes or the colors. It was something he couldn't figure out. She didn't even look like Tricia anymore. She looked like somebody else.

On Sunday, he almost lost to a nobody in the first round of the qualies but somehow got by him. He started Monday's second round seeing the ball as big as a grapefruit, exploding off his racket into sections of unreturnable pulp and seeds. He was not only getting to impossible shots but doing something with them, even off balance, even on the run. With a 6–4, 6–2 win over a thirty-year-old trying to make a comeback, he moved on.

Before and after every match, sometimes even during changeovers, his eyes crawled the bleachers, row by row.

Neither he nor Tricia knew where the other was staying. When he saw her, if he saw her, it would be at the tournament.

Tuesday, he sat in his room at a Holiday Inn, watching rain, as relentless as his sadness, cancel all play. He was well rested for the main draw, but so was Alex Lamotte, a pro ranked inside the top fifty. Terry played the most physical match of his life—three hours of long rallies, with shots clipping the corners and painting the lines. At the net, his touch had never been so soft, and luckily, his serve was on. He and Lamotte split the first two sets, and though he had to save four match points in a killer tiebreaker, Terry took it 10–8 and the match 7–5, 5–7, 7–6.

In his room, he fell back on the bed. He was through to the second round. If he could win one more match, maybe he'd still have that wild card in the Open qualies, maybe Nona hadn't given it back. He didn't even know who he was scheduled to play tomorrow and was too tired to get up and look at the draw. He sighed. If he could win tomorrow, and win a hundred matches after that, maybe he could forget the match that hurt so much—the one he'd lost to a guy in Houston, whose name he'd never even know.

Across the net from Terry stood the 1977 Wimbledon qualifier who had played his way into the semifinals before losing to Jimmy Connors in four sets. Eighteen years old and just out of high school, he'd been the youngest player in history to make the Wimbledon semis.

In the spring of 1978, Terry had watched that same player win the NCAA Championships as a Stanford freshman—win *the* match, as it was called, defeating John Sadri of NC State, 7–6, 7–6, 5–7, 7–6. Four hours and fifteen minutes. 144 points to 143.

John McEnroe had turned pro following that victory, and now, four months later, he was ranked fifteenth in the world. He wore a red headband, and his reddish-brown hair was long, shaggy, and as unruly as he was. Not more than five eleven, Terry guessed. One sixty at most. Slight. Scrawny. A lefty.

"Fucking wizard," Terry muttered after only three games.

McEnroe had an uncanny court sense, knowing instinctively where to place shots. He had lightning reflexes, incredible touch, and an arsenal of impossible angles. He was quick. He was surgical. He had no weaknesses.

Serve and volley, slay and viscerate, Terry thought. *No, eviscerate.* That was the word, and that's what he was—eviscerated. His guts were lying all over the court, shriveling in the sun. So were his nerves and his brain and his balls. He couldn't settle down, couldn't get his first serve in. Not that it mattered. McEnroe cracked returns off his firsts as if they were seconds. And McEnroe's serve, though not powerful, was as pinpoint accurate out wide as down the T.

McEnroe took the first set, 6–0. A big fat bagel. Not even twenty minutes long, or short.

Terry opened the second by holding serve for the first time, but only after saving five break points, running down every unpredictable ball, playing patient defense, and attacking every opportunity he was given. At fifteen minutes, that game had been almost as long as the first set, but the glimmer of belief it gave him—coupled with a few lapses from McEnroe—saw him through to a 7–5 win in the second.

They played to 4–all in the third without a service break before McEnroe disputed a call—questioning, whining, then aggressively arguing that Terry's serve had been wide. Good, Terry thought. He's pissed off. But the incident didn't hinder his opponent as Terry hoped. It pumped him up. McEnroe played the next four points with vengeance but couldn't take Terry down.

"Five–all," Terry said, still believing as he stepped to the service line. He double-faulted. Love–15.

He served a let, a fault, and a shallow second. McEnroe knifed a return. Love–30.

Deep trouble. Facing the sun, eyes burning, Terry hit a killer serve, wide to McEnroe's backhand to start the longest rally of the match. Thirty-three strokes and one unforced error. Terry, not McEnroe, made it. Love–40.

Triple break point. He felt fear on his face, knew McEnroe saw it. He readied himself and saved the first break point by rifling a body serve and rushing the net. Caught off guard, McEnroe netted a forehand. Terry saved the second, again coming in. He barely caught McEnroe's up-the-line pass but punched it safely back crosscourt and out of reach.

One more and he'd pull even at deuce. He didn't dare charge the net again, unless he blasted the serve of his life—which he didn't. McEnroe took the ball on the rise and slammed it at an impossible angle to Terry's backhand. He stretched and thought he had it. But his ball struck the net cord, teetered eternally, and fell back on Terry's side of the court.

Broken. Down now, a set and a break.

McEnroe. Serving at 6–5 for the match. Inventing shots and angles: 15, 30, 40–love. Game, set, match.

It was over. Just like that. Just that serve. Just that return. Just that plunk of the ball on the wood of his racket frame instead of the pop of the ball on strings.

It was over, and it was McEnroe's: 6–0, 5–7, 7–5.

Handshakes—McEnroe, the chair umpire. Terry had to look down to keep the water out of his eyes. Not tears. And for the first time in his life, not shame. Just wet, steamy sorrow finally released—not for the loss of a match but the loss of the girl he loved.

He sat down in his sideline chair, put his rackets in his bag, pulled the sweatbands off his wrists, and pulled off his shirt. He dug in his bag and said, "Fuck." He hadn't packed a second shirt. He listened to the crowd ten feet behind him, filing out of the stadium. It was a drone for the most part, but a few individual voices soared, and every other word was McEnroe.

Some cheery bozo called to him, "Good match. Nice try."

He draped the strap of his bag over his shoulder, and was heading for the locker room when someone called, "Hey, you." Called it loudly from high up in the stands. "Hey, shirtless."

He couldn't believe how quickly she bounded down the steps or how quickly he met her at the half wall between the bleachers and the court. He couldn't believe what he saw.

"Jesus Christ, Tricia, what happened?"

Two hours later, he was staring again at the discoloration on the right side of her nose—the mix of yellow and green so pale he might not have noticed it if her swollen lip hadn't spotlighted it. No way she'd stumbled into something in a dark hotel room in Houston.

"What in Jesus God's name are we doing here?" She laughed, and the slice in her lip opened and began to bleed again. He gave her a towel from his bag. "Why are we at the University of Georgia?"

"This is where I'm gonna tell you the big idea. We're gonna walk around campus in a while, but first I wanted to come here." Together they looked up at the Henry Feild Tennis Stadium, which he was sure was the best in the country. "The NCAAs were played here the last two years, and they'll be here next year too" he said, eyes bright, "when I win, capping off my great senior year. Come on." She'd taken a cab to the tournament, so he led her to the Mustang he'd rented for the week. "I miss my car," he said and chuckled at the look she gave him. "Our car. Okay, your car. This rental is a piece of crap."

"Hmm. Do you love me or my Porsche?"

"You. And I'm glad I lost that match. 'Cause now I know

you love me too, win or lose."

Athens, he remembered as they began to walk, was a damn good college town, and UGA, a great school—great campus, great athletics, and rowdy, devoted fans. For years before the stadium was built, he'd been told, students watched tennis matches from Kudzu Hill behind the courts, with coolers full of beer, and the kind of roaring cheers and jeers usually reserved for football games. To celebrate the stadium's completion in '77, Georgia had invited Southern Cal, the reigning NCAA men's tennis champs, to play a special dedication match. It had been tight, but the Bulldogs—Tennis Dawgs they were called—had sent those West Coast boys packing, shocked by defeat and a barking crowd. Texas had great fans, sure. But Georgia was fucking amazing.

"Let's sit," Tricia said, nodding at a bench on the edge of a shady quadrangle. "We've walked for an hour, and it's pretty here."

"Know what kind of buildings those are?" he asked as she looked around the grassy park.

"Greek Revival? The columns—"

"No."

"Not Greek Revival? Then what?"

"Old."

"Very funny. But correct. Probably late nineteenth century."

He made small talk, knowing it was procrastination dressed up as words. His right foot began to work, bouncing his leg up and down until she put her hand on his thigh.

"Drumroll, please. The big idea is?"

His eyes followed a student walking toward them—dark hair and eyes, short skirt, long legs. She smiled and walked on but glanced back over her shoulder twice. "Cute," he said.

"I'm sure she thinks you're cute too."

"A lot of pretty girls in Georgia."

"And in Texas? Are you trying to make me jealous?"

"No. I'm stalling." He sat up straight, crossed his arms, and told her everything he'd learned about UGA while hanging out during the championships. "They've had this tradition here forever, that when Georgia wins a football game, freshmen ring the bell at the chapel all night long. And remember streaking? A few years back? This school holds the national record. Fifteen hundred people got naked together and ran around campus."

"Now that's impressive," she said wryly.

"It's nice here, Tricia, don't you think?"

"It's beautiful. I love the architecture. The history must be very rich."

"I knew you'd like it." A clock chimed and students, alone, in pairs, and in groups, began spilling into the quadrangle, on their way from one class to another or into the weekend ahead. One group walked lockstep with an attractive, middle-aged woman, pleased to keep her classroom lecture going. "Tricia." He had to look away to get through it. "Tricia, I want you to come to Austin with me." In return, he got a look as empty as he'd ever seen from her.

"Terry—"

"Let me finish. That's only the selfish part, for me. The other part is for you. I want you to get your doctorate. Because you want to, because of how much you love books and poems, because of your parents, and because you'd be so happy teaching. I can see you right here or anywhere. I know you should finish it—for you. So why not Austin?"

Across the quadrangle, two guys were laughing at what must have been a great joke. Or they were laughing at him. Or maybe Tricia was laughing inside and he was somehow hearing.

"Terry—"

"Don't talk. Just think about it. No snap decisions, especially if you're snapping to a no." He paused. "Don't even say yes or maybe—not until you're sure." He watched her hand take his, mindful of the blisters. "It's too late for you to get accepted this fall, but you can start in January. And you might be able to get a graduate assistantship and a stipend." She raised her eyebrows and he said, "What? You think I don't know words like stipend? I told you I've been working on this idea. I know the chair of the English department because I almost lost my scholarship over English 101. There was a shitload of reading, but my coach is a friend of hers and got her to help me out with a tutor. She has a ten-year-old son with a wicked forehand, so I coached him some. So I happened to talk to her the other day—"

"You happened to talk to her? You mean you called her?"

"Yeah." He seemed to have crossed a forbidden line. She looked insulted or—hell, he had no idea how she looked. "I know you don't need money, but a stipend couldn't hurt, and you'd get to start teaching right away." The big idea was beginning to shrink. "I'm going back to Austin, Tricia. You've never said you'll come see me. You've just said you want to remember me. You can say anything else you want to and kiss me in the corner, and I may be stupid, but I don't think you want this to be over any more than I do." He stood up. To move, pace, fold, tug, unfold. "What does that look mean?"

"You told me not to talk." She held out her hand. He sat back down. "You can talk as long as you don't give me an answer yet."

"I don't have an answer yet, but I want to tell you that after Houston I went to Austin. I spent four days there."

"Four days?" He frowned. "You're kidding me, right? Why?"

She shook her head. "I had things to think through on my own, and I chose to do it there. I did what we've just done. I walked around campus. I walked miles around campus every day. I went to the library, the English department, the tennis courts. I thought about you."

He looked up at the bluest sky he'd ever seen, felt the sun

on his face. "If you come with me," he said, "I—You've gotta know I'm just talking Austin. I don't have anything to offer, nothing more planned. I don't have Nona now. I don't know if I can make a living playing pro or not, but even to try, I'll need money I don't have." He waited, thinking Porsche, beach house. He waited like a tennis brat for her to offer to help him. "I can't see past Austin. That's all I've got."

"You've got me."

He had a sense of things happening too fast and wanting them to happen faster. "Okay. That's the big idea. Your turn. Kiss me in the corner."

"At the beach house," she said. "Let's go back to Kiawah."

He closed the bedroom door and waited. She sat on the bed, hands in her lap.

"Terry, I have something to tell you."

"Talk louder. I can hardly hear you." But he could plainly hear the coursing of fear through his veins. Through his chest. His head.

"This must be how you feel," she said, "when you're facing match point, and you know that no matter what, you have to hit the ball."

"Then just hit the fucker and let me return it." But she didn't speak, move, or blink her anxious eyes. "I can handle it, Tricia. Okay?"

"I've lied, and I hate myself for it."

"Just tell me."

She nodded. "Terry, there is—"

"Stop," he broke in. "I'll tell you, okay? It will be easier. 'Cause I'm not as stupid as you think, Tricia." He leaned back against the door and waited the twenty-five seconds allowed between points. He shifted his weight to the balls of his feet, leaned slightly forward, tried to look ready.

"There's somebody else," he said. She didn't respond. "There's Tom-Dick-or-Harry."

She said softly, "Jack."

"Jack," he repeated. The name made it real. It hurt, but at least it was said and was done. He'd gotten the kiss, and it was just what he'd thought. All he had to do was hold serve. The umpire called time. He sat down beside her. "Jack, who goes to sleep afterward. Jack, the rotten choice."

"Yes, that is Jack."

"He lives in New York."

"Yes."

He bounced the ball six times, held it against the center of his racket. "He loves you."

"Yes."

He tossed, drew his racket back. "And you love him?"

"Yes. No." She braided and unbraided her hair. "Maybe. Maybe in some way I do."

"But not like you love me." His voice had gone soft and his heart, loud. Boom, slam, beat.

"I've never loved anyone like I love you, Terry."

He squared his shoulders. "He doesn't understand you like I do, Tricia. He doesn't love you or treat you like I do. He sure as hell doesn't know how to make love with you. And this is the hardest one, because it's unforgivable." His voice rose in disbelief. "He hit you, Tricia."

"Just once."

"Which I would never do."

"I know."

"Look at me." He moved his lips gently around hers, starting and ending with the split. She put her arms around him. "You broke up with him, but he wants you back. Or you haven't broken up, but you want to."

"Yes."

"And come to Austin with me."

"Yes."

It had been muffled, but a yes. He smiled at her. "What did I miss?"

"Terry." She took his hands.

Oh fuck, he thought. He'd missed something big. "What?"

"Terry, promise me what I promised you today—no snap decisions. Promise you won't say or do anything until you think things through." Her voice trembled. Her hands began to shake.

"Promise you'll give me time to explain. Promise you won't leave. Promise you'll stay with me tonight."

His voice was strong. "I promise."

"The car," Tricia said. "It's Jack's car."

"Okay." He'd known from the beginning it was way too much car for her.

"This is Jack's beach house."

"Okay." He waited. Waiting was killing him.

"Terry," she said, "I'm Jack's wife."

Stop there, he wanted to say. *Jesus. Stop.* But he couldn't manage a word and Tricia seemed unable to handle the silence.

"I'm married, Terry. I'm married."

He walked to the bedroom door like he walked to the net when he'd lost. Like he was beaten, but okay. Like it didn't matter. Knowing all he had to do was shake hands and get away. Get to the shower.

"Terry, you promised."

Without looking back, he mustered the will to say, "I'm not leaving. I said I wouldn't, didn't I? But I gotta be by myself for a minute."

He slammed the bedroom door behind him so hard he thought it had splintered and come down. He bolted up the stairs. He ran through the empty guest bedroom to the bathroom, still slamming doors. To the toilet. To his knees. He threw up, then dry heaved again and again, waiting for his heart to come out.

He listened, heard Lynn's and Tricia's voices downstairs. He flushed the toilet and stood up. Smelling, tasting, swallowing puke. He gagged. He rinsed his mouth out. He locked the door, stripped, listened to Tricia sobbing until he couldn't stand it.

In the shower, he closed his eyes and leaned his head back, letting the water rush over his face as he listened to her knocking—knuckles, palms, fists? He pressed his forearms against his ears, and when he finally released them, he heard only running water. He backed into a corner of the shower and, squatting, slid to the tile floor. Cold on his ass. So cold in the corner. He drew in his feet. He clutched his knees.

What a dumb-ass he'd been—sitting in her reading circle, reading the idiot kids' books she assigned, listening moon-fucking-struck while she read aloud to him, while Wendy read to Peter, the little lost boy. What the fuck did she read to her husband?

For nearly three months, he'd been driving another man's car, living in his house, sleeping in his bed, and balling his wife. No wonder the bastard had hit her. He should have hit his sinning, whoring wife.

Tricia was his *wife.* Tricia was *married.*

Tricia was standing there—crying and walking toward him through the steam. "How did you get in here?" he shouted, words shredding his throat. "Get out."

She froze. Her face was red, her eyes swollen. Still dressed in a T-shirt and shorts, she stepped into the shower and sat down too, catty-corner from him. She put her feet inside his, leaned forward, and put her hands on his knees.

"I am so sorry."

He didn't hear her. He read the words on her lips. He looked at her through the shower stream, through white lines on the court and black lines on the page. He hoped she knew that the water in his eyes and on his face was only the shower.

She turned around, and still sitting, slid back against him, draped her arms outside his legs, held his shins. He put his hands on the floor, changed his mind, and wrapped his arms around her. She turned her lips to his ear. “I love you.”

“I know. I—” No fucking way he could say it, even though he wanted to. Didn’t matter. She knew.

“I’m going to leave my husband.”

“Tricia.”

“Please.”

“About Austin.”

“Please.” She took his hand, placed it between her breasts.

He felt fright in her heart, laid his head back against the tile. “This changes everything.”

“I always knew it would,” she said.

Together, clothed and unclothed, they sat in the shower until the water went cold as stone.

CHAPTER 11

In the morning, in our crypt of a beach house, Terry sat on the floor in front of the television and the Atari VCS that Tricia had bought him before we went to Nona's. He turned on Air-Sea Battle but never touched the joystick. He stared at the screen, ignoring my attempts at conversation, nodding yes or shaking no to my questions. Tricia responded with polite lethargy but initiated no interaction with me or Terry. There was no hand-holding, lap sitting, kissing, or touching. They didn't do the cheek thing, and for the first time, the bright, palpable connection between them had burned out, leaving their eyes full of ashes.

"I'm going to the beach for a while," I said.

I changed and grabbed a towel. On the deck, I picked up a chair and set out. I stopped at the top of the dunes, baffled by the landscape.

A wrack line stretched up and down the beach as far as I could see—a mass of seaweed several yards wide and as high as two feet in places. Even from the dunes, I could smell the detritus, could smell the summer and the seventies. For all our navel-gazing narcissism, and searching for self- and sexual fulfillment, the approaching close of the Me Decade was feeling like the summer's close. Both were snakes' nests of deception and disillusionment. Morality had slithered away long ago and taken meaning with it.

Sitting in my chair, wondering how bad our bad ending might be, I watched seaweed swirling in the cresting waves before they washed it ashore to rot and die.

Hours later, I approached the deck slowly, not wanting to disrupt the earnest conversation finally under way. I had a sense of progress if not resolution. Still, neither of them smiled as I climbed the steps. Terry went to the beach, and I sat down alone with Tricia for the first time since Nona's.

"Houston," I said. "Tell me."

I already had Jack's version: he had called me from the hotel as soon as she'd left him there. Now, as I combined her account with his, similarities exceeded differences. But the differences were what mattered. I suppose the truth lay somewhere in the middle, without angry reds and blinding whites, without the midnight-black of selective memory, without the grays they dabbled in to muddy their guilt and failures. Prosecutor and defender for both, judge and jury for neither, I deposed and cross-examined her as diligently as I had deposed and cross-examined him. Husband and wife were equally convincing.

I know this much to be true. Both Jack and Tricia were apprehensive. Jack said "nervous": he knew the summer had changed her and didn't know what to expect. Tricia said "uneasy": she hoped to shore up her courage to divorce him but was afraid Patricia would intervene.

He didn't meet her at the airport as promised. He'd reserved a limo to bring her to the restaurant where he was waiting.

First glimpses.

As she followed the maître d' to his table, Jack found her classically beautiful, as always, but with a sexiness that was new. He thought it was the tan. She was wearing blue, his favorite color, and the sterling pendant he'd given her for her birthday. She looked like she'd stepped out of Vogue rather than off a plane.

Tricia saw Jack in the flicker of the three tall candles. She thought he looked thinner and that his hair was grayer, but he was handsome and familiar in every way: custom-made suit, white shirt, silk tie, a Scotch, a cigarette. He looked overwhelmed but flashed a smile.

They embraced and clung to each other longer than either had intended. They began a stilted conversation, but relaxed over dinner and a California sauvignon blanc he'd discovered and known she would love.

He wanted to listen first, which was a first, and she realized how little she could reveal about life on the island. When she defaulted to her reading list, he remained surprisingly attentive. He asked questions, and though she thought them superficial, she wasn't sure.

He talked about clients—mostly new ones—and ad campaigns, how well I was doing with Kiawah. She asked about the audit. He asked to save that for later.

Waiting for dessert, and bolstered by a fourth Macallan 18, he confessed feeling like they were on their first date.

She said she felt that way too. "I will never forget how you coerced me into dinner and turned on your unqualified charm for twenty-four hours straight."

"I am much less sure of myself tonight," he said.

She found herself wondering if she'd had too much wine, in spite of lessons learned at Nona's. She wondered if sex with Jack would be different now, if she would come, and if she would cry.

She had crème brûlée and coffee.

He had coffee. And a cough. It was shallow, but once it kicked in, it lingered.

"Bronchitis," he said, and looking away, he unloaded. "I'm selling a fifty-one percent interest in the company."

She went blank, face and mind, for a moment. He turned his eyes back to hers, and took a long sip of Scotch.

"I'm in a goddamn mess. I have no choice."

"I'm sorry, Jack," she said, meaning it. She asked to hear more, saying she wanted to understand and help if she could.

He was touched but said, "It's complex. You only need to know that I will stay on as president and CEO for three years after closing. After that, I may sell the rest of it, or if I'm able, buy it back." He cleared his throat and, looking pained, swallowed several times. "This has changed everything—my priorities, me." He loosened the knot in his tie slightly. "I want to slow down, and for the first time in my life, I want children."

When she began to cry, she knew he thought she was overjoyed. But she was drowning in his sea change, even though Terry had taught her to swim. Murphy—or God—never ran out of wrenches and temptations.

She stopped crying and drank a glass of port. He drank a Rusty Nail. Both were drunk when they left for the hotel.

From that point forward, their accounts differ. What happened in Houston became an accusatory he-said, she-said tale.

Jack said:

The moment he opened the door of their hotel room, Patricia announced she wanted a room with two beds, or her own room, because she'd grown accustomed to sleeping alone. Once inside, he told her she was ridiculous. Then he apologized. Three goddamn times. Three. He tried to kiss her—tenderly, he said.

"I won't," she said. "You've had too much Scotch."

He was confounded. "Won't what? Kiss me? Have sex with me? Share a room with me?"

"I've got my period. I know you don't—"

"Are you refusing me?"

"Yes. I'm saying no."

"With your newfound independence, Patricia, get your own goddamn room." He had kept his voice steady and quiet, but might have sworn under his breath as he calmly—calmly—left her side.

But Tricia said:

Once inside the room, he backed her against the wall. She'd forgotten the harsh demands and taste of his mouth, the urgency of his hands. She felt violated. She forced herself to ask—*ask*—if he would stop. And she asked if he would mind getting another room, a double.

"Explain this to me," he said, "because I don't understand. You are my wife. We've been apart for nine weeks." Then he shouted, "Are you refusing me?"

She told him she had a right to say no and she was getting another room.

Jack said:

When she brushed past him to call the desk, he lost his goddamn temper. He grabbed her wrists with his left hand, and in trying to fight him, she fell back against the wall. He'd never seen her like that, and in the scuffle, he grabbed the neckline of her dress and ripped it open.

Tricia said:

As she struggled to escape him and start toward the phone, he called her "a ridiculous excuse of a wife." That he was wild-eyed, and that if he'd killed her, he would have been acquitted for temporary insanity. That she was frightened. He began to cough, allowing her to break away, but he grabbed the V-neckline of her dress and ripped it. The bodice fell away.

They concurred that the jellyfish sting suspended time.

According to Tricia:

She began to cry, because she knew that, except for the sting, he would have raped her. "What have you done to yourself?" he asked, as if it were her fault.

"I was swimming, Jack. I was stung."

"Swimming, playing tennis, finding yourself on an island—all so you can refuse me?"

She knew the look, saw the fuse sizzling. She knew how to

stop it but couldn't bring herself to beg. "I refused you because I can't stand you."

The veins at his temples darkened. He clenched his jaw.

Silently, she counted backward from ten. At four, Patricia interceded. "I didn't mean it, Jack. I'm so sorry."

But according to Jack:

He saw the worst of the welts on her breast. Shocked, he slipped the dress off her shoulders. She looked as if she'd been whipped. His recollection of their dialogue was much like hers, except:

She did not stop at "I cannot stand you." She added, "In bed. I can't stand being touched by you. I hate it. I always have."

She was so loud, Jack said, so belligerent and drunk, that he was sure someone would come to their door. He had no choice but to shut her up. He backhanded her across the mouth and nose. Both bled profusely. She probably should have had her lip stitched.

They ended up in an overstuffed chair and a half. She cried and he held her. She said they could never make things work.

He apologized, tried to explain the stress he was under, and talked about the sea change. He wanted a child, he said. He wanted to give her a child. And he wanted her because he loved her.

They got into bed and lay like dead bodies on the funeral pyre of their marriage. Jack said he remembered looking at the clock as late as 3:40 a.m.; Tricia said she remembered 4:15.

Jack said he lay thinking of things he wanted to tell her but couldn't bring himself to.

Tricia lay thinking of Terry's hands, she said. Of Terry sometimes asking her to keep her eyes open when they made love.

When she woke the following morning, Jack was talking on the phone.

"Aaron, what if?" he was saying. He laid out scenarios she couldn't follow. All she heard was "What if? What if?"

She stopped listening. What if Terry didn't want her forever? What if she asked and he said no? What if there were too many pretty girls in Texas or on the pro tennis circuit? What if Tricia/Patricia came out of the summer alone?

It didn't matter. Gingerly she ran her fingers over the bruise on her face. She had to do it but wasn't going to now, now that he'd struck her for the first time. Today she would only hint. Her unshakable decision and explanation would come in a letter she'd write from Kiawah, where she would be miles away and safe. Then she would leave the island, maybe even hide until his explosion was surely over and he'd accepted the change.

By the time he hung up the phone, Jack had found a way to restructure and rescue the company and Tricia had packed and was ready to go. Back to the island, she told him, to finish the summer, to decide if the marriage could be saved and if she wanted to try.

They told me, separately, every word they'd said, every thought.

"Patricia, you have every right to walk out." He took a step forward and she flinched. "Christ. I'm inept. I admit it. I don't know how to make you happy, not instinctively. But hear me, princess, I will learn." He forced a limp smile. "If you think we need counseling . . . I'm willing. I want to give you a family. Isn't that what you want?"

"You're saying that now? It's too late."

He looked at his watch. "What time is your plane?"

She shook her head sadly. "That's not what I meant. It's too late in our marriage."

"I'm not even fifty."

"We have too many problems."

He held out his hands to her but she wouldn't take them. "I won't let you leave."

"The flight's at eleven. I'm going to be on it."

"I'm not talking about Kiawah." He threw his hands up. "Our marriage. I won't let you leave our marriage. I won't give up our marriage any more than I'll give up TCC."

"You love me as much as the agency? Lovely, Jack."

"That's not what I meant."

"This is hopeless. We're hopeless."

"No." He turned to the wall, slammed it with his fist. "No." He placed both palms on the wall, took a step toward it and, elbows bent, leaned in. He hung his head, then laid his forehead on the wall. She squeezed his shoulder as she walked past him to answer a porter's knock, and turned back to her husband after her luggage had been rolled away. Jack had recovered, but he looked like a stranger—hapless in pajamas instead of a suit.

"I can save my company," he said. "For Christ's sake, let me do it. Then I'll give everything to our marriage. I'll save it too. Whatever it takes."

"I'm going to Kiawah, Jack."

"Please give me a chance."

"I'll think about what you've said."

He nodded, as if relieved, as if sure he'd convinced her, and like always, won. "I'll come in two weeks," he said. "Labor Day weekend, as planned."

When Jack called me from Houston to tell me his version of what had happened, he also told me that weeks ago he'd rejected the plan Aaron Silver had devised in New York.

"I couldn't do it," he said. "It was criminal. I'm not a thug. I'm not my father. My only other choice was to let TCC go so I found a buyer, Lynn. I have a contract ready for execution and a closing in October. But I won't have to do it now. The change in Patricia changed me too—invigorated me, made me want to fight again. I talked to Aaron this morning. I've found a way to hang on."

I congratulated him, and he told me what he had not told his wife, saying someone needed to know.

He had seen Adam Scofus the day before. He had a mass in his right lung and was having a lung biopsy on Monday morning at 10:00 a.m. The procedure was simple, the recovery quick—an overnight stay in the hospital followed by a few days of recuperation in the hotel. He didn't expect complications, though he hadn't stopped smoking as ordered. He had hoped to have Patricia with him but she'd gone back to Kiawah. He would fly back to New York on Friday alone and to Charleston on the first of September for the holiday weekend.

I processed little beyond mass and biopsy. I sank to the floor, sat with my back against the wall. "You need to tell her," I forced myself to say. "She deserves to know." I urged him to call the airport, have them page her. I asked him to let me tell her when she got back to the island, but he was determined not to manipulate her with a possible malignancy.

"Shall I come to Houston then?" I said.

"Why? It's a bronchoscopic biopsy, a thirty-to sixty-minute procedure."

"I don't like empty hospital waiting rooms while anyone is under general anesthesia. Including you, Jack." He said nothing. "Especially you."

And there it was. Cards on the table. Unintentionally, but in those last two words, he and I both heard everything I'd sworn never to feel. I waited for him to fire me for falling in love with him. Instead, he lit up and inhaled.

"Dear God, Jack. You've got to quit. Please."

It wasn't business anymore. It was love and fear. It was Jack. It was me.

It was Tricia, who cared as little about him as she did about TCC.

"May I come to Houston?" He smoked, and I waited, biting

my lip, chewing my knuckles, squeezing my eyes shut against tears, acting like his wife.

"Lynn," he said, sounding like a father. "You understand me better than anyone else does or ever will. But I understand you too, better than you understand yourself."

"Do you understand that I—"

"Listen to me, Lynn."

I held my breath to hold back—God forbid—a sob. I pulled in my knees, tilted my chin toward the ceiling. It was a TCC commandment: no matter what happens, do not cry. Not in his presence. He hated tears.

"If you forget everything I've taught you about advertising," he said, "about the industry or running a company, that's fine. But remember this: You do not love me. You do not want me." He paused, giving weight to what would come next. "What you want, Lynn, is to *be* me."

I lay down on the floor, alone in the house and my life. He went on.

"And you have the brain, and the drive, and the will to do it. You can lead. You can manage.

You could run my agency, or your own. You don't love me. You want to *be* me."

I rolled my head side to side in dizzying disagreement as silence pushed us further apart.

"Lynn," he said. "I've asked too much of you for far too long. I'm sorry. I'll have a helluva learning curve, but in fairness to you and my wife and for the sake of my marriage, from this point forward, I won't need your help with Patricia. I'm on my own."

I knew then I had to leave the agency and wondered whether two weeks' notice would be fair.

On the deck, watching Terry ride out the summer and

seaweed, wave after wave, I confirmed for Tricia that a sea change had occurred, that if she'd ever doubted that Jack loved her, she could not doubt it now.

She frowned, her eyes dark with sadness. "Part of me is sorry, even mourning. Part of me is afraid of him, of his temper. I'm going to write to him tonight, a long letter. I'll tell him it's over and why it would never work, though I don't know how to explain things in a way he'll understand."

I resisted the impulse to say: *I don't know how to tell you he has a tumor in his lung.*

"But I have two weeks to figure things out." She turned her gaze to Terry, and a few waves later, added, "I have fourteen days, but I need your help."

Your husband needs yours. He's sick. He needs you. I only thought these things.

"Terry is leaving tomorrow. He'll go home for a week and then to Austin. I'll go back to New York, get a lawyer and file. I'll have to fight Jack, won't I?"

She didn't wait for an answer, telling me without words that she didn't need my help. "Starting tomorrow, Terry doesn't want us to see each other or even talk by phone until the divorce is final. I won't go to Austin until then."

I watched Terry walk toward us, looking like Adonis. I thought about Jack, who had asked too much of me. I looked at Tricia, who had overcome Patricia, and suddenly I was weary of them all. Terry smiled at me. He kissed Tricia lightly and dropped to one knee, a shackle of seaweed around his ankle, just below a jellyfish sting. *He is marked,* I thought. *Doomed.* He kissed her as if he couldn't stop, as he always had, as if I weren't even there or didn't matter. "I'm going to get a shower," I said.

For too long I'd lived in the middle of Jack and Patricia, and Tricia and Terry, consumed vicariously by the pleasures and pains, ups and downs, and thrills and abuses of their relationships. While I knew in my heart that all three loved me as I loved them, I felt used, used up, alone, and no longer needed.

I decided I should go back to New York the following day, regroup on Sunday, and on Monday start looking for a job and a life. I stayed in my room for hours. I tried to draft a letter but couldn't get beyond *I'm writing to resign.* I tried to work, to nap, to pack my clothes. In the late afternoon, I gave up and went downstairs to an empty house.

I didn't know where Tricia and Terry had gone.

But I did know after answering a phone call that Tricia didn't have fourteen days, or even fourteen hours. She had two at most.

Jack had changed his mind. He was in the airport. In Charleston. He wanted me to pick him up.

I tried to tell myself this was Tricia's problem—lie, sin, issue. But it wasn't. I'd deceived Jack too. I remembered the hurt in his eyes when he discovered Bill Kiernan's failure of loyalty and I remembered his anger. How much greater this hurt and anger would be. There was Houston too now, the latest footstep he had followed along his father's road.

You want to *be* me, he'd said, and I tried to, with all my left-brained might. But I couldn't think calmly and develop a plan. All I could do was panic.

With the Mustang no longer in the driveway, I assumed Tricia and Terry were returning it. To Hertz? At the airport? They could have saved me a trip. But they would have needed the Porsche for the drive home, and it was in the garage.

I called the tennis pro shop, but Terry wasn't there and neither was Baze. I wasn't sure Terry had even told Baze she was married. I wasn't sure he'd mustered the tolerance for the *I-told-you-so* sure to come from his friend who had called her bad news from the start. I called the villa but no one answered.

I began filling garbage bags with Terry's things, wondering how he would feel about being trashed, or more aptly, erased. I started with the bathroom—toiletries and the jock strap on the doorknob—then went to the bedroom for clothes, tennis magazines, a can of tennis balls, his course catalog. I drew the first bag closed and started a second with *Peter Pan*; I knew the book was hers but associated it so strongly with him that it had to go. I emptied the top drawer of the bedside table, glad to have found a bag of pot.

I started toward the kitchen, lugging two bags behind me. Sunlight darted through the sliding glass door, caught the crystal jar on the coffee table, and bounced like a laser into my eyes. The Peanut M&M's were the deadest of giveaways. Their happy primary colors screamed kid, college kid, a kid in a candy store, a lost boy, a lover boy, in love with another man's wife. I emptied the M&M's into the bag with his clothes.

I disconnected the Atari, added it to the bag. I packed up albums—*Ol' Waylon* and Kenny Rogers's *Love or Something Like It*—while imagining Patricia explaining a newfound love of country music to Jack. She might manage that but would be hard-pressed to claim Jethro Tull, Pink Floyd, or the Who as favorites. I took Springsteen and left Streisand. Took KC and the Sunshine Band, left the soundtrack of *Grease*.

Two gallons of milk in the refrigerator looked wrong. So did the beer. Ice cream? Garbage disposal. Flip-flops on the deck, stray wristbands on the living room floor, a roach clip in an ashtray, and I was through with Terry. I set the overnight bag he'd taken to Atlanta, his tennis bag, and both trash bags in the foyer.

I turned my attention to Tricia but left things as they were. A tennis dress wouldn't raise suspicions. The summer clothes, which were definitely not New York or anything I would have purchased for her, were believable manifestations of her new self.

I locked Terry in the trunk of my car to bake and suffocate. I could lie about traffic jams and car trouble. I could say I had to go to elaborate, time-consuming lengths so as not to spoil Jack's surprise. But I could not show up at the airport more than an hour late.

I stopped at the villa and left a note on the door: *Baze—Find Terry and keep him away from the beach house. Wait for my call. I'll explain. —Lynn.* I hadn't risked leaving a note for Terry or Tricia at the beach house. I couldn't be sure they would return before I did, with Jack. I drove a mile or two off the island before realizing Jack would need to put his luggage in the trunk. I turned around and drove back to the villa, where I left Terry's things unattended outside the front door.

"God," I murmured, getting back in my car. "I will never pull this off."

Unknowns and variables made the drive to the airport the longest forty minutes I'd ever spent in a car. I wondered if I could earn redemption by telling Jack the truth on the way to the island; I wondered if Nona had somehow reached him and told him; if melting chocolate would irreversibly stain Terry's clothes; if Tricia, should she return before I did, would deduce why I'd evicted her lover; if Jack already had a prognosis from Scofus; how I would feel when I saw him.

Standing on the sidewalk, his bags on a cart, he looked hot, tired, thin, and impatient.

"Hello, Lynn," he said as he got into the car. He complained, but with a smile: "What took you so long?" He waved my apology into acceptance, smoked, and coughed.

"The biopsy?"

"Waiting on results."

"Honestly?" I thought he was lying.

"Scofus will call. From this point forward, though, it's Sloan Kettering. Adam will consult. If I'm in New York instead of Houston, I'll work more productively. The restructure is a go, and I'll fry Bill Kiernan's ass in the process."

My circuitous route through downtown Charleston gave him ample time to detail strategy and tactics. As he assessed key issues, options, and risks, I ran a mental gamut of what he might walk into at home—anything from apparent normalcy to hot sex under way on the kitchen floor.

"For most of the summer," Jack said as I pulled into the driveway, "I've felt I was going to lose what it has taken me twenty years to build, everything I've fought for and worked for and that is exclusively mine. But I'm back, Lynn. Goddamnit, I'm back."

And he seemed to be. I silently ran through Tricia's litany. *I-me-mine power. Control. Caretaking. A proclivity to intimidate. Conceit masquerading as confidence. Duplicity. Machine-gun laughter. Fast, cold, humiliating. Lovemaking, the same.*

And something else that I couldn't remember or refused to.

He opened the car door for me. "I'll come back for my luggage. I want to see her."

I followed him to the door; he turned the knob. Locked.

"I don't think she's here," I said, handing him my key. He inserted but did not turn it. He turned to me instead.

"Where would she be?"

I have no idea how long I contemplated my answer.

"Lynn?"

But long enough for me to remember *the something else.*

"Lynn?" He dropped his hand to his side.

"I think she has a tennis lesson."

Extreme volatility.

§

I unlocked the door and stopped behind him in the foyer, thinking he was reacquainting himself with his second home, taking in the view across the room, or maybe remembering, as I was, the last time he'd been there with me. But when I stepped to his side, I realized he was captivated by his wife, coming over the dunes. Alone. In the sliding glass frame and unaware, she climbed the steps and dropped the beach bag on the deck. The summer was in her hair, the sun was in her skin, the island was in her lazy movement, and Terry was in her blood. Jack saw all but the last.

"Kiawah agrees with her," he said, still unmoving.

A year ago, even in the same white bikini, she would have appeared Princess Grace pretty, sculpted, and virginal. Now she exuded a primal desire, begging to be sated.

The sting had disappeared excepting three broad pink slashes across her breast and two on her inner thigh. As she brushed sand from her feet and ankles, the right strap of her suit slid from her shoulder. Without adjusting it, she jumped into the deep end of the pool, disappeared, reappeared, and swam to the ladder.

"Jesus God," I read on her lips as she saw us. Forgetting her towel and bag, forgetting she was wet, she joined us inside.

"Hello, princess."

"Jack," she said as he crossed the room to embrace her.

Over his shoulder, her eyes asked frantic questions I couldn't answer. He hugged and kissed her, and still holding her, explained why he was early. She gushed about happiness and surprise, eyes racing around the room, appreciating my work. She led him to the bar.

"Why don't you fix a drink, Jack? While I change." She called from the bedroom. "Lynn, can you come here for a moment?"

"Fix me a drink?" Jack said, leaving me for her.

I heard the bedroom door close, and moments later, a relentless hacking, which forced him back to me. I gave him water instead of Scotch, but he couldn't shake the cough. It lasted long enough to enable her to dress and return to us.

"Are you all right?" she asked.

"Yes." He looked at me. "Or I will be, with a Scotch."

I went to the bar, thinking he'd mistaken her unease as concern for him.

"I've seen a doctor, Patricia. I'll be fine."

But Patricia was nowhere to be found. I handed him a drink and watched guileful Tricia. She massaged his back, asked what she could do for him, what he wanted for dinner. As Jack pulled her into his lap, guile became sacrilege: she kissed him as if he were Terry. In disbelief, I locked the front door. Uselessly. Terry had a key.

Jack's cough put an end to the kiss. The flight had been a bitch, he said, the layover, too long. He didn't want to go out for dinner—not at the club, and definitely not in Charleston. She offered to make omelets.

"Omelets?" I echoed.

Jack was amused. "A new skill?"

She answered, "Yes."

We had no cheese and Jack needed cigarettes.

"You want them," I said, "You don't need them. Please."

He laughed. "I want, need, and will have them, Lynn."

I volunteered to go the store. I wanted to get away, stop by the villa, find Terry and Baze. But Tricia volunteered to go with me, and Jack, though tired, didn't care to be left behind. After a circular discussion, the three of us piled into my car.

That is why I was on hand, as was Baze, when Patricia's husband met Tricia's lover.

In our cart were fresh mushrooms, spinach, a dozen eggs, and a block of sharp cheddar. Jack added a carton of Viceroys, and Tricia a loaf of bread, but that was the beginning of a spree: bananas, a gallon of ice cream, and four large bags of Peanut M&M's. Either she expected to banish Jack within the hour and welcome Terry back home, or she had decided to declare war and lost her mind in its fog.

"Oh. Laundry detergent," she said.

I turned the cart into the adjacent aisle and stopped so abruptly that she and Jack, three steps behind, bumped into me before halting and pulling even.

In Baze and Terry's cart were four New York strips, two twelve-packs of Michelob, and a six- pack of Heineken. Terry, who was reaching, ironically, for a box of Cheer, took stock of the situation a few seconds later than the rest of us.

God bless Baze, who said, "Hi."

And Tricia, still fighting, lying, and staving off her alter ego, said, "Hi Baze. I'd like you to meet my husband. Jack, this is Chris Bazemore."

They shook hands, and because Baze and Terry had stopped by the courts for a hit after returning the Mustang to the airport, because they were tennis attired and sweaty, Jack said pleasantly, "You're the tennis teacher."

Baze was going to say yes, assuming it would be safer, but Terry spoke up: "No, I am. I'm her teacher."

"Jack Curren." He extended his hand.

Terry started to put the detergent in the cart, changed his mind, and still holding it in his right hand, took the Heineken out of the cart with his left. And there he stood. I imagined him saying he couldn't shake the hand that had struck the woman he loved. And there we all stood, dangerous seconds ticking by, until Terry regained his reason or lost his nerve, put the beer and the detergent in the cart, and accepted Jack's still-outstretched hand.

"Terry Sloan."

The look on his face was worse than what Tricia called his triple break point look, and the heart on his sleeve gave out a soundless *what the fuck*? He looked stoned, but he wasn't. He was a fawn in the headlights—no, a boy in the gleam of her wedding rings.

"How's she doing?" Silence.

"She's doing great," Baze said. "Helluva backhand."

"Really?" Jack seemed pleased.

"She'll backhand you to death."

Jack looked at Tricia, who was looking at Terry, who was looking at the floor.

"Put the Heineken back," Baze said. "Go get some St. Pauli Girl."

"Yeah." But he didn't move.

"We've got everything," I announced, turning to go.

"Tricia, are you coming tonight?" It was a squawk, thin and reedy, from Terry. "At eight? For your lesson?"

Jesus Christ, I thought. *She's going to say yes.*

Instead, I heard machine-gun laughter. "Not tonight. I just got in from New York."

"I'll call you, Terry." Her return of squawk was high and guilty.

"Get the beer," Baze said.

And I said, "Let's go."

Jack took Patricia's hand and led the way. I followed on their heels. Terry called my name, but I didn't stop. I walked on, listening to Baze.

"Damn, Terry. A tennis lesson? Eight o'clock at night? Hey, wait, man. Don't."

At the register, we took our places in what felt like a police lineup or a line of prisoners, bound and facing a firing squad: Jack first, then Patricia, our cart, me, Terry, clutching the Cheer again, and Baze, empty-handed. He'd abandoned their cart amid the soaps, mops, and cleansers, which would never freshen our air, wash out our dirt, or bleach our stains.

While Jack and I faced the cashier, Tricia stared at the automatic door. Exit. Out. Over. I glanced at her, then at Terry, and back at her. Jack lit a cigarette and held it between his lips as he took cash from his money clip. She turned her head slowly and slightly toward Terry.

"Don't," I ordered. She stopped. She didn't.

"Lynn," Terry said. I shook my head without looking his way. I heard a shallow breath, full of panic.

"Don't," Baze said. "Don't say anything." And of course Terry said, "Tricia."

"Don't," I said.

And of course she did. She turned. And Jack turned too.

"I've got eight in the morning open, if you want your lesson then."

"She doesn't," Jack said.

"I can't," said his princess.

"Yeah, okay."

I looked from Terry to Tricia, praying they wouldn't do the cheek thing, and I looked at Jack. He threw a final glance at Terry, without suspicion, malice, or competitive fire. He did not see an enemy, a threat, or a rival. Just an annoyance. A harmless, pesky fly.

We turned out the beach house lights at ten—after omelets, after Patricia pretending to read W. S. Merwin while Jack and I reviewed photos for the cover of the new Kiawah brochure.

I couldn't sleep. I called Baze in the middle of the night, but he said he couldn't talk: he was on a suicide watch, and the guy he was watching had gotten fucked up, taken the bicycle, and disappeared.

"I'm going out to look for him. And get this: he said he

didn't understand what had happened, but he wanted to fucking kill somebody; he just didn't know who. I voted for Tricia. Do you want to vote?"

He hung up, and I continued to hold the receiver. I heard a door open downstairs. I heard a door close. Front, sliding, master—I didn't know which. I heard someone moving about. I didn't know who.

At the railing of the catwalk, I looked down through the darkness of the house to the deck. I saw the orange glow of Jack's cigarette, a beacon that drew me to him.

"I can't sleep," he said as I sat down beside him. "Time zones?"

"Time zones. Cancer. The company. Take your pick."

I'm writing to resign.

But I wasn't sure I'd be able to. I felt the pull of how things had always been, of whatever it was about Jack.

I'm writing to resign because I fell, Jack. I never thought I would. But I did.

"Did you tell Tricia about the tumor?"

"No."

I felt privileged and smug.

"Suppose it's inoperable," he said.

"Is it?" Barely able to make out his features in the shifting moonlight, I had no idea if he would answer. I took the cigarette from his hand. "I'm smoking this so you won't. I'm trying to save your addicted ass." He chuckled, and I felt closer to him than I had in months. "Did you hear from Adam?" I reached across his body for the ashtray, slowly and by design. "Has something changed? You sounded optimistic this afternoon."

He didn't answer, leaving me certain only of a change in the air. The night smelled of rain. Palms clattered. Waves crashed. Noisy and close to the dunes, they suggested a spring tide.

Suddenly I wanted TCC back; I wanted him back at his desk; I wanted our relationship back. But most of all, I wanted him well again.

"Shouldn't that kid have called her Mrs. Curren?"

My heart jumped like a toad. "Isn't that what he called her?"

"No. He called her *Tricia*. Like you did a moment ago." He lit another cigarette and extinguished it, seeming as addled as Terry had been with the detergent and beer.

"You misheard. I said *Patricia*."

"And I misheard him too?"

He turned toward me, and I looked straight ahead. The moon appeared and disappeared in windblown clouds, like a dolphin swimming in the ocean. I tried to concentrate on the dunes, but the play of light was intermittent and Jack's voice, spellbinding.

"Lynn."

He slid his hand onto my back, and at the nape of my neck his fingers began a massage, pleasurable and therapeutic. When I had taken his phone call in the afternoon, I had raised my shoulders, forced their blades toward one another, and maintained that posture until now. As he worked on the muscles of my neck, I released them, let taut go slack. I relaxed my throat, tongue, and jaw. He spread his fingers out wide across the back of my skull, pressing them and his palm firmly against my head. I rested my uneasy mind in the strength of his hand, thinking that the things I loved in his touch were likely the things Tricia hated.

"Lynn." He leaned toward me, his breath warm along my jaw. I refused to face him, yet felt my mouth open in anticipation.

I'm writing to apply for things as they were, Jack.

"Is she sleeping with him?"

"No." My response was as automatic as the tightening of his

fingers in my hair. With a sudden yank, he forced my chin toward the sky. I arched my back and lifted my rear, trying to relieve the pressure and pull.

"Lynn?" Another yank almost snapped my head off, but he let go and apologized. He picked up a drink I hadn't noticed on the table and finished it. "Don't lie to me, Lynn. My CFO is one thing. My wife is another. But you, Lynn. For Christ's sake." He walked to the edge of the deck, tossed the ice cubes from the glass to the sand below. Little more than a shape in starlight, abandoned by the cloud-covered moon, this vacuous shell of a man turned and faced me. "Is he fucking my wife?"

God. I was sick of the whole damn thing. "Lynn?" said the shadow, sick and humble.

"Don't be ridiculous, Jack."

"Lynn?"

"Of course he is."

I tried to decide why I'd told him. Possibilities:

I couldn't lie any longer.

He trusted me. I couldn't lie to his face.

I fell victim to old habits, to his easy control.

I was afraid of him.

I was sure he already knew.

I was sick of the whole damn thing.

I loved him. I hated him.

I wanted to save their marriage. I wanted to blow it apart.

I wanted the chance I could never have as long as he had Patricia.

I did not want to be him.

I wanted to love him.

And I wanted him to love me.

I waited for my turn as his victim. But he rose. He spoke weakly, with openness he'd never shared, and with obvious difficulty too. "I can feel this thing inside me. It's eaten my company, my marriage too. They're all one insidious, malignant thing now, and it's going to take me down."

He is broken, I thought.

"I'm going back to bed. To Patricia."

He is defeated. He is done.

"I won't let her leave me."

"Jack." I had to say it. "I . . . don't . . . think—" I spoke slowly but wasn't sure he was putting my simple words together. "I don't think you can stop her."

He told me, and the night, and the ocean: "I don't want to be left." A wave crashed. "Lynn." Then another. "Are you inside my head?"

"Yes."

"I don't want to be left," he said. "Alone."

To die, I heard as he went back inside.

I waited several minutes before assuming watch in the hall. I waited to hear Jack's accusation, her denial. Waited for his rage, her weeping. For rape or a beating. I waited for conversation so deadened by the closed door that I had to guess at its meaning—confession, apology, reconciliation? I waited to be needed and heard nothing at all.

I saw Terry at first light, lying on his side in the dunes, one arm above his head as if grasping for something just out of reach. I tried to rouse him, gave up, called Baze, and got his machine. "Damnit, where are you?" I said. "I need you. Terry's here, Baze. Here." I laid out details and concluded, "Please get to the beach and take him home."

The sky lightened, Jack and Patricia slept on, and Terry didn't twitch. I began to fear he'd overdosed and was dying while I twiddled my useless female thumbs and waited on a man to save the day. I went back to the dunes and shook his shoulder. I repeated his name until he grunted and rolled onto his back. He put his hand to his forehead to shield his eyes from my halo of rising sunshine. “What are you doing, Terry? You’ve got to get out of here.”

He sat up slowly, the right side of his body completely covered in sand—sand in his hair, eyebrows, at his temple, on his cheek, in his stubbly beard, even on his lips. The pungent smells of liquor and body odor were seeping from every pore.

He gestured toward the house. “All night long, I watched out.”

“No, you passed out.”

“Well, I’m watching now.”

“Can you even see straight?”

“He might try to hurt her when she tells him about me and her. He hits her.”

“No, he doesn’t.”

He looked indignant. “Whose side are you on?”

“No one’s side. He loves her. That only happened once. He doesn’t hit her.”

“He does, and I’m watching out.” He dropped his head to his knees. “I’m gonna puke.”

“What did you drink? Or take?”

“Every-fucking-thing.”

“Go back to the villa, Terry,” I said. “Throw up there.”

“Don’t watch me puke, Lynn.”

He got up on his knees, retched again and again, and when nothing came up, sat down in the sand. I glanced at the house expecting to see Jack and/or Tricia on the deck, but there was no sign that either had stirred.

“Where’s your bike, Terry?”

“I don’t know.”

“Did you ride up the beach? Where’s your bike?”

“On the side of the house.”

“Jesus.”

"Just go, Lynn, okay?"

"I'll go, if you'll go. To the villa. Go now."

"Okay," he said, exasperated. "As soon as I puke. But watch out for her till I get back."

"You don't need to come back. You need to go home."

He shouted, "O-fucking-kay."

As I started toward the house, a light went on in the kitchen. I didn't look back until I reached the deck. Over my shoulder, I saw Terry—lying on his back, arms and legs sprawling, looking as relaxed as if he were sunning. He was sleeping again.

A light was on in the hall as well as the kitchen. Their bedroom door was closed. The Porsche was not in the garage. I had no way of knowing who had left until Jack emerged from the bedroom an hour later. In the rumpled clothes he'd worn on the plane, he sat down in the kitchen. I had showered, dressed, and drunk three cups of coffee.

"Where is she?" he said.

"The store, I think. We're out of half-and-half."

"We were at the store yesterday."

"We didn't think of it then."

"Where is she?"

"I don't know, Jack. Sit down."

I glanced at the clock—eight thirty—and over Jack's shoulder at the dunes. All I could see were legs—Terry's, knees to feet. I imagined him rolling around as he slept, caking himself with another layer of sand. I imagined Tricia looking for him at the villa, the courts, on the beach.

I gave Jack a cup of coffee. Black.

"I don't know what to do." He drummed his fingers on the table. "I don't know why I didn't suspect it. Or why you didn't tell me, or give even a hint."

"My useless emotions," I said. "Guilt for what you and I

had done. Regret. And, Jack—" I didn't think I could shatter him further. "She is happy."

"What do I do?"

I sighed. "I can't help you anymore."

His eyes filled with tenderness for me, by which I was touched and for which I was grateful. "I understand."

We didn't speak again until he had smoked a cigarette and finished his coffee. He said, "There are no towels in the bathroom."

"The dryer then. Shall I—"

"No, no. I'll get one."

"Your robe is upstairs." I watched him move away from me. "That's a spare. I have another."

Double entendre, and though unintentional, it made me doubly sad. A moment later he came back into the kitchen, towel in hand.

"I don't know what to do."

It hurt me to see him so helpless. So thin, sick, and gray. He looked at the ceiling. I waited, embarrassed for him, but when he leveled his eyes again, I realized I hadn't checked the dryer the day before.

"Does he drop off his clothes for his laundress? Or has he been living here?"

These are the things that amazed me:

Tricia walked in at that moment.

She took a carton of half-and-half from a grocery bag.

She didn't take off her sunglasses, and Jack didn't ask her to.

She didn't argue when Jack suggested they go back to New York right away.

Jack became preoccupied with getting her books back to the city.

Neither of them saw what I saw.

Baze appeared in the dunes and somehow got Terry to his feet.

Terry swayed, resisted, argued, took a swing at Baze, missed, and face-planted in the sand.

Baze threw his hands up and left. *Left*.

Terry rose, climbed to the top of the tallest dune, and stared at the beach house as if he were king of the mountain and the road and all he surveyed.

He started toward us in slow heavy steps.

Patricia was still wearing sunglasses.

Jack was pretending nothing was odd or wrong.

Jack had left the chain saw in the city.

Jack—Sea-Change Jack—was going to accept what had happened. Accept his princess as an adulteress and laundress with a live-in lover and let it all go without a word.

"I'm going to get a shower," Jack said to his wife. "Then I'll pack your books. Lynn, call the airline."

I went to the phone in the kitchen, thankful for a reason to turn away from the glass, from my view of Terry. Terry closing in. T minus thirty seconds. Counting.

Jack started down the hall. Tricia took off her sunglasses and looked at me with mismatched eyes. She had fallen back into the river. She was numb but floating with the current. She had not forgotten how to swim.

She whispered to me, "I'll go to New York. I have to. I'll tell him there. I'm afraid here. Whatever happens he can't find out about Terry. Whatever we do, we have to get out. Get away. Please, let's get off of this island."

"Tricia," I said softly, but I stopped before telling her Jack already knew. *She's right,* I told myself. *We have to get away before the summer implodes.*

"Delta Airlines. This is Janet. How may I assist you today?"

"Jack will need a towel," Tricia said, walking to the laundry room.

"No," I said loudly, giving the word emphatic, unmistakable shape on my lips. And again, close to shouting, I said, "No."

Everyone stopped—Jack in the hall, Tricia at the dryer after opening the door, and the man I was actually trying to deter: Terry came to a halt on the deck.

"May I assist you with a reservation?"

Jack saw Terry.

Tricia took one of Terry's T-shirts from the dryer, wadded it into a ball, pressed it to her cheek, and began to cry. Three sobs, though quiet, drew Jack back to the kitchen.

"Delta Airlines. Janet speaking. May I help you?"

I hung up the phone and looked at Jack, who understood for the first time that his wife loved the man she'd been sleeping and living with, the one on the deck; the one pulling off his T-shirt and using it to brush sand from his face before putting it on again; the one who was young, fit, and strong, with a long healthy life ahead of him.

She loved him. Jack knew it. And he played the only card he had. He coughed, and as if he had willed it, blood spattered his chin and shirt.

"Patricia, I'm dying."

"Jack," she tried to say. But his name was a wisp of air on her lips. She shook her head in shock, guilt, sorrow, and some remnant of her childhood's faith in him.

He began giving her—and me—the information he had, as methodically as if he were Adam Scofus, MD. The tumor in his right lung was malignant and too close to the trachea to be operable. Two lymph nodes were positive. Stage 3 cancer. Radiation would buy time. Adjuvant therapy— chemo—was an option, if he could tolerate it and chose to. Textbook case: Six months. A year at most.

I studied my hands. Patricia hid her face in hers. And Terry knocked on the sliding glass door.

Patricia, seeming not to have heard the knock, went to Jack.

Jack gave me a nod. “Get him out of here,” he said, teeth clenched, lips tight.

I went to Terry. I slid the door open a few inches. “You have to leave.” I closed the door and turned my back as Terry looked across the room and into the kitchen where Patricia was crying in Jack’s arms.

“Shhh,” he said, stroking her hair. “I need you to be strong for me.” Her sunglasses fell from the top of her head as she looked up at him. She smiled as best she could and stopped her tears. She still had not seen Terry. “We need to go home,” Jack said. “Pack your things, princess. As soon as Lynn gets us a flight, the three of us will go to the club for breakfast.”

He coughed again. I thought he’d faked it. Behind me, I heard Terry open the door. “Move, Lynn.”

When I didn’t budge, he said it again, and Tricia turned toward him, eyes opening Jesus God-wide.

“Pack,” Jack said. “I’ve got this. I’ll handle him.” With stiff hands on her shoulders, he shoved her toward the hall. She took three steps and stopped as Jack moved to the center of the living room. I held my position at the door.

Jack’s voice was staff-meeting steady. “Why are you here? What do you want?”

“To talk to Tricia.”

“There’s no one here by that name.” Polite but unyielding.

I moved left, allowing Terry inside. Four sets of eyes fell to his feet and the sand on the carpet. He seemed suddenly unsure of himself, and though Jack was yet to shower, shave, and dress in fresh clothes, he projected intelligence and a strong sense of self.

Terry looked past Jack to Tricia. "Did he hurt you?" She shook her head. "Did you tell him?"

"No." She cast her eyes down.

"That's why I came. To help you tell him."

"Tell me what?" Jack asked, recapturing Terry's attention. He pulled his lighter and a pack of cigarettes from his shirt pocket and offered one to Terry. The gesture caught Terry off guard: he considered accepting but then refused, and Jack laughed softly before lighting up. "Are you here for your laundry?"

"I—what?"

"Lynn, get his clothes."

I started toward the dryer.

"Patricia, pack. We're leaving."

I stopped just shy of the kitchen, waiting for her to obey, but she was paralyzed by the danger or absurdity of the situation: The four of us in one room, the bizarre dialogue, the confrontation, the absence of anger and fisticuffs. We had only shock and sand, a cancer-ridden husband and a hungover lover, guilt and extraordinary need. In all four corners of the room, in all four hearts, we had love and desperation.

"Don't get his clothes," Tricia said quietly to me. "I don't want you to."

I turned back around on the chessboard as the pawn in the middle. I looked at the knight in sandy armor.

"I'm in love with Tricia," Terry said. Jack laughed with his eyes. "I see that."

"I love Tricia." He turned to her, expecting *I love him too.*

"She'll send you a postcard from New York."

"She's not going."

We watched Jack smoke. One slow drag. Two. Three.

"You're deluded," he said to Terry. "You're laughable."

I looked at Tricia and saw her doubting the dream for the first time, seeing a boy who would never read Tolstoy or Virginia Woolf, not because he chose not to, but because he wasn't able; seeing a collegiate tennis player with a professional pipe dream and a need for Nona or someone like her; seeing an athlete who had the upper body of *David* and the legs of *Hercules* and knew a lot of pretty girls in Texas.

"She's going with me," Terry said. "To Austin. She's going to grad school, like she wants."

"Really?" He fired a round of rat-a-tat-tats.

"I am, Jack." She was breathless with fright.

"Don't be ridiculous, Patricia."

"I'm leaving you," she said.

He seemed unfazed. He laughed again, but this time without ammunition. "Fine. If that's what you want. But be sure."

I believe to this day that if things had stopped there, Jack would have let her go. His façade was not yet tarnished, and his ego seemed, though it wasn't, intact. He was afraid of his illness, but he'd face it alone, summon his final *whatever it takes.*

But Terry was soaring now. Game, set, match.

"You don't understand her," he told Jack. "You don't even know who she is. She's told me things she's never told you or anybody. And she'll never tell you. Only me. I'm first and only."

Jack looked at me for confirmation and I shrugged. He looked at Tricia.

"Yes," she said, but she had hesitated.

Jack looked at me again, pleading with his eyes. He gave out a short dry cough.

"She doesn't love you." Terry proclaimed. He might as well have fist pumped.

"Stop," Tricia murmured. Then she said firmly, "Don't, Terry. That's enough."

Terry seemed to be dancing up the centerline. "I asked her once. You know what she said?"

Jack coughed again and turned to Patricia.

Terry leapt over the net. "She said yes, no, maybe."

Jack whispered to his wife. I heard. Terry didn't. "Please, Patricia. I am sick. I don't want to be left."

"She said maybe she loves you. But she doesn't. Tricia loves me."

"Patricia," Jack whispered, "I am dying."

With that, Tricia gave in to Patricia and to a cloudburst of guilt and fear, straight over center court.

"And you hit her," Terry yelled. "You fucking hit her."

"Oh get out," Patricia cried. "I can't do it now. I tried but I can't *now*. Do you understand what I'm saying? *Now*, I just can't."

Silence thundered. Shock struck like lightning.

"What?" Terry said, triple break point in his eyes.

"Get out, Terry."

"Tricia, wait."

"It's over. We're done. Now get out."

Jack coughed up a spot of blood for good measure. Terry went to the deck, and facing the ocean, stood still.

Patricia, still crying, wiped blood from Jack's mouth with curious fingers.

"I'd like to get breakfast," he said.

I followed Patricia down the hall. She wanted to shower, she told me, to start the day over— and the summer, and her life over. As she disappeared into the bathroom, I went to the bedroom deck. I saw Terry on the beach, sitting on the swing where he and Tricia had sat together so often.

I felt Jack beside me. I don't know how. At the same time I felt numb all over. "Scofus called?" I said woodenly.

"I called him," Jack said. He tilted his chin toward Terry. "What the hell is he doing?"

"I don't know. I'm going upstairs." Upstairs, to gather myself so I could help him, to get it together so I wouldn't cry.

"Get the flight," he said, and as I left the room, he added, "and show tickets for tomorrow."

"Tomorrow is Sunday. A matinee?"

"Something she'd like to see. Something I'd like, if there is such a goddamn thing."

I took a long hot shower—my second of the day. When I was dressed again, I went back to my desk, but instead of calling for flight reservations or play tickets, I flipped through my Rolodex for Adam Scofus's number. I'd never met him, but we'd spoken often on the phone, and though I knew Jack would be furious, I dialed.

"Lynn," he said, "How are you? I assume Jack told you what we found."

"Yes. Patricia asked me to call you. She wants to make sure she understands the situation exactly as you related it to Jack. She's afraid he's keeping something from her. She wants clear notes on everything you told him." Dead silence. "If that's permissible. I certainly understand confidentiality, and I can have her call you personally if you'd prefer." I tightened my grip on my pen. "Is this inconvenient? Do you have time now?"

"It won't take much time," he said. "He called me this morning before rounds and I told him four things. One, if I ever see him smoking a cigarette again, I'm going to beat his ass. Two, Rick Roberts is the surgeon at Sloan Kettering I want him to see, and I'll call Rick on Monday morning. Three, the tumor is a hamartoma that should be excised as soon as possible. And four, of course, it's benign."

I walked to the window.

Where there's a problem, I could hear Jack saying.

I tried to tell myself he had committed no greater

transgression than Patricia and I had. He'd just done it all at once, with one nasty lie, instead of meting out an untruth over months. But he'd claimed to be *dying.*

Whatever it takes.

I looked at the beach. Terry was no longer there. I considered telling Jack I knew, or telling Patricia, or telling both. But all I wanted was to get them on a plane and away from me. I was sure he'd want me back in New York too now, sure that my promotion had arisen from his desire to have me oversee his wife, not a new account, on the island. I made their reservations for a one o'clock flight. It was already ten thirty. I would insist on staying behind to ship the books, make sure the beach house and Kiawah account were in order, and drive the Porsche back by midweek.

I'm writing to resign.

I went downstairs, where Jack was in the kitchen, taking off his shirt.

"Ruined," he said, tossing it in the trash. "I'm coughing up so much blood I don't see how I'll make it six months."

I glimpsed the shirt before the lid of the can snapped shut. He was right: a lot of blood.

He disappeared down the hall and reappeared fifteen minutes later, having showered and dressed, looking refreshed and—damn him—relaxed. Then Patricia joined us, hair done, makeup done—eyes lined, shadowed, thick with mascara. Both eyes blue. Literally. Figuratively.

The shirtwaist dress she was wearing made me think of her island clothes. I hoped she'd leave them at the beach house forever so the ones in the dryer wouldn't be lonely.

Jack smiled at Patricia and me. Smiled and said, "Let's go eat."

I stayed in the terminal until their plane had taken off, and on the drive home stopped by the villa. I was hoping Baze had put Terry on a plane too, to Austin. I needed to sit alone with my friend and tell him everything. I knocked but no one answered.

I sat on the deck of the beach house for hours, knowing I couldn't eat or sleep. I left four messages on Baze's machine, but he didn't call until nine.

"I need to talk," I said. "Can you come over?" I wondered why he had to think about it.

"I'm hanging out with Terry."

"Can you break away?" I wondered why he'd spoken so softly.

"No."

"Just for an hour?" I felt selfish but couldn't stop myself. "Even an hour would help."

"Where in the hell is Tricia? Where's Jack? Or is it Dick?"

"In New York. They're gone. If you could—"

"I'm in Charleston. I'm with Terry."

I sank in a pool of rejection. Jack had chosen Patricia; Patricia had chosen Jack; Baze had chosen Terry; and no one had chosen—would ever choose—me.

"We're at the hospital," Baze said.

What's wrong? and *What happened?* dissolved like the acrid medicinal powder of a capsule on my tongue.

"Terry rode his bike home this morning, and about a mile from the beach house, he was hit by a car."

"Oh Jesus."

"It was still morning—maybe ten. I was going back to the beach again to try to get him to leave, and I found him sitting on the side of the road, bleeding like hell but conscious. He said the car was going really slow when it hit him. It just kept going."

"Oh my God."

"Hit and run. On Kiawah Drive. Imagine that."

"No, that's impossible, Baze." I had driven to and from the

club for breakfast, to the airport and home again, and had seen no trace of an accident on the island's main road.

"Strange thing, though." Sarcasm oozed through the phone line, filled my ear like an abscess. "There wasn't a scratch on the bike, nary a one. And Terry's in intensive care."

The lights were low in the ICU waiting room, and the temperature felt just above freezing, even at the door. At the far end of the room, in one corner, an elderly man slept soundly in a chair; and in the other, a doctor spoke earnestly to a middle-aged couple while the woman nodded and cried. On my right, a campsite had been deserted: a pillow and blanket had been left on a couch, pages of the *News and Courier* had fallen to the floor, and two Styrofoam cups of black, surely cold coffee sat on an end table.

Baze had hung up as soon as he'd told me. I'd known he wasn't going to call back. And he'd known I would come. I sat down beside him on the black vinyl couch to my left. He looked tired and disheveled. We didn't say hello or try to smile.

"I don't know how to call his mom," he said. "I called the house in Orlando, and his dad said she left him. They're divorced now. I don't think Terry even knows. That must have been why she was calling the villa so much, but Terry never called her back. His dad said he has no idea where she is, which I'm sure is a lie. And—get this—his dad says, 'Keep me posted.' Terry's in a coma, and he wants me to keep him posted."

"A coma."

"A medically induced coma. But just the same—keep him posted? And the prick is a doctor. He's a surgeon."

I took his hand. "Tell me."

With difficulty he catalogued the injuries. "Both eyes are swollen shut and purple; the left is worse than the right. There's a cut across his chin with a ton of stitches. His right cheek is broken, and they'll have to wire it back together."

"His cheek."

"Yeah." Baze touched mine.

"Ironic." I touched his.

"He has two cracked ribs and one broken rib. All on one side. I've forgotten which one. There's a little bleeding—" He stopped, let go of my hand, leaned his head back against the wall. "His brain is bleeding."

I watched the doctor leave the room, and when the woman sobbed sharply, Baze sat up again and pressed his palms together. He didn't seem to be praying but trapping control, which had wavered with his last four words and threatened to depart.

I was praying.

"Bleeding, but not too much. It's subdural, they said, which means it's in a layer of tissue around the brain that protects the brain, except for a really bad hit, in which case, the brain bounces around, hits the skull, and bruises and bleeds. Since the skull can't expand like muscles or skin, the blood gets trapped, and the brain can swell." He paused. "Am I making sense?"

"You're doing fine."

"That's what the first CT scan showed, some bleeding, a little swelling. They did a second one just before you got here, and nothing was getting worse. They induced the coma to give his brain plenty of oxygen. If there's enough oxygen, there won't be any damage, or as much damage. Less damage, faster healing. Tomorrow they'll do another scan, and if things are still looking good, they'll gradually stop the drip and bring him out of the coma."

"What kind of—" I couldn't say *damage.*

Baze battled the situation in the only way he could. "I'm predicting a one hundred percent recovery, which is not only possible, according to the neurosurgeon, but probable." He made a circle with his fingers and thumb. "Zero damage. A bagel. He'll be banged up and confused at first, which is normal, but then he'll be okay."

"Good," I said, as if he already were.

"When I found him, he was sitting on somebody's lawn, bleeding like crazy, all over his face and head. I got him in the car, grabbed some towels at the villa. I couldn't see waiting twenty minutes for an ambulance to get to the island, so I drove him here, which might have been a mistake. They might have sent a helicopter. Did I make a mistake?"

"No," I said, with confidence I lacked.

"As soon as we turned on Bohicket Road, he passed out, which scared the shit out of me, but he came to after a couple of minutes. He kept passing out and coming to. He passed out just when I pulled up to the emergency room, and they took him in."

I took my turn, leaning my head back, looking for the same courage and composure Baze had found on the ceiling. "He wasn't hit by a car."

"I know."

I rolled my head to the side and looked at him. "You're sure?"

"Yep. First, there was the unscratched bike. Second, the docs said the injuries were inconsistent with an accident. Third, he looked like somebody had beaten the shit out of him. And fourth, when I asked him what had happened, he said, 'Nobody hit me. I got hit by a car. A yellow VW.'"

"I have so much to tell you."

"I've definitely got some time, because until I can find Two Ls, I'm staying right here."

"I've got beer in my car, if you want to take a break."

"Cold?"

"Yes. I brought the cooler."

My eyes followed his to the large round clock on the wall—bright white face, big bold numerals, short stubby hands marking minutes and hours, a skinny second hand ticking off time we could see and hear. It was the kind of clock you'd watched as a kid in class, waiting for the bell to ring and the school day to end, waiting in a place where you didn't want to be, waiting to get on with whatever was next.

It was 10:55 p.m. ICU visiting hours were restricted: only family members could see patients, only one at a time, only at 8:00 and 11:00 a.m., and at 4:00, 8:00, and 11:00 p.m. Baze suggested I claim to be a cousin.

"Why? He's unconscious."

"I think he hears me and knows I'm there."

"Tubes?"

"He's on a ventilator, so there's a tube in his throat and an oxygen mask. Catheter. IV." He must have seen apprehension in my eyes; he saved me from having to admit I'm squeamish and prone to fainting. "I'll be back."

He pressed the rectangular button on the wall outside the unit, said his name and Terry's into the intercom, and waited for the heavy double doors to swing open.

I don't know that Baze was right about everything, or anything. But drinking Heineken in my car in the hospital parking lot, windows down, the night warm and damp, I listened without argument. He insisted on calling Jack *Dick*, and I didn't object.

Yes, he said, we were morally and legally obligated to take Dick's blood-soaked shirt out of the trash and to the police. Assault and battery was a criminal offense.

No, we weren't going to, because Terry, the dumb-shit, wouldn't want us to. Terry was either ashamed of losing both the girl and the physical fight in one day, or he wanted Tricia to be happy and have what she wanted, even if she wanted Dick. Terry preferred to have been defeated by a car, and Baze had obliged. A yellow VW, he'd told the docs and police, early morning, no witnesses.

No, Baze told me, we didn't need to look for blood on the beach. Even if we found it, even if we had the shirt, even if we could talk Terry into pressing charges, it would be he said, she said. Dick could claim anything, and who would believe Terry? He'd had a helluva drug cocktail in his blood when he was admitted.

No, we weren't telling Tricia what had happened. She might come back to the island, and if Baze ever saw her again, he'd make her look worse than Terry did right now. She'd chosen Dick, not Terry. Tricia was out.

No, I shouldn't tell Tricia that the tumor was benign, Baze said. If I did, I'd be so deep in their shit I'd never find my way out. I needed to quit stirring it, wash my hands of it and them forever. Tricia would have to figure that out on her own.

No, we couldn't tell Helen Sloan the truth, the whole truth, and nothing but the truth, if and when we found her. She didn't know about Tricia and didn't need to know. We were sticking with the yellow car.

And yes, Baze said, he could guarantee me a job with a really good midsize ad agency in New York, with branches in Chicago and Atlanta. One of the co-owners of the agency was the father of his fiancée.

"Your *what?*" I said.

"Annie," he said. "It's not official yet, but it's happening—ring for Christmas, wedding in June after graduation. I'm going to work for her father in Chicago. The family business I told you about. Annie's going to law school at Northwestern."

I got out of the car and leaned against it, feeling weaker than I had in the face of the drama and trauma of the day. I knew our bantering, though it had carried an edge and a dare, had been exactly that and nothing more. Yet I felt hurt, as if I'd lost yet another man to another woman. Worse, Baze had taken an unethical tumble in my eyes, as Jack had. He joined me at the side of my car.

"You lied, like the rest of us."

"Terry didn't lie, except to Nona. And I didn't lie. It just never came up, Lynn. And besides, Annie and I were spending the summer apart for a reason. We'd gonc through a rough patch in May. Things were stale. We were scrapping all the time. So we were taking a break, going out with other people when we wanted to. Everything was up in the air. I didn't need to talk about air, did I?"

A siren whistled far away, grew louder, began to scream. We waited without speaking for the inevitable arrival of a white van with red flashing lights. We watched the flurry of activity surrounding another victim, rescued, unloaded, and wheeled inside.

"But you're getting married."

"We decided two days ago. I didn't lie, Lynn. But I'm sure as hell lying now—about a phantom yellow car." Silence. "About you."

"Is there a punch line?" I asked, but he wasn't smiling.

"I haven't mentioned you to Annie. She'd think you and I are too close. She'd think you're dangerous. And for me, you are." He lingered for a moment in this unexplored territory of earnestness before darting home. "That's why I never tried to vaccinate you. I knew if I tried—" He paused for timing and a grin. "You'd let me."

"I might have." My laughter met a quick death in midair.

In the amber glow of streetlights, Baze looked worn and ragged. He seemed to be holding on by only the thin, fraying thread I'd clung to in the early morning. There was a kiss at the end of it, and we both felt entitled: we had been thinking, talking, and joking about it all summer; we were stuck in a calamity together; we didn't know what else to do; and we wanted to. He drew us together in an instant and we were held together for a long time by a kiss that was comforting and tempting, spontaneous and predestined too.

"Let's go in," I said, breaking out of another middle waiting to ensnare me. I took his arm and we walked toward the hospital. The lack of conversation was maddening. "Tell me about Annie, Baze." But he didn't.

Our steps rang like muffled bells in long wide halls, empty now excepting a nurse in one wing, an orderly in another, and two interns in the third. The PA clicked on and doctors were paged. At nurses' stations, staff gathered, talked, and laughed. Too loudly perhaps for patients who needed to sleep.

Let them laugh, I told myself. This is their TCC, their daily grind. They are effective and task oriented. They are meeting objectives in the face of such vast collective illness that they should be forgiven for forgetting that pain is individual and that vulnerability, nakedness, dependence, and fear are personal. I hated thinking of Terry that way—in need without the woman he loved.

"We have to call Tricia."

"No, Lynn. Don't. Please. She's the worst thing that could have happened to Terry. She doesn't need to know what's happened to him now. Come on, Lynn. Are you with me on this?"

In the thick of conspiracy sealed with a kiss, I nodded.

"We're not calling Tricia unless we have to. Unless he dies or something. He dies, you call."

Four days went by.

CHAPTER 12

The phone rang. In darkness, Patricia heard Jack's gruff hello and, "Where are you? And why are you calling at quarter of twelve?"

She stared at the alarm clock's green numerals, their glow intensifying with his anger.

"It's Wednesday. We agreed you'd be back in the office today and you weren't."

She sat up in bed as Jack paused. Since she'd been back in New York, she'd been furtively trying to call Lynn, and Terry, and even Baze. She'd reached no one and no one had responded to her messages.

"No. You cannot, Lynn," Jack said. "She doesn't care. Do you understand me? Patricia does not care."

But Tricia did. She turned on the lamp, tried to make out Lynn's words.

"You had no right. I want you out of my house and off that hellhole of an island."

"Give me the phone, Jack," Tricia said.

He hung up, stood up, and planted himself at the bedside table as the phone began to ring again.

She threw back the covers, and he said, "Don't try to answer. I'll goddamn kill you."

She felt dizzy with thoughts of Houston, but the phone's after-midnight, something's-wrong ring meant tragedy was probably on the line too. The need to know pushed her forward.

"So help me God, Patricia, I'll beat your head in. I will hurt you. Like I hurt him."

She stopped. "Hurt who?"

"After he ran from me on the beach."

She tried to believe he was lying, but the scene was too easy to visualize. The phone stopped and began again. She felt as though she needed her hands to move, to part curtains of thick stifling air in the room. They hung before her in endless rows, with Jack and the phone beyond.

He shouted above its clanging. “He ran like a pup.”

“I am not running, Jack.” Her voice was wobbling in volume and tone, but she persevered. “I am going to answer the phone. Whatever you did to him, do it to me, if you want. I’m going to answer.”

He slapped her halfheartedly, but she didn’t flinch. He drew back his arm, balled his fist, and held the threat. When she didn’t duck or step back, he let his hand fall.

“Go downstairs,” she said.

“I don’t know what you want from me anymore.”

“Go to the study, Jack.”

“I don’t . . . Christ.” He put on his robe. “I’ve never known what you want.”

“Go somewhere. Anywhere. Go to the office.”

“I didn’t hurt him,” he said. “I roughed him up a bit. That’s all.” As he picked up his cigarettes and lighter, she picked up the phone.

She could not conflate Jack’s confession and Lynn’s words, startling deep scratches on an album, excruciating to her ear: Accident, bike, car, brain, bleeding, swelling, coma, confusion, agitation. Tumor. Lung. Benign.

When the conversation ended, she sat on the bed, remaining as calm and determined as she had been with Jack, knowing she’d at last arrived at that place in herself she’d been seeking. Still, the wait for the call that Lynn had said was coming was long and difficult.

“Tricia,” Baze said. “I’m here with Terry.”

“He’s all right?” She held her breath. Something inside her threatened to rupture.

"He's okay, but agitated. The doctors think everything will come back to him over the next few hours or days, but right now, he can't remember what happened. Lynn is here. Terry's mom is here."

Helen, she thought. *Hell-en*. "What does she know?"

"Only that he thinks something's happened to you and that he's not going to rest until he knows you're all right." Silence. "And that he loves you." A second silence. "I'm going to put Terry on the phone so you can tell him you're safe. Don't overload him with anything else. He's supposed to remember on his own. Understand?"

"Yes." She waited. She heard Terry breathing.

"Tricia?"

"Hi, baby." She couldn't say more. She'd heard a break in his voice. A clean break, though. She could seal it, save him. "I'm fine, Terry. And I'm on the way. I'm coming back."

"When?"

"I'm in New York, but I'll be with you by afternoon."

"Where are you?"

"New York."

"Are you coming back?"

"Yes," she said, patient but alarmed. "I'm on the way."

She stayed upstairs until the cab arrived. Jack was coughing as she stepped into the study with its dark, paneled walls. On his desk were a stack of files and an open portfolio of storyboards he'd brought home from the office. A cigarette burned in the ashtray. In pajamas, sitting in his high-backed leather chair, he looked up and over his readers. At her suitcase. At her.

"I'm having surgery at eight Friday morning."

"I know."

"The tumor is benign."

"I know that too now."

"It's still major surgery."

"I'm sure you'll be fine."

§

In the elevator at Charleston Hospital, she tried to prepare herself for seeing Terry. In pain, beaten, and confused. She pressed the button for the fifth floor but got out on the third by mistake. She rang for and boarded another car and didn't realize until the bump of landing that she'd traveled back down to the lobby. The doors opened and she almost collapsed.

She and Terry—Terry in his forties, his curly hair short and darker—locked eyes. Neither moved until the door began to close. He caught it with his hand and stepped inside. He had the same broad shoulders. His khaki trousers fit snugly across his thighs. He reached for the fifth-floor button. Already lit. He glanced at her again.

She was sure he knew who she was. Terry had been agitated, had asked for her, and Baze had called. They knew she was coming today. Still, he unnerved her when he said, "Tricia?" He sounded like Terry, and she answered yes in a whisper that even she barely heard.

The car stopped at the second floor to pick up a priest, at the third for a nutritionist and a social worker, all identified by hospital badges. Somewhere along the ascent in the now-crowded elevator, she let down a pair of tears, and the man, who stood close beside her now, with his back like hers against the wall of the car, took her hand and held it until they stepped onto the fifth floor together.

"Five twenty-eight," he said, gesturing toward the hall straight ahead.

She looked into familiar hazel eyes. "Are you going in?"

He shook his head. "I'm going to wait here for Helen. Terry's better now, so she's able to be worse, to break down. Everything's caught up with her."

"He's better?" She brushed her cheeks, hoping to blend out the streaks in her blush. She'd known not to wear mascara.

"Much. The phone call was a big help. We're glad you're here. Helen and I. We've heard a lot about you from Baze and Lynn. I'm Mike, by the way."

He didn't offer his last name.

She didn't ask. She only smiled. "You're Terry's father."

He looked uncomfortable. "Yes."

She tapped on the partially open door and entered a space of palpable stress and exhaustion. Lynn, Baze, and Terry's mother broke their huddle, and she measured degrees of sleeplessness by the dark circles beneath their eyes. She saw a nurse, whose large frame, thin lips, and severe frown conveyed authority. Across the small room, she saw Terry—flat on his back, his face battered and swollen cobalt blue, his chin bisected by a crooked line of stitches, his fingers clawing at the keypad on the hospital bed.

She felt faint but moved forward. She hugged Baze, who was slow to reciprocate; Lynn, who wrapped warm arms around her; and Helen, who introduced herself, thanked her for coming, and embraced her as if she might never let go. The nurse looked disgruntled.

Beside the bed, Tricia placed her hand over Terry's. She looked down and smiled. He looked up in wonder. She pressed the button, and as the bed hummed and brought them face-to-face, they both fought tears. She lowered a side rail and sat down. She kissed his forehead, and with respect for the stitches in his chin, she brought their lips together.

"Where's the orchestra?" Baze said from the corner. Looking back over her shoulder, Tricia saw him exchange glances with Lynn, and their eyes, though rolling, were filling too. Helen's were flooding. The nurse looked annoyed.

"What happened?" Terry's voice was weak. "I thought that—Tricia, did I wreck the car?"

"No, baby." She lightened her tone. "The car is fine. So am I."

"They keep saying I was riding the bike. But I can't remember."

The nurse stepped forward, shoulders high. "According to Dr. Hempstead, you're not going to remember unless you get plenty of rest. This is too much stimulus," she said, waving her arms at the group. "There are too many of you here at one time."

"Get her out," Terry said to his mother, but Helen was already ushering the nurse, Baze, and Lynn to the door. "You go too, Mom."

Helen turned to Tricia. "I can come back in an hour or so. One of us will need to stay overnight. Last night, he tried to get out of bed twice. He didn't know where he was."

"I want Tricia to stay," he said. Helen nodded with a willing abdication of control. "And don't ask the doctors when I can play tennis. You asked the brain doctor, Mom. That was stupid. The bone doctor is the one who'll know, but I don't want you asking. Not while I'm lying here without even my mind in one piece. Chill, Mom. Take a break. You need it."

"All right." She walked to the bed. She placed her hand on his shoulder, but he didn't react. She leaned toward his forehead, but he said "don't," and her pursed lips went back into a line that sagged at the corners with worry and age.

Tricia watched the exchange, or lack of exchange, knowing that the smallest of the nesting dolls inside him, the one that held the key to his baggage, was his mother. Another was the man she'd met in the elevator.

Helen left wordlessly, and Tricia couldn't help saying, "She loves you, baby. She wants to help. Can you trust that she's trying, even when she makes mistakes?"

He sighed. "If I trust her, it's because I trust you."

He touched her cheek and waited, eyes expectant and

hopeful. She knew how to reassure him, to tell him that nothing between them had changed, that she could see beyond his bruises. But she was afraid to touch what was broken and the blue ridge left in its place.

"They can't put it back together," he said. "It's, like, smashed. But it won't look too bad once the swelling goes down."

"Does it hurt?"

"Some. And my head sometimes. The doctor said I might get some migraines. My ribs hurt all the time." Without warning, she shivered. "Are you cold, Tricia? Or do I look that bad?"

"No, baby. Not to me."

"My mom wouldn't let me look in a mirror at first, and Baze says I look damn good now compared to at first. I've been asleep for four fucking days."

"I know."

"You're smiling."

"Only because you're sounding like yourself again."

"Only because you're here." He raised a finger, motioned her closer, and kissed her. Then his entire body seemed to sigh and sink deeper into the mattress. "Tricia, I can't take this shit. They won't let me out of bed even to pee, and I've got nurses wanting to bathe me and shave me. The doctor says the memory thing happens to most people in a wreck. Like, you remember seeing the car coming straight at you but not the crash or what happens afterward. But usually it all comes back." Silence, then: "You're staring at my chin."

"I don't mean to."

"You want to see my side?"

Following his directions, she helped him lean forward, hating to see him wince, to hear him grunt. She untied the gown and slipped it down to his waist. He lay back on exhibition, and she studied the canvas of his ribs and torso, the abstract swirls of color from the palette of rage, the art of Jack Curren. *My husband,* she thought. *My ex-husband. I'm leaving him. I've left.*

They turned toward the door as a nurse came in. "This is Nan," he told Tricia, "the only nurse I like around here."

The only young nurse, Tricia thought as they exchanged hellos. *The only pretty nurse.* Dark hair, bangs and a ponytail, blue eyes shining.

"I'm going to take out the IV," she said to Terry. "That should make you happy."

"That pill would make me happier." He eyed the inch-high paper cup she'd set on the over-bed table.

"How severe is your pain?" She removed the tape and needle from his hand. "On a scale of one to ten, with ten as unbearable."

"Nine. What is that pill anyways?"

"Percocet." She handed it to him with a cup of water. "Buzz if you need me."

He thanked her and watched her walk out. "Baze says N.A.N. means nice-ass-nurse. Not meaning she's nice, even though she is, but meaning that uniform's tight and she has a nice ass."

"Don't make me jealous."

"I won't." For the first time, he laughed. "But she does. The other nurse, he calls B.A.N., which stands for big-ass-nurse, or bad-ass-nurse. Her name's Bess, or maybe Boss."

Tricia laughed with him, as if they were sitting in bed at home or sitting on the beach or floating in the ocean with their arms around each other, as if the summer were just beginning.

"Will you put me back down? 'Cause I'll get tired soon." His mood flattened with the bed. "What I hate most is when the doctor asks me my name and what year it is and who the president is, like I'm an idiot."

"But you know, right?"

"I know most things."

She wanted to stop there. The afternoon light, streaming through half-open blinds, cast the shadow of every slat on the wall. She liked the golden warmth; she needed the peace.

But Terry went on. "I know the grocery store. You were with him, and I saw your rings and his ring, and you left me there. I didn't know what had happened or what to do, except to get fucked up."

She wanted to explain that Jack had arrived early, that she hadn't known what to do either. But Terry took a sharp turn, left her between the aisles.

"Tricia, my mom's acting weird." He yawned. "I thought she'd be pissed when I told her about you, but she wasn't."

"Did you tell her I'm married?"

He seemed already groggy as his lips started toward a smile. "Tricia, you're smart, but you've got no common sense. I'm gonna make peace with her, like you want, so there's no way I'm telling her that." His eyelids began to blink. "You don't mind staying, do you? I know you brought something to read. W. S. Merlyn or somebody."

She smiled. "Yes, Merwin. I'll go to the car, get my tote bag, and be right back."

"Good." His eyes were half closed now, like the blinds. "I want you to stay. And I want to remember."

In the hospital's dimly lit chapel, she tried to pray, but erratic thoughts shattered concentration like pebbles shattering stained glass: Terry, memory, Jack, surgery, assistantships, applications, divorce.

She bought a wilted spinach salad in the cafeteria but wasn't able to eat.

She went to the hospital's lobby, where Tillie the All-Time Teller wouldn't give her cash, and where, from a pay phone, she tried to call Lynn at the beach house. Both lines were busy. She tried again and then listened to the signal. It began to sound like machine-gun laughter.

She watched others walk away from Tillie with stacks of crisp bills and realized Jack had cut off the phone lines, closed her checking account and probably her credit card accounts too.

With twenty-two dollars cash in hand, she went back to 528.

CHAPTER 13

He woke in the night, managed to sit up and swing his feet to the floor. He needed to pee, but not in the plastic jug. He wanted to walk ten yards to the bathroom and pee, standing on his own two feet. But a grenade exploded behind his forehead.

He looked at Tricia, scrunched in the recliner, and decided not to wake her. She'd had to fly from New York and probably hadn't slept much in that frigging chair.

New York. Wait. New York made no sense. She wasn't planning to go to New York until he'd left for school; she shouldn't—

His thoughts detoured to the grocery store, and he realized she'd gone home to the city with her husband.

But wait. The swing. Something about the swing.

He buzzed for the nurse and Nan came in. She lobbied for following orders at first—for the jug—but gave in. She wasn't very big, he noted, as he put his arm around her shoulder and she slid her arm around his waist. He tried not to lean on her too heavily but couldn't help it. She'd been right. He shouldn't have tried it. He was too dizzy to stand alone, so he peed with her holding up his gown and watching. What the fuck else could he do?

And what the fuck was this thing that had happened to him? Why couldn't he remember? Nan was walking him back to the bed.

He was walking to the swing. He was sitting on the swing.

He was high, but not on Percocet. He was fucked up, mixed up, shocked, sad.

"Stay," he said as Nan pulled the sheet around him.

"I have other patients."

"I'm going back to it and I'm—" *Scared*, he wanted to say but didn't have to. Nan nodded.

Someone was behind him, running in the soft, thick sand. He turned, expecting Tricia and got Jack instead, sucker punching him in the face, starting the unfair fight that was over even as Terry hit the sand. He tried to get up, made it to his hands and knees.

Jack pulled the swing back. Jack let it fly.

Terry threw his arms up too slowly. There was pain in his chin and blood everywhere.

Jack pulled him up. Jack beat him down. Right. Left. Forehand. Backhand. Jack grabbed his hair. Jack slammed his head into the swing's wooden A-frame again and again until Terry could barely see. He crawled, stood, tried to run for dunes, fell.

"My wife. You were fucking my wife."

Terry struggled to his knees, to his feet. Terry ran, tried to run, as best as he could. Jack followed, walking and shouting. Terry climbed the dunes, fell, rolled down to a driftwood log.

Jack pulled him up. "Don't hurt me." Jack beat him down.

"Please don't kill me."

Knees. Feet. Jesus. Had Jack done this to Tricia? Fear. Pain. Jesus. Was Jack going to? Jack was kicking him. Heel and toe.

"Don't hurt Tricia." Ribs snapping. "I love Tricia."

"If you ever go near my wife," Jack was shouting, "I will kill her. Not you. Her. Kill her."

"Are you okay, Terry?"

He looked up at Nan. "Yeah," he said, his voice strained. "I got it back. Most of it anyways." All but one big piece—the one between the grocery store and the ass kicking.

"Do you remember the accident?"

"A Volkswagen. A yellow Beetle. It grazed me, and I hit the street hard. I couldn't see the license plate or anything else."

"The police will want to talk to you when you're able."

Tricia moaned softly and opened her eyes. She gave him a puzzled look and the missing piece of the puzzle.

In the beach house. With Tricia, Lynn, and Jack.

Thinking he'd won. Like with McEnroe. So fucking close. So fucking sure. Jack whispered to Tricia. What the hell had he said?

Tricia caved. Tricia sobbed. "Oh get out. I can't do it now."

From the recliner, Tricia smiled at him. She sighed and went back to sleep.

"It's over. We're done. Now get out."

He turned to Nan. "Will they let me go now that I remember? There's no more tubes or anything. Can I go?"

"That's up to Dr. Hempstead. He'll probably want to observe you a few more days and do a final CT scan before releasing you."

"But they can't keep me here, can they? Like, if my mom—well, I'm twenty-three. So I can do whatever I want, right?"

She frowned. "You can leave AMA—against medical advice. But you've been through a lot. Please don't."

"Nan, thanks for staying." She had the bluest eyes he'd ever seen. Even in the room with the lights down low, he could see clear through them, see his way out of this place. "Will you be here tomorrow?" He could tell she didn't want to answer.

"I'll be back at three in the afternoon."

"Will you write down your phone number?"

"Why?"

"I might need some help."

When Tricia woke the next morning, she looked worried—but not about him. She looked a million miles away. When he told her to take a break and come back around five, she agreed, just like that, like she wanted to get away from him. Like she didn't want to look at him anymore. His busted cheek, his sewn-up chin. Like she was only there because his mom, Lynn, or Baze had asked her to come. She looked like she felt sorry for him.

When he called Nan, she agreed to come in early. The cop bought into the VW story and closed the case. Baze said he would come at ten and bring him some clothes.

He forced down eggs, peed in the jug, and lay still. He needed to conserve his strength for the walk with the physical therapist that was planned. And for getting out of the place.

But then the bone doctor came in and things turned. Sank. He said it would be eight weeks before Terry could pick up a racket, twelve before he'd be one hundred percent. The pain came back so hard and fast that he wished the cocksucker Jack had broken his neck and he was dead like the seagull that had started it all. He wished he could kill himself and leave Tricia a note telling her he'd gotten the idea from Konstantin in Cheekhov's play.

"I'm not going back to Austin," he told Baze. "Not looking like this and having everybody asking what happened. I can't play tennis for months."

"You have to go back. You have to enroll, even if you can't play, or you'll lose your scholarship." Baze waited. "You mean you'll wait a week and come back? Late enrollment?"

"I guess."

His friend whistled softly. "If that's what you want. But you'd better check on enrollment because there's a cutoff date. And check with Coach." Again Baze waited—for nothing. "What exactly are you planning to do?"

"I'm going home. With Two Ls." In spite of the circumstances, he enjoyed the rare moment of speechlessness from his usually unflappable friend. "I've got to go somewhere," he said, "till I can get a grip."

Baze looked at the pillow, blanket, and book in the recliner. "What about Tricia?"

He needed to tell the whole story, at least once, to somebody. To Baze, Lynn, Nan, his mom, the man in the moon. To somebody because he could no longer tell the person it was so easy to tell things to. He thought he'd do best if he said it fast, but the words came out clay-court slow— clay court in misting rain, the ball heavy and sitting up high, waiting for somebody to slam it back into his gut.

"Her husband beat the ever-loving shit out of me, and I don't want any-damn-body to know but you. I got hit by a car, okay? I don't want to see Tricia. Ever. I can't. He said he'd kill her if I ever got near her again. And most of all, Tricia picked him, not me. She's his wife. Get Lynn to help if you have to, but make sure Tricia stays away until five, like she said she would. That will give me plenty of time to get out of here."

"With your mom?"

"Yeah." He wanted to scratch his chin. The stitches were beginning to itch. He leaned back against the pillow. "You ought to try this Percocet."

"I don't want to, because it's got you thinking crazy. Listen to me, Terry. You've got to go back to Austin. I can wait a few days. We'll go together. As soon as you can. Tricia won't matter anymore in Austin."

He focused his gaze on a speck on the wall. He thought about tennis. Down the tubes. And a great senior year. Up in smoke. And the slice in his chin that would leave a scar. And his cheek that would always be smashed. And the break and cracks in his ribs that would take months to heal.

"I'm fucked." He squeezed his eyes shut. "I am so fucked." The Percocet was working but only on his physical pain. He thought about Tricia. Fuck Tricia. But he loved Tricia, loved fucking her. He loved her way too much. He'd never get over Tricia. "Baze."

"Yeah, buddy."

His tongue felt thick. "Is my mom here yet?"

"I don't know. I'll check."

He looked at the speck again. The speck, the smudge, the mess, the hole in his life. It could only be filled by someone who loved him.

"I want my mom," he said.

He slept until the mattress shifted as his mother took a seat on the bed. He looked up and blinked at the smile he'd never been able to believe in.

Skip practice? Not if you love me. If you love me, you'll go, little ace. Hmm? She might as well have added, *If you'll go, I'll love you too. If you win, I'll love you more.*

"Baze said you wanted me."

"I do." He saw that he'd made her incredibly happy with those words. He pressed the keypad. He sat up straight to help himself be straightforward. "Mom, I'm screwed up worse than ever, in every way I could be. I've always been screwed up, and I'm sorry about things I did that were . . . wrong or mean. I'm sorry about how things always were with us and—"

"Not now, Terry. There's no need. I'm sorry too, but we'll talk later. Right now, we need to get you well."

"I'm better."

"We need to get you back to Austin."

"I've—"

"Back in school."

"I remembered—"

"Back on court. Where you belong."

He fell back into the pillows. She patted his cheek. The good one. Like he was still little ace. He listened to Tricia: She loves you, baby. She wants to help. Can you trust that she's trying, even when she makes mistakes?

"Mom, I want to come home for a while. I want to be with you. Maybe six weeks. Or six months." He thought her eyes would fill with emotion, but they filled with what looked like panic instead. "I need to come home. I need you right now." He tried to laugh, to pretend that the no in her eyes was a joke. "What? You don't want me to come home?"

He imagined himself still hooked up to machines, imagined the red line—his heart line— zigging and zagging so wildly that the monitor exploded.

"Terry." His mother stood up.

"Can I come home?"

"No. I—"

"No?"

"You can't come home because—"

"What?" He had to yell. "What?"

"You can't—"

"Please." Still shouting.

"No," she cried.

He rolled to the side of the bed, yelping at the pain in his ribs. He slammed the heel of his hand against the bed rail and yelped again. He clutched the bed rail, panting and feeling like a dumb trusting dog, chasing his tail, chasing a car, run over again by a yellow Beetle. He pushed the breakfast tray by the bed to the floor.

"You can't come home." Her shriek, not his hand, seemed to push the over-bed table into the wall. "At least not to Orlando, to the home you know. I've divorced your father."

Bess the Boss hustled in. "What's the commotion?" She looked at the tray, cold scrambled eggs on the floor, and the puddles of milk and orange juice.

"It slipped," Terry said. "That's all. Everything's great in here."

"Then tone it down." She nodded at the floor. "I'll send housekeeping."

He turned to his mother, who pushed Tricia's sweater and book aside and sat down in the recliner. "I was going to tell you the day of the final, when we went to lunch, but you had to bring Nona McClelland along. I've called you every day at the villa, but you were never there."

"I was at Tricia's."

"Why, for God's sake, couldn't you call me back?"

"I'm sorry." His gaze tagged along with hers through the half-closed blinds. He wondered if the weather had cooled while he'd been in a coma and trapped here. "It's a sin, Mom. Divorcing him. But it's not like I'll miss him." Silence. "You're living somewhere, right? Can I come there?" He waited as long as he could. "Just for a week?"

She twisted the cuff bracelet on her arm. "I'm in Savannah."

"Can I come to Savannah?" The bracelet went round and round, shimmering like Tricia's rings. "You don't want me at all?"

"Terry, I have something to tell you."

Zig and zag went his heart.

"Terry, I've remarried. I'm married."

A tornado touched down in his head, sucked up his brain, spun it, and slammed it back into his skull.

"Mike and I both want you to come to Savannah."

"Who's Mike?" But he knew, and she knew he knew.

"He wants very much to get to know you. This would be a good time."

He lowered the bed, loving its groan, wishing it wouldn't stop at 180 degrees. He wished the whole damn bed would just keep going. All the way through the floor and the other floors, down to the lobby, to Neverland and never-have-to-come-back-land.

"Terry, you will love Mike." His mother came to his side again. "He's in the waiting room. He's been here as long as I have. If you'll give him a chance, he'll be as happy as I will. He wants to help you. If you'll accept him, then yes, come to Savannah with us."

He looked at the ceiling, wishing for sky. "Mom, I'm beat up. My head's screwed up. And you want me to come home to some place I've never been and some guy I don't even know? You think I can handle that right now?"

"Then I'll rent a place for just you and me."

He saw in her eyes that she really would do it. And that she really didn't want to. "I'll go back to Austin," he said, knowing he wouldn't. "I know he's what you've always wanted."

"The way you and Tricia feel about each other is exactly how—"

He held up his hand. "Ask Baze about Tricia, Mom. Next time you see him. Tell him I said to tell you because I can't." One more roll. Away. Back to his broken side.

Boss Bess returned. "You're going for a walk in a few minutes. Then you're going to sit in the chair for a half hour."

"Great. That's just great."

She mistook his sarcasm for agreeableness and smiled at him as she left the room.

"Mom." He didn't look at her. "Let me do this walking thing and sleep awhile. Come back, at three. Exactly three. Got that?"

She let her hand rest on his shoulder. "Terry, I have something else to tell you."

"No." No more corners. No more kisses. "Please. Not now."

"Mike and I feel you should know that he is your—"

"Mom," he said loudly as she said "father." He heard the same swell of emotion in her voice that he felt in his chest. "I know who he is and I'm glad for you. And him too. But I need you to let me be for a while." He put his hand on hers as he'd refused to the night before. He kept it there until she left him.

"Are you ready to walk?" the physical therapist asked, but

looking at him closely, changed the question. "Are you in pain?" She handed him a Kleenex.

"Allergies. My eyes keep watering. 'Cause I'm allergic." *Or 'cause I'm fucked,* he thought, *'cause I need to get away and have only one place on the planet to go.* "I've gotta make three phone calls first. Can you give me five minutes?"

He asked Nan to bring paper so he could write notes. No, not those kind of notes, he assured her.

He asked Baze to make absolutely sure Tricia didn't come back until five. "And I want you to come here at three and sit my mom down in the waiting room and tell her every fucking thing. Tell her Tricia's married and that her husband did this to me. My mom needs to know and I can't tell her. I don't want to see either you or my mom until you've told her. Please just do what I say, okay?" And though skeptical, Baze agreed.

Then, the most important call. His fingers quivered as he dialed nine for an outside line. His hand trembled as he dialed zero for operator. His arm shook as he gave her the information. His body quaked as he waited.

He heard the click of connection, the familiar "hello," the operator's introduction. "This is a collect call from Terry Sloan. Will you accept charges?"

He drew as deep a breath as his busted ribs allowed and prepared to wait.

There was no hesitation. "Certainly."

He tried to cover the animal sound in his throat.

"Angel? Oh, angel. What is it?"

Dear Nan,

Thank you for coming early and writing down what I say for these stupid notes, 'cause I'm too weak. And 'cause I'd mess up the d's and b's, like I told you. Write exactly what I say, okay? I know this is weird that the very first one is to yourself. But anyways, thanks.

Your patient, Terry

Dear Mom,

I am glad we are starting to get things talked out between us. I am sorry I can't meet Mike, my father, yet. But I will one day.

I hope you don't get too mad at Tricia. She's had a lot of problems in her life. But I wanted you to know the truth about what happened with me and her, and why it wasn't gonna work. But the main truth is that if it hadn't been for Tricia, you and me would have never started talking and getting closer like we are now. And we'll get more closer. I'll come to Savannah, but it might be a while. I love you.

Your son, Terry

Baze,

Thanks for being my friend. I mean it. I wish I'd listened to you about the bad news from the start. Tell Coach and everybody about the yellow VW, so when I come back, with a scar in my chin and a smashed cheek and half a brain, they won't ask why. Tell Freddie he is one lucky prick, because if I hadn't got hit by a car, I'd be playing number one this year and he'd be playing two. See you in Austin. Soon, I hope. Hook 'em Horns.

—TS

Dear Obi-Lynn,

I don't know what I would have done without you this whole summer, or how the hell you put up with me and Tricia sometimes. You were a good friend to her, and I hope you always will be because she's probably still a kinda sad person inside herself. ~~And tell that asshole husband of hers that if he~~ ~~ever hits~~ You were a good friend to me too. And when all this shit started coming down, I didn't know what to do. Especially when I started remembering everything. I wished I could talk to you, but then it came to me that I just have to go. Take care of Tricia for me. Because you know I really love her. So. Anyways. Catch you on the flip side, Obi-Lynn. Maybe NY? U.S. Open?

Your friend, Terry

Dear Mike,

I hope to meet you soon. ~~I know~~ I don't know what to say. I know you're a good tennis player, so maybe we can go for a hit someday in Savannah.

~~Your son,~~ Terry

Dear Tricia,

You know that I love you. I think I have gotten to know you really ~~good~~ well, and I thought what you wanted was me. But now I know it's him. And that's good and right. I'm glad you went back to New York to work things out with Jack. Because you're married. And what we did was wrong. I won't say it was a sin because he treated you bad and I loved love you so much. But I did something I promised myself I'd never do in my life, because of my mom and how much I hated her for it and how much she hated me and hurt me and made me play tennis all because of Mike, my real father. I didn't ever want to cheat with somebody or bust up a marriage, so I'm glad you're back with him, and I hope he'll treat you good. But if he doesn't, or if he hits you or hurts you ever again, you've gotta divorce him. Promise? And it won't be a sin. I would know, right? 'Cause I'm a good Roman Catholic boy. Ha! I guess I better haul ass to confession.

Just kidding. But also not. Maybe it would help. 'Cause me, I'm beaten up and hurting in lots of ways and places, besides the ones everybody can see. I know you're hurting too, and it's not like this is all your fault. But I've gotta get this summer behind me, like it was just a shitty first set, and make up for it with the second. I want to get on with my tennis. And with school, which I know you'd want me to. And my life. You really helped me, Tricia. With all those things. With myself, and tennis, and even my mom, which I know you wanted to. And I hope I helped you too.

I can't believe how things ended up, but I guess I should have seen it coming. 'Cause that's just Cheekhov, right? By which I mean, that's just life.

Anyways, I know you pretty ~~good~~ well, Tricia. Like, I bet you're crying now. But don't, okay? Just always remember me and how much I love you. And know I always will.

I could write about 20 more pages but I'm about to make The Great Escape. *So thanks for loving me. And thanks for the summer and the thimbles and telling me your secrets and listening to mine. I'm gonna put my finger on my cheek for the very last time now. I hope you'll do the same and say "too."*

—Terry

CHAPTER 14

Tricia arrived at the beach house around 9:00 a.m., just after Baze had left for the hospital with clothes for Terry. I encouraged her to take half a Seconal to make sure she'd catch a few hours of sleep.

"You're overtired," I told her.

"I'm worried," she said, and she told me what Jack had done.

I continued organizing my Kiawah files for my replacement at TCC, whomever he or she would be. I was dropping the best of the 35-millimeter slides into a carousel when Baze stopped by at two. He'd gone to the hospital, back to the villa, and was going to the hospital again, as he'd promised Terry. He wanted me to go with him, and since Tricia was now sleeping so heavily that I didn't think she'd be awake even at five, the appointed hour for her return to 528, I agreed to go with Baze and give her a wake-up call around three thirty.

By the time he and I were halfway to Charleston, I was afraid I'd made a mistake: What if the ringing of the phone didn't rouse her or the lingering effects of the drug impaired her driving?

Nurse Bess met Baze and me at the nurses' station to tell us we couldn't see Terry. "A procedure is under way," she said, folding her arms.

"Another scan?" Baze said.

"That's privileged information. My patient has privacy rights." She escorted us from the hall to the waiting room. "Here," she said, "for now. Right here."

"Yes, ma'am," Baze said, saluting her, and as she turned,

the four fingers at his forehead gave way to one finger.

"This is going to be a helluva party," Baze said as the elevator bell gave out a muted clink. "Guess I'll see who's at the door."

He rose as the doors slid open. He led our first guest, Helen, to the far side of the room. I picked up a magazine but its pages might as well have been blank. I couldn't stop glancing at them, and every time I did, Baze looked more awkward and Helen more distraught. I heard him say "Patricia," then "married," then "lied."

The elevator bell, or doorbell, rang. I welcomed Mike, who had dropped Helen off and parked their car. He looked at Helen and Baze and me again, and asked what was wrong. He looked down the hall, as if expecting to see Terry rolled out of 528 on a gurney and on to surgery or the morgue. Bess was on guard.

Helen's transformation into Hell-en was instantaneous. She said nothing, but her eyes cursed and her body tightened. She needed an outlet for her anger, but unlike Jack, who'd had Terry, Helen had no one to strike. Tricia wasn't there.

I glanced at my watch—three o'clock. I thanked God for Seconal.

But then the bell clinked.

Tricia smiled—at Mike, me, Baze, and Helen, in turn. As she stepped off the elevator, Helen leapt from her chair, and Mike leapt between lioness and prey. With strong hands on Helen's arms, he asked what was wrong, but her eyes were fixed on Tricia.

"How could you do that?" She struggled to break free. "How could you lie to my son?"

Mike lost his grip on one arm, but squeezing the other, thwarted Helen's lunge. She couldn't get to Tricia, who was shocked and stammering. Unable to slap, spit, or scratch, Helen cried, "Married? Married and lying to him for months?"

If Terry's mother had been civil, Tricia might have crumbled in apology. But Helen's wrath looked so much like Jack's that it provoked a different reaction.

"I did what *you* did," Tricia said. She glanced at Mike.

Baze stepped into the fray with a paltry, "Wait a minute."

"I lied to my husband, but never to Mike. You lied to Terry. You hurt him."

"You've always hurt him. You abused him."

"Don't accuse me."

"You damaged him."

"*You* damaged him. Go in that room and look at my son."

"You damaged a child. A boy. You almost destroyed him."

The doorbell rang. But this time, Mike, Baze, and I turned toward Bess, on the march in the middle of the hall. I marveled at her combat readiness. "You people have to stop this," thundered the army of one.

Helen and Tricia had fallen silent in the ring, and Baze, turning back to the prizefighters, saw what was delaying round two.

"Nona," he said. "Hi, Nona."

She stepped off the elevator like the guest of honor. I stared with everyone else as she pulled up, her ballerina's breastbone high. Her long arms were at her sides in a first-position curve and even her feet in flat black sandals turned out. Perplexed but poised, her eyes open wide, she posed in her short black skirt and white linen blouse, amid our gray confused surprise.

"Where is he?"

Helen and Tricia attacked with outbursts so much alike that I couldn't tell what was being said or by whom.

"Mrs. McClelland?" Bess bellowed above the cacophony. "Come with me."

The two of them started down the hall, and as Helen broke free to pursue them, Mike threw his hands up. "What in the heck is going on?"

Bess stopped, turned, and with her girth, road blocked Helen. Nona pranced on to 528.

"This is the craziest damn thing," Mike said.

And Bess roared: "I am charged to protect the privacy of my patient. And Mrs. McClelland is the only one he wants to see."

"Your patient is my son," Helen said, her voice edgy. "Mrs. McClelland is no one."

"No one," Tricia said, trembling.

"No one," Helen shouted. "She has no right—"

"My patient has rights," Bess said, a booming contralto.

Beyond her, we glimpsed Terry in a wheelchair pushed by an aide—out of 528, past the nurses' station, and into the elevator reserved for hospital personnel. He glanced only once in our direction, saw Mike, and turned his head. Nona followed the wheelchair, and they were gone. Bess spread her arms in her own game of red rover, dared Tricia, who had started forward, to come over. "He checked himself out," she said, seemingly honored by her insider's role. "He arranged for Mrs. McClelland to pick him up."

"Jesus God." Tears in her eyes and looking like she was going to faint, Tricia protested but let me lead her to a chair.

"She can't take my son," Helen said.

"Do something," I said to Baze. He and Mike rushed toward the elevator. "They'll get him," I told Tricia.

But they stopped as Nan appeared.

With more stage presence than Nona, the young nurse emanated kindness and inspired calm. "He remembered what happened," she said, smiling. "I know you're thankful for that. And I have something for each of you." She fanned blue envelopes out like a deck of cards. "Don't worry. He's safe. He promised me."

Helen challenged, "And who do you think you are?"

Nan was the dealer. She didn't have to answer. "Terry has told you in these notes what he needs from all of you. It's important to him that you know how he feels."

She led us to chairs in the waiting room and sat with us. She distributed the notes, starting with Tricia.

"I have to go—"

"No, no," Nan said gently. "Read first. Please. He wants you to."

With our notes in hand, we began to read. The sounds of bells, buzzers, and beeping machines grew faint. We read and reread. We read each other's, even Helen and Tricia.

"He loves you all," Nan said. Her eyes circling to Helen's, Baze's, mine, lingering on Mike's, and ending with Tricia's. "I could tell as he told me what to write. He didn't intend for you to all be here at once. He'd planned to have left long before you came. But Mrs. McClelland was late." She looked at Tricia and said gently, "You were early. But maybe it's best this way, since you all love him too." She had the comforting skills of a chaplain, and as she went on, the respectful straightforwardness of a physician. "He'll be away for a while with Mrs. McClelland."

"Away where?" Tricia said, her voice weak and small.

"How long?" This from Helen, sounding desperate.

"I don't know. Mrs. McClelland said they're going straight to the airport from here. She said to tell all of you he'll be in touch soon."

In an atmosphere increasingly funereal, Nan escorted us as a group to the elevator. We rode in awkward silence until Mike made a more awkward stab at normalcy. He brought up the U.S. Open, which would begin in a few days. He and Baze talked woodenly about the new USTA National Tennis Center, the probability of a Borg-Connors final, and Borg's slim chances on the hard court surface.

Helen and Tricia joined forces against Nona, conferring

about their common enemy. I thought about Terry and waited to hit the ground floor.

It was August 24, 1978, one week before Jack had been scheduled to arrive on the island. Labor Day would come and go. So would that thief of a summer—stealing a job, a doubles partner, and a son; swindling a marriage, a cheek, and part of a lung; plundering love and lovers; leaving us all with uncertainty and change; forcing us all to begin again.

Tricia had the window. I had the aisle. The sky was irreverently bright. At twenty-five thousand feet, I was thinking about cleaning out my office at TCC, hoping I could do it before Jack recovered and returned. My ears were popping. I swallowed but without relief as Tricia tapped my arm. Her voice sounded distant above the drone of our flight.

"I'm filing for divorce as soon as we get back."

I nodded and said, "I am too."

The phone was ringing as I unlocked my apartment. Aaron Silver was calling and asking loudly if I knew how he could reach Mrs. Curren. He needed to arrange a meeting, he said, regarding the divorce. They planned to file next week.

"Is she staying with you?" He didn't wait for an answer. "Jack would like her to have her books right away. We'll have them delivered. There are forty-five boxes."

"Fine," I said, but it wasn't. My apartment, with a living/dining area, a kitchenette with a window, and a bedroom, was only five hundred square feet. "Good-bye, Aaron."

I knew by my new roommate's eyes that she'd heard everything, and I braced for an onslaught of questions: Jack was filing? Would that hurt her? What would a lawyer cost? How would she find one? But the questions were in my mind, not hers.

"I'll go with you to meet with Aaron."

"No, Lynn. I can handle it. You have your new job."

"I'm going with you," I said. "Aaron Silver is a son of a bitch."

At the end of my first week of work, Bob McHugh called me to his office. He asked how things were going and I gave him a truthful assessment. I loved the job and the corporate culture, so different from TCC.

I thought I might come to admire him and learn from him too, in this new place where my goals were the same but the light was new. It was warm and steady, not fiery. Glowing, not blinding. I was clear-eyed now and would stay that way. I didn't think I'd even have to try.

The agency wasn't as large and didn't have a stellar client list like Jack's, but McHugh and Brown produced excellent work without the intensity and stress that started at the top of TCC and filtered down. I'd breathed those toxins for years like secondhand smoke.

"We're a good fit for you, Lynn," Bob said, "and you, for us. You're going to do well."

"Thank you, Bob. And thank you for the opportunity."

"I think I need to thank Chris," he said, standing, smiling.

"Chris?" The photo on his desk caught my eye. "Oh, Chris. Yes. And I hope to meet Annie soon." I studied the faces of his five daughters and tried to decide which one was Annie, but all had dark, mistrusting eyes and such seriousness even in their smiles that I could not imagine any of them with Chris Bazemore. I decided I didn't know him as well as I thought I did and probably never would: I hadn't heard from him since returning to the city. If I'd lost him, I'd lost a friend. That was all we were and were meant to be. I was twelve years older. But he'd helped me touch something new and different, some wisp or curl of a thing. Something sweet I couldn't absorb then but could almost taste now as it evaporated in the air.

"We are proposing an uncontested divorce," Aaron Silver began, his hands folded upon a file on his desk. "You'll find, Mrs. Curren, that Jack's offer is generous, in light of your actions."

Tricia started to protest, but I laid my hand on her arm, and Rick Lynes, the attorney I'd helped her find, gave her a low, subtle wave.

"New York is an equitable distribution state, with equitable meaning fair, rather than equal. The law lists many factors for determining what is equitable, and I'll lay out those that are relevant. There is the duration of the marriage, a mere three years. The health of both parties, and Jack's surgery must be taken into account. The income and property of each party at the time of the marriage, and at the time of the commencement of this action; you brought and contributed nothing material to the marriage. Nor have you contributed directly or indirectly to his career—also a factor. Even your services as a spouse and homemaker could be deemed unsatisfactory and inconsequential." Aaron moved on to the factors for determining spousal support and belittled her, even while admittedly establishing a clear case for Jack to provide compensation. "We must consider the present and future earning capacity of both parties and the ability of the party seeking maintenance to become self-supporting. Having no prior work experience, you are seriously handicapped, Mrs. Curren, and further limited, Jack tells me, by your inherent inability to relate to others, particularly in social settings, and by your odd penchant for solitude."

Rick spoke up. "Those things constitute an indisputable need, which obviously Mr. Curren understands and with which even you, Mr. Silver, apparently agree."

"I do. Your ability to become self-supporting, Mrs. Curren, is qualified by the period of time and training necessary therefore. I understand you're planning to go to graduate school in Austin, where your—What shall I call him? The young man with whom you willfully committed sexual intercourse while married to Jack?"

"Call him her friend," Rick said, leaning forward.

"You and your friend mentioned that to Jack at the beach house—that you were going to go back to school. Your friend, with whom you voluntarily committed acts of adultery—defined in Subdivision Two of Section 130.00 as acts of sexual intercourse, oral sexual conduct, or—"

"We know the state laws," Rick said, just as I was deciding that he was far too passive to tangle with Aaron or Jack. "This meeting is over. Mail the proposed settlement agreement to Mrs. Curren with a copy to me."

Mrs. Curren was changing colors like a chameleon. She had turned pink with embarrassment, red with anger, and pasty white with what I feared was surrender.

"I've drawn up only the complaint," Aaron said. "Jack asked me to conduct this meeting before drawing up the agreement. The viability of The Curren Company is uncertain, and Jack is attempting to work through personal financial difficulties as well. But he is offering Mrs. Curren her separate property, of course, and $120,000 annually for three years, payable monthly."

I had no idea what Tricia was thinking when she said, "I don't want anything from Jack."

"Yes, you do," I said quietly.

"Yes, I do," she said.

"Against my strongest recommendation, Jack has directed me to ask if Mrs. Curren wants or feels entitled to anything else."

"We'll confer and get back to you," Rick said.

But Tricia said, "I want the car."

Aaron's bushy eyebrows crawled like gray caterpillars toward each other in a frown. "The Porsche?"

"Yes."

He looked annoyed as he dialed Jack's direct line at TCC. It was nearly five o'clock. In a rush of sadness that surprised me, I imagined Jack at his desk, loosening his tie.

"She wants the Porsche," Aaron said. A moment later, he thanked Jack and hung up. "He's fine with that. I'll mail the agreement for review and signature."

As we walked home, Tricia turned to me only once.

"Terry loves that car," she said.

CHAPTER 15

Austin was sunny and cloudless. Fall semester had just begun. Tricia was excited and accepted— a PhD candidate, for whom a teaching assistantship was no longer critical to enrollment in January. She would have ten thousand dollars a month. And wherever Terry had been with Nona, now he'd be back at school.

At the tennis courts, the Longhorns were at work. She spotted Baze and Freddie, but not Terry.

Her head throbbed with every whop of a ball as she waited for practice to end.

"Tricia." Baze came to a standstill.

She'd planned to avoid him. He hadn't called Lynn or returned her calls, and Lynn had been hurt. But Tricia had no choice. "Where is Terry?" she said.

Baze unzipped a pocket of his bag, took out a Longhorns hat, and put it on. He dropped the bag to the ground and said nothing.

"Where is Terry, Baze? Is he still hurt?"

"He didn't come back."

She felt the confused breath of Texas, blowing hot and occasionally cool with a hint of fall. "You're joking. I'm dying inside and you're joking."

"Did he tell you he was coming back? Did he even talk to you after he remembered what happened?"

"Where is he?" she demanded. "I've filed for divorce." She thought that surprised him. "Terry wanted me to come to Austin with him. We'd planned—"

"When did you plan? Before it all happened? Or after?"

"Before," she admitted. "But he'll want me now."

"He's not here, Tricia. I don't know where he is."

"You don't know, or you won't tell me?"

"I don't know. He wouldn't say. We talked a few days ago, and he said he wasn't coming back to school. That's all I know. Two Ls called me too. She doesn't know where he is either."

She wanted to cry, but her eyes had been desert-dry for weeks. "Give me Helen's number. He'll have to call her sooner or later. She's his mother."

"I don't know her number."

"You're lying."

"She remarried. I don't even know her name."

"You're lying. You know it. Give me the number."

And Baze exploded. "Why? Haven't you done enough? What the fuck do you want, Tricia? To pick at the carcass?"

She heard a flapping, felt a hot swoop, a pecking at carrion in her chest, not Terry's.

"Sorry," Baze said, eyes regretful. "I shouldn't have said that." At the cranking of a car and clipped call of a horn, he glanced at a 280ZX nearby, waved at the girl at the wheel. He turned his cap around backward. He looked at Tricia again, his eyes sad now. "I'm sorry. He's not here. He wouldn't want to hurt you, Tricia, but he's been through a lot. You both have. We all have. It was a cluster fuck of a summer, and Terry had to move on. Maybe he'll come back. Maybe he'll call you. Maybe not. Maybe he'll keep playing hide-and-seek or—"

"I don't think he's playing, Baze. Or hiding. I think he's lost. In every way." She thought she saw a flash of concurrence in Baze's eyes, thought he would say he would help her find him. Instead, he responded to the Z car's commanding blast.

"That's Annie. I can't keep her waiting." He started toward the car but stopped ten yards away. "You've filed for divorce?"

"Yes."

"You're going back to school?"

"Yes." She looked at the empty courts. "But I don't know

where now."

"You've got a lot going for you, Tricia. He'd be really proud. He'd want you to do what he's doing. Keep on keepin' on. Keep moving forward. Like in tennis—you have to always move forward, always try to get in, to get to the net."

"He'll call me, Baze. He'll come back."

Baze looked away. "On and forward, Tricia. Especially forward."

This isn't Chekhov, Tricia thought on the flight to Savannah. *This is theater of the absurd, and I have the leading role.*

She called Lynn first and told her quickly what had happened; then, with her heart beating even more quickly, she asked, "Do you, for any reason or by some blessed stroke of good fortune, happen to know Mike's last name?"

"Terry's father, Mike? No. I don't think I ever even heard it. He was Mike. Just Mike."

"I'll have to call Nona," Tricia said, and hung up the pay phone.

She dialed directory assistance, but as she feared, the number was new and unlisted. She had no choice but to go.

Her knock brought Ola Mae to the door, but she looked at Tricia through the sidelight, shook her head, and walked away. Tricia rang the bell and knocked. Then she hammered the door with her fists. Rang, knocked, hammered. Over and over.

At last, Ola Mae opened the door, bringing with her the scent of clean floors and polished furniture. Tricia caught a whiff of lemon as Ola Mae's fists went to her hips. She rocked onto her toes and back on her heels, then settled into flat-footed confrontation.

"I need to see Terry."

"No ma'am. No ma'am," Ola Mae semi-sang. Her cadence

was, “No Sirree.”

“I need Terry. Now.” The word rumbled like snare drums, like the programmatic head roll of Berlioz’s *Symphonie Fantastique.* The fourth movement’s Dies Irae was about to begin. Day of Judgment. Day of wrath. She heard the dance of the witches that followed. Nona’s dance.

“Lord, child, please. Mr. Terry’s not here. Miz Nona’s got him in Bermuda, and once that mama of his sends his passport here, I’m to send it to Bermuda so they can go to France.”

“To France?” Tricia said dully.

“So you better quit your trespassing.”

“I’m not trespassing.” Indignation. “I’m visiting. I’m looking for Terry.”

“Trespassing.” Ola Mae rocked up and back again.

A car pulled into the driveway, and without the accompaniment of a siren, bathed the white stucco walls of Nona’s home in flashing blue. Tricia felt sick.

“Miz Nona said if you or that mama darken this door, I’m to call the police on you. Miz Nona’s talked to the chief. She’s got her connections. You’re about to be arrested.”

Tricia heard the voice of a dispatcher on the radio, a car door opening and closing, footsteps.

“Miss,” said the officer behind her.

She imagined handcuffs, fingerprints, a cell, bail, a court hearing, a police report in a newspaper. A question on a job application: *Have you ever been arrested? Convicted?*

She turned to the young man in uniform, who hadn’t rehearsed his dialogue and dropped his line. He said nothing and she improvised to help him. “I’m leaving now. I won’t come back. I can’t come back, can I?”

Here was absurdity beyond any playwright—beyond Albee, Stoppard, or Beckett. Every required element of the genre was present: outside forces beyond her control, loss of hope, loss of meaning, and silence before the final curtain.

§

Austin. New York. Iowa City.

Tricia made her decision in November, alone at a concert, between Beethoven and Mozart, in the darkness of Avery Fisher Hall. She went back to Lynn's apartment and found her friend curled up on the sofa, wearing pajamas and watching Johnny Carson as Carnac the Magnificent. Tricia looked at her home of the last three months, felt the glow of gratitude.

"Lynn, you've been a sister to me."

"Been?" Lynn said, eyes curious.

Tricia turned off the television and sat down beside her friend. She unbuckled the ankle straps of her shoes and slipped them off. The heels were thin and high. Her feet were tingling. She wiggled her toes against black nylon and flexed her feet. "I'm going to Iowa," she said.

"Iowa? As much as you love New York? What happened to NYU? Why Iowa?"

"Closure. To be happy in a place where I once was miserable. I was reclusive and friendless there as a child, and even in college and grad school. I'm determined not to be now." She hoped for acceptance and support, but Lynn seemed upset and retreated to the kitchenette for a cup of tea. Tricia waited a moment and followed.

"Do you want some, Tricia? Chamomile?"

She declined, and the conversation stalled until the teakettle whistled. She went to the table, and Lynn joined her there with an oversize white mug, its navy-blue TCC logo chipped and faded. Together they stared at the tea bag. They watched it change clear, steamy water to a mild-mannered green, as if the process were as remarkable as the Iowa decision.

"Peter Rabbit's mother gave him chamomile tea," Tricia said, smiling. "After his mishap in Mr. McGregor's garden."

"Only you, Tricia," Lynn said, her smile halfhearted. She

removed the tea bag with a spoon. She added honey. “I’m happy for you—you know that—and for how things are falling into place.” She added a slice of lemon. “But you’ll be so far away.”

“We’ll stay in touch. I’ll visit.” She hadn’t expected Lynn to need reassurance, or the two of them to sit without words through a slow cup of tea.

“It will be easier there,” Lynn concluded. “To get beyond Jack. And Terry. That’s what you need, isn’t it?”

“I suppose.” She managed her own halfhearted smile. “I’m tired, Lynn. I have to go to sleep.” Lynn grabbed her hand as she rose and laced their fingers tightly. “You’ve taken good care of me,” Tricia said. “You can let go now.” She kissed her friend’s cheek. “Thank you for everything, Lynn. I love you.”

But she didn’t go to sleep.

She went to Terry. That night as every night. But only for an hour.

It was the promise of that hour that allowed her to pin him to the backcourt of her awareness at all other times. She never lost serve, never let him break her—never let Peter break through to the nursery of Wendy’s new life, to distract her or impede her plans. She kept his shadow in a drawer, knowing he would come back for it, knowing she would sew it back on for him and give him a thimble, knowing they had plenty of time to fly. She kept the drawer closed until bedtime, then took out his shadow and lay down with it. Alone, her head on her pillow, she traced the silhouette from his shoulders to his waist and followed the outline of his thighs. Undercover and under the covers, she embraced him and called up every moment in memory.

They walked the beach. He held her in his arms in the ocean. He taught her to swim. She watched him play tennis. She read aloud to him. They made love.

She closed her eyes and her senses sharpened until she ached inside. She touched him, her fingers awed and eager, and was touched by him, her flesh responding, her hips arching. She tasted him and offered herself at his table. She breathed in the smell of the sun on their sand-sprinkled skin, the fragrance of their sleep and sheets, the scent of his sweat and their sex, and the freshness of showering together. They laughed and played like children. They talked with intimacy impossible for either of them to have known without the other.

Vividness. Accuracy. Detail. Color. Light.

If she could get things right—the blue of the island sky, the sheen of the summer, the gold in his skin, the touch of his callused right hand—if she could think about him well enough and long enough, she believed she would dream about him. But she never did.

Instead, as weeks passed, he took gradual ownership of that hour like a final set—slowing it down, stretching it out, staying longer each night, refusing to leave. He began to control the points. He let their arguments slip in. He hit hard, bombarding her with things that hurt: the look on his face when she'd told him she was married, the hospital, his cheek, his ribs, Nona, the escape, and his blue-paper good-bye.

He struck up rallies of questions with wicked backspin, questions she didn't want to ask herself or hear. Where was he? With Nona?

Or with someone new? Was she pretty? Was she kind? What was he doing, feeling? Was he happy? Was he okay? He offered no baking soda paste to deaden the sting of unknowns, no ointment to calm her unbearable itch. Even one answer would have soothed her, but he gave her none, and she couldn't close out the match.

Eventually her imagination took up a racket, blasting shots at her from every direction, from baseline to net, from good to bad, from the extraordinary to the mundane—from Terry winning Wimbledon to Terry brushing his teeth.

Terry was with Nona on the Mediterranean coast; Terry was home and at peace with Mike and Helen, in a place she did not know. Terry was on his way to New York, even as she lay there. Terry was leaving a court somewhere on the WCT tour, tennis groupies at his heels. Terry was smiling at a lot of pretty girls, in Texas, in Georgia, all over the world. Terry was winning. Terry was losing. He was slaying his demons. He was coming undone. He was getting things together. He was falling apart.

But the best and worst of her imaginings concerned the day-to-day, the at-that-very-moment things. He was sleeping, his lips slightly parted, his breathing heavy. He was waking, eyes blinking at the morning, arms stretching, lips forming a sleepy, imperfect, enchanting smile. He was putting on his shoes, going out for a run. He was going for a hit, practicing his serve, playing a match. Somewhere. Without her.

Last of all came the overheads smashing down, the hopeful lobs she managed, ending the match with her score at love, with the possibility of never finding him or seeing him again.

She'd forced herself to give up Seconal, so for weeks she used books to fight the loneliness of restless nights. Then her weapon of choice became her dissertation.

Sometimes, along with her index cards, she would take Terry's note from the metal box. She would unfold it, and knowing where every word lay on the page, she would drop her eyes to the ones she wanted. She would read the sentence highlighted in her mind forever, the one that followed *Dear Tricia.* She would drag her finger across the page. *You know that I love you.*

She would turn out the light and lie down in bed. She would think of the scar the stitches might have left on his chin, touch the jellyfish scar on her breast, and wonder what he would have to muddle through in order to arrive in the right place, as she had.

Dear God, she prayed, *let him get there. Let everything be okay.*

She would give him time. Six months? Nine? But no more than nine. If he didn't find her, she'd find him. For now, though, she would wait. It would be hard, but at least she had Anton.

CHAPTER 16

He looked in the mirror at the scar in his chin—thinner, but still the first thing anyone would notice. At least the surgery was behind him, thanks to Nona, and the stitches out. At least his cheek looked almost normal. At least they were back in the States, back at Nona's.

Bermuda had been good, he was thinking, highs in the seventies, nice breezes. The resort had been classier than any place he'd stayed in his life, with staff acting as if he and Nona were the only people there. The Cambridge beaches had been beautiful, but the sand hadn't looked pink as Nona had promised, except at sunset, when he'd had a few drinks.

He'd walked the golf course with Nona when she played, wishing he could try it, but afraid of the pain in his side a tee shot could bring. She'd let him putt for her sometimes and called him a natural on the green.

They had joked all week about men wearing shorts and knee socks.

"Men's hose," Nona had said with a laugh, "not socks. And how I'd love to dress you that way, angel, since you're the only man on this island who doesn't have legs like twigs."

He ran his fingers over the scar. Who was he kidding? It looked like shit. It looked as bad as he felt, standing there with the hangover and the headache that were always hanging on, that never quit. Ever since the hospital, he'd been in a stupor.

He'd felt that way in Bermuda. He'd felt that way in Marseilles. No. Worse in Marseilles. Marseilles had sucked. French was a second language for Nona, and she'd spoken it nonstop—even when they were around people who could speak English, even with her friends, who must have been filthy rich like her, because they lived in a mansion overlooking the harbor. Every time Marie and Georges—who he kept calling George by mistake—would start a conversation with him in English, Nona would butt in and take over in French. He might as well have been deaf. He wished he'd been deaf at the opera.

Outside Nice, he and Nona had stayed in a villa. On the Mediterranean beaches, he'd felt stupid with topless Nona. He'd watched girls, thinking he could be getting laid, thinking about two people doing it without being able to speak each other's language.

Thinking. Thinking of Tricia.

Thinking of her now.

He splashed warm water on his face and reached for the pale blue hand towel on the silver ring. It was monogrammed with his initials—so was the bath towel, so were the pillowcases.

Normandy, which had been his idea, had been the best part of the trip: the museum, Omaha Beach, the cemetery, and the towns nearby, which he couldn't pronounce right—Cherbourg, Arromanches, Caen, Rouen. They'd stayed at a bed-and-breakfast in Bayeux, where nobody spoke English. He'd gone out alone for an early morning run, even though the clouds were dark and threatening rain. There were fields on either side of the winding road, and they'd turned different shades of green as streaks of light broke through the clouds. He'd been trying to remember the names of all the greens in the Crayola box of sixty-four when a rainbow came up and made him forget everything except how happy he was at that moment, in a place he'd never been before, heading for a town as old as the Middle Ages, running hard and fast, his ribs barely hurting, nobody knowing how to find him.

But he'd gotten lost on the way back and hadn't been sure anybody understood him when he asked for directions. He'd wandered around for an hour before he'd found his way, and

Nona had been pissed because he'd run without her.

He'd tried to make it up to her in Paris. While she was trying on dresses in Galeries Lafayette, he'd slipped away to buy her a bottle of Chanel No. 5, the only parfum he'd heard of. He'd wished as he walked to the register that he could give it to Tricia instead. But he didn't know where Tricia was, or who she was with or not with. Maybe she'd divorced Jack after all. Or maybe she'd started believing what Terry had said about sin and decided to stay married forever.

The clerk had swiped his credit card, which was really his mother's card, and handed it back to him, rattling off French and broken English. All he'd picked up was *over limit.* He'd hated Nona in that moment because he needed her—for money as well as the language. Because he didn't have a dime or a franc or a fuck to his name.

That night, he'd asked if they could go home, and to his surprise, she'd said, "Of course, mon something-or-other." Mon, which meant "my," and something-or-other, which sounded like fee, but couldn't have been because it wasn't in the French dictionary. It was one of those words she said all the time but wouldn't translate when he asked her to.

He turned out the light.

Downstairs in her sunroom, Nona was sorting through mail and magazines that had accumulated while they were away.

"I'd kinda like to drive over to Charleston," he said.

She looked at the clock. "We'll go tomorrow."

"You don't have to go with me." He imagined she was wondering why he'd dressed in khaki pants and a polo. "If you wouldn't mind letting me use your car."

"Charleston? Or Kiawah?"

"I said Charleston, didn't I? It's just something to do, Nona."

"Patricia is in New York."

"Who said anything about—"

"I have friends in New York who know the Currens. They've reconciled, angel. They're together and happy."

He shrugged leaden shoulders. "Good. That's what I told her to do in that note. I'm glad."

Nona closed *Architectural Digest* and folded her hands over the cover. "The Davis Cup tie is at Mission Hills in Rancho Mirage, the first week of December. McEnroe, unlike his highness Connors, has agreed to play. Would you like to go, angel?"

"I'd like to go to Charleston." He waited. She glared at him. "Can I please use your car?"

"Be back by six." She gave him the key. "We'll go out to dinner."

She knew he needed cash but made him ask. She took ten twenties from her wallet and placed them in his beggar's palm one at a time. "Thanks," he said, and to make his next question seem like an afterthought, he started toward the door, stopped, and turned to her. "Did you call your doctor friend?"

"Yes."

"Did he write those prescriptions, like you said he would? Without me having to go in to see him?" He knew she wouldn't answer. "Did you get me some refills? 'Cause my ribs are still hurting. And I'm still getting headaches." Seconds ticked by. "I need my pills."

"Two a day, Terry. Take with food. That means dinner, angel. At six."

If Nan the nurse had said yes when he'd asked her if she wanted to get a beer, if she hadn't just started dating someone she really liked, then the whole damn thing wouldn't have happened.

He wouldn't have bought a six-pack and a cooler, or driven to Kiawah to get reefer and coke from the guy he'd bought from at the beginning of the summer and when Jack came back.

If he hadn't gotten stoned and done a couple of lines, he wouldn't have driven to the beach house and looked in through the sliding glass door at the empty bookshelves. He wouldn't have walked in the dunes, found the driftwood log Jack had crashed his head against.

If he hadn't gotten fucked up, he wouldn't have started shaking so bad that he had to sit down on the swing and smoke another joint to calm down. If he hadn't drunk a beer to top it off, he wouldn't have forgotten dinner at six and walked the beach for miles and smoked another.

If Nona had been waiting to ream him out like he'd expected, he wouldn't have had to wake her up and ask for his Percocet. If she'd given it to him, he wouldn't have gotten so pissed off that he slammed her bedroom door on his way out.

If he hadn't stumbled in the hall, she wouldn't have followed him up the stairs into his room and started firing questions faster than he'd driven home: Where had he been? Why was he late? Why was he drunk? What was he on?

If he hadn't fallen to the thick white carpet, she wouldn't have helped him up and to bed like a kid. And if he hadn't fumbled with the buttons on his shirt, she wouldn't have helped him, asking if he was so drunk he couldn't get undressed.

If she hadn't spoken French when she reached for his belt, he wouldn't have told her to leave him the fuck alone. And if he hadn't been dizzy and had to lie down, she wouldn't have sat beside him and said what she did, words so mean she seemed to be shouting even though she was talking so softly he could barely hear.

"Do you know what you were to Patricia? You were a whim. A lark. An amusement."

"Talk French, Nona. 'Cause I don't want to hear this."

"That's how she explained you to Jack, as her dumb-jock fantasy come to life."

He closed his eyes, knowing he should never have told Nona the truth about what had happened and how much he loved Tricia. He nestled his busted cheek into the pillow, but Nona slid her hand under his face and turned it back to hers.

"Regarde ta mère, mon ange. Mon petit garçon. Mon pauvre fils. Qu'est-ce qui ne va pas? Tu as besoin de savoir qu'elle ne t'aime pas. Mais moi, oui. Je tiens à t'aider et à prendre soin de toi. Elle a failli te détruire. Il est temps d'oublier Patricia à jamais."

He opened his eyes. The sheets were damp. "I don't feel good."

She wiped sweat from his forehead. "Qu'est-ce qui se passe?"

"I don't know what that means. But something's wrong."

"Laisse-moi t'aider, mon ange." She took a pill from the pocket of her robe, put it in his hand, went into the bathroom, and filled a cup with water.

Nona was the angel now—dressed in white, her feet hardly touching the floor as she came back to the bed. She must have looked like that when she'd danced in New York. Like a ghost you could see through. Like this wasn't even happening. He raised himself up on his elbows. She sat back down and helped him get the pill and water to his mouth. Pills. She gave him another. After he'd swallowed the second, she ran her finger over his still-wet lips. Slowly.

You're sick, he wanted to say, *you know that, Nona?* But he didn't dare.

He thought of the twelve hours just past, and in that quick flashback, realized there was only one *wouldn't have* that really mattered: if Nan wouldn't have said no, if he'd had some time with her, he would have asked if he might be getting hooked on those pills and what she thought he should do.

"Il est temps d'oublier Patricia à jamais."

He only got one word of it. "Are you sure she's with Jack?"

"Yes, angel. I'm sure. But you won't hurt forever. Now try to sleep. Sweet dreams."

Don't, he thought. *Please don't.* He would have said it aloud if the pills hadn't worked so fast. And if he'd said it aloud, she wouldn't have kissed him like that before she left him alone in the dark.

He walked to the window, looked out at the morning. He laid his hand on the pane as if to touch October, the best month of the year in the South. He looked at the river and ripples in the pool. Leaves, though still green, were quivering in the breezy face of fall.

He wondered if he'd ever go home again, to his mom and the man he couldn't call Dad. Who'd never wanted him, never cared, never loved him.

He wondered which Nona was waiting downstairs—the warden, the mother, or the one who had kissed him good night, with her tongue so deep in his mouth. He wondered if she'd still sponsor him. Wondered what those French words meant.

He wondered what Tricia was doing at that moment—if she was in New York or maybe on a trip like he had been, in another country, in another time zone. He wondered if she was awake or asleep, what the weather was like, if she was hot or cold or in the rain.

He wondered if the motherfucker Jack was treating her good now. He wondered when Jack would give her the kid she wanted, knock her up so she'd never leave him. She'd stay, always stay, for the sake of her kid. He wondered where the Currens would have Thanksgiving and what her husband would give her for Christmas.

He wondered what he himself would give her for Christmas, if he could. But he had no money, other than Nona's, and no way to get a present into Tricia's hands.

He'd never be able to hold those hands again. Or touch her again. But maybe he'd see her again. Someday maybe. Somewhere.

In New York, if he were playing in the Open.

And maybe it would be enough just to know she was near him, that she was in the same city as he was, that she was at home, in a bookstore, in the stands.

Hey, you. Hey, shirtless.

Hell. Fucking hell. He'd settle for anything.

I love the smell of you.

He'd settle for being in the same city, state, or country as Tricia. Same world. Same universe. Something white on the ground below caught his eye. A seagull alone, hopping on the grass.

Left behind maybe. Lost. With no idea what to do.

He went downstairs to tell Nona he wanted to turn pro.

CHAPTER 17

Tricia left for Iowa on January 1, 1979, a day earlier than planned and a day before Baze and Annie's engagement party. In her departure I saw an attempt to shed the last of her summer skin. The scales and dead cells were still there and itching. I'd known by what she'd pointed out as she read the Times while I was getting ready for work in the mornings: The Yankees' World Series win. The Who choosing drummer Kenny Jones to replace Keith Moon, who'd died from a drug overdose. The sudden death of Pope John Paul I after a mere thirty-three days in office. The selection of the Longhorns for the Sun Bowl. The U.S. Davis Cup victory over Great Britain in Rancho Mirage.

I was living alone again when I received a package in the mail on the second of January. Because there was no return address, I was curious as I cut through the strapping tape and ripped through brown paper. The box inside was sloppily wrapped in red-and-green plaid paper. No ribbon. No tag. A note from Terry instead.

Obi-Lynn. Can you get this to Tricia for me somehow? Without him knowing?

I realized he didn't know about the divorce, that Baze must not have told him.

P.S. I am drunk or I wouldn't be doing this.

P.P.S. I am mailing this from Melbourne. Aussie Open. — Terry

Melbourne and Iowa City.

A tennis pro. A PhD candidate.

On the circuit and back in school. All was well.

I opened the box, and bewildered, tried to see love, sentiment, or a faint hint of passion. Instead, I smelled soggy insult and bitterness.

At my short squatty garbage pail in the kitchen, I stepped on the lever, raised the lid. Looking at the nastiness of dead poinsettias, banana peels speckled black, cantaloupe rinds, and other leftovers in the can, I hesitated, held back by a waft of salty sweetness from the contents of the box.

But the socks and wristbands, worn and unwashed, were intended to offend her, I decided.

Though they weren't degradable like everything else, I dropped them in the trash.

Jack began calling in February, once a week at first, then biweekly for a while. He wanted me back, he said. He could not abide TCC losing me to McHugh and Brown.

I told him he'd manage and he did—holding on to his company amid rumors of Chapter 11 bankruptcy, capably testifying and producing all documentation needed to convict Bill Kiernan of embezzlement while absolving himself of all wrongdoing. Like the entire industry, The Curren Company was helped by the dissipation of the public's mistrust of advertising, a metastasis of its mistrust of government in the aftermath of Vietnam and Watergate. I sensed even then a good year for TCC, and knowing Jack, I wouldn't have been at all surprised if 1979 brought TCC record annual billings.

In mid-May, at the end of her first semester, Tricia spent a week with me in the city. I met her at my apartment when she arrived and within minutes decided she'd never been happier. It wasn't the precarious exuberance of June and July 1978, but a healthy, stable happiness. I'd sensed it for months as a long-distance doubter, but over a quick lunch, I became a true believer. She couldn't stop chattering even to nibble at the chicken salad I'd picked up at a deli.

"Classes are going well," she said, her gray eye as bright as her blue one, her voice effervescent. I drank her happiness like champagne. She went on. "I may have been a mouse in a corner once, but I'm a lioness in the classroom now. I'm contributing so much to discussions that I have to remind myself not to monopolize them. I'm working as feverishly as you and Jack always worked, and loving it." Happy tears glistened. "And I have friends, Lynn. Not friends who are as close to me as you are. But good friends. I'm spending time with them. Going out."

I smiled. She had summered, wintered, and survived 1978. We all had. It was spring now. We were all better off. I had McHugh and Brown. Baze was getting married. Terry, according to Baze, was in Europe for the clay-court swing of the tour. And Tricia had a new empowered self.

She picked up her fork and put it down again. "I have friends who read Cheever and Updike and Greene, who want to talk about Henry James and E. M. Forster. I'd still rather go to a play than a party, but wherever I am, I don't feel inadequate or odd, as I always did with Jack."

"Speaking of plays," I said, glancing at my watch, needing to get back to the office. "What do you want to see tonight? *Fosse's Dancin'* or *They're Playing Our Song*?"

"Neither," she said. "Let's stay here and catch up. Let's just talk."

"Perfect," I said. "I've had a long week."

"I need to talk." She paused. "About Terry."

"All right," I said, wrestling with surprise and knowing I'd be grappling with curiosity until I heard more.

I went back to the office for what became a terrible afternoon. I tried to help a colleague with a new client whose product had begun losing market share shortly after we'd been hired. We presented a list of five problems we planned to address. I kept the sixth to myself: the product's key competitor was represented by the best agency in the business, TCC. We worked with them for hours, answered every question, and made commitments we knew would tax us and our creatives. Still, we lost them. There was nothing to do but go home.

As I approached the break room, on my way to the elevator, I heard my name and stopped in the hall. I eavesdropped on two male coworkers, one of them calling me a ballbuster, the other betting that I'd sleep my way to a vice presidency at McHugh and Brown in no time, before Bob McHugh was too old to get it up.

I also needed to talk now and hurried home to Tricia. She was waiting for me just inside my apartment door. She looked shocked, her face a glaring white.

"What is it?" I asked. Someone was sick? Hurt? Dead? "Who is it?" Jack? Terry?

She took my wrist with her damp, sticky hand. Her other hand was tightfisted. She pulled me to my kitchen table. At my place, she'd positioned my cutting board. And in the middle of that plastic milk-white board, she'd positioned a two-by-three-inch card, to which a spare button was attached—a button that had come with a dress I'd worn only once. She opened her fist and five matching black pearl buttons rolled over the white linoleum floor.

"I'm sorry. I'm so sorry." Apologies tumbled from deep inside me, whispered but wholehearted. I lost count of them. Not that it mattered. There could never be enough. And none of them seemed to reach or touch her.

"Stop," she finally said. "Just stop. Just tell me how it happened."

I tried to imagine recounting the first time for her, but didn't want to even think about it. I'd shut it out of my head. "What good would it do?"

"Maybe I'll understand. If I understand, maybe I can forgive you."

I shook my head. "There's no point."

I wished she were Jack. I wished she'd shout and hurt me like he'd hurt Terry. I wanted her to grab my shoulders and shake me, clench my hair and smash my head into the wall. I would welcome that. I wouldn't resist.

"Then tell me why, Lynn."

I wanted her to rip out my hair as Jack had ripped yellow yarn from the head of the doll she treasured. I imagined the ragged holes he'd made of her eyes. I saw the doll's soft limbs ripped off and her body and heart laid bare, exposing every pulsing fiber inside.

"I was in love with him," I whispered.

She sat down. I felt I should ask her permission to join her, even though we were at my table, in my kitchen, my home.

I started to sit, but she said, "No." She looked up at me, her eyes dark, the champagne flat. She turned her eyes back to the button before her. "I was reading *The Iowa Review*," she said, trancelike. "I wanted to clip out a poem. I needed scissors." She'd opened what I call my miscellaneous drawer—flashlights, candles, screwdrivers, a hammer, nails, extra keys, and extra buttons, most of them on cardboard tags. "I saw it," she said, and she went on, her words as gray and irregular as unhewn granite. "I raided your closet. I threw everything down. Everything you wear. I couldn't help it. I found the dress. I saw— I cut the buttons off."

I fumbled for something to say. "I haven't worn it since the—"

"Since the day you were in my bed?"

I fumbled again, missed again. "I should have thrown it away."

"So I'd never know?" She rose. "You're just like him. Ruthless, duplicitous, ugly inside. Self first, whatever the cost."

"I loved him."

"And that's supposed to make it okay?"

"All he wanted was to make your marriage work. I tried to help him understand you."

"While you were making love with him? Really, Lynn. Please." She walked to the front door, picked up her pocketbook and suitcase waiting there. "I'm leaving," she said without looking back.

I removed the black pearl button from the card in front of me. It felt cold one moment, hot the next. It froze in my hand so hard and deep that I thought I'd need to have it surgically removed. It burned my flesh like a blowtorch, burned through muscle and bone. I walked to my bedroom and stopped at the door.

My dresses and suits lay in a haphazard pile on the floor. The arms and legs of coats and pants were at odd angles, as if limbs inside were broken or dislocated. But they were my clothes, not Jack's. This was my apartment, not his townhome. Almost a year had passed since I'd seen Patricia sitting on their bed, button in hand, tears in her eyes. I knew I'd never see her again.

Terry was a groomsman at Baze's wedding, the Saturday of Memorial Day weekend. The best-looking groomsman, the flirt, the one every bridesmaid eyed during the ceremony. The groomsman who shed his jacket as soon as he arrived at the reception while the maid of honor removed his bow tie. The groomsman every girl in a magenta taffeta gown, sash tied in a large stiff bow in the back, dragged onto the dance floor at least once. The groomsman I couldn't get to even to say hello to. Who avoided me all night long.

Terry was the groomsman stumbling so badly by the time the bride and groom cut the cake that all the pretty maids had lost interest. The groomsman who couldn't catch the garter Baze threw directly to him. Who was so drunk by the time Baze and Annie dashed through a rice shower toward a waiting limo that he had surrendered to a wing chair in the lobby, a bourbon on the rocks on the table beside him. Terry was the groomsman who ran his fingers over the satin stripe on his pants as if to help him remember where he was, who took a pill from his pocket and swallowed it, just before calling my name.

I'd planned to at least mention Tricia when I saw him but decided against it as I approached. "Hi, Terry."

His eyes were half closed. "Do you ever see her?"

I don't think he realized he'd omitted Hi, Lynn. "I saw her a few weeks ago." He stood up. "You want a drink?"

"No, thanks."

"You want to dance?"

"Do you? You look like you're going to fall over."

He laughed. "No, I'm good. Want some champagne?" He leaned left, then dropped back in the chair. "Can you help me? I tried to go to my room, but the key wouldn't work."

I helped him up, to the elevator, and to what he was pretty sure was his room. He slid the key into the door slot—upside down, backward, upside down again. He stopped trying and turned to me.

"So how's Tricia? Big?"

"Big?" I repeated.

"You can't fake me out, Lynn. I heard about the baby."

"There's no baby," I said. "Tricia's in Iowa. In grad school. And divorced, of course."

My words were wading through puddles of bourbon in his brain when the door opened from inside, bringing us face-to-face with Nona McClelland. She looked at me first, eyes wide and hostile, then at Terry. Without a word she slapped him, hard enough to turn his head. I had time to see the imprint of her hand on his face before she slapped him again.

"Brat." One more slap. "Bastard."

She grabbed his shirt and pulled him into the room. A single. A king-size bed.

On my way back down to the lobby, the rumble I heard and the tremor I felt had nothing to do with the elevator. They were another aftershock of the summer of '78. The last one, I hoped.

On July third, Terry's father made his way—through the fog of my surprise and the crowd in LaGuardia's international terminal—to me.

"Baze called us after he called you," he said, "to let us know. Baze didn't think we should come, but Helen did." He waited for reassurance I couldn't give him and went on. "Helen's at the hotel. I wanted to be the one to meet him here. I think it's best."

I tried to be gentle but my tone was sharp. "Best for you or for Terry?"

He studied the chair beside mine as if it were one of a kind and dangerous. "For both of us." He started to sit, but I stood up. "Helen's my wife now. Terry's my son. We've got to get to at least a civil acceptance of that."

I couldn't hold back. "This isn't the time, Mike."

"He's my son," he said. "I think it is."

The silence between us was so powerful that it began to spread. We were in LaGuardia and yet I heard nothing—no arrivals or departures on the runway or in the air, no last calls for boarding, no bustling travelers with rolling luggage or briefcases or New York souvenirs, no conversations. I heard nothing until Mike said my name. His eyes took on the tentativeness of Terry's as he asked if he could buy me a cup of coffee. With a half hour to spare, I agreed.

We found a restaurant nearby, and Mike stared into his cup as if it were a wishing well and he might see a penny he'd thrown strike bottom. When he looked up again, he told me his and Helen's story. It had begun like Terry and Tricia's—a nineteen-year-old tennis pro in Fort Lauderdale; a neglected, unhappy twenty-four-year-old woman, answering the whims of a workaholic surgeon by night, needing something more. Mike didn't know she was pregnant, he said, when he left Lauderdale to take his shot at professional tennis. Eight years later, their paths crossed again.

"I couldn't deal with it at first—a kid out of nowhere." He looked pained and penitent. "A kid playing tennis, being pushed way too hard. I saw what she was doing to him. I wanted to help, but Helen was drinking by then, and I had to help her instead of Terry. I stayed in the shadows, watching my son play, feeling proud one minute and like a criminal the next. Like a coward." He came to an emotional conclusion. "So Terry and I have come full circle. I couldn't deal with his existence. Now he can't deal with mine."

I offered honest comfort. "He will, Mike, but it's going to take time. And it's not going to be tonight."

He finished his coffee. "You're easy to talk to, Lynn. Why is that?"

"God. I don't know. I live in the middle of other people's problems."

He smiled. "Who do you talk to when you have troubles?"

"I don't."

"Don't have troubles? Or don't talk about them?"

"The latter," I said, open and vulnerable in the presence of this man I hardly knew, this man with Terry's smile. I changed the subject. "I'm very worried."

He massaged his neck and left shoulder. "Me too. I don't know what in the hell to expect."

But I did. I remembered Terry, drunk, high, and covered in sand, walking boldly toward the beach house.

I'm in love with Tricia.

"It's almost midnight," I said. "We'd better go."

Mike paid the two-dollar charge for our coffee and left a dollar tip. I suppose he thought he was leaving a quarter on the table instead of a newly minted Susan B. Anthony dollar. A woman on the face of a US coin. It had only taken two hundred years, or close to it.

"Baze didn't give Helen many details," Mike said as we sat down at the gate. "What in the hell did Terry do to provoke that woman?"

"After he lost in the qualifying tournaments at the Queen's Club and Wimbledon—"

First round, Baze had said, bagels and breadsticks.

"Nona showed up unexpectedly in London and found him—"

So messed up, Baze had said, that he couldn't remember what he'd drunk, smoked, snorted, or shot.

"He was in his hotel room, in bed with a girl."

Baze had said two.

"He took a shower," I told Mike, "to sober up, and when he came back into the room, Nona had taken his things and was gone."

At 12:01 a.m., the plane landed. Weary but happy passengers filed out of the tunnel toward smiles and open arms. As their entrances into the terminal grew sporadic and stopped, Mike and I looked everywhere but at each other. The crowd dispersed. The noise decreased.

Terry, assisted by a flight attendant and another passenger, was the last one off the plane.

"Happy fourth," Mike said absentmindedly. Spellbound, we watched the man at Terry's side coax him into a chair as the flight attendant scanned the remnants of the crowd. I nudged Mike and started forward, but now that I needed him, he held back.

I walked toward Terry—flip-flops, tennis shorts, T-shirt, unshaven, the unpleasant smells I'd expected. But this time, he had sweat on his forehead and neck, goose bumps on his arms, and a runny nose. As I drew closer, I heard him ask for a blanket. He saw me and slumped forward. He pressed the heels of his hands against his closed eyes.

"Terry." I knelt beside him, but he wouldn't look at me.

"He got sick on the plane," the attendant said quietly. "He went into the bathroom and never came out. We had to go in."

"Where's home?" the man asked, taking a pen and prescription pad from his coat pocket. "Savannah," Mike said, at my side now. "We're flying tomorrow."

I waited for Terry to leap out of the chair and shout, *no, fuck no, no way in hell I'm going with you.* Instead, he shivered with chills.

"He's very ill. There's an all-night convenience shop near baggage claim. Pick up some Benadryl. Give him two for sleep. He may have more nausea or diarrhea, so get something for that and something for pain. The aching will get much worse." He folded the prescription in half. "This is for two Percocet to tide him over. Get it filled first thing tomorrow. Let him have them and a beer if you have to. Get him home and to a detox unit, preferably in a rehab center. If you need a referral—"

"We've made arrangements."

Again I waited for Terry to explode. Instead, behind his hands, tears started and flowed.

"Call my office if I can help you," the doctor said to Mike. He squeezed Terry's shoulder, nodded at me, shook Mike's hand, and gave him the prescription and a business card.

Mike thanked him, the attendant left, and the three of us were alone in the area except for a custodian, a pilot passing through, and a few stragglers looking on. Mike mouthed, *What now?*

I sat on the floor. "You'll be okay, Terry." No response. "Obi-Lynn says so." A nod.

Mike took the chair beside Terry's. "Whenever you're ready," he said. "No rush."

With the tail of his T-shirt, Terry wiped his nose and tears. "Sorry," he said, rising.

"Let's get your bags," Mike said.

"I don't have any bags." He looked at Mike. "Or clothes. Or any-fucking-thing." His jittery hands fished in his pockets. "All she left me was cash for a cab, my passport, and this."

He handed me a piece of paper that he'd folded into a one-inch square. He stared at the floor as I skimmed what Nona had written—the flight number, departure time, and a good-bye: *Maybe your beloved Patricia will meet you at LaGuardia, since you've never quit thinking about her. Maybe she can love you—addicted, alcoholic, pathetic, and losing. I can't.*

I gave it back to him, he passed it to Mike, and tears began again.

"I'm sorry," he said, and though he looked at neither of us, I knew the apology was intended more for Mike than me. "You don't need this shit. I'm acting like a two-year-old."

"I wasn't around when you were two," Mike said, outwardly casual and, I sensed, inwardly overcome. "I owe you."

He put a conciliatory arm around Terry's shoulder and patted his chest twice in a way that reminded me of the aftermath of the Wimbledon match I'd caught on television earlier that day. They looked like winner and loser at the net until Terry dropped his head, nuzzled his father's neck, and cried a little harder. Together the three of us started to short-term parking and my car.

At the hotel, Terry cried again, in his mother's arms this time. I went to the front desk for a toothbrush and razor for him, asked about pharmacies nearby. Back in the room, Helen was tucking him in bed like a child. She stepped away so that I could tell him good-bye.

"I feel like I'm two," he said quietly. "You know what two is, don't you? 'Two is the beginning of the end.'"

I didn't know what he meant. From the corner of my eye, I saw Mike fold his arms. I expected him to tug his earlobe.

"Maybe two is the beginning of a beginning," I suggested.

"Tricia would love this," he whispered. "Me and my parents." He motioned me closer, wrapped his arms around me and pleaded, "Don't tell her you saw me. Please, Lynn. Tell her I died. Tell her I killed myself. 'Cause I don't want her to ever see me like this. Or ever see me. Or know. Don't tell her what I am. Or where I am. Don't ever. Promise me, Lynn."

I tried to straighten up, to wish him good luck and tell him I'd talk to him soon, but he wouldn't release me until I gave him what he wanted: "I will never tell her, Terry. I promise."

I always remembered what he asked of me that night. He never remembered asking.

CHAPTER 18

Detox was hard. Rehab was harder. This, he decided, was the hardest of all: sitting on his ass every day, not wanting to do anything, or just standing at the bay window of the condo at The Landings on Skidaway Island in Savannah, where Mike was the director of tennis; Mike asking every day if he wanted to go for a hit; his mom asking every day if he was depressed.

"Nah," he said. So many times. So many days.

"You've got to do something, Terry," she finally said, and Mike nodded.

He sat down at the breakfast table where they were eating crunchy cereal. He listened to the annoying sound, wishing for the Walkman his mother had bought him. He began tilting the saltshaker, balancing it, spinning it, counting the seconds until it fell over. One, two, three. Crash. Then all the way to five. He tried again.

"You'll feel better if you get out for a change," his father said.

And his mother: "Why don't you hit with Mike?"

He stopped the spinning, picked up his makeshift top, and set it back on the table. "Mom, I don't ever want to pick up a racket again."

She went to the toaster. No one said anything until she returned to the table and gave him two slices of toast. He looked up at her, and she said what he'd always wanted her to say, "That's fine, Terry, if that's what you want."

He reached across the table for the tub of butter, and his hand stopped. It hung in the air like a marionette's, attached to strings that someone wouldn't release—strings that might never be released. He stared at the familiar label—Good, Better,

BEST BUTTER, the beautiful little girl with Heidi braids, smiling and winking. The wink must have been Jack Curren's idea, when he stepped in to take charge of a photo shoot and a crying child. When he stepped in and took over her life. Told her to wink and cover the gray.

Tricia at seven.

Twenty-seven by now, he guessed. He didn't know her birthday. Didn't even know. He blinked back tears.

"Whatever you want, Terry," his mother said, giving him a bowl of cereal. "Whatever you need."

"What I need," he said. "What I need is to put everything as far behind me as I can get it. I want to go to the beach today, to Tybee Island, and ride some waves. I want to find some special school and learn to fucking read." He stared at his cereal, dipped a spoonful of milk, turned it over, watched it splash. He did it repeatedly, waiting on his mother to tell him not to play with his food. He pushed the bowl away and looked at her. "I want to go to one of those meetings with you." He picked up the saltshaker, spun it—one, two, three seconds. He looked at Mike. "Someday, maybe, I want to go for a hit with you. Maybe." He exchanged the saltshaker for the pepper shaker, spun it, set it upright, and staring at it, said, "I want to go to a lawyer." He looked up in time to see his parents exchange worried glances. "'Cause what I want most of all is to change my name. My last name." He looked directly at his father. "I want Hesselbach. I want yours."

CHAPTER 19

"Thinking Retirement? The Alternative to Crowded Florida," I said to the committee at The Landings on Skidaway Island. "The headline is strategic, simple, memorable." I smiled. "And inarguably true."

I wasn't sure I'd clinched the account on the basis of McHugh and Brown's background, client list, or the marketing plan I'd presented. But I was certain I'd clinched it with the ad campaign for this private golf and tennis community. The president of the land development company was nodding, the vice president of marketing was thoughtful but smiling, and the director of sales looked ready to pull a pen from his pocket and sign the proposed retainer agreement even before I went back to New York.

"How did your company hear of McHugh and Brown?" I asked the director of sales as he walked me to my car. It was a question I always asked but seldom with as much anticipation as I felt then. He answered as I'd hoped he would.

"Our director of tennis. He said the agency's first-rate and so are you."

"Mike?"

"Mike Hesselbach," he answered. "He's a friend?"

"Yes."

"It's six, but he's probably still at the courts," he said, "if you want to say hello."

I followed his directions to the tennis center, parked my rental car near the pro shop, and rolled the window down. With the presentation behind me and stress fading like the afternoon, I listened to birdsong I knew, looked at the oaks and Spanish moss. I closed my eyes, thinking of Kiawah.

If I got The Landings account, then Kiawah Island would be a competitor. McHugh and Brown would take on The Curren Company. I would take on Jack and wasn't afraid to.

Kiawah. One hundred fifty miles from The Landings, 365 days in my rearview mirror. But when Mike—Hesselbach, I knew now—stepped out of the tennis shop, the summer of '78 slipped around my shoulders again. I wished for Terry walking behind him, holding Tricia's hand, and Baze, joking and making them laugh. I got out of my car. Mike saw me and we exchanged smiles.

I had a plane to catch but time for a quick trip to the Marshwood Clubhouse for a drink. We sat on the back patio overlooking the eighteenth green of one of two Arnold Palmer courses. He asked about the presentation. I said it went well and thanked him for the recommendation. I asked about Terry and he winced.

"He was terrific. He was going to meetings with Helen. He'd enrolled in a few classes for the fall at the community college here. He even came back around to tennis. We were hitting every day, played some doubles for fun."

I couldn't understand why Terry had become past tense.

Nearby, a couple rose from their table. In an obvious effort to procrastinate, Mike waved them over and introduced me. They chatted with him about the upcoming members' tennis championship and, after a few minutes, left us.

"Terry's okay?" I said. "He is or *was* terrific?"

He squinted at the green, though it was shaded and we were too. "The doc at the clinic said it's normal. A kid goes through rehab, gets home, and feels great. He has everything so under control that he thinks half a beer won't hurt."

Wings outstretched, a snowy egret glided to the lagoon between the patio and the green to feed. Mike used its graceful flight and landing as another reason to stall.

"But it did hurt, as did the other half, and we were headed to hell after that. He started lying to Helen, saying he was sober and clean. Helen was too intense. They both were. He quit talking to her, and when he talked to me, all he said was that he didn't give a shit about anything anymore."

In shallow water, the egret took slow, high steps on legs so thin they were almost invisible. It stopped and stared into the dark green water, waiting with enviable patience.

"I started to call you," Mike said. "I got your number from Baze. I thought maybe you could talk to him."

"I'd be glad to try." I glanced at my watch. Atlanta to New York would be easy, but I doubted there were many, if any, flights from Savannah's small airport to Atlanta in the evening.

"Terry thinks the world of you." He added, "Obi-Lynn."

The corners of my happy smile were held in check by a rush of emotion I couldn't explain, something as deep as my concern for Terry. Deep but different. I shook it off. *Of course I care about Mike,* I told myself silently. I cared about Terry, and Mike looked and sounded like Terry, had spoken my name with Terry's tentativeness.

I took my Day-Timer from my purse and looked at tomorrow's schedule. "If I can change my flight—"

"No need," he said. "We're past that now. Helen took him back to Willingway. That's where they are now. It's a different program this time, eight weeks instead of six."

"If you ever need me," I said, "please call." I put my planner away.

We finished our drinks and walked to the parking lot, stood together at my car.

"I wanted Helen," he said. "I wanted Terry just as much. Because he's my son. But there was more to it than that. Something drew me to him. I don't know what exactly."

"He's vulnerable," I said.

Mike looked away. "Aren't we all?"

I must have looked insulted instead of surprised when he

turned his eyes back to mine.

"I'm sorry," he said. "I meant most of us are."

"I need to go." I reached for the handle of my car.

"Old-school," he said, his hand covering mine.

I let him open the door. I swung my purse to the far seat, where my passenger and companion—my briefcase—was waiting. He closed the door, and I rolled down the window for good-byes.

I was tentative now. "Do you see me that way?"

"Vulnerable?"

"No. In," I said. "Invulnerable." *A cold, hard woman?* I wondered. "A woman without needs?" He took a step back, folded his arms, like Terry used to do.

He considered me intently, smiled, and said, "No."

CHAPTER 20

A dozen times on the flight to New York, Tricia wanted to close the Raymond Carver short story collection, show the cover to the chatty woman beside her, and point to the title: *Will You Please Be Quiet, Please?*

"There. Look," said the woman. "If you're going to the Open, you'll want to see."

Terry wasn't playing. She'd learned that from *Tennis Week.* And, from the plane, her bird's-eye view of Louis Armstrong Stadium showed her the enormity of her task. Each of the thousands of dots inside it emphasized her idiocy. Believing Terry was one of those dots and that she was fated to find him was folly.

Or maybe it wasn't, because in the crowd at LaGuardia, as she headed toward baggage claim, she literally stumbled into one of the only two people of the city's seven million that she'd prayed she wouldn't see.

"Patricia," Jack Curren said.

Silently she cursed the power that had brought them together and turned her into a pillar of salt. She was no one's wife. She was Jack's ex-wife. He was paralyzed too. Only the business associate beside him moved. In a black pantsuit, magenta blouse, and pumps, the pretty brunette eased her hand out of his.

"Hello, Jack," Patricia managed.

"How are you?" he said.

"I'm well." She wanted to tell him how well—U of I, PhD, 4.0—but could only stand there, hating him for what he'd done to Terry and for looking healthier and happier than she'd ever seen him. At least he had the good grace to appear confounded and unable to take charge of the situation. He fumbled.

"You know Ellen," he said, nodding at the woman beside him.

Ellen? Tricia wanted to say. *How in Jesus God's name would I know Ellen?*

"Ellen Cabot," the woman said briskly. She took Tricia's hand with a grip that was far beyond firm, that said I'm a woman in a man's world, as good as the best of them. Bone crushers, with something to prove, Lynn always said. Ellen said, "And it's Patricia?"

"No," she said. Jack looked sheepish. "No, it's Tricia. Tricia Wyngate. Excuse me."

She felt the pull of pay phones as she moved on. How automatically her fingers would dial the familiar number, how badly she wanted to say: *You won't believe who I saw, won't believe what he said, and who is this bone-crusher Ellen?*

The luggage carousel circled. Kiawah waves built and crashed. She'd told Jack she was doing well, told herself the same thing every day. She had her work, friends, colleagues, her dissertation committee.

But the Iowa winters were bleak, and she didn't have Terry. Tears ebbed and flowed. She didn't have Lynn.

Three months before, Tricia had changed her number to unlisted to stop Lynn's calls. She'd returned every letter unopened.

But if they could patch a quilt from the tatters of their friendship, even a fragile, threadbare thing rather than a source of warmth or comfort, she had to call her and try.

The familiar hello jabbed like a needle, but Tricia persevered. "Hello, Lynn." The words sat frozen and stung her lips like ice before melting into a sigh. "I'm here in the city." She waited for Lynn to help her with this mending, but there was only silence that Tricia couldn't interpret. Stunned, grateful, or angry silence? "I hope . . . or I thought . . . May I stay with you?"

Lynn's yes was so excited that Tricia qualified her intentions. "I don't want you to take vacation days. Nights will be enough until we see how things go. I'll manage to entertain myself during the day."

She managed by taking the subway to Queens at 9:00 a.m. and back to Manhattan at 4:30 p.m. Between trains, she wandered the grounds at the USTA Tennis Center in Flushing Meadows.

Every afternoon she washed away the heat and disappointment before Lynn came home so she didn't have to talk about where she'd been and why. Night after night, square after square, they worked together. Tricia was certain their stitches would hold in the future but equally certain they would unravel if they spoke of the past. She couldn't revisit 1978 aloud with Lynn, couldn't even tell her about Jack—and Ellen—at the airport. And she could no longer talk to Lynn about Terry.

On her last day in the city, Tricia was in Louis Armstrong Stadium for the Open's all-New York final. But she saw only a few points between McEnroe, who'd grown up in Queens, and Brooklyn-born Vitas Gerulaitis. During play, she scanned the faces of spectators. During changeovers, she walked the stadium's steps up and down, with an image of Terry tattooed on the pupils of her eyes, with thoughts of Terry, only Terry. He had drilled through her bones and was thriving in her marrow. There could be no remission.

She was miserable by the time she got back to Lynn's—her fair skin sunburned, heels blistered, legs cramping. She found herself thinking that she could trust Lynn again, that she should talk to Lynn about Terry, that Lynn would hug her, understand, and help her find him.

But she was also thinking Virginia Woolf had been right when she wrote "there is no end to the folly of the human heart."

She felt too foolish to tell Lynn what she'd been doing for the last seven days. Too foolish to admit that, if she had to, she would do it for the rest of her life.

CHAPTER 21

From that point forward, they flew into and out of my life as if I were the central hub of an airline: Jack, professionally; Baze, when he and Annie were in the city; Tricia, twice a year; and Mike, on behalf of Terry. Just to let you know, Mike always began when he called.

They touched down and took off at random, with no one air-traffic controlling.

There were blue-sky flights with smooth landings.

There were long, grueling flights.

There were tailspins in turbulence and recoveries. Above all, there were missed connections.

While they flew, I climbed. Successfully. I'd been bristling at the glass ceiling since I'd first heard the term that year and wasn't sure what I'd find at the top of McHugh and Brown's ladder. But I'd been promoted from assistant to account exec within my first nine months there, and with my feet arched comfortably around corporate rungs, I was determined to find out.

Whatever it takes, I said to myself.

Jack Curren was right. I wanted to *be* him but a better version of him: honest, ethical, moral; taking advantage of no one, respectful and fair to all.

I awaited 1980 at home, alone, smoking, no champagne, Times Square seeming a continent away. On the radio, Al Stewart drifted into "Time Passages" as I pondered the present.

Our jeans had lost their flare, maybe our lives had too. Jeans were straight legged now. Calvin Klein, which had its own agency in-house, "obliterated the boundaries of acceptable sexual content in advertising," Jack Curren noted while speaking at a year-end professional luncheon. He'd scolded Klein for the traffic-stopping Times Square billboard featuring model Patti Hansen on all fours, logo on her hip pocket. Then, after noting that the company's jeans sales had exceeded over $60 million that year, he'd flashed his irresistible smile and added, "Of course, I'd be proud as hell if that account and board were mine." Great laugh line. Greater applause for one of the industry's revered leaders.

The ERA was on life support, having failed in March as expected, still three state votes short of ratification. Though a new deadline of 1982 should have given me hope, it didn't.

As the Times Square ball began to descend five blocks away, I picked up Newsweek's December 31 issue but couldn't get past the cover—the faces of thirty of the American hostages in the American Embassy in Tehran. Held since November. No sign of release.

Terry was a different kind of hostage. In rehab again. A third time.

Happy New Year.

I went to bed.

I heard from Mike the night before Valentine's Day.

"Just to let you know," he said, "we're picking up Terry tomorrow. We're all hoping three's the charm."

"Just to let you know," Mike said, in late March, voice breaking. "Helen is dying. Bilateral breast cancer." I muddled through questions, he through details. "Terry is taking it hard."

I looked at the glass of cabernet I'd just poured, made it splash like Christ's blood on white porcelain, turned on the water, detoxed my sink. "He's not drinking, is he?"

"No," Mike said. "But he can't talk about it. There's a

support group. I've said we should go together, but every time I bring it up, he says no. He's either at Helen's side or he's on a tennis court, taking his anger out on the ball, blasting it really."

"Tennis could be therapeutic for him right now."

"I've been coaching him a bit," he said, and in his tone I heard a modulation to another key. "No reason, really. He says he'll never go back on tour. I talked him out of his wooden racket and into graphite, oversize. It's perfect for him and where the game is headed."

"Tennis is therapeutic for you too, Mike. I hear it in your voice." Our silence, even more than our words, closed the miles and months between us. "Can I help?" I asked him. I was disappointed that he didn't answer right away. "Should I call Terry?"

"I thought about that," he said.

Gripping the receiver with my shoulder and chin, I took a cigarette from a pack on the counter. My lighter was in the bedroom, so I dug quietly in a drawer for matches.

"Or about having you ask Tricia to call."

I decided against the cigarette. "You'd have to ask Terry first. I promised him—"

"I asked Helen first and she said no. She was adamant. Helen wants Terry all to herself right now. It's like she's trying to make up for the past with every bit of the future she has left."

I closed the drawer—my miscellaneous drawer—and thought of my friends. They weren't star-crossed lovers. They were universe-crossed.

"So, would it help if I talked to him?"

"No, I—"

He sounded weary now, beaten down.

"What would help, Lynn," he said, "is if you'd just keep talking to me. I'm scared for both of them. Nobody here has had time to get to know Helen. And nobody anywhere knows Terry like you do."

Except Tricia, I thought.

Mike went on. "When we're all three hurting bad, I feel like, even though I've been here three years and know three-fourths of the community, nobody really even knows—" His voice broke.

"You don't have to say it, Mike. I get it."

It wasn't that I could finish his sentences like Jack's but that I felt that way too. Excepting Tricia, no one knew me either.

The calls came at random and gradually slowed over the next two months. By fall Helen was one of ten patients of a recently founded organization: Hospice Savannah. The country was deep in the throes of the second oil crisis of the decade. The economy was mired in stagflation and record high interest rates. Unemployment was rising. The presidential campaign was in full swing. And Reagan ads were asking if we were better off than we were four years ago.

Better in what way? I wanted to ask. Helen wasn't, Mike wasn't, Terry wasn't. Tricia? Maybe.

And me? A vice president at McHugh and Brown? Maybe. Maybe not.

Tricia defended her dissertation in July—brilliantly, according to her committee. In mid-August she donned her tam and robe, shook the dean's hand, and began looking for a job. On the day of her first interview, she mailed me a photograph along with a note that read: *Don't laugh. This is really me.*

She was power dressed in a gray suit with a peplum jacket, and I hoped the likely male department chair who would hire her would do so for her brain, not her breasts. Her enviable waist looked smaller than ever, thanks to shoulder pads, like those Velcroed into everything in my closet, ranging from the size of saucers to salad plates. Her hair was still long and straight rather than chin length and permed like mine.

P.S. I'll come up for a week at the end of the month, but don't take vacation. I'll need 9:00 to 5:00 every day for the library, for an article I'm writing. We career girls will play at night, like last year. —Tricia.

She stayed with me from the twenty-sixth of August to the thirty-first, or from the first round of the U.S. Open through the round of sixteen. Over the course of the week, she was a study in pink—her face on Wednesday, shoulders on Thursday, arms on Friday, sandaled feet on Saturday. I didn't ask how she was getting sunburned in the New York Public Library or why she wouldn't admit what she'd been doing, which she must have known I'd surmised.

Following her lead, I didn't mention the Open.

Honoring my promise to Terry—and to Helen too now, and Mike—I didn't mention his name.

In October when Mike called, I was in Tokyo, leading a McHugh and Brown team on the agency's first international account.

"Just to let you know," he said to a machine instead of me. "Helen is gone."

He'd called me at home rather than work, so his message was days old when I heard it.

"I'm taking a leave of absence from The Landings," he went on. "Terry and I are leaving for Europe on Sunday. He played a few challenger tourneys over the last few months. Helen asked him to. He even won a couple. He's got the points now for a string of Grand Prix events." A pause. "He's ready. Helen would want us to go."

I hung up with two thoughts, both painful.

I had missed the funeral I'd planned to attend.

My career was a lousy husband.

"Dysthymia," my doctor said in the second week of 1981. "Depression. Mild but chronic."

I wanted to suggest that the problem was something else, to say no, it's just January, in the way that Baze had once said it's just August. But I didn't argue. I knew she was right.

"I can write a prescription," she said, "or you can take better care of yourself. Don't try to stop smoking right now. We'll work on that later. But get more exercise, more sleep, and something other than work in your life."

I thanked her, and began to work harder, making sure I earned every penny of my almost-equitable pay, allowing no time to ponder my solitary life.

Mike and Terry flew into a black hole just after Mike proudly let me know that Terry might break into the top one hundred by the end of the year.

Baze circled the edge of my radar screen until Easter, when I turned it off. He and Annie were having problems, he said in my office, and he needed advice.

"I work for her father," I told him. "I can't help you. Please don't ask."

"Work comes first, Lynn, right? Always first."

I tried to call him later, tried several times. But I never reached him, and I let it go.

Only Tricia, soaring, remained in touch. She accepted a tenure-track position, not at a quaint liberal arts college in the Northeast as I'd expected, but in the Department of Comparative Literature at the University of Georgia in Athens. She was more interested in setting up her office in Park Hall than in finding a place to live, but after three months in a Holiday Inn, she began looking for a house to rent.

Over a weekend in February, I helped her move to

Greensboro, Georgia, a small hilly town with a lake and not much else, twenty minutes from campus. She'd chosen the house, she said, for the built-in bookcases and shelves in almost every room. In spite of them, we ran out of space with two boxes of books yet to unpack.

"Here," she said, pointing to two kitchen cabinets with glass doors. "Why not? It's only me here. I need one plate, not a set of china."

Saturday night, too tired to do much else, we settled into the camelback loveseat we'd found that morning at a garage sale to watch movies on HBO.

"Not this," she said as *The Turning Point* began. "I've seen it. It reminds me of Nona."

"Nothing else is on," I said, though I dreaded the emotional conflict between lonely, single, aging ballerina Anne Bancroft and her friend and onetime competitor Shirley MacLaine, who had given up her career for marriage and children. No woman, it suggested, could have it all.

"That's the first time I've ever seen you cry," Tricia said as the movie ended. She handed me a Kleenex from the box she'd nearly depleted in two hours' time.

Just as I was Tricia's first overnight guest in Greensboro, she was scheduled to be mine, in my new two-bedroom condominium on Forty-Seventh, in early September.

I'd bought it in June, and the change had helped. So had a second assistant at work.

The problem with Tricia's visit was that I wasn't there. I was in Miami as a last-minute substitute for Bob at a weeklong conference. I'd left on Monday and returned home early on Saturday the fifth, expecting to have at least one afternoon and evening with Tricia before she went home on Sunday. But I found only traces of her in my new home: a thank-you note on my refrigerator and a stack of magazines in the guest bedroom.

I knew by the one on top—*Novel: A Forum on Fiction*—that she hadn't intentionally left them for me to read. I continued through the stack, sliding each one onto the bed: *American Literature. The Comparatist. The Georgia Review. The Iowa Review.* I stopped at the next, though it wasn't the last.

U.S. Open 1981, USTA National Tennis Center, September 1–13.

She might as well have left me her journal.

I opened the official program and read the names she'd highlighted. They were scattered in the ATP rankings list. They followed one another in the alphabetical list of players: Sadri, Saltz, Saviano, Scanlon, Segal, Simonsson, Simpson, Smith (Jonathan), Smith (Stan), Solomon, Stadler, Stefanki, Stewart, Stockton.

Terry wasn't playing. I wondered why and wondered whether Tricia's disappointment had become so unbearable that she'd gone home a day early.

I made a pot of coffee, and waiting for it to brew, flipped idly through television channels. On the local news, I saw Vitas Gerulaitis hit a forehand past Ivan Lendl.

A few minutes later, Peter Jennings informed me that Sandra Day O'Connor was likely to be confirmed as the Supreme Court's first female justice, and that the National Centers for Disease Control had announced a high incidence of Pneumocystis and Kaposi's sarcoma in gay men.

Power off.

Coffee made me think of my desk and what would have accumulated in five days' time. I decided to drag myself to the office, thinking I'd rather face the chaos on Saturday night—and Sunday, if necessary—than first thing Monday morning. I packed Tricia's magazines into my briefcase so I'd remember to mail them to her and walked down Forty-Seventh.

As I approached the Gotham Book Mart, I stopped under the "Wise Men Fish Here" sign, and looked at the window display: Maya Angelou's *The Heart of a Woman.* The book, which I could mail with the magazines, would make a nice apology to the houseguest I'd deserted, who loved the poet's "Phenomenal Woman" and sometimes quoted lines from "Still I Rise."

I stepped inside the Gotham and discovered the cruelest of missed connections.

Standing in mid-aisle with a book in hand, Terry turned when I said his name and drew back. He looked like a schoolboy caught where he shouldn't have been. I felt like the hall monitor dispatched to escort him to the principal or to detention.

"What are you doing here?" he managed.

"I live here, remember? New York City. I live three blocks away. What are you doing here, Terry? Are you here for the Open?"

He broke into a smile. "I guess you could say that." He stepped forward and hugged me, cautiously, then warmly.

"I was on my way to the office," I said, "but I stopped to buy a book for—" I paused, wondering how he'd react. "For a friend."

Book. Friend. Tricia. The progression of his thoughts was apparent in his eyes, and I followed it to the book he reshelved: *The Compass Flower,* W. S. Merwin. Now he'd really been caught, red-handed, red-faced.

I watched his Adam's apple rise and fall, twice, before he said, "Did she ever come here?"

"Yes. So did Albee, Auden, Bellow, Capote—she used to recite the list of writers who came here." I thought of the other list in my briefcase. "You've found her favorite store."

"Good," he said softly. He looked at the shelf and talked to Merwin, not me. "I figured if I checked out enough bookstores that sooner or later I'd be breathing her air. If she came here, she breathed in air and breathed it out. It's still here." His voice was otherworldly distant. "Pathetic, right?" He waited for Merwin to answer. "All I want, all I've got is her air." He drew in a breath. His shoulders rose; his chest expanded and collapsed. He ran his fingers up and down the book's spine, as if it were her spine. "Maybe she pulled this one out to buy but remembered she already had it and put it back. So this is how I touch her now. The only way I can."

Poised to accomplish the happily-ever-after ending that no one else had been able to, I silently congratulated myself. "I have her number, Terry, if you want to call her. I know where she is." He took the book from the shelf again, flipped through it, and began to read to avoid my question. "She hasn't dated anyone since she left Jack." I grew impatient with excitement. "Don't you want to see her?"

"I can't, Lynn." He looked at me again. "I've got my shit together for the first time in three years, and just thinking about seeing her makes me want to have a drink."

Self-congratulation became self-doubt. Still I said, "Do you love her?" He didn't answer. "If you love her, why don't you go after her?"

He had a list of reasons at the ready. "'Cause loving her almost got me killed, and losing her did kill me. Killed who I used to be anyways. And 'cause she picked him, Lynn, not me. Do you know what that did to me that day?"

He seemed not to know Jack had said he was dying. "But, Terry—"

"He said he'd kill her if I ever got near her again."

"But Jack remarried. He wouldn't care. Jack has a wife and twin daughters now. He—"

"'Cause it's been three years, Lynn. She's different. I'm

different. I'm an alcoholic. I'm in recovery, but I'm an alcoholic."

"That wouldn't matter to her."

"I got it from my mom. Tricia wants kids. I don't want to pass it on to a kid. Not her kids. I love her too much."

"That doesn't always happen, Terry. If you—"

"I can't, Lynn," he said, voice rising, eyes frantic. "And I can't listen to this. I'm clean and I'm sober, except for her. She's worse than Percocet and blow and beer. It's sick how I love her."

"But she loves you too." I was determined, but he was desperate. "I gotta go."

"Wait," I said.

He considered, but then said softly. "It's her serve, Lynn. She's gotta—I always wanted—" He put the book away. "I always thought she'd come after me. And she didn't."

"She's been trying to find you."

"Not very hard. She could have asked you, Lynn. You were talking to Mike for a while."

"But I couldn't have told her," I said. "You had me swear not to."

His eyes went blank, his lids blinked nervously. He didn't have to say *What?* to let me know he had no idea what I was talking about.

"Terry," I said. I had to lay my briefcase, an attaché case, on the floor to open it. An elderly couple turned into the poetry aisle as I knelt. They stepped over my feet as I slid the latches open. They were between Terry and me as I pulled out the program, between Terry and me as I said: "Tricia has been looking for you since—"

"I'm suffocating, Lynn. I gotta get out of here."

He started toward the door and, panicking, I lost twenty seconds to nervous hands and uncooperative latches I couldn't close. I scooped up my briefcase and, drawing it to my chest, I rushed from the store, program in hand.

I saw Terry at the corner a half block away, getting into a cab. I fought my way through the crowd as best I could without full use of elbows and hands.

In a flash of foresight, I saw the collision like a driver might—my collision, head-on, unavoidable, a nanosecond away. The man, whoever he was, was burly, scowling, and rushing, rushing not like me, but unintentionally at me. He knocked my briefcase from my arms. My breastbone and heart were bashed, if not from the blow, then from the sight of my notes from the Miami conference, airborne and scattering in a laughing breeze.

I watched in disbelief, knowing I should recover what I could. I watched paper birds fly. I let them go. I abandoned my briefcase on the sidewalk and ran after Terry.

The cab was at the curb, waiting for a break in traffic. I rapped on the glass of the back window and Terry rolled it down. "What the hell—"

"Take this," I cried. "It's Tricia's. Please take it."

I shoved the program through the window as the cab screeched and pulled away.

The last place I expected to be on Sunday morning was subbing for Bob again, but he'd called, and at 1:00 p.m., I was entertaining a client in Louis Armstrong Stadium at the U.S. Open. Courtside section. Row twenty-four.

"I have to confess," I said as I sat down, "I haven't been following the Open. I was in Miami last week. Who's playing?"

"Jimbo," said the client's wife. She, not he, was the obvious fan. "Connors."

"Connors and who?" I asked, but I didn't need to. My eyes had fallen on Mike and Baze, below us, in the player's box.

"Terry Hesselbach."

"Hesselbach," I said, and smiled. "Of course."

"He's only ranked around 100, but he's playing great. And here he is, the round of 16. With Jimbo."

I wanted to excuse myself and go down to say hello, but there were ushers posted at both players' boxes, wearing the blue shirts and white shorts of event personnel, and looking much more diligent than those posted above us at the entrance to Section 32.

I'd forgotten my sunglasses, and the blazing sun forced me to squint through the long, tight first set as Hesselbach—not Sloan—came from two breaks down to win it 7–5.

In the second, Jimbo began going for bigger shots, which paid off with a quick break of serve. But Terry broke back, and they played from 1–all to 6–all before a bewildered crowd.

"This is mind-blowing," said the client's wife.

In the tiebreaker, Terry was on fire. He had Connors serving at 2–5, and after what did appear to be a bad call for 2–6, Jimbo flicked a bird at the linesman and began working the crowd to lift his game. Four blistering winners later, at 6–all, the number four seed was strutting and grabbing his crotch, while Terry looked at Mike for supportive nods.

The match hit the two-hour mark, the sun was straight up, and the temperature well on its way to the forecast of ninety-seven. I wondered if the weather of the six days before had been as brutal during Tricia's fruitless search.

As the players changed ends, I reached for my pocketbook and ChapStick. I dropped the tube as play resumed and was leaning over to pick it up when a whoosh of alarm swept through the crowd. I looked at the court, afraid that Terry had fallen or was cramping or had missed an easy shot. But the cause of the whoosh was not on court. It was above us.

I turned and looked up. At Tricia. And with everyone in our section, I watched, rapt.

Never mind that she was blonde and beautiful. Never mind

that her high-waisted shorts and top with scooped neckline were stuck to her body by more sweat than Connors and Terry combined had generated. Never mind that she was "built like a brick shithouse," as someone behind me said. Tricia was breaking the rules.

She was walking down the stadium steps, not at the 12-point changeover but during play, ignoring the ushers—"Wait, miss. Wait!"—and the security guard—"Stop. You can't do that." When the guard began to pursue her, she ran.

Ran like Cinderella from the palace when the clock struck twelve, but toward her prince, not away from him, losing not a glass slipper but a sandal. She paused a few rows above me, allowing me and spectators nearby to see that something was wrong with her face. She hurried on, stopped dead still, and collapsed.

I heard "heatstroke and hallucinating" from the guard, heard the static of his handheld radio and the call for first aid. I made my way to the end of our row, glancing at the court, where play had come to a halt. Players, chair umpire, linesmen, ball boys—all had turned toward the commotion.

Connors began raising hell about the interruption.

Terry shouted to Mike and Baze, "Is that Tricia?"

Connors yelled that Terry was being coached from his box.

Terry shouted, "Asshole. Shut the fuck up."

The umpire leaned toward his microphone and gave Terry a warning for audible obscenities.

Connors coaxed the crowd to an ear-splitting jeer.

Terry started toward his box, looking ready to mount the fence and climb into the stands.

The umpire announced a second warning.

Baze and Mike began waving to Terry, trying to send him back to the court.

The umpire gave Terry a penalty point, which gave Connors a set point.

The crowd began to boo.

The umpire gave Terry a penalty game—or penalty tiebreaker—which gave Connors the second set. He ordered Terry to return to the service line or be defaulted.

Terry looked from the court to Mike, to the court, to the stands, to me, to the court, and to Mike, who was pleading.

The crowd thundered for the match they'd paid to see, and as Terry walked slowly back to the service line, Baze started up the steps and I continued down.

We reached Tricia at the same time, a beat ahead of first aid. As the techs lifted her onto a stretcher, Terry shouted to Baze from the court, "Is it Tricia?" As Connors, tennis bad boy and master of antics, conducted the crowd to a dissonant crescendo, Terry shouted again, "Is it her?"

Baze shouted back, "No."

I shouted at Baze. "My God, don't lie. Don't tell him that."

And Baze shouted at me. "He's about to be defaulted. What do you want me to tell him?"

Tricia raised her head, a bare inch off the stretcher. "Tell him to finish the match."

At the first-aid station, a nurse sponged Tricia's arms and legs with cool water. I studied the blisters on her face. They looked like water droplets, too many to count.

Her temperature of 103 meant heat exhaustion, not stroke, and no trip to the emergency room. With one ear, I listened to instructions for her care; with the other, to the conversation of two spectators, passing by on their way to a concession stand, voices amplified by the stadium's inner caverns.

"Damnedest thing. Last set, Hesselbach was holding at love, every time he served."

"Now he's broken at love. Every time."

At home, I helped Tricia undress and sat beside the tub

while she soaked in cool water.

"I thought you'd left," I said. "Your note on the refrigerator—"

"My flight is tonight, but I checked into a hotel yesterday. I didn't want you to see me when you got back from Miami." She gestured toward her face. "I didn't want you to know what I'd been doing all week, for the third year in a row. I felt so ridiculous." She held her breath, leaned against the back of the tub, drew in her knees, and slid into the water. I watched the bubbles of exhalation, watched her resurface. "I'd walked the grounds all morning," she said. "I went to the stadium one last time, hoping he'd be in the stands." She smiled dreamily. "And there he was. Not watching. Playing. *Playing.* With a different name." She looked at me and laid her temple on her knees. "He'll know to come here, won't he?"

"Yes. I've left a message at the players' hotel. And Baze and Annie will know. Her father knows my address." I helped her into one of my nightgowns and into bed. I misted her face with water from the plastic spray bottle I used to mist my failing plants, had her drink a glass of water. "Try to sleep, Tricia. I'll wake you when he gets here."

She nodded. "You're sure he'll come?"

"Yes." I closed the door and began to wait, hoping I was right.

CHAPTER 22

She thought she heard her name. Barely, but she heard it. She was underwater. A pool, the ocean— she wasn't sure. But someone was beside her calling her name.

"Tricia."

She opened her eyes but couldn't see clearly. Salt water? She tried to blink it away as she heard Terry's voice, lost in years and changing tides. She wondered how her own voice would sound. She wanted to hear it in the present, in the now of this room at Lynn's, where the pale tan walls behind Terry were filling in like a Polaroid photo.

She asked him, "Did you win?"

"Did I win?" He chuckled. "No. I got my ass handed to me on a platter."

"Because of me? You were fine until I—Terry, I'm so sorry."

He shrugged. "There'll be other matches. But I gotta admit, Tricia, you turned that one into a match I'll never forget."

She took his hand and pulled him toward her. He took a seat on the bed and she looked at him closely. There were deep lines around his eyes. *Too much sun,* she thought, *too much tennis. Too much hurt?* A thin gold chain around his neck led her eyes to a Saint Christopher medal caught up in the V of his starched collared shirt. Things were different. Even his name.

She ran her finger over the scar in his chin and wondered about scars she'd left inside him, wondered if they had healed. She sat up and raised a shoulder so that the strap of the nightgown slid down her arm. She peeled the neckline down to show him the scar at the top of her breast. In a rush of emotion, she remembered the excellence of his touch and was afraid it too might have changed. He raised his hand and let it fall. She saw triple break point in his eyes, the look she knew so well. And she knew she loved him, changed and unchanged.

CHAPTER 23

She was waiting, but he could not touch her. He was unsure of himself, afraid of arousal he wasn't ready for. But an irresistible ache pulled him toward her. Slowly, lightly, he kissed the rosy stain of a bittersweet summer. To his surprise, what he felt was not desire. It was something richer, layered, complex. He'd sensed it first at the Vendue Inn, and it had never left him. He'd tried to bury it when they were apart, but it hadn't died or even slept.

The hell of hibernation was over. Summer was back. Summer was forever now.

There were tears in her eyes when he looked at her again. "Don't cry, Tricia. Okay? Wrinkling your face like that is gonna bust those blisters."

"Let me cry," she said. "I can't help it." She nodded toward a canvas bag on the floor—eight by ten, shoulder strap, U.S. Open logo. "Will you hand me that?"

"You gonna read to me, Tricia?" He picked up the bag, expecting it to be weighted with books. To his surprise it was light. Keys jingled inside. Or maybe change. He imagined a wallet inside and a tube of sunscreen, empty for days and not replaced. "They sell hats at the Open too, you know." He thought she'd laugh, but she was solemn and purposeful as he handed her the bag.

She removed a page torn from a newspaper, tabloid-sized and folded many times. It looked fragile as she opened it and gave it to him. He looked at the ATP rankings, and when she asked him to, looked at the date. November 20, 1978. His name wasn't there.

"I've kept it with me for three years. I wanted to make sure

I had it when I found you, so you'd know how long I've looked for you. Always here in New York. But other places too. I couldn't go to many tournaments from Iowa or Athens. I tried so hard," she said, tears still streaming. "Terry, why did you change your name? Terry Hessel—Hessel what?" And for the first time laughter floated on tears. "Is it back or bock?"

"Bock. Rhymes with lock, sock, jock." He paused. "With a lot of things." Again, her laughter. The sound he loved.

"I wouldn't have picked it," he said, "except that it's Mike's name. Mike, my father. Kind of an ugly name, I know. Nobody would want it but me."

He'd served. Dinked it in the middle of the box. It was such an easy return. But for a moment he wasn't sure the ball was coming back. Silence. Then she hit it down the T to him, as clean and solid and sweet as could be.

"*I* would want that name," she said.

"Be still a minute." He grinned. "I'm looking for a spot without a blister and . . . there. There's one." He touched her cheek with the tip of his finger and turned off her tears. "That means I want to kiss you."

She touched his cheek. "You don't have to ask, you know."

He put his finger to her cheek again, took it slowly away. "I'm making sure you're real."

Finger to cheek, hers to his. "Me too."

"One more thing, Tricia."

Again he touched her cheek, and this time, he let his finger rest there.

He waited until she touched his.

Waited until she said, "Too."

CHAPTER 24

I stared at the closed bedroom door. I'd been as noisy as possible getting ready for work, slamming doors and drawers, clanging pots and pans while unloading the dishwasher. Either they were sound asleep in each other's arms, or awake and ignoring me. In spite of all I'd done for them over the years, individually and together, they weren't going to tell me what had happened, what had been resolved. It was maddening.

It was also eight o'clock and time to go. To McHugh and Brown. To chaos on a desk I couldn't see the top of. To messages written on while you were out slips and recorded by a new, not always reliable, VMX voice-mail system. To accounts, clients, creatives. To a vice presidency in the offing. To my life.

Even more maddening: I didn't hear from them all day long. When they finally called, they didn't call at the office but at home. Their messages went unheard until I'd closed out a ten-hour workday.

"Obi-Lynn," Terry said, "everything's great. To the max, I swear. Me and Tricia haven't stopped talking since last night. Well, except to—" He laughed. "Fill in the blank. Anyways, I've told her everything that's happened in the past three years—except detox and rehab. I don't know how to. I can't exactly say, 'My name's Terry and I'm an alcoholic.' You said it wouldn't matter to her." He paused. "But are you sure? Call me."

Tricia, exuberant, said, "Terry and I are in Charleston. The Vendue Inn. We only have three days before I have to get back for school. And he has a tournament in San Francisco. Lynn, those three days may be a honeymoon. We've called around and found a little town called Ridgeland close by. You can get a marriage license and get married in the same day. I know you'll say we should wait and be sure, but we've waited three years." She paused for a breath. "I don't need your advice. Or, I suppose I do. But what I'd rather have is your blessing, Lynn. Call me?"

I laughed. I took a weary, temporary step out of the middle. I would call them, but not tonight. I would call and say, "Trust yourselves. You know what you want, have always known. Do what you want and need to do."

I listened to the third message.

"Lynn, this is Mike." Long pause. "Just wanted you to know." And longer pause. Audible breath and sigh. "I'll be in the city for a few more days, and I'd like to see you. Nothing to do with Terry or Tricia. I'd like to see you. Just you. If you'd like to see me."

I thought of Tricia and Terry. Of faults and double faults. Of breaking and holding. I thought of unlikely love. Forbidden and obsessive. Impossible but unshakeable. Dreamlike and cheek-touch real.

Mike's was the call I returned.

I guess it's my story too, after all.

AUTHOR'S NOTE

For many years, I had the privilege of marketing The Landings on Skidaway Island in Savannah, Georgia, for the community's developer, The Branigar Organization, Inc. And I have always loved Kiawah Island, where most of *Breaking and Holding* is set. I've depicted these communities as further along in development than they were in 1978 and have creatively relocated a swimming pool, golf hole, and tennis court or two. The headline Lynn uses for The Landings—"Thinking Retirement? The Alternative to Crowded Florida"—was a successful one used in marketing the community for many years. Austin Kelley, Inc. was the advertising agency for The Kiawah Island Company in 1978 and continued their fine work until the 1990s.

Though I don't play tennis, I am an exuberant fan, as anyone who has ever had the pleasure (or displeasure) of watching a professional match with me will attest. I've done my best to be true to the sport and historically accurate but have taken a few liberties as well. Apologies to Mike Cahill, who actually played Jimmy Connors in the round of 16 of the 1981 U.S. Open but is replaced by Terry in this novel. And though John McEnroe did play a tournament in Atlanta in 1980, he obviously didn't play Terry in 1978. I've used these players and others by name to lend authenticity, but major characters on court, on Kiawah Island, and at The Landings are fictionalized.

ACKNOWLEDGMENTS

Kind thanks to all who played a role in bringing *Breaking and Holding* to readers:

Amy Condon, Lyn Gregory, Tina Kelly, K. W. Oxnard, and Nancy Brandon—the bright, talented, nurturing members of my writing group, the Savannah Scribes.

My agent, Cassie Hanjian—patient, wise, and always there for me, 110 percent of the way. Lake Union Publishing, especially Danielle Marshall, Kelli Martin, Tiffany Yates Martin, Scott Calamar, Rebecca Jaynes, Danielle Fiorella, Gabriella Dumpit, Brent Fattore, and the marketing team.

Bill Hoppe and Lane Curlee, my tennis experts.

Adam Davies, whose wisdom and line edit improved the novel early on in important ways.

My dear friends and sisters, who read the manuscript in its original hefty form; including those tireless readers who never said no when asked to tackle revision after revision.

My mom, who said, "Oh, yes you can," every time I doubted that I could.

My son, Colin, who supported me in his inimitable, steadfast way.

My daughter, Sara Jane, whose note of encouragement (circa 2012) is still pinned to my bulletin board, and who read, listened, consoled, and celebrated with me so many times that all I can say is, "How did you do it?"

And Mike, my husband. How did I get so lucky?

ABOUT THE AUTHOR

Photo © 2015 Robert S. Cooper

Judy Fogarty lives, writes, reads, and runs on the historic Isle of Hope in her native Savannah, Georgia. She holds a master of music degree from the University of Illinois and has served as director of marketing for private golf and tennis communities in the Savannah/Hilton Head area. *Breaking and Holding* is her debut novel. With the invaluable support of her husband and two children, Judy's work on her second novel is well under way.